W9-BNS-887

Also available
in Random House Large Print

MURDER ON THE POTOMAC

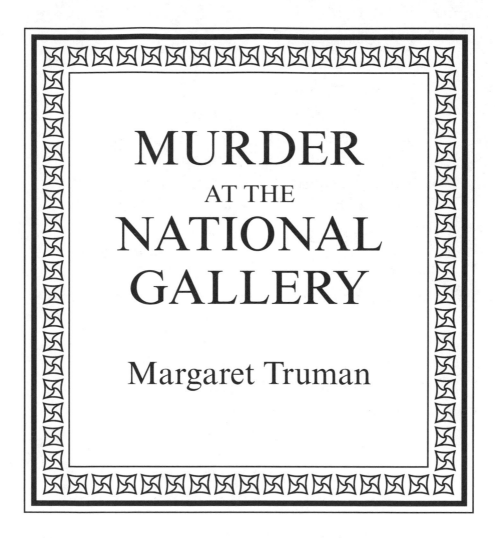

MURDER
AT THE
NATIONAL
GALLERY

Margaret Truman

Published by Random House Large Print
in association with Random House, Inc.
New York 1996

Library of Congress Cataloging-in-Publication Data
Truman, Margaret, 1924–
Murder at the National Gallery / by Margaret Truman.
p.   cm.
ISBN 0-679-75884-4
1. Smith, Annabel (Fictitious character)—Fiction.
2. Women art dealers—Washington (D.C.)—Fiction.
3. National Gallery of Art (U.S.)—Fiction.
4. Large type books.
I. Title.
PS3570.R82M7543   1996
813'.54—dc20   95-50059   CIP

Random House Web Address:
http://www.randomhouse.com/

Printed in the United States of America
FIRST LARGE PRINT EDITION

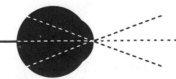

This Large Print Book carries the
Seal of Approval of N.A.V.H.

MURDER
AT THE
NATIONAL
GALLERY

ONE

⊠ ══════════════════════════════════════ ⊠

COSENZA, ITALY

WHO WAS Mattia Preti anyway?

That was all Saltore had time to think about as he ran to keep ahead of the three men.

Breathing hard, he thought next: *What had he done to deserve this?* He'd asked only for what was fair. They'd told him to steal one painting, but he'd stolen three. Steal one, you get paid for one. Steal three, you get paid for three. Fair's fair. Simple.

He'd been stealing for them for over two years. He was good at it. They always told him that. Mostly he stole cars to order, turning them over to his gang, run by local hoods and tithed to Luigi Sensi's Naples empire, *Camorra,* which had customers waiting for the green Fiat or silver Lamborghini. Sometimes he stole silverware and cash from the homes of the rich on hilltops overlooking the Tyrrhenian Sea or from guests at the seaside hotels built to accommodate the increasing flow of tourists into the arch of Italy's boot.

But cars were his specialty. He'd never stolen art

before because no one had told him to. He didn't even like art.

Saltore pressed the paintings close to his chest, huffing harder now, and ran up a narrow winding street leading from the old section of Cosenza, across the Busento River, to the more modern city.

Who *was* Mattia Preti?

He'd never even heard of him. All he knew was that he was told to sneak into the monastic complex of San Francesco di Assisi and remove a painting by this guy Preti. But once he saw how easy it was to pull one from the wall, he wanted them all. More money for him. But the priest came by; Saltore wasn't about to get into a confrontation with a priest. Bad enough at confession.

So he took off with the three paintings and dutifully delivered them to his brooding boss at the cafe, as usual. But when he balked at turning them over unless he received triple pay, his boss, whose reputation in southern Italy had not been built upon diplomatic negotiation, pulled a gun. That sent Giovanni Saltore running from the cafe, with his boss after him, joined by two colleagues who'd been sipping espresso at a nearby table. All this for three ugly paintings that were too old to be worth much, painted by some dead old guy.

Although young, Saltore was not in good shape. His legs went leaden, and each breath drove daggers into his lungs. They caught him when, not thinking, he found himself in a dead-end alley. The three men, guns in hands, walked slowly toward him, backing Saltore against the cement wall. They smiled and softly muttered insults: *"Imbecille buon a nulla!"* Useless imbecile. *"Alienato!"*

"Crazy? You want this junk?" Saltore shouted. He threw the three small paintings to the ground. "Take them. Not even pretty. No good colors. I don't want them. You don't owe me nothing. *Niente!*" Nothing.

His boss picked up the paintings, casually examined them, tucked them beneath his arm, and, as casually, turned and slowly walked away, leaving Saltore with a profound sense of relief. He grinned and raised his hands in a gesture that said all this was just an exercise, a silly mistake. *"Scherzo,* huh?" Just a joke.

He widened his arms and approached the youngest of his pursuers still in the alley. They'd gone to school together. "Hey, Gino, my friend," Saltore said, flashing a broad smile and shaking his head at the silliness of it all. As he reached to embrace his schoolmate, both revolvers fired at once. Their bullets struck Saltore in the chest within inches of each other. He dropped to his knees. The smile was gone, his eyes were wide with disbelief. Still, he held his arms out. Why? the open arms asked.

He was answered with two more shots, this time to the head.

The last thought Giovanni Saltore had before crossing the threshold into that other, better life promised by his church was: *Who the hell is Mattia Preti anyway?*

LONDON

On the day that Giovanni Saltore's art education ended in an alley in Cosenza, Italy, Lord Adam Boulridge, descended from the Duchess of Monmouth, and whose castle on the Northumberland coast was in such disrepair that it was deemed unsafe for tourists and had been condemned, received a late-night visitor. He and his guest spent an hour looking at Lord Adam's collection of paintings by British artists, including a stunning Gainsborough landscape, a departure from the painter's more famous portraits; a Hogarth party scene dripping with social commentary; a tranquil Richard Wilson lakeside scene that had been badly damaged by one of hundreds of serious leaks in the castle's roofs; and a George Romney portrait of a young lady, painted toward the end of the Raphael-inspired artist's life, when his technique had clearly waned. Dozens of other paintings hung haphazardly on the castle's cracked walls. Many were not lighted; Lord Adam trained a flashlight on them for his visitor's benefit.

Following this hour of art appreciation, they retired to Lord Adam's study to negotiate the terms. Lord Adam would take a two-week holiday. In his absence, his visitor would return to the castle and remove the most valuable of the paintings. Upon his return, Lord Adam would be appropriately aghast at the brazen theft of British treasures and would promptly report it to Lloyd's of London, which had insured the paintings for all these many years, or, as some Englishmen put it, donkey's years.

PARIS

Also on the day Giovanni Saltore lost his life, Jacques Saison put the finishing touches on a copy of Vermeer's *The Concert,* the original having been stolen years before from Boston's Isabella Stewart Gardner Museum. Saison had been provided with excellent color slides of the painting by his client, of whom he had not, of course, asked questions. Once he'd been given the "commission," Saison had scoured Paris for just the right old painting, not for the painting itself, but for the canvas that would approximate the age of canvases used in Vermeer's time. He'd found an especially smooth one consisting of twenty-six threads per centimeter to the warp and twenty-four to the weft. Not perfect, but close enough.

Within days he'd painstakingly stripped the original painting from the canvas, and, using a variety of chemical substances, further brought the canvas to its necessary "age." He then smoothed it, using a pumice-stone, which also served to soften the threads to better accept his, Saison's, "version" of *The Concert.* Finally, after experimenting for days to obtain precisely the right proportions, he worked a mixture of rabbit glue, gypsum, and anhydride into the canvas with a paintbrush. Now, a month later, he stepped back to admire *his* "Vermeer." Perfect.

That came as no surprise to Jacques Saison. He belonged, after all, to an elite fraternity. The world's finest art forgers were not organized into a guild, but they might well have been. Famous in a small circle, infamous in the larger one of art police.

What a shame, he sometimes thought when drinking, that he could use his prodigious talent only to copy the works of others. Try as he had since his early days as a student, he'd never been able to come up with an idea of something worthwhile to paint on his own.

But painting on someone else's own, so to speak, paid well.

CINCINNATI

Cindy Whitlock and her husband, Harry, proudly hung the print of Jean-Honoré Fragonard's *A Stand of Cypresses in an Italian Park* above the couch in their den. They'd chosen this particular print at the flea market because its sepia tones would go nicely with the orange-and-white zebra pattern of the couch. They'd paid thirty dollars for it. They could have opted for Rembrandt, Degas, or some pretty landscapes by Thomas Cole, all prints reproduced illegally in New York City and sold by flea-market vendors across the country.

TOKYO

Giovanni Saltore, even if new to the group, wasn't the only art collector to die that day.

While his wife and two daughters prepared dinner in the kitchen of their opulent home out-side of Tokyo, wealthy Japanese businessman Yakoto Kayami, dressed in a pure white kimono of Samurai style and sitting on a small white carpet, his legs bound with rope, removed white tissue paper from a short sword on the floor in front of him, lifted the sword so that its point faced his large belly, and fell forward onto it. Better to die than to face the shame of it having recently been revealed to him that his extensive art collection, considered one of Japan's finest, consisted mostly of masterpieces forged and stolen.

NEW YORK—A WEEK LATER

The International Arrivals Building at Kennedy Airport was busy. This Friday afternoon, among hundreds of passengers deplaning from the Alitalia flight from Rome was Carlo Giliberti, Italy's cultural attaché to the Italian Embassy in Washington, D.C. His trolley was laden with luggage, including an oversized black-leather portfolio. He chatted amiably with the Customs inspector.

Nearby, a short young woman with a large bosom, wearing jeans and a T-shirt with a mildly obscene message on it, and sporting multiple earrings, was taken aside and searched by a female inspector in a private room reserved for such activity. An instant breast reduction occurred when three small plastic bags of marijuana were removed from her bra.

Carlo Giliberti reached the taxi line and gave the driver the address of an art gallery in New York's Soho district, where he soon delivered three unframed paintings by the seventeenth-century Italian artist from Taverna, Mattia Preti, that had been concealed between worthless papers in his portfolio. He thanked the gallery owner for the envelope filled with cash, took another cab to LaGuardia, and boarded a Delta shuttle flight to Washington.

All in all, just another week and several scenes in the swirling world of international art.

TWO

THE NAVAL OBSERVATORY—
WASHINGTON, D.C.

ANNABEL'S EYES opened wide, her laughter irrepressible. "You still have *that?*" she said.

"Of course I do," said Carole.

The two women sat at a long French pine kitchen table in the "Admiral's House" on the grounds of the Naval Observatory on upper Massachusetts Avenue. The so-called Category II Historic Landmark house had been the official residence of the vice president and family ever since Congress decreed it to be so in 1974.

Annabel picked up the faded Polaroid to examine it more closely. "You had so much . . . hair then," Annabel said.

"And less weight. Don't be tactful." Carole Aprile was the wife of the vice president of the United States, Joseph Aprile. "Can you believe we ever looked like that?"

"No."

Carole Aprile, then Carole Peckham, and

Annabel Reed, now Reed-Smith, had been college roommates. The photo showed them printed and painted for a dorm Halloween party.

"Burn it," said Annabel.

"Never. I can always use it to blackmail you with Mac. More coffee?"

"Thanks, no. So, Carole, tell me more about this intriguing assignment you've handed me."

Both women turned as a Secret Service agent passed outside the kitchen window. "I'm still not used to having strange men surrounding me day and night," Carole said. Her husband and the president he served had come into office slightly less than a year ago.

"We would have welcomed it back when that picture was taken," Annabel said.

"You bet. I'm so pleased you've agreed to serve on the commission, Annabel."

"I was flattered to be asked. Mac and I were pleasantly surprised when the president announced that the White House would *have* an arts commission. The arts weren't on anyone's priority list in the last administration."

"And still aren't in Congress. Maybe we can change a few minds. This Caravaggio exhibition is a wonderful place to start."

"It must tickle you to see Caravaggio come to Washington," Annabel said. "Your master's thesis on him was a real valentine."

"Got an A, too. Well, an A-minus. He's always fascinated me."

"He's beginning to fascinate me, too, ever since you asked me to get involved. I've done some reading about Caravaggio and his work. A monumental talent—"

"Just the word. And certifiable nut. Look, Annabel, let me be a little more candid than I was when I asked you to be my liaison to the National Gallery and the Caravaggio show. There's more involved than I let on."

"Oh? I will have more coffee. Half a cup."

Carole poured. She'd excused the member of her household staff who'd stood by to serve the two old friends. Carole Aprile was known to be as much of a hands-on "second lady" as her husband, the vice president, was known to be more than an accessory to the president. Still, the fifty-ish black woman hovered outside the kitchen in the event she was needed.

"You're probably aware of problems we've been having with the Italians. They accused one of our embassy people there of spying . . ."

"I also read about the bribery charges against those defense contractors—"

"Business as usual, they say, bribing foreign governments to get big contracts—"

"And the drug-trafficking stories."

"And more. We've got a lot more going with Italy than most people think. We've also got a sizable Italian-American population, most of whom voted for this administration. The point is that we don't need some scandal to come out of the Caravaggio exhibition. Cathy Eder is doing a good job as my official contact with the Gallery. But that's the problem. She's official. Not privy to everything going on behind closed doors over there. You, on the other hand, might be more readily accepted because of your stature in the arts. And as my college chum."

"It sounds a little as though you want me to . . . well, would 'snoop' be the appropriate word?"

Carole smiled. "Not at all. Maybe a little. Court Whitney is an enigma. Do you know him?"

"Barely. A few social meetings. I know Luther Mason a lot better."

Carole sat back and sighed. "Ah, dear, sweet Luther. I love him."

"So do I, in a metaphorical sense. He was very supportive when I opened my gallery. Still is, even though pre-Columbian art isn't his thing."

" 'His thing.' Michelangelo Merisi Caravaggio. That's his thing. If he isn't the world's leading authority on Caravaggio, he's one of two or three. Curating this exhibition is the highlight of an already highlighted career. He's in heaven."

"Good for him. You say Whitney is an enigma. Why?"

"He's hard to read. From what I hear, he's doing a good job as the Gallery's director. But Cathy told me last week she senses some sort of rift between Whitney and Luther. And the other senior curator, Paul Bishop."

"Artistic temperaments at odds?"

"I was hoping you'd tell me."

"After I do a little snooping. Okay. I have my first meeting there tomorrow morning. I'll report back."

"Great. I just want to be sure everything will go smoothly with the Caravaggio show. I'll feel more secure knowing I have a trusted friend on the scene."

"I'll do my best."

They stood outside together in warm sunshine, flanked by two Secret Service agents. The car sent by Carole Aprile to pick up Annabel that morning pulled into the driveway. Annabel looked up at the house's façade, an unattractive melding of Victorian, Queen Anne, and French Provincial. "Interesting architecture," she said.

"A typically tactful comment," said Carole, grinning. "It's not exactly a well-tossed salad, is it?" The sun kicked off the sheen in her blonde hair, now worn short and stylish, in contrast to the wild and wooly mane of her college years. Carole Aprile was four inches shorter than the five foot, nine inch Annabel Reed-Smith. The VP's wife wore a smart, knee-length dress. Annabel's suit was beige linen, her blouse copper-colored.

"My best to Mac," Carole said as the driver

opened the car's door for Annabel. "How is he?"

"Fine. Grumbling now and then about the current crop of law students' attitudes, and forever promising to paint the house. He refuses to hire someone, he's not really retired, races to every crime scene at the mildest cry for help, so it never seems to get done. Say hello to the vice president for us."

"When, and if, I ever get to see him. Thanks, Annabel."

Annabel's final words before the car door closed were, "And burn that Polaroid."

THREE

THE NATIONAL GALLERY
OF ART

COURTNEY WHITNEY III patted senior curator Paul Bishop on the back. "Consider it a good news, bad news thing, Paul. The bad news? Another voice to be heard, another set of eyes looking over our shoulders. The good news? Genuine interest in what we're doing by the White House itself. Mrs. Smith certainly isn't a bureaucrat like Cathy Eder. As I understand it, she and Mrs. Aprile go back to college together."

"Hardly a reason to have her assigned as liaison," the short, burly Bishop muttered.

"It doesn't matter what you or I feel about her involvement, Paul." Another slap on the curator's broad back. "Let's welcome her this morning with open arms. She's a charming lady and extremely attractive. Even knows something about art."

"Maybe that's why Luther's so pleased with her coming here."

Whitney laughed as he removed his suit jacket from an oak coat tree in a corner of his office, one of three new suits recently arrived from his Savile

Row tailor-of-choice, Tommy Nutter. "I suspect the last thing on Luther's mind these days is attractive women. His love affair with Caravaggio is all-consuming. Besides, Mrs. Smith is happily married. Or so I hear. By the way, did you see this?" He handed Bishop the latest edition of the monthly bulletin *Stolen Art Alert,* compiled and distributed by the International Foundation for Art Research. Bishop quickly perused the list of recently stolen art, grunted, and said, "Three Pretis, huh?"

"Among other things. Come on. They're waiting for us."

The National Gallery's Exhibition Committee met every three weeks in a tastefully furnished conference room on the seventh floor of the gallery's East Building, a few doors from the director's office. Upon the arrival of Court Whitney, the National Gallery's director, the seven permanent members of the committee took up proposals for exhibitions that had been suggested by the gallery's curatorial staff or curators from other museums wanting cooperation. This morning, however, Paul Bishop began by voicing his continuing objection to an exhibition already installed, the early works of French artist Dubuffet, which had been donated to the Gallery by retired art dealer Stephen Hahn and permanently installed in the East Building. "Dubuffet!" he snorted. "An untalented mudslinger. The public may be brutish, but even *it* has disdain for *art brute.*"

Others at the table winced, smiled, or sat back, breathing patience through their nostrils. The Dubuffet exhibition was reality. Why continue to protest? To make his point, they knew. Paul Bishop was a man consumed with making his point about anything and everything.

The gallery's deputy director, Naomi Warren, quickly advanced that morning's agenda. After much discussion, an exhibition of African art was shelved until it could be determined if administrators of the National Museum of African Art, across the Mall, would be interested in collaborating (and wouldn't find their noses too far out of joint). A decision on an educational exhibition suggested by Paul Bishop featuring works of the *Nabis,* particularly the influence of Japanese art on that iconoclastic turn-of-the-century school of painting anchored by Bonnard and Vuillard, was also postponed. It would first have to be determined how many representative pieces of art were available for loan before discussions could continue.

"Well," Whitney said from the head of the table, "I suppose we should get to today's main topic, the Caravaggio exhibition." He asked Naomi Warren to bring in Annabel Reed-Smith.

Annabel, in a tailored brown skirt, white button-down shirt, and softly shaped camel-hair jacket, entered the room with confidence and easy grace, someone at home in unfamiliar places and with unfamiliar faces. The red hair with which she'd been born had burnished over the years into copper. She wore it full, creating a glowing frame for her creamy, unlined face. Her eyes were, of course, green, as if ordained, and large. Her nose, ears, and mouth had been conceived with a stunning sense of proportion.

Annabel Reed had once been one of Washington's leading matrimonial attorneys, known for sympathizing with the pain men went through in divorce, as well as the suffering of her female clients, many of them well-known Washington figures. But her passion had always been art, particularly pre-Columbian.

An elderly curator of Dumbarton Oaks's pre-Columbian collection retired and opened a gallery to fill his days. But running a business became overwhelming to him—more accurately, to his wife, who wanted him with her in the garden—and he sought a partner. Enter Annabel.

She eventually bought him out, maintaining her law practice while running the gallery. A year later, she took down her shingle and became a full-time, and blissfully happy, gallery owner.

The men at the table stood. "Please, have a seat," said Whitney, having buttoned his suit jacket for the few seconds his midriff was exposed. "A pleasure to see you this morning, Mrs. Smith. You know some of us. I'll let the others handle their own introductions."

Annabel pleasantly returned greetings and took a chair next to senior curator Luther Mason, who kissed her on the cheek. "Good to see you," he said.

"First, Mrs. Smith, let me welcome you to this meeting of the exhibition committee." Whitney had unbuttoned his jacket. "Sorry to have asked you to remain outside, but we try to keep the discussion of proposed exhibitions to a minimal number of people."

"Hardly an unpleasant wait," said Annabel. "Not that I was surprised, but there are lovely pieces of art everywhere, in every hallway, above every desk. It must be a delight working in a museum, surrounded by such beauty."

"There are those who view our surroundings as a perk of working at the National Gallery," said Whitney. He added, "Of course, there are others who would prefer higher pay."

"Insensates all," Paul Bishop muttered.

"Hard to understand why anyone would want health insurance with all this art around," said George Kublinski, chief of the National Gallery's Design and Exhibition Department. Kublinski was a cherubic man with animated blue eyes and a seemingly unlimited reservoir of humor and energy. His large collection of splashily colorful suspenders was a personal trademark.

"Employees are a bother, with their incessant demands for survival," Luther Mason said, with a warm smile.

Annabel noted that senior curator Luther Mason and director Courtney Whitney were built along the same lines, both tall and reed-thin, enabling them to model their clothing nicely. But that's where the similarity ended. Whitney had a full head of brown hair flecked with gray. Mason's male-pattern baldness had progressed to the middle of his head. Was he allowing it to grow long enough at the back to drape over his shirt collar in an attempt at compensation? Or was it, as an occasional detractor commented, Mason's gentle rebellion against Washington's conservative image? Curators in New York might get away with long hair, but few would in the nation's capital. That day Luther wore jeans, a red-and-blue-check button-down shirt, rumpled tweed jacket, maroon knit tie, and tasseled loafers, sans socks.

But it was the marked difference in their facial expressions that struck Annabel. Whitney had lank lips; the hinges at the corners of his mouth didn't allow his lips to part very far when smiling, resulting in what appeared to be pained, insincere smiles. Luther's smile, on the other hand, had an openness to it that was, at once, inviting and genuine.

Whitney directed the meeting back on course. "As all of you are aware," he said, "the new administration has expressed a keen interest in the artistic life of this nation. Among many things President Jeppsen has managed to accomplish in the early days of his presidency has been the establishment of the White House Commission on the Arts, spearheaded by Vice President and Mrs. Aprile." He looked to Annabel. "I understand the first person Mrs. Aprile called was you, Mrs. Smith."

"Carole Aprile and I were college roommates," Annabel said. "And please call me Annabel." As she mentioned her personal history with Carole Aprile, she wondered if her appointment to the commission might be viewed by some as an example of bureaucratic cronyism, a pal's patronage. She let that thought pass. What did it matter what anyone thought? The fact was that after having abandoned a lucrative career as a matrimonial attorney, and with the unbridled support of her husband, handsome, urbane law professor Mackensie Smith, who'd closed his criminal law practice to teach after losing his first wife and son in a Beltway accident, she'd indulged her dream of opening a pre-Columbian art gallery in Georgetown. It had flourished, along with her stature in Washington's increasingly vibrant arts community.

Whitney continued: "Mrs. Aprile has appointed Mrs. Smith—Annabel—as White House liaison to the Caravaggio exhibition. Needless to say, there are significant political ramifications to this show.

Those of you who have been dealing with the Italian government know how difficult they've made it for some of the Caravaggios to travel here, and then on to the Met, and London. I'm personally gratified at the level of interest shown by the White House in resolving these problems, and I know I speak for everyone in this room, Annabel, in welcoming your direct involvement."

"I'm glad I can be a part of it," she said. "Ever since Carole—Mrs. Aprile—asked me to become involved, I've been reading more about Caravaggio. Not only a master, a controversial fellow as well."

Luther Mason laughed. "A gentle characterization from a gentle lady," he said. "Just because Caravaggio was in the habit of killing people shouldn't taint our opinion of him."

Until his death a dozen years ago, Roberto Longhi had been considered without peer as a Caravaggio scholar. At his passing, that appellation was passed to Sir Denis Mahon, although a growing number of unofficial judges of such things had come to view Mason as being, at least, on a par with Sir Denis. Mahon was in his late eighties; unless he possessed centenarian genes, Mason would find himself standing alone one day as Caravaggio scholar *par excellence.*

There were, of course, dozens of others with a deep knowledge and appreciation of Caravaggio's work. But they were bunched well behind in second place. Mahon and Mason had already crossed the finish line.

Remembering Carole's comment about her staffer's report of a rift among the gallery's hierarchy, Annabel made it a point to observe the interplay between Whitney, Mason, and Bishop. There was a certain tension, she decided, but nothing overt. Paul Bishop's responses to comments made by Mason tended to be curt, even gruff on occasion. But Bishop was gruff with everyone. And Whitney demonstrated at times what Annabel thought might be a patronizing patience with Mason. But on the whole, the gallery's director and his two senior curators acted like the busy professionals they were. At least that was Annabel's perception.

What she didn't know—yet—was that Luther Mason disliked the new director intensely—"Oh, for the good old days of Carter Brown and Rusty Powell" (Whitney's predecessors), he told discreet friends.

During a lull in the conversation, Paul Bishop said, without provocation, "Can you believe that moronic critic in the *Times* years ago who actually tried to find a comparison between Dubuffet and Rembrandt, of all things? Just because they both favored brown, and heavy textures, hardly begs such a comparison. Maybe it was that Rembrandt preferred old models, and Dubuffet enjoyed bloated, deformed ones."

Whitney sighed. He knew that Bishop was annoyed now that the meeting's focus had turned to the Caravaggio exhibition, in which he would play only a minor role. Worse, it promised to be the crowning achievement of Luther Mason's twenty-two years at the National Gallery. Gravel in Bishop's craw. Meanwhile, Mason enjoyed the unbridled respect of the gallery's vast staff. More important, he had the faith of a number of the institution's most powerful members of the Board of Trustees. Mason could do no wrong in their eyes. That's why Whitney picked his arguments with Mason carefully.

Knowing that Whitney disliked Mason, Bishop had made a point of getting close to the new director and enjoyed his disparaging offhand comments about Mason. But those were private moments. In the National Gallery of Art's hierarchy, Luther Mason stood tallest. And the Caravaggio exhibition would only elevate his reputation and stature to new heights.

Whitney cleared his throat. "We would all appreciate an update from you, Luther, on how things are progressing with the exhibition." To Annabel: "We've been working on this show for almost two years. Six months to go, which in this business is getting down to the wire."

Mason opened a leather-bound legal-sized book, removed half-glasses from his pocket, placed them on the end of his nose, and silently

surveyed his notes. Satisfied he'd sufficiently readied himself, he took in the others at the table: "I
would say that things are progressing quite nicely.
I'm leaving this evening for Rome. I think final
arrangements will *at last* be made with the Borghese Gallery for the three works it's loaning us—
The Little Bacchus, St. John the Baptist, and *David
with the Head of Goliath.* Donald and his people
have made two trips to the Borghese. I believe you
have their reports. It's their professional judgment
that those three paintings can be safely traveled.
You are aware, of course, that Donald insists that
special climate-controlled boxes be constructed
here." He looked at Whitney. "It is my understanding that you have approved the construction
of those special crates."

"That's right, Luther. Please move along."

Annabel heard the unnecessary sharp edge to
the director's voice.

"The Registrar is currently putting final touches
on the agreements with the Uffizi, the Her-
mitage—although Lord knows the Russians have
been, as usual, infuriating in their demands—the
Louvre, and the National Gallery in London.
We've run into a number of unfortunate snags
with Galleria Doria-Pamphili concerning *Penitent
Mary Magdalene* and *Rest on the Flight to Egypt.*
Because they're in private hands, an additional set
of egos have had to be dealt with. Bad enough to
deal with the bureaucrats thrown in the way by the

Italians, without having to salve pompous private citizens. But still, they are the owners, lawfully, I might add, unlike the Russians." He sighed deeply, as though seeking something from an inner reservoir. He found it. "Carlo Giliberti has been extremely helpful in these matters."

Giliberti, one of Luther's close friends, had been running interference for the National Gallery, through the Italian Embassy in Washington, since the idea of a Caravaggio exhibition was first raised.

Mason's briefing of the exhibition committee lasted another ten minutes and was surprisingly efficient; and underneath, the joy at the prospect of being surrounded by Caravaggios shone through everything he said and had already accomplished. When he was through, Whitney turned to design chief George Kublinski, who spread a set of preliminary drawings of the exhibition on the table.

Initial debate about where to hold the show within the National Gallery's two buildings had been spirited, sometimes rancorous. The East Building, the newer of the two, had more available exhibition space. But because it was primarily used to show the works of more contemporary artists, Mason held fast to his insistence that to place the works of Michelangelo Caravaggio in such a modern architectural setting would be a form of blasphemy. He prevailed, and plans proceeded to use a gallery in the West Building to showcase Caravaggio's works—his artistic output amounted to no more than fifty paintings, according to those who kept score. Approximately thirty would soon hang in the National Gallery.

"I'd like to raise an issue," said Naomi Warren.

"Yes?" Whitney said.

"I had a meeting earlier this morning with the Education Office concerning materials to be distributed to schools. They're concerned about how to handle Caravaggio's tumultuous personal life. He's hardly the sort of role model for the million or so school kids who'll be reading these materials."

"Simple," said Paul Bishop. "We leave out everything having to do with those he murdered, his homosexuality, his dastardly behavior with family and friends, and his subsequent drug-crazed death on that beach." His tone was smug, arrogant.

"Absolutely not," Mason said, closing the cover of his leather-bound book with unnecessary force. "Are we mounting what is perhaps this institution's most important exhibition in years, or are we running a board of education?"

"I think Naomi's point is valid," Whitney said.

"I think not, Naomi, but the point is absurd," said Mason. "Who are we to separate the man from his work? Should we purge any mentions of the Sistine Chapel from the history texts because

Michelangelo was gay? Caravaggio was a bona
fide genius. Geniuses walk their own path. We're
not approving his *life.*"

Whitney suggested to Naomi that they schedule
a meeting as soon as possible with the Education
Department. Mason's face mirrored his pique at
the director's response. He stood and said, "I believe we've covered everything of substance for
now. Will you excuse me? I have to finish preparing for my trip."

"First class, of course," Bishop said.

Mason turned to Bishop, smiled, and said, "Yes,
Paul. First class." It was as if he had said: First
class for those involved in first-class curating. But
he added: "At no extra cost to the taxpayers." And
left the room.

The meeting lasted only a few minutes more.
When asked whether there was anything Annabel
wished to convey on behalf of the White House
Arts Council, she said only that Carole Aprile had
written her master's thesis on the work of
Michelangelo Caravaggio. "I would say her interest in this exhibition is more than a passing one."

"Wonderful to hear that," said Whitney. "And
thank you for joining us, Annabel. I look forward
to many more meetings with you. Would you come
to my office for a few minutes?"

Once there, he asked, "Think that distinguished
husband of yours can spare you now and then?"

"Spare me? From what?"

Whitney smiled. "Not spare you *from,* Annabel. Spare you *for* a few trips on our behalf."

"Trips? Where am I going?"

"I spoke with Mrs. Aprile this morning. She agrees that having you accompany some of our people to Italy for final negotiations on the Caravaggio exhibition makes sense. You wouldn't be traveling in an official capacity, of course. But you would add a sense of direct involvement by the White House, which might help us get over a few remaining hurdles with the Italian government."

"I'd love it," said Annabel without hesitation. "I assume I'd be traveling with Luther Mason."

"And others. Have a problem with Mason?"

"Oh, no. I've known Luther for years. Brilliant and pleasant to be with. No, no problem. Would *he* have a problem having me tag along?"

"Why would he?"

"I don't know. This woman representing the White House meddling in what is very much his domain."

"Don't give it a second thought. Too late for you to go with him tonight. Or could you swing it?"

"Afraid not."

"I'll have Luther put together a fast itinerary covering the next few months. You take a look at it and pick your spots to participate."

"Fair enough. And thanks again for all your courtesy this morning."

"My pleasure. Oh . . . mind a suggestion?"

"Of course not."

"We never call ourselves a museum, Annabel. New York's Metropolitan is a museum. Lots of things from all the ages. We just collect pictures, and some sculpture. We're a gallery. Not a museum."

"I'll remember that," said Annabel, wondering whether he was trying to be helpful or had issued a mild rebuke. Or both.

"Best to your husband."

"He'll enjoy hearing from you. He loves the Gallery—and hates museums."

"How did it go?" Mackensie Smith asked after he and Annabel had been seated for a lunch of almond chicken salad at C. F. Folks, on Nineteenth Street, below Dupont Circle.

"Fine," said Annabel. "Pretty big brains and bigger egos in the room this morning. Put some politicians to shame."

Mac chuckled. "Luther Mason?"

"Everyone. Luther. The new director, Whitney. Who sends his best. Another curator named Bishop. Some sparks flew."

"Sorry you got involved?"

"Absolutely not. I enjoy sparks now and then."

"On the Fourth of July. And as long as they don't land on you. Sparks can burn. Start large fires."

"I can handle it."

"I have no doubt about that, Annabel. Never have."

"Whitney wants me to accompany Luther and others on some of the trips to Italy," Annabel said. "Sort of lend a presence on behalf of Carole and the White House."

"Makes sense. When are you leaving?"

"I don't know. They're putting together a list of scheduled trips. I'm to choose which ones to take. Join me? We haven't been to Italy together."

He dabbed at his mouth with his napkin, sat back, and sighed contentedly. *"Sei la più bella ragazza del mondo,"* he said, a big grin on his handsome face.

She laughed. "I forgot. You speak some Italian. Let's see. You think I'm beautiful. The *most* beautiful woman in the world?"

"Si. Vuoi venire a vedere i miei tatuaggi?"

"You've lost me."

"I asked if you'd like to come up and see my tattoos."

"Your tattoos? Why would you—?"

"Just a phrase I happen to remember."

"You don't have any tattoos."

"I know. Should I get one?"

"No."

"I'd love to go to Italy with you. I can accompany you as your spouse. Maybe they have a museum tour for spouses, and a shopping mall."

"I certainly hope so."

"Should I pack this afternoon?" he asked.

"You're already packed." Mac Smith always kept a suitcase packed "just in case."

"Italy," he said to no one, returning to his lunch. "Sounds lovely. Eat your salad, Annabel. It's very good, and not at all Italian."

FOUR

⊠ ———————————————————— ⊠

THAT NIGHT—DULLES
INTERNATIONAL AIRPORT

CARLO GILIBERTI was waiting when Luther
Mason arrived for their Alitalia flight to Rome.
Mason would have preferred flying another carrier, on which he'd accumulated more frequent
flier miles, but that wouldn't have been politic. Alitalia had joined a growing list of corporate sponsors of the Caravaggio exhibition and had been
designated the official carrier of the art for the exhibition. It was expected, although unstated, that
Gallery staff use the airline whenever possible. In
return for this consideration, the airline had insti-
tuted its own quiet policy of upgrading senior
Gallery personnel to first class.

The Italian cultural attaché and the senior curator were a study in opposites: Mason looked every
bit the professor, or gallery curator. His double-
breasted navy blazer was sculpted to his tall, slender frame. His shirt was a blue button-down
model, his tie a muted blue paisley. He wore gray
slacks and brown walking shoes with thick crepe
soles. Mason held to what had become a hope-

lessly old-fashioned belief that one should dress nicely when traveling. His only fear of flying was that he would be seated next to someone wearing a tank top, sandals, and a baseball cap worn backwards, and who wanted to talk.

Giliberti, also thin, was considerably shorter. His suit was silver gray; hundreds of tiny metallic threads woven into the cloth shimmered in the overhead lights. The collar of his white shirt rose unnaturally high at the back of his neck. His tie was a palette of reds, greens, and yellows, his shoes highly polished black loafers with paper-thin soles. The cultural attaché's swarthy face had a chiseled quality, the nose large and prominent, some acne pitting scarring his cheeks. His hair was coal-black, wavy, and wet.

Their traveling styles were different, too. Mason sat in his preferred window seat in first class, where he was less likely to be called upon to chat. The more gregarious Giliberti, a familiar face on Alitalia, was especially friendly this night with one of the flight attendants, engaging her in long, animated conversations. Mason contented himself with reading magazines and reports he'd carried aboard in a well-worn expandable brown-leather briefcase. Giliberti watched the movie, a current American comedy with Italian subtitles, its racy scenes deleted in order not to offend the flying public.

Mussolini would have been proud, Mason

thought, as the aircraft pulled up to the gate precisely at its scheduled arrival time at Rome's Leonardo da Vinci Airport, on the coast, fifteen miles east of the city. With Giliberti leading the way, they were sped through Customs and into a waiting government Mercedes that took them to the Valadier Hotel in the heart of the Eternal City. The Valadier, once a brothel, was Luther Mason's place of choice when in Rome. Its transformation into a luxurious hotel, with the largest bathrooms in the city, was inherently appealing. But it was its location that he especially enjoyed. Situated just below Pincio Hill, the Valadier was only a short walk to the splendors of Villa Borghese's sumptuous grounds and esteemed museums, as well as the popular Piazza del Popolo.

"What time is our meeting?" Mason asked as he prepared to leave the Mercedes.

"Two hours," replied Giliberti. "I'll pick you up at ten-thirty."

Mason followed the bellman and his luggage into a lobby gleaming with marble, polished brass, expanses of mahogany, and overflowing arrangements of fresh flowers. He was shown to the room he always tried to reserve, one of three with a terrace overlooking the Borghese gardens. He slowly and carefully unpacked, neatly arranging socks, underwear, and shirts in dresser drawers and positioning his hang-up clothing in the large closet so that the garments were equidistant from each other.

After a quick shower, he opened the door to allow room service to deliver coffee and fresh pastries. Ninety minutes later he joined Giliberti in the waiting car.

MINISTERO DELLA CULTURA

Alberto Betti was as corpulent as Carlo Giliberti was thin. Perhaps *round* was a better adjective to describe the minister of culture, whose office in the seventeenth-century Palazzo di Montecitorio was proportionally large to accommodate him, or so it seemed. Minister of Circles, Luther Mason thought, for Betti appeared to be constructed of a series of them, the type drawn by young children on stick figures. There was a circle for his head, almost perfect, its upper curved pate disturbed by strands of thinning black hair. A larger circle defined his torso and was covered by a drab, wrinkled blue suit—enough material to make four suits of average size, Mason mused. The circles were supported by short tree trunks for legs inside his trousers. Like most overweight people, Betti tended to perspire and to breathe laboriously. The long, slender black cigarettes he chain-smoked didn't help.

In all his trips to Rome, Mason had never met Alberto Betti. Giliberti always took care of details involving the Italian government, including the payment of an occasional "gift" to an unnamed government official to, as Giliberti would say, *"ungere."* Grease the palm. Never large sums. Petty graft, small enough for Mason to include on his expense account under "miscellaneous." That was what bothered him most. To compromise one's principles and reputation for such minor money was doubly distasteful to him. If you were going to steal, which he had never done, aside from penny-candy thefts as a small boy, at least steal big.

The globular minister of culture sat heavily behind his desk and asked, *"Caffè?"* Giliberti accepted, Mason declined. As they waited for Betti's secretary to bring the coffee, Giliberti and Betti engaged in a spirited conversation. Mason, who had a working knowledge of Italian, quietly listened to their banter about women, the most recent of many political upheavals in Italy, food, and again, women. After coffee had been served, Mason asked Betti, in Italian, whether the problem of the "six-month rule" had been resolved.

Betti looked to Giliberti, smiled through fleshy lips, and raised his hands in a gesture that asked, "What is the answer?"

"I explained to Mr. Mason on the flight here, your excellency, that it appeared to me, based upon our last conversation, that a solution was at hand. But as I also explained, it is not as easy to bend the rules these days as it was before the current situation."

Mason knew the "current situation" referred to a series of Mafia scandals that had rocked both the Italian government and big business. The pressure was on. Rules, even the most archaic, were now being followed to the letter after decades of breaking them as a matter of national pride.

"But as is always the case," Giliberti said, directing his comment to Mason and raising his eyebrows, "there is always the possibility of *l'eccezione.* An accommodation." To Betti: "Am I correct, your excellency? *Fra amici.* We are among friends."

Betti said, *"Si,"* shifted his bulk in his chair, and ran a finger between his circles, his collar, and the folds of his neck.

Giliberti smiled broadly at Mason. "You see, Luther, we are not nearly as unbending as you might previously have thought."

"Let me be direct, Minister Betti," said Mason. "Are you saying that an exception to the six-month rule will be made for our Caravaggio exhibition?"

The top circle broke into an arc resembling a grin. "The six-month rule is not without merit," he said, pudgy hands taking flight. "You are certainly aware, Mr. Mason, that Italy is rich in artistic treasures. Does not this nation possess more great works of art than any other? We must have rules."

Mason controlled a growing anger and frustration as he nodded. He didn't need lectures from a fat politician whose only connection with the art world was to stand in the way of progress. But he knew what was coming. This time he had traveled to Rome prepared for it.

Betti continued: "All the world wishes to borrow our masterpieces. All the world's museums want them displayed on their walls. You are no exception, you and your National Gallery." He chuckled. "Obviously, a man of your artistic sensibilities understands the need for a country of origin like Italy to enact all possible legislation to protect its treasures."

Mason's stomach growled, matching his mood.

"This is especially necessary with an artist of Caravaggio's stature and talent. His works rank among civilization's finest. From his early days in Milan until his tragic death at the age of thirty-nine, he created the most inspired religious paintings of all time. There were those who were less than kind in their judgment of his work. Giovanni Baglione wrote that Caravaggio had 'ruined the art of painting.' Another, your Mr. Ruskin I believe, no, the English person, said he found Caravaggio's work to represent—let me see if I accurately recall what he said—he said it represented 'horror and ugliness and filthiness of sin.' But the more enlightened admirers of his work . . ."

Mason seriously wondered if he could contain

himself any longer and not bolt from the room. What an insult to have this bureaucrat lecture *him,* Luther Mason, on the importance of Caravaggio. As far as he was concerned, no one in the world—including any Italian—knew more about the artist than he did. His expertise was acknowledged internationally. He'd written the definitive book on the artist's work. His papers appeared in dozens of scholarly journals. To be subjected to this sham violated every one of his senses.

But he stayed, his face expressionless, his posture rigid in the overstuffed chair, his belly burning.

"You and your superiors have found the arrangements suggested to Carlo to be satisfactory?" Betti asked, as much with raised eyebrows as with his voice.

Mason thought he might choke on the word: "Yes."

Betti said to Giliberti, "It will be carried out as instructed?"

Giliberti's reply was an enthusiastic affirmative.

"Splendid," said Betti, pushing himself up by placing his hands on the desk. "When reasonable men who share an appreciation of true genius and beauty can sit and rationally discuss such matters, a satisfactory conclusion is almost always reached." He extended his hand to Mason. "It is my sincere hope that your Caravaggio exhibition in Washington will be the highlight of that esteemed institution's long and illustrious history."

"I'm certain it will be, Signor Betti."

Mason waited in the reception area until Giliberti joined him. "You see, Luther? I told you
everything had been worked out."

They lunched at an outside table at Piccolo
Mondo, on the Corso, the famous thoroughfare
once used by ancient Romans for horse racing,
now home to countless restaurants and cafes.
Mason ordered cold pasta with tomato and basil,
while Giliberti indulged in a heaping plate of *coda
alla vaccinara;* Mason found the thought of eating
oxtail off-putting.

"Are you sure you don't want me at the meeting
this afternoon?" asked Giliberti, referring to a
three o'clock date Mason had at Galleria Borghese.

"Not necessary."

Had he been entirely truthful, Mason would
have admitted he'd had enough of his Italian
friend for one day.

"Tonight? You have plans?"

"To read, and to go to bed early," Mason said.

"If you change your mind, call me."

As they finished their coffee and waited for the
check, Giliberti leaned across the small table and
said, "The minister is a sensible man, *si?*"

"The minister is an unprincipled slob," Luther
replied.

Giliberti recoiled in mock horror, then laughed
too loud. "Luther, even though we deal with great
art, we also must recognize that it is a business, this

loaning of paintings from one country to another.
So a little money will pass hands from your country to ours, from someone there to someone here.
Where is the harm in that? It is done every day, *si?*
In your country. In my country."

Mason's bottled-up anger at what had transpired that morning now came from his mouth in
a low, steady stream. "Carlo, we are talking about
transporting precious, priceless paintings by Caravaggio from your country to mine to be put on
display at the National Gallery. Because of your
arbitrary rule that no art treasure may be out of
the country longer than six months, and because
the exhibition will travel to the Met and to London, we must again crate those precious paintings
at the end of six months, put them on planes, and
return them to Rome, where they will sit in your
depressing airport for twenty-four hours to satisfy
some stupid law, and then be flown back to the
United States. Transporting those priceless works
once is dangerous enough. To subject them to unnecessary packing and traveling is idiotic."

Giliberti started to speak, but Mason continued. "On top of that, money is to be paid to certain unnamed individuals in your Ministry of
Culture—*tangentopoli!*—bribesville—paid to have
the rule bent so that the paintings can be placed in
greater jeopardy, and—"

The waiter placed the check in front of Giliberti, who didn't make a move. Mason dumped an appropriate pile of *lire* on it, stood, and said, "You must excuse my moment of pique, Carlo. It was a very long flight, and an even longer hour with your minister of culture, who, by the way, hardly deserves the title. He bought the position, you say? I believe it. I'll be in a considerably better mood after I get a good night's sleep."

"Of course, my friend," Giliberti said, following Mason to the sidewalk. "We will breakfast together?"

"If you'd like."

"I would like very much. We must leave early to allow time for the drive."

"All right. Now excuse me, Carlo. I have a dreadful headache," said Mason, sounding to himself for a second like the classic disaffected wife.

"By all means. I am just so happy that things went well this morning with his excellency." Giliberti held open the door of the waiting Mercedes, but Mason shook his head. "It's only a few blocks to the hotel. A walk might help clear my head. I'll see you at the hotel at nine for breakfast."

"I shall be there. Enjoy your evening in Rome, *amico. Ma sta attento o te ne pentirai!*"

Luther didn't have to be reminded that crime was rampant in Rome.

In retrospect, Luther was sorry that he'd been cross with his friend. He'd been losing his temper with greater frequency lately. But who could blame him? The mounting of the exhibition at Mason's curatorial home for the past twenty-two years, the National Gallery of Art in Washington, D.C., was the most meaningful event of his professional life. It was also proving to be the most difficult of the many exhibitions he'd curated.

It was hard enough navigating the tricky waters of foreign governments and international art dealers to pull together a show of this magnitude. But now there was the added complication of the new director, Mr. Courtney Whitney III.

From Mason's perspective, Whitney's talent was limited to wooing wealthy patrons of the arts and schmoozing with members of the Board of Trustees at interminable cocktail parties and dinners and weekends in the country. But did he have a genuine appreciation of the art that hung in the gallery he directed? Hung anywhere for that matter? Not as far as Luther was concerned.

It had been Mason's dream that the Gallery one day own a work by Caravaggio as part of its permanent collection, and he considered not owning one a representation of the Gallery's glaring weakness. The National Gallery possessed a still life that had once been thought to have come from Caravaggio's hand, but subsequent analysis cast serious doubt on its provenance.

And years ago, former National Gallery director John Walker had bid seriously for Caravaggio's

Saint John the Baptist. But not seriously enough. It went to Kansas City's Nelson Gallery–Atkins Museum. After stepping down as director, Walker often cited losing that painting as one of his greatest professional disappointments.

Aside from the intense personal pleasure Mason would take from having many of the petulant genius's works occupying the walls of the National Gallery for the six months of the exhibition, he also hoped that one of the lenders to the show, possibly a private dealer, would be sufficiently impressed by the gallery's professional approach to will a Caravaggio to it. It had happened before— but never, unfortunately, with a Caravaggio.

The three o'clock meeting with a curator and the administrative head of the Galleria Borghese was over in fifteen minutes. There were only a few details to iron out, which Mason knew when he planned this trip. The meeting could easily have been accomplished by telephone. But using the phone would have meant not making this particular journey to Italy. Of all the trips Luther Mason had taken there over the years, this one had to be made.

FIVE

THE FOLLOWING MORNING

CARLO GILIBERTI was late for breakfast, something to do, he told Luther, with an unexpected and thoroughly delightful meeting with a female friend he hadn't seen in years—*"Bellezza rara, Luther, a raving beauty"*—who was reluctant to have him leave her apartment that morning. Luther had already eaten and was waiting in the lobby, his suitcases at his side. The Italian cultural attaché's penchant for being late was pathological. And so routine it no longer annoyed Mason.

They placed the luggage in the rear seat of Giliberti's red Fiat convertible. Mason folded his lanky frame into the passenger bucket seat, secured the seat belt, and clenched his teeth. Under ordinary circumstances, he would have insisted that Giliberti arrange for a government vehicle and driver. But this was not an ordinary circumstance.

From the moment Giliberti slapped the gearshift into first and pulled away from the curb, Mason's apprehension was understandable. Giliberti was a pure madman behind the wheel, perhaps no more maniacal than the million other drivers in Rome that morning, but sufficiently demented to cause Mason to wince and to tighten his stomach muscles as though preparing to pull G-forces. No matter how often Mason asked Giliberti to slow down, it only inspired the Italian to go faster.

They roared south out of Rome on the A2, the honey and pomegranate hues of the city, the ancient red brick and gleaming white marble and steel of skyscrapers sliding by in an Impressionistic blur as they headed for the less congested *Lazio,* that large region surrounding the city. Another request for Carlo to drive slower was met with a laugh and a surge of the powerful engine.

"We aren't meeting him until dinner," Mason said over the whoosh of wind. "Why are we rushing?"

"We are not rushing, Luther. We are going for a ride. Sit back. Relax. Italians are born to speed."

And to lose wars, Mason thought grimly.

They said little to each other as they passed the Alban Hills on their left; to their right was the beginning of the Tyrrhenian Coast, home to sun-seeking hedonists.

They passed through the town of Frosinone and continued southward into the Campania region until reaching Naples, where they exited the A2. Giliberti followed narrow, winding local roads down along the Amalfi coast, passing Mount

Vesuvius and going through the city of Pompeii, then heading directly south to the pastel seaside resort village of Positano. They checked into the Poseidon, on the coast road near the San Pietro.

"What time are we meeting with him?" Mason asked as they checked in.

"We made very good time, huh?" Giliberti said. "We will meet at eight. Would you like some feminine companionship this afternoon? Positano has the loveliest of *puttane.*"

A prostitute was the furthest thing from Mason's mind. "No," he said. "I'm still fatigued. A nap is certainly in order, maybe a swim in the pool."

"As you wish. One thing concerning our dinner this evening."

"What is that?" Mason asked as a bellman approached to take their baggage.

"The gentleman you will meet is deceiving in his appearance. He is an old man, Luther. Such men are often thought to not pose a threat to anyone. Too old. Too feeble. But he is very powerful in this part of Italy. His connections are strong. Those who work for him are extremely loyal."

As the bellman walked away burdened with their bags, Mason lingered behind with Giliberti. "Be direct with me, Carlo. What are you saying?"

"I am saying, my friend, do not enter into this meeting unless you intend to go through with your plan."

"I made it clear from the beginning," said

Mason, "that it would depend upon my evaluation of what he has to offer."

"Of course, of course, and that is still the understanding. Tonight, you and he will break bread and get to know each other. Establish trust. That is very important to the *Camorra*," he said, referring to the Naples Mafia. "Signor Sensi rules with—what do you say?—with the iron fist. He must trust those with whom he does business."

"And so must I, Carlo."

"Go. Swim. Take your nap. I am confident everything will turn out exactly as you wish."

Mason was alone in the pool. He swam laps until a shoulder cramp sent him to a chaise for a half hour of sun. He returned to his room, sprawled on the bed, and fell asleep. Soft, fragrant breezes drifted in from the terrace through the open French doors.

That evening, Luther and Carlo walked to a restaurant called Covo dei Saraceni, where they were ushered to a table already occupied. He was, as Giliberti had said, an old man. He had the face and hands of someone who'd spent his life doing hard manual labor in the sun; his brown skin had the quality of elephant hide, his face was molded into dozens of lumpy planes. The fingers were gnarled, his gray hair unruly. He wore a suit that had been bought many harvests ago; the points of the collar on the once-white shirt were curled. His tie was a mustard yellow and carelessly knotted.

He reminded Mason of a groundhog.

Aside from a cursory interest in those physical details, Mason was more aware of two young men seated behind the old man at their own small table. He didn't know, of course, that one of them had recently gunned down a former schoolmate, Giovanni Saltore, in an alley in Cosenza, an act for which he'd been rewarded by a promotion to Signor Luigi Sensi's cadre of personal body-guards.

Giliberti introduced Mason to Sensi, but Sensi waved away Mason's outstretched hand and mumbled something in Italian, gesturing for Mason to sit to his left. Giliberti took the chair opposite.

Sensi virtually ignored Mason throughout dinner, speaking to Giliberti in a tired, low, raspy voice. There was no menu. Regional dishes—pasta *all'amatriciana,* made with pancetta and local pecorino cheese; pasta *all'arrabbiata,* which Giliberti explained had been made "angry" with hot peppers; roasted artichokes, tripe; and saltimbocca, slices of veal, cured ham, and sage leaves in a hot sauce—were brought to the table one after the other. The two young men ate what looked to Mason to be spaghetti.

Once dessert had been cleared, the old man leaned in Mason's direction. "So you want to do business with me," he said in hesitant English.

Mason nervously glanced left and right. For the first time he realized that adjacent tables had deliberately been left unoccupied, even though a knot of people waited at the front door for vacancies. *"Si,"* he said in a barely audible voice. The old man fixed him in a cold stare. Mason cleared his throat and repeated, *"Si.* Yes. I would like to do business with you, Signor Sensi, provided, of course, that what you have for sale is—well, is what I want."

Sensi's hand gesture to Giliberti said that he was about to enter into a difficult discussion. He looked at Mason again: "But I do not understand the terms you offer, Signor Mason. No. *Non capisco.* I do not understand. You will forgive me, but I am an old man."

Mason looked to Giliberti, whose face was serious. "Didn't you explain to Signor Sensi about how we would proceed?" he asked.

"Of course. But what you suggest is unusual. Not the normal way Signor Sensi does business."

Mason's stomach had knotted, and he felt woozy. He'd sipped only half a glass of red table wine, so he knew his discomfort wasn't from alcohol. His face felt hot; was he visibly flushed? he wondered. He started to explain to Sensi how things would progress but stopped in midsentence. The truth was that in this circumstance, and under these conditions, he was incapable of rational dialogue.

Giliberti jumped in. "Signor Sensi, I realize what my good friend has proposed is highly unusual. But you and I have done business before, huh? Many times. And we have never had trouble between us. Am I correct?"

The groundhog nodded.

"And so I come to you with my friend, Mr. Mason, who is respected in the United States as a man of honor and integrity. He has carefully thought about what he proposes and has explained it to me in great detail. I understand what it is he wishes to do. I support his plan. I only ask that you trust him as an extension of your faith in me."

Without warning, Sensi motioned for his bodyguards to stand. He placed his misshapen hands on the table. "Then we will do business," he said to Luther. Sensi was up now. One of his guards handed him a cane, and he slowly lumbered away from the table, the young men following closely behind.

Mason drew a deep, audible sigh of relief. Giliberti said, "See? I told you I could arrange it."

"But what about my opportunity to examine it?" Mason said.

"Oh, I am relieved you did not insult him by questioning that," Giliberti replied. "Everything is arranged for tomorrow morning. You will see it then. Now, I suggest we celebrate."

By the time Mason extricated himself from Giliberti at a lively, loud discotheque on the water's edge, where they were joined by a voluptuous young blond woman whose only interest seemed to be to hang on Giliberti—who said she was a cousin he hadn't seen in awhile—his head was pounding, and a fiery heartburn had set in. He was also drunk, a condition he hadn't experienced in years until getting better acquainted with Giliberti, and stumbled twice on the way up the steep steps from the waterfront to the hotel.

He stood on the terrace outside his room and looked over the tranquil, shimmering sea. He had done it. All the months of planning were now about to be converted into action. How long had it been since Carlo Giliberti first told him of the existence of the painting? Six months? Seven? There had been two previous trips to meet with the old mafioso, Luigi Sensi, but each meeting had been canceled at the last minute. "He is a very cautious man," Carlo had explained. And ruthless, Luther knew. He'd never before met anyone involved in organized crime. The Mafia? La Cosa Nostra? He didn't even know the proper term. If he'd been told a year ago that he'd be sitting down to dinner with such a man, he would have scoffed at the suggestion. If he'd been told he would be poised to do something . . . irregular beyond that, that, too, he would have dismissed as folly.

But here he was, in Italy, having come from dinner with a "Godfather"—was Sensi called that?— should he have kissed his ring?—and about to meet with him again in the morning.

He sat and wrapped his arms about himself. He suffered, at once, a rush of excitement tinged with almost religious joy and a powerful feeling of dread. Then he started to shake. His stomach went into a spasm that caused him to double over, followed by nausea, and soon its release in the bathroom.

He fell onto the bed in a cold sweat and continued to shake until sleep calmed him.

The Italian sun had not yet made an appearance when Giliberti and Mason drove away from the hotel in Giliberti's Fiat. The forecast was for a sunny, pleasant day with low humidity.

Because Giliberti seemed unsure of the route, he drove more slowly than usual. Mason was not displeased, and neither was his stomach. They passed through lush farmland as they traveled inland from the coast, past fields of sheep and large grape arbors that looked like aircraft hangers, and through thick forests of umbrella pines and cypresses.

By the time they turned off the main road on to a rutted dirt path wide enough for only a single automobile, the sun had come up, and Giliberti was able to turn off his headlights. They went a hundred yards before reaching a break in the heavy vegetation lining the road. Giliberti turned through the opening and proceeded on yet another dirt road until arriving at a rambling, ramshackle farmhouse covered with vines. Two large dogs of mixed origin, one yellow, the other black, came around the side of the house and barked as the men got out of the car. Giliberti noticed the apprehension on Mason's face and told him in Italian that they wouldn't bite.

The dogs, tails wagging in energetic circles, followed them to the front door. Giliberti knocked. The door was opened by an elderly woman wearing a black dress and white apron, a white net on her hair. She was stout; her face was sweet. The two young men who'd protected Sensi at the restaurant came up behind her. Giliberti said something to the woman in Italian, and she stepped back to allow them to enter.

Inside, there was a musty coolness, and the strong odor of garlic and stale tobacco. The woman disappeared to the left; Mason and Giliberti followed one of the two men to the right, into a living room overflowing with old furniture. Drapes were drawn tightly over every window, keeping the room in virtual blackness, broken only by two lamps in opposite corners that spilled small amounts of yellow light onto a worn red carpet. From one of the darkened corners came the voice of Luigi Sensi, who sat in a chair that all but swallowed him.

"Ah, Signor Sensi," said Giliberti. "We are early. I apologize for that."

The old man struggled to his feet and leaned on

the cane that had been hooked over an arm of the chair. "Better to be early than late," he said gruffly. To Mason: "You have come."

"Yes."

Sensi hobbled from the room and out the front door, Mason and Giliberti behind him, followed by the two young men. This day, without their suit jackets, the bodyguards' shoulder holsters and revolvers were plainly in sight. The dogs joined the entourage as Sensi led it across the broad front yard and through a series of grape arbors fat with fruit. The guards opened large doors to a barn partially collapsed at one end, and they entered. The smell of hay and manure was pungent. Sensi gave an order in Italian, and the two men went up a ladder to a loft. Mason heard them rummaging about. Eventually, one descended the ladder; the other handed down a large rectangular object wrapped in burlap.

Sensi instructed the young man to unwrap the object near a broken window that allowed a shaft of light to illuminate a small portion of the darkened barn. He motioned for Mason to come closer. "Look," he said. "Come see."

Mason felt as though his shoes were glued to the floor. He was weak from his physical illness the night before and from the hangover he'd suffered since waking. But something other than those maladies kept him from stepping forward. Sensi had beckoned him into the holiest of churches, into a sacred shrine of a lost civilization. Although the only light cast upon the object came through the window, the entire area seemed to glow.

"Yes, let me see," he said, his words breaking the inertia. He stood at Sensi's side and looked down at the thing that had brought him to this rundown farmhouse in southern Italy. His gasp was involuntary. He pressed his lips tightly together to keep any further sounds from emerging.

Sensi was amused at Mason's behavior. "Come closer," he said, gesturing toward the painting. "Examine each inch. Touch it if you wish."

The chore of examining it cleared Mason's head, gave him purpose. He went on one knee and did what Sensi had invited him to do, using a magnifying glass he'd pulled from his pocket.

When he stood twenty minutes later, Sensi broke out in a broad grin that exposed yellow teeth with gaps. It was the first time Mason had seen the old man smile. Ordinarily, when someone smiles, it gives comfort and assurance. But this did not. Mason turned away.

"Okay?" Giliberti asked.

"Yes. Okay," said Mason.

"It is a deal, Signor Sensi," said Giliberti.

"I would like to leave now," Mason said, taking quick steps out of the barn and toward the car.

Giliberti ran and caught up with him. "Do not offend him, Luther. He has been most gracious. You must thank him properly."

Mason stopped and looked at his friend. "And how do I do that?"

"By expressing your appreciation for allowing you to come here. For the pleasure of having dinner with him last night. For honoring you with his trust in this business deal."

When Mason turned to do so, he saw only the back of the old man entering his house. "You thank him for me the next time you see him," he said.

It wasn't until they were almost back in Rome and heading for the airport that Giliberti once again brought up Mason's lack of courtesy. "You are much too nervous, my friend," he said. "But if you continue to act with such animosity toward your benefactor, I cannot guarantee what will happen."

"Benefactor? He is an old, ugly mafioso who steals and plunders and murders."

Giliberti let the comment go until he pulled up in front of the Alitalia terminal. As Mason got out and removed his luggage from the rear, Giliberti leaned across the seat. "Remember one thing, my friend," he said. "Signor Sensi may be old and ugly. He may murder and steal. But he is a man of honor. And you have chosen to do business with him. I suggest you become a man of honor yourself."

Mason didn't know how to respond.

Giliberti laughed. "Don't take me so seriously, Luther. And relax. Everything will be fine."

"You've made all the arrangements for the painting to go to Paris?" Mason asked.

"Of course. It will be there in the morning. By special courier."

"And you will be there to see that it is handled properly?"

"Again, my friend, I say not to worry. I have taken care of every detail. Go. Catch your plane. Safe trip. I will be back myself in a few days and we will have dinner. To celebrate. At my house. My wife will cook a fine meal. She asks for you often."

SIX

THE NATIONAL GALLERY OF ART
—WASHINGTON, D.C.

DID CARAVAGGIO know in gouache heaven that the art he created three hundred years ago would spawn so many meetings in a city that didn't even exist in his time?

George Kublinski, chief of design and exhibition, gathered a group around him in an empty room in the East Building of the National Gallery to demonstrate a fiber-optic lighting system he'd designed especially for the Caravaggio exhibition to avoid potentially damaging heat. Kublinski was acknowledged throughout the international museum world as the preeminent expert on new lighting techniques. It was no surprise that he worked for "America's Museum," affectionately so-called despite technically being a gallery. Its reputation for excellence in art conservation and restoration, scientific testing, packing, shipping, and, because of George Kublinski, lighting, was without peer.

The group surrounding Kublinski included interested employees, and design and exhibition experts from elsewhere who'd traveled to Washington to learn more about fiber optics.

As Kublinski conducted his demonstration, several meetings were taking place within the institution.

Agents from private insurance companies, and Gallery attorneys, met with representatives of the federal government to finalize details of insuring the Caravaggio paintings while in the Gallery's possession. Because most of the works would come from other nations, the federal government would indemnify the bulk of the exhibition through the Federal Council on the Arts, administered by the National Endowment for the Arts and augmented by private insurers.

In another office, in the East Building's basement, the National Gallery's top security brass huddled with the deputy administrator to review security plans. The gallery's "cops" prided themselves on never having lost a work of art since the Gallery opened in March of 1941. The only "breach" of security in its fifty-four years had resulted in an *addition* to the gallery's collection. A young Washington artist had spirited one of his paintings *into* the West Building and hung it on a wall alongside the works of the great master painters. It remained there until a sharp-eyed security guard noticed one too many "masterpieces."

The security meeting concluded with a tentative

schedule to provide most of the three hundred guards with a short course in Caravaggio and to arrange for increased practice time on firing ranges around the city. Until recently, the National Gallery had had its own range. But after years of use, tests showed the ground to contain a shockingly high lead level, and it was closed.

The director's office on the seventh floor of the East Building was also the scene of a meeting between Director Courtney Whitney and Senior Curator Luther Mason.

"Luther," Whitney said in a tone intended to pacify, "I understand your concerns about including Caravaggio in the computer system. And rest assured I would like to accommodate you. But I'm afraid my hands are tied. The trustees are one hundred percent behind the Micro Gallery. They are not about to make exceptions."

He was referring to the National Gallery's newest innovation, a privately funded computerized visitor's center in which gallery-goers could sit in front of computer monitors and use touchscreen technology to create their own personal tours of the vast gallery without ever leaving their chairs. Older curators, Luther Mason very much included, were aghast at the notion of pixelizing masterpieces. But the project had many advocates. To Mason's chagrin, Whitney had eagerly embraced the concept and had pushed to get the system up and running as quickly as possible. Luther had been informed of the decision first thing that morning, the wrong time to lay such unpleasant news upon him. For one thing, he did not much like mornings. For another, he'd been awakened before the alarm by a call from Cynthia, the second former Mrs. Mason, who informed him that she intended to hire a lawyer to pursue half of his personal art collection.

"That was determined in the final divorce decree," he said sleepily.

"That was determined before I learned you'd lied about its worth, Luther. You defrauded me."

"No, I didn't—goodbye, Cynthia." Fact was, he hadn't lied. His small collection was well chosen but mediocre at best in market value.

Another prebreakfast call came from his only child, Julian, son by his first marriage, to Juliana. Julian, an artist, strugging, naturally, needed money.

"I just gave you money," Mason told him.

"I need more. Supplies don't grow on trees. The landlord's bugging me. I have to find a new place. I need more room."

I need—I need. Luther promised to think about it.

And now this. Caravaggio reduced to bits and bytes and manipulated by a "mouse."

"Bad enough this is happening to any work of art in this institution, Court," he said. "But to subject Caravaggio to this technological abortion is something I simply cannot, and will not, live with."

Whitney checked his watch. They'd been talking for a half hour, and he'd grown tired of the debate. "I'm afraid we're going to have to end this conversation," he said. "I'm running late for another meeting. No matter what your views, Luther, Caravaggio in the Micro Gallery is, as they say, a done deal."

"Nonsense! You can still stand your ground with the trustees."

"I prefer to pick my battles with them, Luther, and this is not one I choose to take on. Besides, if it's good enough for the National Gallery in London, it will be good enough for the National Gallery of the United States. End of discussion."

Whitney had conducted the session in shirtsleeves. He took his jacket from the coat tree, slipped it on, and checked himself in a mirror. The director's concern for his appearance only further upset Mason. He knew he could do little. He was, after all, an employee, and the man about to walk out the door—how he hated the thought—was his boss.

In a final attempt at conciliation, Whitney stepped behind Mason and placed his hands on the curator's shoulders. "Luther, don't let this issue taint your achievement of bringing Caravaggio to America. Like it or not, we both work for the trustees. They have spoken in all their infinite wisdom, and you and I must abide by their decision. By the way, is everything still on track?"

Whitney removed his hands, and Mason stood. "Yes, Court, things are going smoothly, aside from some loose ends to tidy up at the Borghese. I'm going to Rome tomorrow to resolve them."

Whitney's expression said that he wasn't pleased. Mason had become a virtual commuter between Washington and Italy since the project began. He'd returned from his most recent trip only days ago.

"A problem?" Mason asked.

"Just a silly thing called a budget, Luther. We're already thirty-two percent over on Caravaggio. Travel costs are far in excess of what was allocated."

The cost of the Caravaggio show had risen with each passing day. That morning's estimate put the total close to nine million. But Whitney chose not to challenge his esteemed senior curator any further. "No problem at all, Luther. By the way, I've told Annabel Reed-Smith that I agree with Mrs. Aprile. Annabel *should* accompany you on some of the Italy trips. Will you be traveling alone tomorrow?"

"No. Donald is coming with me to take a final look at *The Entombment* at Vatican Pinacoteca. It's the only work we seem to have any serious debate about. He's still not sure whether it's prudent to travel the painting. I think he's being overly cautious, but that decision is his, after all. He'll be going on to Malta to make a final decision on *Saint Jerome.* He might be right about that one. It's in dreadful shape. Even if he does decide it can travel, the amount of conservation and restoration that would have to be accomplished in Malta could prove prohibitive."

"I'll see if Mrs. Smith is free to join you on the trip and have her coordinate with your office. Thank you for all your good work, Luther. Not only do the trustees appreciate it, you have my personal gratitude." With that he was gone, leaving Mason standing alone in the middle of the office, thinking: *What happened to his concern about the budget?*

The National Gallery's Office of Special Events, always busy choreographing its many social events, grappled with planning a black-tie dinner that had been injected into the schedule at the last minute. Ordinarily, only one dinner would be held to celebrate an upcoming exhibition at which the lenders of works, the trustees, and an assortment of government and industry movers and shakers in the D.C. arts scene would gather. But the trustees, prodded by Courtney Whitney, decided to host a second bash in advance of the official opening dinner and had persuaded the corporate sponsors to foot the additional bill.

Mary Helm, head of the department, met with representatives of the outside catering service. The menu would, of course, be Italian, without reverting to gastronomic clichés. A three-course Venetian meal was chosen because the caterer felt it would be more delicate, subtle, and lighter than fare from other regions. Each dish would be renamed to coincide with the theme of a Caravaggio painting—Antipasto *Medusa, Sleeping Cupid* Baked Scallops, Smoked Lamb Soup *Salome,* Veal with Tuna Sauce *Emmaus,* and for dessert, *Boy with a Basket of Fruit,* with its suggestion of cannibalism. Finding subject matter in Caravaggio's works not dealing with crucifixion, incest, or murder was a challenge.

Raul Sebastian, head of the Gallery's music department, was given the assignment of providing appropriate background sounds during the cocktail hour. Sebastian was a man known not only for his musical expertise, but for never allowing a simple project to remain that way. Despite the minor role music would play, he agonized over the choice of Italian composers to feature. Italian Renaissance? Or Baroque, with more music from which to choose? Renaissance composer Don Carlo Gesualdo, whose madrigals and motets were primarily vocal, but whose personal life paralleled Caravaggio's? Gesualdo had had his unfaithful wife and her lover murdered. The Baroque Jean-Baptiste Lully, born in Florence but who wrote French opera? Sebastian pointed out in a memo that Lully died of gangrene after accidentally smashing his foot with a staff used to pound the floor when his musicians did not keep correct time.

"How about Vivaldi?" Mary Helm suggested.

Sebastian dismissed her suggestion. "Why do you suggest him? Because he wrote four hundred concerti? No. Vivaldi wrote one concerto four hundred times!"

He settled on Corelli and instructed a chamber group culled from the National Symphony to rehearse sections from the composer's twelve concerti, as well as *La Folia,* to be performed by a violinist with piano accompaniment. So much for background music, unlikely to be heard consecutively or attentively by anyone other than the musicians.

"Mac, it's me."

"I gathered as much," Smith said to his wife after taking her call in his home office. "Recognize your voice anywhere, Annabel."

"What a relief. Mac, I just received a call from Court Whitney at the National Gallery. He wants me to accompany Luther Mason—tomorrow—on a trip to Italy. Think you can break loose?"

"For some reason, Annabel, I always have trouble with people who give me too much advance notice. Tomorrow? Can't. That lecture I made the mistake of agreeing to is coming up fast. I'll need every minute I can steal to get ready."

"Damn."

"I suggest you go, discharge your official duties on behalf of the United States, enjoy yourself, buy something pretty on the via Condotti, and hurry home to me."

"Why do you always make it so difficult for me to live my life?"

"Because I love you. You say you leave tomorrow? Let's celebrate with dinner out tonight. I don't suppose you'd be in the mood for Italian food?"

"I'm *always* in the mood for Italian food."

"Sounds like a corny lyric to a Dean Martin song. Soon you'll be up to your pretty neck in the real thing."

"You're right. Let's make it sushi."

"You know I don't eat sushi."

"But I do. We could go to Sapporo. The one on M, not Pennsylvania. I can satisfy my sudden urge, and you can have tempura."

"Seven?"

"Let's make it six. I have to pack."

"Okay."

"Mac, one request while I'm gone."

"Yes?"

"No *tatuaggi*."

"I can't get a tattoo while you're gone? I was thinking of a heart with your initials in it."

"Were you?"

"Or maybe a depiction of one of Caravaggio's paintings."

"Uh huh."

"Which do you prefer, Annabel?"

"Make one permanent mark on that skin I love to touch and you're the former Mackensie Smith."

"You have a talent for taking all the joy out of a man's life, Annabel. See you at six. And by the way, I love you."

SEVEN

ROME—TWO DAYS LATER

I'LL LEAVE you to your work," Annabel told
Luther Mason. It was an hour into their flight to
Rome, and they'd been talking since leaving Wash-
ington.

"Yes. I really should get this written before we
arrive. I give the lecture the day after we get back.
Annabel, I can't tell you what a pleasure it is to
have you with us."

"I'm delighted to be with you. I just wish Mac
had been able to come."

"Another time, I'm sure." He opened his briefcase, put on his glasses, and went back to writing
his lecture on the influence on Caravaggio of
Peterzano, Figino, and Jacopo and Francesco
Bassano.

As Annabel browsed through a magazine, she
cast an occasional glance at her companion. The
more time she spent with Luther Mason, the more
he impressed her. Not only was he an expert on
Caravaggio, his enthusiasm for the subject was
contagious. He'd traced the artist's life for her in

considerable detail, linking his works to periods in his tumultuous personal life.

On her way back from a restroom visit, Donald Fechter beckoned her to the empty seat next to him. Fechter had come to the field of art conservation from a background that included a Ph.D. in chemistry and a stint as a college professor. To Annabel, he looked more the rugged, middle-aged pugilist than a man who'd spent his life in intellectual pursuits. That, as she eventually learned, his favorite leisure pursuits were mountain climbing and white-water rafting came as no surprise.

Fechter proved to be as engaging a seat companion as Luther Mason had been for the first hour. By the time the captain announced they were beginning their descent, Annabel had learned a bewildering amount about conservation and the National Gallery's approach to it. Fechter supervised fifty-four specialists in matting and framing, textiles, oil, and watercolor, three-dimensional objects, and pure science. He was accompanied on this trip by two assistants, carrying with them a variety of scientific instruments to measure humidity levels and pH factors, a portable X-ray machine, and a book Fechter claimed was his traveling "bible," *The World Weather Book.*

Carlo Giliberti met them at Leonardo da Vinci Airport and deftly navigated their passage through Customs. Mason sat in the front passenger seat of the chauffeured Mercedes. Annabel,

Fechter, and Giliberti shared the roomy rear seat. Fechter's two assistants were driven into the city in a rented minivan.

Annabel found Carlo Giliberti to be charming—maybe a little too charming—*insincero,* Italian for not always meaning so many flowery compliments. Yet she enjoyed his company, his enthusiastic chatter, his overt love of Rome and its people. He assured Annabel that he and the car and driver were at her disposal and that he would take personal pleasure in escorting her about the city during any free moments.

It didn't take Annabel long to discover that she would have plenty of free moments in which to take him up on his offer. After a much-needed nap in the Valadier Hotel, she accompanied Mason to the noon meeting at the Church of San Luigi dei Francesi, lender to the exhibition of *The Martyrdom of Saint Matthew* and *The Inspiration of Saint Matthew.* They were there less than a half hour. From what Annabel observed, everything had been worked out long ago; the visit was pro forma, the conversation with church elders nothing more than a pleasant exchange about Caravaggio's importance.

Next, they went to the Galleria Doria-Pamphili, where Caravaggio's *Penitent Mary Magdalene* hung. There, too, Caravaggio's impact upon art was briefly discussed, along with the splendid weather Rome was enjoying, the Italian soccer team's chances in the World Cup, and the Pope's book and its multimillion dollar advance and bestseller status.

That was it for the first day. Tomorrow, Mason told her, they would meet briefly with officials at the Galleria Borghese. The rest of the time in Rome was Annabel's to enjoy. Because Mason was preoccupied with what he termed "personal commitments," and Don Fechter was busy making final inspections of works to be crated and sent to Washington, as well as preparing for his trip to Malta, Annabel took Giliberti up on his offer to play escort. She'd expressed interest during the ride in from the airport at seeing the sculptures in the Museo Torlonia, one of the largest private collections of antiquities in Europe, and open by appointment only. *"Non è problema,"* Giliberti said, a favorite expression, and they spent a pleasant two hours admiring the collection.

That evening, neither Mason nor Fechter was available for dinner, so Annabel dined with Carlo at Hostaria L'Angoletto, a small restaurant near the Pantheon. He was twenty minutes late but contrite. Annabel said she wanted to eat light, but Carlo would not hear of it. "I will help you finish what you don't eat," he said, ordering *puntarelle*— crunchy stalks of chicory dressed with anchovies, crushed garlic, olive oil, and vinegar; *peperonata*— chicken stewed in roasted peppers; and two pasta dishes. A satisfying bottle of a red Torre Ercolana, from the hills of the Castelli Romani southeast of the city, nicely complemented the meal.

He kissed her hand in front of the hotel and said he would pick her up the next morning in time for her eleven o'clock meeting. Annabel made a mental note: Carlo at 11:00 A.M. Or 11:15. The minute she was alone in her room, she called her husband.

"What time is it there?" he asked.

"About eleven. How are you?"

"Fine. I had a good day. One of my students actually made sense this morning. Oh, I took Rufus to the vet. He twisted his hind leg. Nothing broken but he's hobbling." Rufus was their blue Great Dane.

"Poor fella. Give him a hug for me."

"Hugging Rufus could put *me* in the hospital. Besides, you haven't been away *that* long."

She filled him in on her day in Rome.

"Sounds like all play, no work," he said.

"Just about. Don Fechter seems busy. Luther? Well, he's busy with lots of personal things." She told him about her dinner with Carlo.

"Watch the hands, Annabel."

"He's a gentleman, Mac. The eyes are in constant motion but . . ."

"Carole Aprile called. Wondered if I'd heard from you."

"Anything urgent?"

"No. I said we'd be talking."

"I'll call her before I go to bed. I love you."

"I love you, too."

"You haven't gotten any tattoos, have you?"

"Just one, a two-foot heart with your initials."

"Where?"

"Show you when you get home. Have a good sleep and enjoy the rest of your time there."

Annabel was pleased to find Carole at home. "Mac said you called," she said.

"Yes. How's Rome?"

"Lovely. I'm not sure why I'm here but—"

"Why?"

Annabel laughed. "A few brief meetings that seem to accomplish nothing, or not much, and lots of free time."

"I talked to Court Whitney today. He raised concerns about the budget for the Caravaggio show."

"And here I am in Rome on taxpayer money. I hope I don't end up being called a 'junket junkie' in some exposé."

"No fear of that. Look, Annabel, while you're there, keep a mental note of how much actual time is spent on business."

"I'm uncomfortable being in that position, Carole. I'd make a bad whistle-blower."

"I'm not asking you to do that. The Gallery's budget really isn't my concern. It's just that Court says Luther Mason is virtually commuting to Italy these days."

"Well, it's his exhibition. I'd be the last person to second-guess him."

"Of course not. Is everything going smoothly with the lenders?"

"Seems to be. Almost too smoothly."

"The government officials involved?"

"I haven't met any, except for Carlo Giliberti."

"Cultural attaché. I understand he's been immeasurably helpful."

"Speaking of smooth, he sure knows his way around."

"I'm sure he does. Anyway, thanks for calling. Maybe we can catch up for coffee when you get back."

"Love it. Good night, Carole. Speak with you soon."

Following the cursory meeting the following midmorning at Galleria Borghese, Mason excused himself—lunch with an old friend—and Annabel set off with Giliberti and their driver. She bought herself a box of elegant stationery, a copy of the art magazine *FMR* at Franco Maria Ricci, and handmade beeswax candles for Christmas gifts at Pisoni. After considerable debate, she also decided to buy Mac a nineteenth-century walking stick that had caught her eye in the window of La Gazza Ladra. Mac never carried a walking stick but had collected a half-dozen of them that he proudly displayed in an antique umbrella stand.

They ended the afternoon browsing art galleries on via Margutta. As they admired a series of Cubist nudes by a young Italian artist, Giliberti whispered, *"E più bella di tutti questi quadri."*

"Pardon?" said Annabel.

"You are more beautiful than all these pictures."

She laughed. "I would certainly hope so, Carlo. Somehow, Cubism has never struck me as an especially attractive way to represent women. But thank you anyway. Time to go."

"*Si.* You will be joining us for dinner this evening?"

"Absolutely. I'm glad Luther can make it. I haven't seen much of him since we arrived."

They gathered for dinner at Andrea, in the via Veneto section, where they had lobster bisque that was, in Annabel's modest culinary opinion, to die for, and *straccetti di manzo con porcini e tartufi,* thin strips of sautéed beef brought to life by porcini mushrooms and truffles.

Everyone was in an expansive mood. Their animated conversation ran the gamut from whether Washington art dealer Chris Middendorf was a genius or a tasteless con man, to new developments in the conservation of old paintings, which set Don Fechter off on a fascinating journey through that complicated, sometimes controversial field. He'd just finished recounting the techniques that had been used in restoring Bellini's *The Feast of the Gods* when Annabel said, "I hate to interrupt, but I have a plane to catch."

Mason checked his watch. "Right you are, Annabel. Your driver can take her, Carlo?"

"Of course."

"My luggage is with the concierge at the hotel," she said.

"You can pick it up on the way," Giliberti said. "I would go with you but I have a date here in the city with a cousin I haven't seen in a long time."

"I'll go with you, Annabel," Mason said, suppressing a smile at Carlo's cousin story.

"No need," she said. "As long as the driver—"

"My pleasure," said Mason. "I'm supposed to pick up a rental car in the morning. I'm taking an extra day to spend with friends in the countryside. I'll pick it up tonight at the airport instead."

Luther said, as they headed for the airport, "I have an apology for you, Annabel."

"Apology? For what?"

"For being so unavailable. I'm not sure I've adequately indicated my pleasure at having you with us on this trip. In having you involved in the exhibition, period."

"You're a busy man, Luther. You have a lot on your mind."

"Which is no excuse for ungentlemanly behavior."

"Say no more. I loved being in Rome, learning more about Caravaggio and seeing how a few of the pieces come together. My appetite for the show has certainly been whetted. I can't wait to see all those masterpieces together in one space."

"Nor can I. To me, as you've undoubtedly guessed, it's not just a show. It's the culmination of a lifelong dream. Of course, being in close proximity to Caravaggio will be only temporary. Six months. But I intend to soak in his genius and beauty every minute he's there."

Annabel found it interesting that Mason spoke as though the artist himself would be present. Such dedication, she thought. It was because of the Luther Masons of the art world that shows such as the Caravaggio ever saw the light of day. America's Museum—sorry, Gallery—was fortunate to have him.

The airport was busy when they arrived. Mason told the driver to wait and accompanied Annabel inside. She checked the departure board. They'd made good time; she had more than an hour before her flight.

Mason excused himself and headed for the Maiellano Car Rental counter. Annabel decided to wait until he'd finished his transaction before getting in line for Customs and Passport Control. She idly crossed the terminal and came up behind Luther, who was going over a map with the rental-car agent. Annabel was close enough to hear their conversation. He was going to a town called Ravello, off the A2, south of Pompeii.

Mason seemed startled when he realized she was so close.

"Long drive ahead of you?" Annabel asked pleasantly.

"No. Just a few hours."

"Thank you again, Luther, for these past two days."

He smiled and shook her hand. "Drive safely," she said. "You know how Italians are on the road."

"I'm well aware," he said. "Carlo missed his calling. I think he got his license at a Monte Carlo rally. Have a pleasant flight, Annabel. At least Mr. Giliberti won't be your pilot."

Of all the places in Italy Mason had visited over the years, Ravello ranked high on his list of favorites. It was situated high, on cliffs above Amalfi, approximately twenty miles northeast of Positano and two hundred miles northwest of Cosenza, where the fledgling mafioso, Giovanni Saltore, had his career cut short after stealing paintings from San Francesco di Assisi.

Ravello represented to Mason almost everything lovely about Italy. He knew he was not alone in that assessment. In 1880, Wagner was so taken by the romantic splendor of Ravello's Villa Rufolo that he exclaimed, "The magic garden of Klingsor has been found." Mason had attended the annual July Wagner Festival held in Ravello on two occasions. And once, during a sabbatical from the gallery, he'd lived there for two months.

He arrived before noon, checked into the Villa Maria Hotel, and enjoyed a light lunch. Later, he sipped a sweet vermouth on the grassy terrace, transfixed by the view before him, the sea far in the distance, framed by the majestic hills of Amalfi.

He spent an hour in the town's cathedral before getting into his rented car and driving twenty minutes to a small church with crumbling masonry. Weeds and vines obscured its façade. A wooden sign that had once announced the times of services was broken; pieces of it lay on the ground.

Mason got out and approached the overgrown front door. He was about to knock when the door opened. A short, spare man wearing a blue chambray shirt, baggy gray pants, and sandals faced him. Mason judged him to be in his seventies. He was mostly bald; hair that appeared to have been dyed black was wet and combed close to his temples. His eyes were small and black, set close together in the thin, angular face. A carefully trimmed pencil moustache looked as though it had been painted on his upper lip with a black felt marker. "Father Giocondi?" Mason said.

"*Si.* You are Signor Mason."

"Yes."

"Come in, come in."

They entered a large room where once pews and an altar had dominated. But that was when the parish had a congregation and before its beloved priest had cut his deal with the Vatican.

Besides being a man of the cloth, Father Pasquale Giocondi had been a thief. Dirt poor, he'd entered the priesthood at the outbreak of World War II as a safer alternative to joining the Italian army and soon discovered there were fringe benefits to having become *Father* Giocondi. No reason to give up his earlier vocation. There were black-market goods to be laundered and sold and favors to dispense to politicians and businessmen. The war was good to Giocondi; he did not celebrate its end. For years afterward he tended to his faithful flock in the small church outside Ravello and took a little extra off the top of the collection plate in return for dispensing his blessings upon them. Eventually, his misdeeds were discovered— and proved by a papal board of inquiry—causing the good father to do what any citizen might do. He hired a lawyer, who hard-bargained with Vatican attorneys: "The church doesn't need this sort of scandal," the attorney told his Vatican adversaries, the wisdom of which wasn't lost on the church's hierarchy. What came out of these negotiations wasn't ideal as far as Giocondi was concerned, but it wasn't a bad deal, either. The parish was scheduled to be closed anyway, its parishioners to be served by a newer facility a few miles away. In order to avoid scandal, the Vatican agreed that Giocondi could "retire" and receive his pension, and they gave him the rundown church in which to live out his life.

He'd lived there for the past seven years, not exactly in a lavish manner but comfortably enough. His status as a retired holy man proved useful at times to certain people in need of a middleman or courier unlikely to challenged. There were the occasional trips to Rome and Milan and Sicily—he never questioned what was in the small packages he delivered to unnamed persons in those places. And there had been the paintings he'd stored in his home, his former church, and that he sometimes transported from Ravello to other towns and cities. That's how he'd met in passing Italy's cultural attaché to the United States, Carlo Giliberti, who took an uncommon interest in this messenger, not of God but of the Godfathers.

"Please, sit down, Mr. Mason. It is my honor to have you visit me," said Giocondi. He motioned to a pair of comfortable upholstered chairs in front of the unused altar.

"I don't have much time, Father Giocondi." Luther reached into the inner pocket of his blazer, removed two envelopes, and handed them to him. "Here," he said. "It's the cash you requested as a down payment and your ticket to Washington. Included with the ticket is a letter of instructions, which you are to destroy once you've memorized it. I believe Signor Giliberti has told you to wear your priestly garments at the black-tie dinner."

"*Si.* I understand."

"I have made arrangements for you to stay at a hotel outside Washington," Mason said. "Those directions are included with your airline ticket."

Giocondi nodded.

Mason checked his watch. "I have only an hour to go over things with you so that you understand precisely how you are to act and what you are to say. I would like to do that now."

"Of course."

"I had understood you speak excellent English, and I can hear why they say that about you."

"Thank you."

Mason looked around the church's interior. "Then we will speak more, but not in here," he said. He had thought carefully about this meeting, about every meeting he was to have from this point forward. You couldn't be too careful. He'd read detective novels in which the unsuspecting were overheard, even tape-recorded, and there were, of course, real-life events in Washington involving taped meetings that had brought down a sitting president. "Outside," he said. It was suddenly an order.

Giocondi led them through a rear door; Mason had to duck to avoid hitting his head. They walked fifty yards from the church to where a cracked and discolored marble birdbath sat at a tilted angle beneath a diseased oak. Three rusting white-metal benches haphazardly surrounded the birdbath.

Mason took a handkerchief from his pocket, wiped off one of the benches, and sat. Father Giocondi didn't bother cleaning his perch. Mason drew a deep breath and swatted at a fly that landed on his forehead. Rehearsal time. Looking directly at Father Pasquale Giocondi, he said, "Shall we begin?"

EIGHT

A FEW DAYS LATER

AT FIRST, Courtney Whitney III, director of the National Gallery, thought the ringing telephone was part of a dream. But he realized that the dream was over. The ringing was a jarring 5:00 A.M. reality.

He reached across his muttering wife, knocked the phone from the small night table, slid down the bed, sprawled across her legs, fumbled on the floor for the receiver, and found it. "Hello?"

"Court. It's Luther."

"Luther? For God's sake, where are you? It's the middle of the night."

"I'm in Rome, about to catch a flight back to Washington. Sorry to wake you, but it's urgent. You know I wouldn't make such a call unless it was important."

"Urgent? Are you sick? Is something wrong with you?"

"No. To the contrary. I have made an unbelievable discovery, Court. You must meet with me the moment I arrive in Washington. Will you come to the airport?"

"Come to the airport?"

"Yes. I don't want to discuss this at the Gallery. Believe me, Court, you'll be pleased you did."

By this time, Sue Whitney had turned on a light and was sitting up. Whitney sat on the edge of the bed, the receiver to his ear, his other hand pressed against his forehead. "All right, Luther, I'll meet you."

"It was Luther?" Sue Whitney asked after Mason had told Whitney when his flight would arrive and had hung up. "What did he want? Too much *vino?*"

"Damned if I know, but I think the man might be on the verge of a breakdown."

Mason cleared Dulles Customs and came directly to where Whitney stood. "Thanks for being here, Court."

"The question is *why* I'm here."

"Let's go to the Delta Crown Room," said Mason. "We can talk there."

Mason flashed his membership card, and they went to a far corner of the handsomely appointed room. They sat facing each other in twin maroon club chairs, and Whitney waited. When Mason said nothing, Whitney said, "You look like hell, Luther."

"I haven't slept much," Mason replied. His eyes were bloodshot; gray stubble on his cheeks had aged him a decade.

Mason placed his elbows on his knees, bringing him closer to Whitney. He said in a fatigued voice, *"Grottesca."*

Whitney's expression mirrored his confusion. *"Grottesca?"*

Mason nodded solemnly.

"Grottesca?" Whitney repeated. "The lost Caravaggio?"

Another nod from the curator.

"Luther, I understand something terribly important is on your mind, and I was willing to come here to find out what it was. But I have a heavy schedule. What about *Grottesca?"*

Mason sat back and closed his eyes tightly. His lips trembled. Was he about to cry? Whitney wondered. "Luther, I—"

Mason leaned forward again, eyes open. "Court," he said, "I have found *Grottesca!"*

Whitney's smile was involuntary. He shook his head in place of words. "What do you mean, you've found it? *Where* did you find it? *How?"*

Mason raised his eyes to the ceiling as though to place his thoughts in a logical sequence before beginning. "It has been in a storeroom in an abandoned Catholic church outside Ravello. You know my fondness for Ravello. I always try to get there whenever I visit Italy. Somehow, when I'm there, a feeling of calm comes over me."

"Yes, fine, Luther. But what about the painting?"

"I met a friend for a drink in Ravello, and he introduced me to an elderly gentleman who is retired from the priesthood. His name is Giocondi. Father Pasquale Giocondi. A humble old man who has lived in an abandoned church ever since his retirement.

"We chatted about many things. Eventually, my friend mentioned my lifelong interest in Caravaggio, and that I was curating a Caravaggio exhibition at the National Gallery." He drew a breath to slow himself. "Father Giocondi waited until my friend left before asking me to come to his church—which is now his home—to examine something he thought might interest me."

"Go on, Luther. I'm listening."

"I went with him. It was only twenty minutes outside of Ravello. Terribly run-down, in dreadful repair."

"Luther, stick to the—"

"Yes, of course. I suppose I have been rambling. He took me into a dusty storeroom littered with junk and had to pull away dozens of boxes and old pieces of furniture to get to the painting. It was flat against the wall, the canvas facing away from me. I helped him pull it out. We took it into the main room, which used to serve as the area of worship for his congregation. I couldn't believe my eyes. I've been studying the *Grottesca* and its disappearance for years. I've read every bit of scholarship ever written about it and had explored all avenues in the hope of one day finding out what actually happened to it.

"And there it was, Court. In *front* of me, in this humble former church, presented to me—placed in my hands—by this retired priest."

Whitney frowned. "Is this priest that astute about art to have realized it might be an original Caravaggio?"

"Yes. Since his retirement, Father Giocondi has pursued the study of art. He's extremely knowledgeable. It's like Italians and opera. They practically breathe it. I was impressed with what he knew."

"What said to *you*, Luther, that this was, in fact, the lost *Grottesca?*"

"Many things. Every scrap of information I've learned about it came into play. For instance, Caravaggio's 1597 *Bacchus* has always been considered the final painting he did in his famous series using the same young boy as a model. Remember? That, too, disappeared but was found in 1917 in a back room of the Uffizi. But my research has told me—and I say this without hesitation or reservation—that *Grottesca* was, in fact, *the* final work using that same youthful model.

"I examined it carefully for an hour, went over every inch. There is no question that the same model was used. Court, the painting is so alive you can feel the thorns trapping the boy and beasts, hear the anguished cries. The medium appears to be walnut oil, although that can easily be determined by Donald's lab.

"The *craqueleure*," he said, referring to hundreds of minute cracks formed by the drying of the oil paints and shrinkage of the pigments, "is definitely what you would expect to find in a work this old. The paint was applied in that same sure, heavy hand that marks Caravaggio's technique. I saw no sign of sketches beneath." Caravaggio was known to avoid using preliminary sketches, attacking his work directly with his paints.

"The brushstrokes are so sure, Court. The stark realism. The harsh, single source of light. It's all so—so—so Caravaggio. Believe me, Court, it is an original Caravaggio. It *is Grottesca!*"

"A remarkable story, Luther. Perhaps too remarkable."

"What do you mean?"

"Finding two lost Caravaggio masterpieces in one decade is just—well, too much to accept."

"*The Taking of Christ?* An important find, yes. But not of the magnitude of *Grottesca.*"

Caravaggio's *The Taking of Christ,* painted over four hundred years before and "lost" for most of that time, had been discovered in 1990 in the St. Ignatius Residence of Jesuit priests in Dublin, Ireland, by an Italian art restorer, Sergio Benedetti, when he was called in to clean a number of paintings hanging in the old Georgian building's dining room. By the time it had been restored and given to Ireland's National Gallery, its worth had been estimated at close to $40 million.

"Perhaps," said Whitney. "What are you suggesting?"

"I am suggesting that we bring *Grottesca* to Washington to anchor the exhibition. A monumental coup for us. One of the world's greatest pieces of art, lost for centuries, is now resurrected—by the National Gallery of Art."

"Whoa, Luther, slow down," said Whitney, using his hand to emphasize the point. "Forgive me if I must inject the pragmatic view that it will take more than your opinion, as formidable as it might be, to authenticate its provenance."

"Of course," said Luther.

"And what makes you think the Italian government, to say nothing of the Vatican, will allow such a priceless treasure to be brought to Washington for exhibition?"

Mason's face said he'd been waiting for that question. His smile was smug. "It has already been arranged, Court."

Whitney said too loudly, "Arranged? What do you mean 'arranged?' "

Mason glanced about to see whether the director's raised voice had garnered attention. Confident it hadn't, he said in almost a whisper, "Carlo has arranged it."

"Giliberti?"

"Yes. I contacted him immediately. Fortunately, he was still in Rome and was able to make an instant overture to his friend, the minister of culture. It will take some money, and there are conditions. The Italian government, in a gesture of goodwill, will allow *Grottesca* to be sent to the National Gallery as soon as conservation has been completed. We will have the work to examine until the exhibition. Plenty of time to further authenticate its provenance and authorship. Then, we will be permitted to include it in the show for the first month, but only for that one month. At the end of that time, it must be returned.

"But think about it, Court. Think of how much interest will be generated in the entire exhibition by this one rare—rare, hell, virtually unseen—masterpiece. *Grottesca*'s glow will light up all of Washington, all of America. Its only appearance in the United States will be at the National Gallery. It won't travel to New York or to London along with the rest of the exhibition. For one month, Caravaggio's greatest painting will rest solely within our walls."

Whitney abruptly stood up, not because he wanted to end the conversation but because he didn't know what else to say. If Mason was right, the National Gallery—under his leadership—would be responsible for perhaps the greatest find in the history of lost art. It could potentially gen-

erate huge donations to the museum. He wanted
to get back to his office to think things out. An immediate meeting with the trustees would have to
be called. With others, too.

"I want to mull this over, Luther. Decide what
direction to take. A lot of decisions will have to be
made, by many people."

"Of course," Mason said, walking with the director from the club and into the terminal.

"Where is the painting now?" Whitney asked.
"In the church with the priest?"

"No. Carlo arranged for it to be taken into cus-
tody by a leading European conservator. He wants
to arrange for private conservation and restoration while details are worked out with the government to allow it to come here."

"You mean I won't have a chance to see it?"

"Not immediately," was Mason's answer. "But
I'm confident that conservation can be completed
in time for it to be unveiled briefly at the dinner. At
least the preliminary work. Carlo is certain he will
receive permission for us to do more conservation
once it's at the gallery."

"We'll need private funds," Whitney said. According to policy and congressional intent, federal
funds could not be used to conserve and restore
works not owned by the National Gallery.

"That certainly shouldn't be a problem," Mason
said. "We'll have donors fighting over each other
to fund the work."

Whitney knew his senior curator was right. "Did you take a picture of it?" he asked.

Mason shook his head. "I was too excited to think about finding a camera. I don't travel with them, as you know. I prefer to record my travels in my mind, not on film."

"Yes, I've heard you say that before, Luther. All right. When will we be able to examine *Grottesca?*"

"As soon as Carlo tells us it's ready to be transported. We'll have it in time for the dinner. I'm sure of that. You know that Carlo and I have worked closely together over the years. He is very much in our corner on this. He'll do what's in our best interest."

"Then I suppose it will have to be that way," Whitney said. "Come on, my car's outside."

"No, Court, I need some sleep. I'll call you at the end of the day."

"Fine. This Father Gicuzzi."

"Giocondi."

"Whatever. It might be wise to have him at the dinner. To tell his tale of the painting. Authenticate what you've told me."

"I anticipated that, Court. He'll come. It's an excellent suggestion. I would like to—I would like *you* to introduce Father Giocondi at the dinner and to announce the discovery." Luther knew there wasn't any chance that he, despite being the one to have unearthed *Grottesca,* would be allowed to make the announcement. It had nothing to do with ego on Whitney's part. It simply was gallery protocol for the director to break major news. In actuality, Mason didn't want to be center stage. Having Whitney do it added an additional third-party endorsement.

"We can work all that out later. Go home, Luther, and get some rest. You deserve it. And as I said before, you look like hell."

Darkness had fallen over Paris as Jacques Saison, who'd been drinking all afternoon, slept on a cot in his studio on rue de la Huchette, above a Greek restaurant, on Paris's Left Bank. He swore as the pounding on his door continued. "Go away!" he shouted.

The door swung open and Carlo Giliberti stepped into the cluttered, foul studio, where the remnants of half-eaten meals had attracted an assortment of bugs, rodents, and other wildlife. They scattered when Giliberti snapped on a harsh overhead light.

The master forger sat up, the words coming more rapidly now. *"Imbécile! Tête de mule!"*

"Hey, my friend, wake up," Giliberti said, ignoring being called a fool and blundering idiot and almost tripping over a toppled chair. "It's important."

"Giliberti," Saison mumbled. He stood, lost his balance, and fell back on the cot.

Giliberti placed the wrapped canvas he'd picked

up from the courier against a wall. "Sober up, Jacques. There is serious work to do."

Giliberti had found it easier than he'd anticipated to cut his deal with Alberto Betti, Italy's minister of culture. And more expensive. His payment to the minister wiped out most of what Luther Mason had put into their joint account. He'd have to hit Mason up for more. You couldn't deal on this level without plenty of lire behind you.

Giliberti started the meeting by saying, "I bring you wonderful news, Signor Betti."

"I always welcome wonderful news, Signor Giliberti. What is it?"

"*Grottesca* has been found."

Betti's face was blank. Giliberti gave him a capsule history of the lost Caravaggio.

"Of course," said Betti. "I was thinking of other things when you mentioned the name. *Grottesca*. Of course. The lost Caravaggio masterpiece."

"That's right, excellency. Your memory is excellent. *Grottesca* is no longer a lost treasure. It has been found."

Betti came forward, his face and voice demonstrating deep interest. "Where? How?"

Giliberti went through his carefully scripted response. The painting had been found by the man Giliberti had previously introduced to the minister, Luther Mason, senior curator at America's National Gallery.

"*He* found it? The American?"

"*Si.*" He went on to describe how Mason had met a retired priest, in whose humble church the painting had been discovered.

"What splendid news," said Betti. He stood and went to his large window, his bulk effectively obscuring most of the light. With his broad back to Giliberti, he said, "Where is this lost Caravaggio?"

"With Signor Mason."

Betti turned. "And where is Signor Mason?"

"I don't know."

"You don't *know?* How can that be? He has the painting?"

"*Si.* But that is not a problem, your excellency."

"Explain."

"Mr. Mason is a fair and honorable man. He asks only that *Grottesca* be allowed to take its place in the Caravaggio exhibition at his museum." Betti started to speak, but Giliberti kept going. "He has asked me to negotiate an arrangement with you. He has taken the painting to a trusted and expert conservator, who will bring the work back to its original excellence. Signor Mason asks only three things. First, that *Grottesca* be allowed to be flown to Washington directly from the conservator. Second, that the announcement of its discovery be made at a special formal dinner at the National Gallery a month from now, in concert with an announcement from your office. And third, that it remain in Washington until taking its place in the

Caravaggio exhibition to be held there six months from now. It will be on display for only the first month of the exhibition. At the end of that month, it will be returned to Italy, where you can bask in the further glory of this incredible event."

"I see," said Betti, lighting a cigarette. "This will not be easy, Carlo. There will be many questions here once we let this be known. Government officials. Our own museum people. The press. Maybe the Vatican."

"Yes, the press will ask many questions," Giliberti said.

"*Rapaci!*" was Betti's reply.

True, the press would be ghoulish vultures, and so Giliberti suggested that while the discovery of *Grottesca* be readily confirmed, all plans for its conservation, restoration, and travel remain a secret. "For security purposes."

"Of course. Highly unusual way to do such things." He lit another cigarette. "Signor Mason strikes a hard bargain. I could have him arrested."

"To what end, excellency? His conditions are small and reasonable. He wants to be recognized for his role in this remarkable discovery. Ego, you know? He has a very large ego."

"You assure me that at the end of the month in America, the painting will be returned here?"

"*Si.*"

"Not one day later. We must arrange to celebrate its discovery."

Pompous ass, thought Giliberti. He smiled and enthusiastically shook the minister's fat hand, thinking that he cared no more about Italy than the rest of the greedy politicians. "You are a great man, Signor Betti," he said. "I must go. I will keep you fully informed of every step."

"Be sure to do that, Carlo. There must be no surprises."

"No surprises, your excellency."

Betti waddled alongside Giliberti to the door. "This will not be easy for me," he said.

"Of course not."

"I will have to accommodate many others. Soothe their concerns."

"Naturally. You need only tell me what resources you will need."

"I will think about that and call you."

"I look forward to hearing from you.

"Your—contribution—will have to be substantial. This is a substantial undertaking. You say Signor Mason will make this announcement at a special dinner one month from now?"

"*Si.* You see how important this is. Usually, only one dinner for the opening. In this case, two dinners. A two-dinner occasion." He laughed. "And it is his intention to bring the priest to Washington for that dinner. The priest must remain in seclusion until then. I will alert Italian media in the U.S. that something special might be announced that evening. Simultaneously, you should have a statement ready to release from you and your office."

"I will do that."

"Good."

"Your friend Signor Mason is to be congratulated."

"I will personally pass along your best wishes and salutations."

"*Grazie.*"

It took Giliberti an hour to sober up Jacques Saison to the point where he understood the assignment. He examined *Grottesca* for a long time, his unshaven face grimacing as he came to recognize the work. "Caravaggio," he said.

"It doesn't matter, Jacques. No questions. All you must do is to create two perfect copies."

"Two? How long do I have?"

"You will have the painting here for almost a month."

"Two copies? Impossible!" He poured himself another *caffè calva* with shaky hands, reversing the usual proportions of thick espresso and Calvados, and offered Giliberti the leftovers of a plate of *pâté en croute.* Giliberti declined, wincing at the tremor in the artist's extremities. Hopefully enough alcohol would steady him, as it usually did with alcoholics.

"Take photographs, Jacques. Use them after I take the original from you."

"And how long do I have to complete the copies?"

"A few months. I will let you know in plenty of time when I need them. Bring in your assistants. There is enough money for whatever and whoever you need. More money than you have ever been paid before. Enough to leave Paris for a six-month vacation . . . more."

Saison now demonstrated more interest. He discussed the techniques he would use and listed those assistants whose talent was sufficient to help with the job, but who wouldn't ask too many questions.

"One final thing, Jacques," Giliberti said as he prepared to leave. "I mentioned enough money for an extended vacation away from Paris. You *will* take that vacation until told you may return here. And you will tell no one where you have gone."

"*Oui.* I understand."

Giliberti called his wife at their residence in Washington to tell her he'd be back the following day. He then hooked up with a friend from Italy, a willowy young woman who supported herself by working in a French bakery during the day and by offering her services as a call girl at night. *His* cross-cultural mission continued.

The next morning, Giliberti decided that this project of Mason's was becoming too complex, too time consuming, and most important, too expensive. If Mason wanted his continued collaboration, he would have to ante up more money. Lots more.

"Sei la più bella ragazza del mondo," he told his "cousin" as he prepared to head for Orly and his flight to Washington. He kissed her.

"Come again soon, Carlo," she said, not believing for a moment that he considered her the most beautiful woman in the world. Typical Italian male *adulazione.* She was a whore and knew it. Pretty, perhaps, but not beautiful. And good at her moonlighting trade.

"Arrivederci, visetto d'angelo."

"Arrivederci, Carlo."

NINE

ORDINARILY, COURT WHITNEY would have called a meeting of all department heads to plan the inclusion of *Grottesca* in the Caravaggio exhibition. But from the moment he committed himself to the terms of Luther Mason's remarkable find and the delivery of the controversial painting, he realized it was necessary to establish a need-to-know system within the Gallery.

Mason's discovery would be formally announced in a month at the first of two dinners. In the meantime, Whitney established a series of restrictions on how interoffice correspondence was to be generated and distributed, and who would be invited to meetings. He wasn't naive enough to think a lid on the project's details could be securely closed and sealed for a month, especially not in the city of leaks, Washington, D.C. But he had to try. And he did.

MEMO

TO: The Director

FROM: D. Fechter—Conservation

SUBJECT: "Grottesca"

Naturally, I join everyone in applauding the remarkable find by Luther Mason of this priceless lost Caravaggio.

But I must raise serious professional objections to the way it is being handled.

To allow such a masterpiece to be conserved and restored by an unknown person, and to be shipped across the Atlantic without careful consideration of its condition by this department, is, in my professional judgment, foolhardy.

My respect for Luther has always been of the highest order. But he is not a conservator. I urge you to intervene in order that I, and my associates, be allowed to examine the painting before *any* conservation work is done on it and before it is shipped to this gallery.

MEMO

TO: Donald Fechter

FROM: The Office of the Director

SUBJECT: "Grottesca"

I have read and considered your memo to me with great care. Under normal circumstances, Donald, you are quite right.

But this is not a normal circumstance. My hands are tied. The conditions set for us to have *Grottesca* on display for one month are stringent and, yes, unconventional. But it comes down to a simply matter of doing it this way or not having the painting. Obviously, the former option is unacceptable to me and the trustees.

You and your department will, naturally, play a significant role in examining, determining provenance and authorship, and final conservation. In the meantime, we all must go along.

MEMO

TO: The Office of the Director

FROM: Paul Bishop, Senior Curator

SUBJECT: "Grottesca"

I must protest in the strongest possible terms this outrageous display of grandstanding by Mason. To allow him to dictate the terms of bringing this work to the National Gallery flies in the face of every professional standard set by this institution.

I must further advise you, Court, that if you allow this to go forward, I will have no choice but to tender my resignation.

MEMO

TO: Paul Bishop, Senior Curator

FROM: The Office of the Director

I suggest, Paul, that you calm down and accept the reality of this most unique situation. I don't like it any more than you do. But the trustees have blessed it. That must be good enough for me, and certainly for you.

Shall I place your threat of resignation in the folder with all the others you've sent over the years? All kidding aside, don't you dare quit on me. I have a feeling that when the dust settles over this *Grottesca* matter, I will need your expertise, and steady hand, more than ever.

Buy you a drink? Or dinner?

It's time we did that again.

MEMO

TO: Courtney Whitney III

FROM: Wolff Grundig III

SUBJECT: "Grottesca"

I am certain that my fellow trustees will soon be lavishing additional funds upon the National Gallery and raising even more to support the incredible work done by you and your staff in bringing one of the world's most magnificent masterpieces to this esteemed symbol of the nation's artistic soul!

BRAVO, Court!!!!

To show my personal gratitude, please accept the enclosed check for $50,000, to be added to the Acquisitions Fund!

You and Susan must come to the house for dinner soon. We have a magnificent '71 J. J. Prum I promise to open for the occasion!

TEN

MAC SMITH handed their engraved invitations to the uniformed guard at the West Building's Constitution Avenue entrance, then he and Annabel passed through a metal detector. The attendance of Vice President and Mrs. Aprile dictated enhanced security; two Secret Service agents with dogs patrolled the perimeter. Mr. and Mrs. Mackensie Smith climbed the stairs to the Rotunda on the main floor, where the predinner cocktail party was in full swing.

"Drink?" Mac asked.

"A touch of white wine."

He slipped between elbows to place his order at one of four bars set up in the West Sculpture Hall. A young tuxedoed man reached over him to snare a *bruschetta* from a tray being passed by a waiter. The small piece of toasted garlic bread, topped with chopped tomatoes and sprinkled with olive oil, disappeared into his mouth in one movement. He smacked his lips and said to those with him, "I know what I'm talking about. I wouldn't kid about something like that."

You know something about gluttony, Mac thought.

The string quartet reached the section of a Corelli concerto marked *appassionato,* causing the young man to speak louder: "His name was Yakoto Kayami. Big-shot businessman, more money than God, one of the biggest art collections in Japan. Somebody got hold of the fact that most of the paintings he owned were trash, or forged, or stolen, or a combination of the above, so he did a hara-kari on himself, big sword right through his gut." He laughed. The women winced. Mac took his wife's elbow and herded her in the direction of another hors d'oeuvre tray skillfully balanced on the hand of a waitress.

"Mac, Annabel," a voice said as they were about to toast each other.

"Hello, Scott," Annabel said to the portly man with silken yellow-gray hair, thick tortoiseshell glasses, and chubby cheeks of high color. His bow tie and cummerbund were created from a multicolored Matisse print, a showy contrast with his black tux.

"Dear lady Annabel," M. Scott Pims said, kissing her hand.

"Not me," Mac Smith said, withdrawing his hand from reach. "I left my papal ring home."

"Pity," said Pims. "I need dispensation tonight from—from something."

"The food?" Annabel suggested lightly.

"Oh, no," Pims replied. "The food is heavenly. Like the crowd." He made a face as if a foul smell had wafted into the room.

M. Scott Pims was Washington's most visible artistic gadfly. He wrote extensively on the arts, his articles and reviews appearing in a wide variety of publications. His books, although never reaching best-seller status, enjoyed splendid reviews and were staples in local bookstores. A weekly program on public television station WETA drew a large audience because of his flamboyant, irreverent, often choleric trashing of the art world. Pims's reputation as a gossip monger and trivia lover was without peer.

"Braced for the big announcement?" Pims asked.

"Big announcement?" Annabel said, glancing at Mac.

"I admire that in a woman, Annabel," Pims said. "Practicing discretion until told it is all right to be indiscreet. Of course you know about it, being in the position you enjoy with the insiders." He laughed and included the room in a sweep of his hand. "And we're surrounded by insiders, aren't we? Ah, well. I shall play along with your admirable façade and pretend you don't know. You won't hear it from me. Excuse me. Must circulate. Somewhere in this drove of pretension is a juicy story of lust, love, perhaps murder, or more. And, of course, I must be the one to reveal it. Pleasant evening, Smiths. And Annabel, congratulations on your new role as ambassador-at-large for the White House. Good luck with the Italians. And keep your eye on Luther. He may seem benign here at home, but once abroad he turns into a carnal beast. Ta ta."

" 'Drove of pretension?' " Mac said, laughing, as they watched Pims embrace a woman who seemed to be made of jewelry. "He's a drove of pretension unto himself."

"I like him," Annabel said. "He's fun."

"I suppose." Mac leaned close to her ear. "Obviously, the big surprise about the lost Caravaggio isn't such a big surprise."

"Which comes as no surprise in this town, or where Pims is concerned. With his network, he probably knew about it before Court Whitney. Besides, he and Luther are very close friends. Court did his best to keep it under wraps, but you know how those things go, especially in D.C., with its committees, networks, people who 'need to know.' It's a wonder it hasn't been in the papers."

"Or on Pims's TV show. There's Billie and Roy heading into that gallery. Let's catch up with them. I need to ask Roy something."

As Mac and Annabel pursued their friends, Roy and Billie Kramer, and while other guests smacked and snacked and enjoyed the Italian wines, National Gallery director Courtney Whitney looked out over the Capitol from the terrace outside his seventh-floor East Building office. He was alone. Down the hall, in the seventh-floor boardroom, Luther Mason and Father Pasquale Giocondi were going over final details of how news of the *Grottesca* would be presented to those gathered.

Whitney's remarkable meeting with a bedraggled Luther Mason at Dulles Airport almost a month ago had spawned an equally remarkable series of events at the National Gallery.

Upon returning to his office that day, and in violation of his commitment to keep those in the know to a small number—he knew that if he didn't bring in the trustees from the start, he might not be around for the Caravaggio show—Whitney convened a meeting that night. Joining him in the boardroom were seven of the Gallery's nine trustees. The two absent members comprised half of the four-person contingent decreed to come from government; the other five had no government connection. Whitney preferred dealing with the government faction, because not being collectors, they tended to defer more readily to his ideas than the others. Besides, the government had little control over the Gallery's daily activities. Its funds were mandated by Congress—changes of administration meant virtually nothing where money was concerned. Of course, there was always the push by a new administration for patronage jobs, all of which were summarily rejected.

Still, it was nice to have a White House like the Jeppsen-Aprile version demonstrating a particular interest in art. No sense turning one's back on it. The executive branch might not exactly feed the Gallery, but there was nothing to be gained, and perhaps much to be lost, by biting its hand.

The trustees placed no stumbling blocks in what had become, by that time, Whitney's shared enthusiasm for bringing *Grottesca* to the National Gallery. There were the expected questions about the unusual circumstances of the painting's discovery by Luther Mason, and the manner in which it would leave Italy for its brief residency in Washington. But Whitney urged that Luther, as a foremost Caravaggio expert, be given a free hand. Once the work was securely in the Gallery, he assured them, he, Courtney Whitney III, would take personal charge.

He asked the trustees for public silence until he made the official announcement at the first of two dinners and ended the meeting with a final comment about the unusual conditions of bringing the masterpiece to Washington: "Unorthodox, perhaps, ladies and gentlemen, but no more so than the artist himself."

The following morning, he chaired a series of meetings, including one at which Annabel Reed-

Smith represented the White House Arts Council. By that time there had been discreet communications between Mrs. Aprile and the council, the National Gallery, and Italy's Ministry of Culture confirming the details of how *Grottesca* would travel to the United States.

The rumor that a world-class announcement would be made at the dinner had resulted in a crush of media requests to attend. The public-information office urged that a press conference be held prior to the dinner, but Mason was squarely against that idea and pressed Whitney to quash it. "So much more potent, Court, to allow the news to emerge from the dinner. The more mystery the better. Build the suspense."

Whitney was persuaded. Only top dogs from carefully selected news organizations were invited to the dinner, and they were asked simply to enjoy the evening—no snooping, no questions, no reporting. But press releases were prepared in advance for handing out afterward.

The question of who would make the announcement about *Grottesca* had also been a topic for debate.

Whitney had thought carefully about it. If *he* made the announcement—which would be expected—it might appear that he was stealing Mason's thunder, something he was perfectly willing to do, provided it didn't look as though he were doing it. He had asked Luther if he would prefer being the bearer of good news. "After all," he said, "it was you who made this possible."

Mason didn't hesitate. "No, Court. It's the director's responsibility and privilege. Thank you for offering, but you're the appropriate person to do it."

Whitney checked his watch. Time to go. As he slipped into his evening jacket and checked his appearance in a mirror, down the hall Luther Mason was in the midst of a heated discussion with the priest.

"Absolutely not," Mason said.

Pasquale Giocondi, who wore his "uniform" for the evening—brown habit, sandals, and a large wooden cross suspended from a leather thong—shrugged and said, "I did not realize when I agreed to do this that so much would be at stake, Signor Mason. You are asking me to take part in a crime, *si?* But for so little money. I must weigh the risk."

"There is no risk," Mason said sharply. "All the risk is mine. All you have to do is say a few words about—"

"A few lies, you mean."

"From what I understand, lying is not alien to you, Father Giocondi. Nor is crime."

Another shrug from Giocondi. "I will not take your insult personally. And I will not go through with this unless you pay me more."

The door opened and Court Whitney poked his

head into the boardroom, a practiced smile lighting his face. "Ready, Father?" he asked. "Your audience awaits."

Giocondi looked to Mason; arched dyed eyebrows asked a question. Luther's face was tight as he nodded. "All right," he mumbled.

"Yes, I am ready, Signor Whitney. I look forward to meeting your honored guests."

Mason stood and waited for Giocondi to do the same. "Court, I think it would be wise to spare the Father from the media who are here. We'll handle all the questions at a later press conference. Father Giocondi should be sheltered from that."

"Probably prudent, Luther. By the way, I've decided that after I announce the discovery of *Grottesca,* I'll introduce you to say a few words and to introduce Father Giocondi."

"I really don't think that's—"

"Spare me your modesty, Luther." He slapped his senior curator on the back. "Come on. The hors d'oeuvres will be gone."

They rode down in the elevator and took the underground moving walkway connecting the East and West buildings. As they stepped off, Giocondi stopped to admire a waterfall created by twenty-four jets of water in the exterior courtyard that linked the buildings. The water spewed six feet into the air and then ran down multiple tiny concrete steps to an expanse of glass that ran floor to ceiling. *"Bello! Bello!"* he exclaimed.

"Come," Whitney urged.

By the time they joined the cocktail party, most of the guests had become aware of a painting covered by a red-velvet drape and mounted on an easel on steps leading up to an inactive fountain in the West Garden Court. It was flanked by two uniformed guards. Spotlights on portable metal stands were trained on the easel but had not yet been turned on.

"What is it?" one person asked another.

"Is this the big surprise we've been hearing about?"

"What could it be?"

"Scott, you must know what's under that drape."

Only satisfied, knowing smiles from M. Scott Pims. "Patience," he replied to those inquiries. "All in due time."

"That pompous, phony bastard," a man said. "He doesn't know any more than we do, just likes to make us think he does."

With the appearance of Mason, Whitney, and the skinny little old priest in brown robe and sandals, attention went to them. People speculated on who the monk was.

Whitney circulated with his wife, leaving Mason and Giocondi on their own. Luther led Giocondi to a relatively quiet area behind the musicians. But he couldn't hide. People kept coming up to congratulate Luther on his success at mounting the

Caravaggio exhibition, which meant, of course, having to introduce Giocondi: "This is Father Pasquale Giocondi," he said quickly. "He's here from Italy and is my special guest this evening." That sufficed for most people, although others attempted to engage Giocondi in conversation. Mason answered most of their questions for the priest.

Eventually, the guests were seated for dinner at candlelit tables of eight in the West Garden Court and the West Sculpture Hall. There was no dais. A lectern and microphone had been positioned to the side of the dry fountain, near the shrouded easel.

Court Whitney, the gallery trustees, and the vice president and other high-ranking representatives from government occupied tables nearest the fountain. A large contingent from the Italian Embassy, including Carlo Giliberti, took up two tables. Luther Mason and Father Giocondi sat at a table surprisingly distant from the center of the action, considering that Luther was, in most eyes, the star of the evening. But he hadn't wanted to be close to others. He chose this table when Special Events was making seating assignments and arranged for Scott Pims, Julian, Luther's son from his first marriage, Julian's date, and three members of his curatorial staff to sit with him and Giocondi. It was, for Luther, a safe table.

Mac and Annabel's table included members of

the National Gallery's senior administrative staff. Once antipasto was served, the topic of conversation quickly turned to the priest.

"Any idea who he is?" someone asked.

The others shook their heads. One gentleman speculated, "Maybe Caravaggio confessed his sins to him."

"The way this show is shaping up," said another, "we could use some heavenly intervention." She was the writer in the Education Department responsible for developing educational Caravaggio materials for schoolchildren. "Caravaggio was a barbarian," she told her dinner companions. "Assault on the via della Scrofa. Imprisoned in Tor di Nona. Attacking people with swords. Murder in Rome. Rape. Thievery. An out-and-out scoundrel."

That set off the usual debate over the role an artist's personal life should play in evaluating his creative output. Another round of discussions centered on whether Caravaggio was homosexual, bisexual, or merely high-spirited. It was a lively and spirited table; the good conversation carried through the meal, until Whitney stepped to the lectern and asked for everyone's attention.

After an interminable number of introductions and acknowledgments, Vice President Aprile spoke: "I'm honored to be here this evening," he said, "but I think Carole is the one to make any remarks about the purpose of the evening. She's the

Caravaggio expert in this family. And, I might add, in this administration."

Carole Aprile pledged the full and continuing support of the White House Arts Council to the exhibition.

Whitney resumed his position at the microphone and said, "Judging from the splendid turnout this evening, having a rumor circulating around town that something important would be announced was good for business." There was some laughter. "I won't keep you in suspense any longer. The fact is that this institution has been instrumental in finding one of the art world's most important lost treasures. Ironically, it is a work by the genius wc celebrate tonight, whose majestic creative achievement will grace these walls a few months from now." He went to the draped painting. The spotlights came on, giving brilliant life to the red velvet. Whitney untied two red silk ribbons and slowly pulled the drape away. Gallery photographers took pictures.

"Ladies and gentlemen," said Whitney, "I proudly present to you Caravaggio's lost masterpiece, *Grottesca.*"

A smattering of gasps from the knowing cut through a muttered chorus of, "What is it? What's *Grottesca?*"

"For some background on the monumental importance of this painting, I'd like Senior Curator Luther Mason to say a few words. As most of you know, Luther is one of the world's foremost experts on Caravaggio and is our curator for the exhibition. Luther's dedication to seeing that Caravaggio is presented in all his glory to the American people at this institution is exemplary. To have accomplished this in one's lifetime is achievement enough. But a month ago, Luther returned from yet another of his many trips to Rome and told me a remarkable story. I wish him to share that story with you now. Luther, the floor is yours."

Mason walked tentatively to the lectern and peered at the crowd. The director's introduction had focused the guests' collective attention on what he was about to say. All eyes and ears were trained on him.

He looked back to his table. His son, Julian, stood and held out his date's chair, and they left the room. "Luther's son looks so *angry,*" Annabel whispered to Mac.

Despite being upset by Julian's untimely departure, Luther cleared his throat and slowly recounted his version of events leading to the discovery of *Grottesca.* When he'd completed his tale, he said, "The parish priest I mentioned, Father Pasquale Giocondi, is here tonight as a special guest of the National Gallery of Art. Father Giocondi, who is now retired, agreed to be here to share in this important moment. It took some real arm-twisting to get him to say something, but I'm pleased he has acquiesced. Father Giocondi?"

There was a buzz from the audience as Giocondi walked purposefully to the lectern. *"Signore e signori,"* he said, "it is a great honor for me to be here this evening as a guest of Mr. Mason and the National Gallery of Art. I also say that it is frightening for a man such as myself, who has spent his life offering humble service to his Lord, and to his flock. Some might think it was—how do you say?—an accident for me to have met Mr. Mason. But I disagree. I believe that God directed me to be where Mr. Mason was on that day because Caravaggio was a true servant of our Lord. He painted with religious conviction and passion. His great talent was given by God to be used in his service. It pleases me to think that I have played some small part in allowing his greatest work of all to be here, to be seen and enjoyed by millions of people."

Applause.

Luther stood behind Giocondi. His broad smile said to everyone that he was pleased with what the former priest was saying. In reality, it was a smile of relief. Carlo had been right. Giocondi was good. Smooth. Appropriately humble, yet demonstrating pride in his contribution to the evening and the coming exhibition. And his English was just right, easy to understand but with enough of an accent to add panache.

Giocondi spoke for another ten minutes, and

Mason's relief was sustained. He stuck to the script Luther had created for him. Everything he said supported Luther's bogus official version of how he'd found *Grottesca,* the chance meeting of the two men in a Ravello cafe, the casual trip Luther took to the old church, his shock at seeing what he believed was Caravaggio's lost masterpiece.

Mason took in the reactions of the audience. Most appeared to be pleasantly spellbound by the little man's spiel. When Giocondi ended by saying, "And God Bless America," Luther stepped to the microphone and said, "We all share in our appreciation of what you have given us, Father Giocondi. You have done a great service to the art world, and to the people of America, as well as to the citizens of your beloved Italy. Thank you for sharing this with us this evening."

The applause was louder and more sustained now. Guests stood.

Mason led Giocondi back to their table. Court Whitney made a few final comments, including inviting guests to enjoy after-dinner drinks and to examine the great Italian paintings in adjacent galleries. *Grottesca* had been covered the moment Giocondi concluded his remarks, and two uniformed guards prepared to spirit it away for safekeeping.

"Nicely done, Luther," Scott Pims said when Mason and Giocondi returned to the table. "Julian expressed his apologies for having to leave so abruptly. Undoubtedly a pressing previous engagement."

People were now descending upon them. Luther decided not to press his luck with Giocondi. He said to them, "Father Giocondi has a heart problem and must return to Rome immediately to continue his medical treatment. He'll be available for questions later, in Italy. Please excuse us."

Mason now wanted—needed—to get Giocondi offstage and away from questions. A sudden, pervasive panic had overtaken him. His heart pounded and his mouth had gone dry. As he herded Giocondi toward a door, Carlo Giliberti sprung from his table and joined them. "Very good, Father," he said. "Excellent, Luther."

Realizing the three of them were, briefly, alone, Mason said, "I think it best to get him out of here. Back to the hotel. Back to Italy as quickly as possible."

"All right," said Giliberti. "I will have my driver take him."

"He wants more money," Mason growled.

Giliberti looked at Giocondi. *"Non capisco, Padre."*

In Italian, Giocondi showed that Giliberti did indeed understand him, and he launched into a loud and animated explanation that only exacerbated Mason's discomfort. He snapped, "I told him I'd give him more. Just get him out of here."

"Father Giocondi, Bob Wetzel, arts editor, *Washington Post.* I have a few questions—"

"Not now," Mason said. "Father Giocondi isn't feeling well. He has a heart condition and—"

"Luther."

Court and Sue Whitney approached. Whitney extended his hand. "Fine job. Fine speech. You too, Father."

"How could this painting be languishing in your church all these years?" Wetzel asked. "Did you know—?"

"He's sick," Mason said into Whitney's ear.

"I'm sorry to hear it."

"Excuse us."

"Where can you be reached?" Wetzel called after them.

No answer from Mason or Giocondi. Giliberti accompanied them to the Rotunda.

"You're pale, Luther," Giliberti said.

"Yes. I—"

"Wait here," said Giliberti. "I will get my driver to take him to the hotel."

"Do it yourself, for God's sake. Just get him *away* from here." Mason's voice was unnaturally high. He disliked sounding pathetic.

"Yes, yes, Luther. I will arrange things," Giliberti said. "But you must calm yourself. People are noticing." He turned to Giocondi. "Please give me a moment with Signor Mason."

Giliberti placed his hand on the small of

Mason's back and pushed him away, leaving the priest standing alone. Two couples approached.

"Don't leave him there," Mason said.

"Luther, *Chiudi il becco!*"

Giliberti's whispered command to shut up jarred Mason. He pressed his thin lips tightly together.

Giliberti gripped his arms. "I will take the Father away, Luther. You go home. I will contact you later."

"All right."

"Good show, Luther."

Mason turned to face Annabel and Mackensie Smith, who were passing through the Rotunda on their way home. "You remember Mac," Annabel said.

"Yes. Of course." Luther was sweating profusely and dabbed at his forehead and cheeks with a handkerchief. Mac was surprised at the wet, limp hand Luther offered.

"Quite an announcement you made tonight," Mac said.

"So exciting," said Annabel.

Mac started to thank Mason and Giliberti for having been such accommodating traveling companions for his wife, but Mason interrupted. "You must excuse us. I—I have someone I must see. Father Giocondi isn't feeling well."

"Congratulations, Father," said Annabel.

"Grazie."

"*Buona notte,* Mrs. Smith," Carlo said to Annabel.

Mac and Annabel watched them walk away.

"The *priest* isn't feeling well? *That* man looks like he's about to drop dead," Mac said of Mason.

"I know. Something is definitely wrong."

"So that's Carlo Giliberti."

"That's Carlo."

"Let's go. Rufus needs to go out."

"So do I. The food was heavy."

"The food was bureaucratic Italian."

Once their blue Great Dane had been walked, and they'd changed into night clothes and robes, Mac poured them each two fingers of cognac and they settled on a couch in the study.

"Do you get the feeling, Annabel, that there's something strange about this suddenly discovered painting?"

She shook her head. "Why do you think that?"

"I don't know. What if—?"

"What if what, Mac?"

"What if it's a phony? A forgery?"

"Impossible."

"Why? Happens all the time."

"Not with an institution like the National Gallery, or a curator with Luther's credentials. Besides, it's a moot point. The gallery will be subjecting *Grottesca* to every conceivable test. I understand other experts will be brought in to lend their opinion."

"I suppose you're right." He sipped, enjoying the burn. "I know one thing for certain."

"What's that?"

"Luther Mason had better get himself to a doctor for a physical. Judging from the way he looked tonight, he might not be around to enjoy his own exhibition."

ELEVEN

GILIBERTI WENT to where Father Giocondi was talking with a knot of guests. *"Scusi,"* he said pleasantly. "Come, Father Giocondi. You will be late for your flight."

"What a wonderful thing you've done," said a woman.

"Grazie, grazie," the priest replied.

Giliberti herded him down the stairs and outside, into the cloudless night. A white Lincoln Town Car stood at the curb. Seeing Carlo, the driver got out and opened a rear door.

"Get in, Father," Giliberti said.

With the priest settled in the backseat, Carlo spoke to the driver: "Listen carefully to me," he said, handing him money. "Take Father Giocondi to his hotel. Stay with him. *Capisce?* Do not leave his side."

"But what if the ambassador asks where I am?"

"I'll take care of it. Do not allow the Father to speak to anyone. *Anyone.*"

"Si."

To Giocondi in Italian: "You were excellent tonight."

"*Grazie.* Signor Mason will pay me more?"

"I will talk to him. You spend a pleasant evening, take your flight home tomorrow. Speak to no one. I will be in touch."

"*Si.* Call me when he has the money."

"*Buona sera,* Pasquale."

As Giliberti sent Giocondi on his way, Luther Mason went to a men's room where he took two Tums and used a paper towel soaked in cold water on his face. Other men came and went. Some congratulated him. Mason struggled to acknowledge their kind words. He felt as though he had no voice. He tried to appear relaxed, but his legs were rubbery, and he leaned on a sink for support.

He eventually regained enough composure to return to the scene of the party, where hangers-on watched guards remove *Grottesca* from its easel and spirit it away to an unspecified safe place. His attempt to calm down had been successful. There was nothing to worry about, he reminded himself over and over, annoyed at his prior loss of confidence. The Caravaggio original of *Grottesca* was now safely in the possession of his employer, the National Gallery. And he was the one who'd found and delivered it, perhaps not the way he'd described it, but found and delivered it nonetheless.

He'd done nothing irregular—yet. And it wasn't too late—yet—to abandon the plan.

Or was it?

The problem, he knew, was that others were involved. He could trust Carlo. But what about the rascal of a priest, Giocondi, who'd already violated their agreement by asking for more money? And the old man, Luigi Sensi, was a mafioso. As long as he was paid what Luther had agreed to pay, he had no reason to upset things.

Of course, the source of the money for Luther to finance the plan, San Francisco art collector Franco del Brasco, was also a gangster. A dressier one, and smooth, with a good cover—a man whose hands and money were dirty. At least that's what Luther had been led to believe. A very rich gangster. No reason for him to cause trouble either.

Still, too many people.

He spotted his friend, writer and broadcaster Scott Pims, speaking with two women Luther recognized as leading gallery fund-raisers, and started in their direction. But he stopped when he saw Carlo Giliberti entering the court. Mason went up to the cultural attaché. "What happened?" he asked, suffering the return of panic. "Where is Father Giocondi?"

"I sent him with Francesco to the hotel."

"Francesco? Who is Francesco?"

"One of our drivers."

"You entrusted him to a *driver?*"

"*Si,* Luther. I saw no need to go with him myself. I told Francesco he is to not allow the old man to speak with anyone, and to stay with him until his flight."

"I wish—"

"Forget Giocondi, Luther. We must talk." He led Mason to the center of the Sculpture Gallery, where catering personnel were clearing and breaking down tables, and then paused at the foot of a Milanese sixteenth-century Venus.

"What is it?" Mason asked.

Giliberti stretched up to Mason's ear. "Money," he said.

"Money? Giocondi?"

"*Si.* And they want more money in Italy."

"*Who* wants more in Italy?"

"Signor Sensi."

"That's ridiculous. I made my deal with him. You said he was a man of honor."

"Yes. But he did not realize the importance of the painting. It is more valuable than you led him to believe."

"I led him to believe nothing, Carlo. I was honest with him. I expect honesty in return."

"A nice sentiment, Luther. But Sensi is not sentimental. You don't have the choice. He can do terrible things to you. To us."

Giliberti looked past Mason and stiffened, his eyes wide. Mason turned. Standing at the other large statue dominating the center of the hall, the sixteenth-century *Bacchus and Fawn,* were two heavy men. Luther remembered seeing them during dinner at one of the Italian Embassy tables.

"What's the matter, Carlo?"

"Them."

"Who are they?"

"Security from the embassy."

"Well—?"

"But they work for Sensi, too. They will bring the money to him."

"I can't," Mason said, anger melding with fear. "I can't."

"There is nothing you can do about it, Luther, except to pay. Or, of course, you can always return *Grottesca* to him."

"I don't *have* more money, damn it," Mason said. "I can't go back to del Brasco and ask for more. He's already advanced me a half million, and I gave Sensi half of that. He won't give me more until he has the painting. Make Sensi understand that."

Giliberti shook his head. "Go to del Brasco, Luther, and get the money. One-half million, American. Sensi will not take no for an answer."

The two men continued to stare at Carlo and Luther.

"I have to go, Luther. I told them you would have the money in three days."

"You told them *what?*"

"Call me tomorrow and tell me you have

worked things out." He walked away at a brisk pace and disappeared into the Rotunda.

Mason stepped into an adjacent gallery and pretended to study Angelico and Lippi's *The Adoration of the Magi.* At that moment, he adored nobody. He looked back. The two men slowly passed, paused to look in at him for what seemed an eternity, and proceeded toward the Rotunda.

He slumped on a bench in the middle of the gallery. The air had gone out of him. He tried to resurrect his earlier thought, that he still had time to call it off. It was a failed second attempt. The reality was he'd stepped into a vortex from which it was getting impossible to extricate himself. As a boy, after seeing a movie where someone was sucked into the ground, his recurring dream had him stepping into quicksand—of university, of scholarship, of the museums and art world, and now, this . . .

He could have avoided the situation, he knew, had he stepped back at any number of junctures. He could have declined dinner with Sensi. But knowing the aged mafioso had *Grottesca*—God, what a powerful motivator—propelled him to that night in Positano.

He could have decided in Ravello not to drive to the run-down church in search of the smarmy priest, Pasquale Giocondi. But he went. He couldn't change that. Even if he could, would he have? If he hadn't he might never have seen the painting, held it in his hands, for even a moment.

Despite those decisions, he still could have bailed out. But his call to Court Whitney, his boss at the National Gallery, had defined his situation, shaped it, thrust him into the role of a pilot who, upon reaching the point of no return on a flight, develops engine trouble and still must continue pushing forward, hoping to reach the planned destination.

He did what he seldom did, ordered whiskey, neat, from a bartender finishing up in the West Garden Court.

"Bravo!" His fleshy friend, M. Scott Pims, placed the fingertips of his right hand to his eyebrow and tossed Mason a salute. "Well done. Having a nightcap, I see. To steady the nerves after your triumph?"

"Where are you going from here?" Luther asked.

"Straight home to beddy-bye."

"I have to talk to you."

"Oh, I'm well aware of that, Luther. Your place or mine?"

"Yours."

The murder of Carlo Giliberti, Italy's cultural attaché to the United States, happened too late to make the morning papers. But radio and television broadcasts had the news.

Mac and Annabel Smith heard it as they were starting to enjoy a second cup of coffee in their kitchen.

Luther Mason heard the news reports driving to work at the Gallery.

The news interrupted an argument between Court Whitney and his wife, Sue, over where to spend an upcoming long weekend.

And Vice President Joseph Aprile received word of the murder during his early-morning briefing.

They all reflected upon having been with Carlo Giliberti hours before his demise. Charming fellow. Who could have done such a thing?

Press reports said that Giliberti had been found in some bushes on the perimeter of Rock Creek Park. The cause of death was a single stab wound. Robbery a possible motive; his wallet was missing. But his rings, Rolex watch, and $485 in his pocket were not.

Law-enforcement agencies generated their own initial theories. Washington MPD's chief of detectives, Emil Vigilio, after observing the body and its resting place in the park, and the wound, commented to fellow detectives that it had all the trappings of a mob rubout.

"Why? Because he's Italian?" a colleague asked.

"No, wiseguy. Because it looks like every mob hit I've seen. In the movies." Organized crime of the Mafia variety was less visible in Washington than elsewhere—Vigilio's experience with Mafia assassinations was limited to dramatized versions.

Wade Johnson, head of the State Department's 1,000-person police force, charged with protecting the lives of the District of Columbia's vast foreign diplomatic community, had a different take on it: "A snow bird looking for cash to snort up his nose."

"What was an addict doing in Rock Creek Park that time of night? It's like asking for it himself. And why not take the rings, the cash . . . ?"

"In a hurry to get home because his mother might worry. Who knows?" Johnson replied before heading for a meeting of agencies that would inevitably end up arguing more about jurisdiction over the case than clues. "Looking for action. Smelling the roses. Got lost. Come on. This meeting should be a laugh a minute."

TWELVE

"CAROLE? It's Annabel."

"I was going to call you. You've heard."

"On the radio. My Lord, what a shock."

"I know."

"To be with him just hours before he's murdered. But that's the usual reaction to anyone's death. The question is *why?*"

"And who. Court Whitney called. He's in a panic."

"Why?"

"He says Luther wants to cancel the exhibition."

"But that would be—"

"I know, I know . . . an overreaction. Does that sound callous? They were close friends."

"No, not at all. Court isn't canceling, is he?"

"No. But he said Luther is beside himself. A wreck. Came into his office insisting the show be scrubbed. Almost as if he wanted to cancel. Then left. Court doesn't know where he's gone. No answer at his apartment. A favor?"

"Sure."

"Try to get hold of Luther. Keep trying him at home."

"All right. What do you want me to tell him?"

"I don't know—calm him, I suppose. It's tragic what happened to Mr. Giliberti, but we need Luther. It's his exhibition."

"I'll do what I can."

"Do you think—?"

"What?"

"That Carlo Giliberti's death might have something to do with the Caravaggio exhibition? The *Grottesca?*"

"I can't imagine. Yes I can. In art circles, the unimaginable is too often normal."

"I read about the huge sums paintings bring these days. Millions for marginal works. Tens of millions for masterpieces like *Grottesca*. People have killed for a lot less."

"I'll try to reach Luther," Annabel said, hunching her shoulders against a chill that had nothing to do with the weather.

"Thanks, Annabel. Call me?"

"Of course."

Annabel tried Mason's apartment but received a busy signal. Frequent attempts over the next fifteen minutes brought only the increasingly annoying busy buzz. She had an appointment at her gallery with a potential pre-Columbian buyer and was running late. Mac had already left to teach a class at GW. She'd try Luther again from the gallery. It was the best she could do. For the moment.

Mason went directly home after meeting with Court Whitney. Blinds drawn, door locked, he sat on the edge of his bed and tried to put his jumbled thoughts in order. Could he persuade Whitney and the trustees to cancel? He felt he had to try. It was a way out for him. Carlo Giliberti's murder had been a terrible blow. At the same time, it offered an excuse to call off the exhibition, or at least to postpone it. *Grottesca* could be sent back to Italy where it belonged. If his moneyman, Franco del Brasco, wanted back what money he'd advanced, Mason would find a way to reimburse him if it took the rest of his life. How could he have been so foolhardy to think he could pull this off?

He went to the living room where he dialed a number. "Mother?"

"Yes."

"It's Luther."

"I know. You're the only person who can call me that."

Luther was used to acerbic responses from her, having grown up as an only child in the home of Joseph and Catherine Mason.

His father had been a professor of agricultural science at Purdue University, in West Lafayette, Indiana. He'd retired from that position but didn't have much time to enjoy his leisure. A massive heart attack killed him three months after his retirement dinner.

Catherine Mason had been West Lafayette's head librarian until her retirement, a stern, sturdy, and proper Baptist woman whose efficiency at running the library compensated for any lack of warmth with its patrons.

"How are you?" Luther asked.

"I am feeling just fine," his mother replied.

He envisioned her sitting in her favorite Queen Anne grandfather chair, next to a small table on which the house's only telephone rested. Chronic arthritic pain in her shoulders, hips, and hands would cause her to sit crooked in the chair, but nothing would be said. Catherine Mason suffered pain well. "How are you, Luther?" she asked.

"Not very well, Mother. I had a great shock this morning."

Her silence invited him to continue.

"A very dear friend of mine was murdered here in Washington last night."

The silence continued until she said, "It seems every time I pick up the newspaper or watch television, someone is being murdered in Washington. They say it's worse even than New York."

"There are too many murders here," Luther acknowledged. "But this was a special friend. His name was Carlo Giliberti."

"An Italian?"

"Yes. He was the cultural attaché at the Italian Embassy."

"And he was your friend?"

"Yes. I was with him last night at a formal dinner."

"Was he murdered at the dinner?" Catherine Mason asked.

"No. Later. In a park."

"What is this world coming to?"

Had she closed her eyes and said it to the God she trusted? he wondered.

"Mother, I thought I might find some time to visit with you."

"That would be nice."

Luther hadn't been back to Indiana in more than three years and suffered perpetual guilt about it. But he always managed to rationalize not making the trip, the most persuasive excuse being that his mother was seldom alone. She'd remained active in the community, especially the church, and he received occasional letters from a neighbor who never failed to marvel at Catherine's busy schedule. There was no physical need for him to be with her, he would remind himself after calling to say the pressures of work precluded him from coming home for yet another Christmas, or Thanksgiving. If she fell ill and needed constant care, he would, of course, be at her side. Like any dutiful son.

The truth was that Mason did not especially want to see her. He loved his mother, but she represented the pain of what he considered to have been an unhappy childhood.

"Would you like me to visit?" he asked.

"Do you have to ask? How is Julian?"

"Fine. Has he called, or written?"

"No."

The hypocrisy of trying to convince his only son, and his mother's only grandchild, to maintain a relationship with her wasn't lost on Mason. Julian seemed even less interested in seeing her than Luther.

"Young people these days," he said, forcing a sardonic chuckle. "You can't tell them anything."

"Do you hear from Juliana?"

The mention of Luther's first wife pricked him. "We talk occasionally," he said. "I thought she kept in touch with you."

"Not as much as she used to." His mother's voice was sad.

Luther Mason and Juliana Moreau had met while graduate fine-arts students at Harvard University's Fogg Art Museum; Luther had spent four unhappy undergraduate years at Purdue, where his father's employment meant free tuition.

He lived at home while attending Purdue. Being a "townie" provided him with a rationale for staying isolated and withdrawn, going to classes and then straight home, the way it had been in high school, where his quiet presence, viewed as aloof and snobbish by some, caused them to call him a momma's boy and even a fag, which wasn't true. The teenage Luther was obsessed with girls and the profound sexual mysteries they promised, spending hours in the library where his mother worked, ostensibly studying, but in fact sneaking into the recesses of the racks that held art books to ponder the magnificent color plates of voluptuous nudes by Titian, Cranach, Gauguin, and Renoir.

But as exciting as the grand nudes by old masters were, there was a large coffee-table book to which Luther found himself returning with regularity. It featured the works of an artist he hadn't heard of earlier, Michelangelo Merisi Caravaggio. The scenes and portraits in the vivid color plates affected Luther far more powerfully than the other books he studied. Although there were no nudes, Caravaggio's paintings exuded a sensuality that physically aroused him. Strange, he thought, because most of the themes were religious. What was it about this artist that was so profoundly affecting? he wondered.

He studied the Caravaggio book countless times, using a small magnifying glass to get closer. He analyzed every detail of the lovely female face in *The Conversion of Mary Magdalene* and did the same with the thick-lipped, epicurean young musician at the center of *The Musicians.*

But it was the face of the young boy in Caravaggio's *Bacchus* that had the strongest impact upon Luther. There were times he stared at it so long that he lost touch with where he was—*who* he was—as though he and the boy model had become one. The book's text indicated that this model had been used by Caravaggio before and that *Bacchus* seemed to have been the last time. But Luther also studied a plate titled *Grottesca* in which the model, he was certain, was the same. *Grottesca* was lost, said the book, its fate unknown.

His mother's staunch religious faith precluded her ever buying her son an art book in which undraped female figures were represented. But because Caravaggio was considered a major painter of religious subjects, she acquiesced to his frequent requests for the Caravaggio book and bought it one year for his birthday. He prized it as another young boy might treasure a baseball glove, a football, or a set of trading cards.

Luther dated a few times while at Purdue, brief relationships that never progressed beyond an awkward kiss goodnight. He would have graduated a virgin had it not been for West Lafayette's dozens of brothels, identified with a yellow light and a house number, each one a fraction. It was in such a house that an older woman initiated Luther into sex. It was, at once, exhilarating and terrifying.

By the time he received his undergraduate degree in literature—further setting him apart from the university's overwhelming population of engineering students—his surreptitious enjoyment of art had blossomed into an appreciation of art itself, and the artists who created it. Luther himself did not possess artistic talent. His crude attempts at charcoal sketches and an occasional watercolor were dismal failures. But he had developed an eye for the work of others—more important, a deep *love* for it—that set his course for the future. His departure from Indiana to Harvard was, as he remembered, "the most important and liberating day of my life."

Juliana Moreau was a serious painter of the Abstract School—Mondrian, Kandinsky, and their disciples. The Czech Kupka, the turbulent Surrealist Masson, and the German Wols were her idols. She showed Luther a series of Wols paintings soon after they met. "They look like malignant growths," he said. Not a suitable remark and not an inspiring start to their relationship, but it progressed nonetheless.

She was a slight young woman with coal-black hair worn long and straight. She was plain in the sense that she did nothing to make herself less so. Luther did not consider her beautiful, even attractive—until she showed a definite interest in him. Once that happened, his visual perception of her changed.

After dating for two months, they consummated what had become love in a cheap Boston hotel. Which meant, of course, in those years, that they would be married, eloping to Maryland the summer following their sophomore year.

Luther was almost paralyzed with fear at the thought of bringing a *wife* home to meet his widowed mother. But it went surprisingly well. Juliana seemed sincerely to like Catherine Mason, developing a comfortable bond with her that sometimes, it seemed to Luther, excluded him. Which was all right. A good relationship between mother- and daughter-in-law took the pressure off.

Graduating from Harvard raised the first serious debate in their relationship. What would they do next with their lives, and where would they do it? Despite Juliana's objections, Luther accepted a post in San Francisco as an apprentice curator in Medieval and Renaissance Spanish Art at the M. H. de Young Memorial Museum. Juliana was unhappy there and not silent about it. After a year, she announced that she was going to Paris to study painting. That she'd made her plans without discussion or warning bothered him, more so than the fact that she would be gone. Their relationship had cooled to that extent. There was no discussion of divorce. It wasn't necessary.

They attempted a reconciliation a year later, resulting in Juliana's pregnancy and the eventual birth of their son, Julian. Some found it strange for a son to be named after the mother, but that mattered little to Luther. Although he loved the child from the first day of his life, becoming a parent did not generate the heightened sense of accomplishment other first-time fathers enjoyed. It had happened, that's all. A natural development in a married person's life. And an added burden, one he was committed to shouldering.

Luther and Juliana lived in relative happiness in California until Julian was two, enjoying the bohemian spirit of the city and its abundance of cultural and social opportunities. And Luther was taking more pleasure from his young son than he'd imagined. The boy was smart and funny. Luther was not the sort of man who laughed often or loud, but Julian made him do that.

Juliana pursued her painting, studying with a San Francisco artist, but she wasn't happy. She missed Paris and urged Luther to leave his job, pack their belongings, and move to the City of Light. Her suggestion had its appeal, but not enough for him to abandon what had become a budding curatorial career. His superiors viewed him as a bright talent who might one day make a significant contribution to the art world.

One day, Juliana said she wanted to visit Luther's mother in Indiana and take Julian with her. Luther couldn't accompany them because of a particularly crowded schedule at the museum, but he wished them a safe and happy trip. Juliana called from Indiana few days later: "Luther, I've decided to go back to Paris."

"Back to Paris? I thought—"

"It's best for everyone concerned. I've discussed it with your mother and—"

"Do you think it's best for Julian?"

"Your mother has agreed to care for him."

Luther caught the next plane to Indianapolis, where his mother picked him up at the airport. Luther was emotional during the ride back to West Lafayette, Catherine Mason calm and stoic as she presented her case for his leaving Julian with her.

"Fine," he said angrily. "The hell with Juliana. But I'm taking Julian back to San Francisco with me. He's my son."

His mother's smile further angered him. It was a smile that said "poor, confused Luther. I know best."

Luther's confrontation with Juliana was heated. He begged her to reconsider, to give it another year with him in San Francisco. Then, he promised, they would go to Paris together. "Julian will be a year older and—"

She replied by closing her packed suitcase and snapping its locks. Luther turned to see Julian standing in the doorway, eyes red and wet. Luther reached for him, but the boy ran to his mother and grabbed her legs. Catherine Mason appeared and said sweetly, "Come, Julian. I just baked peanut butter cookies for you."

Julian looked up at his mother, who smiled and

nodded. "They're your favorite," she said, giving him a squeeze. To Luther as Julian ran from the room: "This is a wonderful place for him to grow up. You're never home, Luther. He needs stability, someone always there for him. Don't look at me that way. I know I don't provide it either. Go back to San Francisco and follow your dream, like I'm doing. Give our son the chance to grow up in normal surroundings. Your mother is a good woman, dedicated to him. We'll both visit often. When he gets older, he can come stay with us whenever he likes."

Luther was gripped with a sense of helplessness. Juliana joined Catherine and Julian in the kitchen, where they ate cookies and played a game with the boy, causing him to laugh with rare abandon. Luther sat on the front porch, their voices and giggles reaching him through the open kitchen window. He heard Juliana tell their son that she was going to a wonderful city called Paris and that he would come visit her there many times. "What fun we'll have," she said. "You'll learn to speak French and we'll take long walks and eat yummy cakes and cookies and . . ."

A taxi picked Juliana up at five that afternoon to take her to Indianapolis and her flight. She kissed Luther on the cheek. "Talk it over with your mother," she said. "Whatever you decide to do is fine. He is your son."

That night, after Julian was asleep in "his bedroom," Luther and his mother sat in the living room. Pictures of his father were everywhere, on the walls and in small oval silver frames on the mantle and piano.

"Juliana is right," his mother said softly. "Not about leaving. She isn't terribly stable, you know, leaving her only child like this."

"Leaving her husband," Luther muttered.

"She tells me you weren't happy together. No wonder, the sort of lives you lead. Out all hours of the night, artists using drugs and drinking. She told me you stay at that museum where you work for half the night. Weekends. No time for him."

"That's not true. Maybe there isn't a lot of time with Julian, but I always try to make it quality time."

That knowing smile again. He hated it, wanted to strike it from her lips.

"I spoke with Reverend Gormley, Luther, and told him the story. He agrees. Julian deserves a decent Christian upbringing. I'll see that he gets it. I'm young and healthy enough to take good care of him."

And lonely, thought Luther.

"Why don't we try it, Luther? You can come take him any time you wish. After all, he is your son."

The next morning Luther called to Julian, who was playing in the pretty yard with a red wagon his grandmother had bought for him. The boy sat on

Luther's lap. "Daddy's going back to San Francisco for awhile, son. He has a lot of work to do and wouldn't be able to be with you. Grandma loves you very much. You stay with her until I come back."

Julian looked at him with expressionless large brown eyes. Luther Mason fought back tears. "Okay, son?"

Julian nodded, ran from the porch, and pushed the wagon across the yard, making motor sounds. Luther kissed his mother and got in a taxi for the trip to the airport. He didn't dare look back.

Julian Mason remained with his grandmother until graduating from high school. In the early years, Luther traveled regularly to Indiana to spend time with him. But the visits became less frequent as time passed, especially after Luther accepted a position in the curatorial department of Washington's National Gallery of Art.

To Luther's surprise and pleasure, Julian decided to pursue a degree in fine arts at George Washington University. That decision reunited him with his father, who by this time had gained his deserved reputation as one of the world's leading authorities on the life and works of Caravaggio. He was also married for the second time, to a woman he'd met at a gallery reception.

Cynthia Walsch had been left a considerable amount of money by her deceased first husband, allowing her to devote her time to favored local charities. She was physically different from Juliana—a big woman, almost raw-boned, with high color in her cheeks and a body that would remain chunky no matter how hard she dieted.

Perhaps Cynthia's most striking feature was her laugh. She laughed easily and often. Luther enjoyed being with someone who found the things he said to be witty. Too, she demonstrated a sexual aggressiveness that pleased him.

The easy laughter and sex vanished after they were married. Although they were together when Julian moved to Washington, it had become a classic marriage of convenience, leaving Luther plenty of spare time to help his son settle into his new surroundings and to get to know his father once again.

"Do you hear from your mother often?" Luther asked him during their first dinner together.

"No," Julian said. "It doesn't matter."

"When are you coming?" Catherine Mason asked Luther.

"I don't know, Mother. I've been spending a great deal of time in Italy getting ready for my Caravaggio exhibition. And now this dreadful murder of my friend. I must go to California soon. Maybe I can stop on the way there, or back."

"Whatever," she said.

"Well, I just wanted to call because—I wanted

to tell you about my good friend being killed last night."

"I am sorry to hear that, Luther. You will let me know ahead of time if you plan to visit?"

"Yes. I will let you know. Take care."

The phone in Indiana was gently replaced in its cradle.

Luther sat back in his chair and closed his eyes against tears that threatened. He was sorry he'd called, even sorrier he'd indicated he might visit her. The truth was he didn't know who else to talk to about Carlo's murder. He had no interest in the gossipy speculation running rampant in the East and West buildings of the National Gallery. He could have called his friend, Scott Pims, but he'd left him only a few hours ago after sitting up all night talking.

By 5:00 A.M., Luther had become sufficiently lubricated by Pims's steady flow of expensive brandy to launch into a long, meandering, self-pitying monologue about his life and the people in it. Mason seldom drank to excess, and only, it seemed, in Pims's apartment, where he felt—safe? With this overbearing, inveterate gossip and intellectual bully with whom he'd become close friends? It was here, in this apartment, plied with brandy, that he'd shared with Pims his dream of possessing *Grottesca* and how he intended to do it.

This particular night, Pims lost patience with Mason's soliloquy. "Oh, for God's sake, Luther," he said, "stop feeling sorry for yourself. You're about to take a dramatic leap into a life of excitement, intrigue, and adventure. Isn't that what you want?"

Mason responded with sudden, unbridled enthusiasm. "Yes, exactly, Scott. That is the point of what I'm doing, isn't it? To light a flame. To take my turn at riding bareback and naked in the moonlight."

Pims laughed and shook his large, leonine head. "You really must come up with a new metaphor, Luther. I'm growing weary of your *Equus* infatuation."

Pims was referring to *Equus,* a play that Luther had seen more than a dozen times. In it, a disturbed young man, treated by a conservative, inhibited psychiatrist, talked with rapture of riding a stallion naked across the field at night, causing the psychiatrist to reevaluate his own life, which lacked the young patient's free spirit: "When will it be *my* turn?" the psychiatrist asked himself. And so had Luther Mason, over and over since first seeing the play.

"Dinner tomorrow?" Pims asked as Mason was about to leave.

"Afraid I can't, Scott. I'm hoping to have dinner with Julian, although you never know with him. He has a habit of not showing up. He's terribly irresponsible."

Another laugh from Pims. "A chip off the Caravaggio block, I'd say."

"I prefer to not think of it that way, but I suppose you're right. I'll call you in a few days."

He went home, napped, showered and shaved, and headed for work.

Usually, while driving to the Gallery, he listened to WGMS, one of Washington's classical-music stations. This morning, he decided to catch the news on WMAL.

The report of Carlo Giliberti's murder almost sent him off course into oncoming traffic.

Who could have done such a thing?

What had happened to Carlo Giliberti in Rock Creek Park early that morning was known to three people—the two men who'd killed him, and who weren't likely to come forth with the information, and Carlo, who was in no condition to. Had they been able to explain, they would have painted this picture.

After his conversation with Luther in the West Sculpture Hall, Carlo had gone outside for a cigarette. His display of calm to his curator friend was a sham. Inside, his nerve ends were sputtering, live wires touching.

That he shouldn't have tried to play both ends against the middle was reinforced when he saw the two embassy "security men" approach.

They declined his offer of cigarettes. "Come, Carlo. We take a ride."

"No. Too late. What do you have, women?" Carlo tried his most engaging laugh. "Not tonight."

"Andiamo!" one of the men said. His voice was hard.

Carlo knew it was useless to argue. He might as well go with them, hear what they had to say, smooth it over, straighten it out. Was it such a sin to try to make a little more for all his hard work? All they had to do was say no. Nothing ventured, nothing gained, as his American friends were fond of saying.

They flanked him as they headed for a dark-blue rented sedan parked on the wide cobblestone road between the National Gallery's East and West buildings. Carlo sat in the front passenger seat. The second man sat directly behind him.

They drove slowly, aimlessly, without an apparent destination. Carlo's chatter was met with grunts. He chain-smoked as they traveled the city's nearly deserted streets.

"Hey, look, my friends, what is this all about? Huh? "It was a mistake, that's all." He turned to the man in the rear seat. *"Capisce?* I was testing Signor Sensi. You know, seeing if he would be generous with me for being so loyal to him. A little more money from him was all I asked for. But I don't want that anymore. No need. I talked to my friend, Mason. He will soon have another half-million American for Signor Sensi. That's right. I intended to give most of it to him. No. I will give *all* of it to him. You tell him that."

When Carlo sent word to Sensi that he wanted more money from the old mafioso or would walk away from the deal, he knew he had little chance of succeeding. Hitting up Luther was a less risky sell. He would lie to his friend, tell him that Sensi was demanding additional funds. Judging from Luther's fear of the old man in Italy, Carlo was certain he'd go to his moneyman, del Brasco, to get it. And if he didn't, what was the harm in trying? Sensi would never know Carlo had used his name in vain to extort a bigger payoff from Luther.

"Be quiet," the driver said to Carlo.

"Sure. Hey, look, my friends, we forget all of this. When I get the half-million from my friend, I save some for you. Enough for you to—"

The man in the rear seat wrapped his left forearm around Carlo's head and thrust a needle-thin stiletto into the back of his neck. The blade entered smoothly and silently into the cultural attaché's cranial cavity, piercing the pituitary and stopping only when the shank made hard contact with Carlo's skull.

Death was almost instantaneous.

Giliberti's final words were obscenities, directed not at his killers but at the artist and current toast of Washington, Michelangelo Caravaggio.

THIRTEEN

THAT SAME MORNING

BY THE time Annabel reached her gallery on Georgetown's Wisconsin Avenue, it had started to rain. The parking lot she used was two blocks away; the only things in shorter supply in Washington than character and integrity, she thought, were parking spaces in Georgetown.

Her hair dampened, but not her spirits, she let herself into the gallery, punched in the code to deactivate the alarm system, turned on the lights, and went to her small office in the rear to settle in for some administrative duties before her buyer arrived. She hoped other customers wouldn't come in. Browsers almost never bought any of the expensive artifacts. Her sales were primarily to a network of collectors she'd established, each name carefully entered into her computer's database, including what she knew of the pieces in their collections, their personal preferences, the financial limits to which they were likely to go, and other pertinent information.

She took a break a half hour later and entered

the showroom, standing in the middle of the large, well-lit space to admire what she'd managed to accomplish. Each work had special meaning for her, making it sometimes difficult to part with them. When she forgot that she was in the business of selling the pre-Columbian art in the gallery, Mac was always there to gently remind her.

She went to what she considered the centerpiece of her current collection, a baked clay, six-inch-high, Tlatilco female figure, unusual, and by extension more expensive, because of its double face. It was a superb example of Mexican preclassic culture, dating back to circa 1300–1700 B.C. She'd negotiated long and hard to purchase it from its previous owner, a wealthy Mexican physician. When the deal was set, she could barely contain her trader's glee. As far as Annabel was concerned, she'd "stolen" the piece; its worth was far greater than what she'd paid.

She'd bought that particular piece before she'd closed her law practice and opened the gallery, having made the purchase purely for personal pleasure, installing it in an alarmed Plexiglas case in her law office. Clients often admired it. Eventually, Annabel began using it to make a point with warring couples—that rather than approaching divorce from two distinctly different standpoints, two faces, it was better for everyone concerned, especially children, that the parting couple cooperate. She was never sure whether the analogy was effective. But she did have an impressive number of divorcing couples come to the bargaining table under less angry circumstances than when first becoming involved with her.

"I trust you slept well," Annabel said to her inanimate Tlatilco friend before returning to her office to resume running figures on a broad spreadsheet.

Fifteen minutes later, a buzzer indicated that someone had entered the gallery. Annabel got up and looked into the showroom. A short man wearing a green raincoat and a Baltimore Orioles' baseball cap closed the door behind him.

"May I help you?" Annabel asked.

"No," he said, shaking his head. "Just looking."

"Make yourself at home," Annabel said, certain he'd come in only to escape the rain. She returned to her desk and positioned herself so that she could watch him.

Annabel glanced down at her work. The next time she looked up, she couldn't believe what was happening: The man had pulled a hammer from his raincoat pocket and swung it with great force at the case, smashing its top and sides and sending the Tlatilco to the floor. The case's special alarm had come to life, its scream bouncing off the four walls.

Annabel gasped. She started to shout, but the words wouldn't come. Springing from her chair, she raced into the showroom. The man had turned and was about to run for the door. "What have you—?" Annabel managed. She grabbed the back of his raincoat collar, spinning him around. Annabel's hand instinctively went up to protect her face as he brought the ballpeen hammer down in a wide, uncontrolled arc, its peen aimed directly at her forehead. The hard metal nob deflected off the back of Annabel's hand, causing it to graze her ear and cheek and land with a painful thud on her shoulder. She fell to her knees as the man stumbled to the door, opened it, and disappeared.

Annabel shook, wrapped her arms about herself, and looked down at the white marble floor. She was surrounded by small pieces of what had been her beloved Tlatilco. She reached tentatively to touch them, then drew back her hand. "Oh my God, why?" she said aloud. She'd knelt on one of the pieces, causing a sharp pain where it cut her knee. Her shoulder ached. She got to her feet and went out to the street, looking left and right. No sign of the man. Across Wisconsin, on the corner of M Street, stood two uniformed Washington MPD officers.

"Help! Help me, please," Annabel yelled.

She and the two officers stood inside the gallery.

"What is it?" one of the cops asked.

"A valuable piece of pre-Columbian art," Annabel replied, her voice trembling in concert with her body.

"And you say this guy just walked in, hit it with a hammer, and left?"

"Yes. That's exactly what happened."

"And then he hit you?"

"Yes."

One of the officers checked the side of her head. Her ear and cheek were red, but the skin hadn't been broken. "Maybe you should sit down," the officer said. To his partner: "Call for an ambulance."

"No," Annabel said. "I'm all right." She looked down at her torn stocking and knee, where the small gash oozed blood that ran down the front of her leg. She pressed a paper towel to her knee.

She pointed to the open door to her office. "I was in there doing some bookkeeping. He came in, stood at the door for a few seconds, then went over and examined the piece. I looked down for a moment. When I looked up, the hammer was in his hand and on its way toward the case. It happened so fast."

"Did he say anything to you?"

"No. I mean, I asked if I could help him, and he shook his head. I think he just said, 'No.' Maybe he said he was just browsing. I really don't remember."

"What did the guy look like?"

"I never saw his face. Not clearly. He had on a green raincoat and a baseball cap. I think it said Baltimore Orioles on it, but I can't be sure. Yes, that's what it said."

"You didn't see his face good?"

"No."

"Hair? Any distinguishing features?"

"If I didn't see his face, I don't see how I could—" She caught her anger. Nothing was to be gained by being short with them.

"And he attacked you?"

"Yes. No. I mean, I don't think he intended to attack me. He was heading for door but I stopped him. I grabbed his coat and . . . he hit me to get away, I think."

"Can I use your phone?" one of the officers asked.

"Certainly. In there."

From beneath a display case Annabel took a plastic bag in which to place the Tlatilco fragments.

"Don't touch them, ma'am," one of the cops said. "Let's wait until we get a detective down here."

She called George Washington University but was told Professor Smith wasn't available. She asked to have him call her at her gallery. "Tell him it's urgent," she said.

A couple of browsers attempted to enter the gallery, but one of the officers had positioned himself at the door. "There's been a crime committed here," he said. "The gallery is closed."

Annabel remained in her office until the buzzer said someone else had arrived. She went to the showroom. "Steve," she said. "Of course. I should have thought to ask for you. I wasn't thinking straight." Detective Steve Jordan headed Washington MPD's art squad.

"This time, for some reason, they put the call through to the right person," he said. "What happened here?"

Annabel explained.

Jordan knelt and visually examined the broken figure. He looked up from his position on the floor and said, "Doesn't make any sense. Why would a guy come in and smash this thing?"

"I wish I knew," said Annabel.

Jordan stood. "I can see somebody *stealing* it. Worth a lot of money, huh?"

Annabel nodded.

"Insured, I assume."

"Yes, but not for its full value." Annabel had meant to increase coverage on that piece along with others in the gallery but hadn't gotten around to it.

"Report said injuries. You?"

Annabel shrugged. "Nothing serious. I tried to stop him and he took a swing at me with the hammer." She grimaced against pain in her shoulder. "Not very bright on my part."

"Get yourself checked out," Jordan said.

A police technician arrived and took photographs. Jordan asked Annabel whether the man had touched anything on which he might have left fingerprints. She said she didn't think so, except for the front doorknob, which a criminalist dusted.

After the uniformed officers and criminalists had left, Jordan sat with Annabel in her office. He took a small tape recorder from his pocket and placed it on the desk in front of her. "Okay, Annabel, give me a complete statement."

When she was finished, he turned off the recorder and sat back. Jordan was a short, compact man with salt-and-pepper hair that closely followed the contour of his temples. He wore a gray tweed jacket, white button-down shirt, and maroon knit tie.

Annabel had known him for three years, ever since he was appointed head of the art squad. Mac Smith's relationship with him went back further, to when the detective worked Homicide.

Jordan had earned, at nights and on weekends, a master's degree in art history at Georgetown University. Other members of his family were involved in the arts—his father edited an art magazine in New York, and an uncle was a painter of minor note in Denver—which helped explain this homicide detective's interest in matters other than murder.

Shortly after earning his advanced degree, the head of the Washington MPD art squad retired, and Jordan got the job. Annabel had heard nothing but praise for his having shaped what had been an ineffective appendage of the police department into an important, functioning addition to it. A number of articles had been written about him, including a piece that recounted his role in recovering a stolen Velázquez. The case had involved close cooperation between Jordan, his counterparts in Spain, and other international art sleuths. The painting was discovered and recovered in Washington, turning Jordan into a hero of sorts, at least to the arts community.

"Strange," Jordan said.

"Very," Annabel agreed. "An insane act. Nothing to be gained. Just wanton destruction of a beautiful object."

"I know," he said. "If the guy wanted to steal it, it would make sense."

"I really appreciate you being here, Steve," Annabel said. "All I hope is that you find the madman who did this. It won't restore the figure, but it will satisfy my need to find out why." She picked up her ringing phone. It was Carole Aprile. "Yes, Carole. Noon? All right. I can be there. What? Oh, nothing. I'll fill you in when I see you. Noon it is."

"Free for lunch?" Jordan asked after she'd hung up.

"Can't. I just got summoned to a noon meeting at the National Gallery."

Jordan raised his eyebrows. "About what happened last night to the Italian cultural attaché?"

"I assume."

"Strange case, too. Homicide has it, but everybody is fighting over jurisdiction. State. Embassy cops. The National Gallery's own police force. FBI. But I'm rung in, too. The guy had something to do with art, so the art squad gets involved. How about later in the day? Can I buy you a drink? Dinner?"

"I don't know, Steve. I was leaving things open. Mac and I had dinner plans but—is there something else on your mind?"

He laughed easily. "I wanted to make you a proposition, hopefully one you couldn't, or wouldn't, refuse."

"A proposition? Sounds intriguing."

"Maybe. I'd like you to come down to headquarters sometime today to look at mug shots."

"To what end? I didn't see his face."

"You never know what you've seen, what your mind's eye might have recorded. At least go through the procedure. We're big on procedure."

"All right. What time?"

"Whatever's good for you. Four?"

"I'll be there."

"An early dinner after?"

"I'll ask Mac. He still doesn't know what happened here this morning. Maybe the three of us can have dinner together."

"The Collector? At six?" he said.

"I'll let you know at four."

The phone rang. "Must be Mac," she said.

"See you at four, Annabel. And have that shoulder looked at."

FOURTEEN

MAC RACED to Annabel's side after returning her call and hearing what had happened. By the time he arrived, the numbness that had consumed her had been replaced by regular pulses of anger.

"Forget the meeting and come home with me," Mac said. "You don't realize what a traumatic thing you've been through."

"I'm fine, Mac. Honest I am. I was lucky. No major damage."

"Raise your arm."

She did, pleased that only a mild ache remained in her shoulder. "See? I'm okay. I don't want to miss the meeting."

"You'll come directly home after it?" Mac said.

"I can't. I told Steve Jordan I'd come down to look at mug shots at four."

"To what avail? You said you didn't see him."

"I know. But Steve thinks I might have seen more of him then I remember. Seeing a face in the mug book could trigger recognition. Please, I'm fine. What I want most is to find out who did this, and why."

They stood outside as a young reporter from the *Georgetowner,* who'd learned of the incident from a friend, arrived to interview Annabel. Annabel graciously put him off. He asked if he could call her at home later that evening. "She won't be available," Mac responded gruffly. "Sorry."

"I'll be home about six," Mac said after the dejected reporter had departed. "I'll have something ready for dinner."

"I almost forgot," said Annabel. "Steve wants to have dinner with us tonight. At the Collector."

"Feel up to it?"

"Yes."

"I suppose so. Meet you there? What time?"

"Six, he said."

"I can make it by six-thirty."

A lingering embrace was a needed balm for both of them.

The noon meeting at the National Gallery accomplished little, in Annabel's view. The topic was, as expected, how Carlo Giliberti's murder might "impact" the Carvaggio exhibition. Not seeing Luther Mason there triggered a reminder that she was supposed to have continued to try reaching him. "Where's Luther?" she asked Court Whitney as attendees trickled into the conference room.

"He won't be here," the gallery director said

abruptly. "Went home sick. Last night's tragic event upset him. Understandable. He and Giliberti were pretty close."

"I understand that he wants to—"

One of two trustees who would attend the meeting motioned Whitney from the room. They'd no sooner left than three Secret Service agents entered, followed by Carole Aprile. She came directly to Annabel. "Thanks for showing up," she said. "Anything wrong? You sounded . . ."

Annabel gave her a thirty-second sound bite of what had happened at her gallery.

"What are you even doing here?" Carole asked.

"Trying to be helpful. I didn't reach Luther. Time got away from me."

"I don't wonder. I spoke with him just before coming here. He's calmed down, although he's talking about canceling the exhibition."

Whitney and the trustee returned and called the meeting to order. It lasted only a half hour. "I understand Luther Mason thinks we should call off the show," Carole said.

"That's correct," Whitney affirmed. "Luther is upset—and he's wrong. The show must go on, as they say."

"Any word on Mr. Giliberti's murderer?" Annabel asked.

There wasn't. Whitney said, "The faster they find who killed him, the better off we'll be. The press is already trying to link up his murder with the exhibition and the *Grottesca*. I got a call from a tabloid reporter this morning. He's doing a piece he's calling 'The Caravaggio Curse Threatens Washington.' Unbelievable. The sooner they pick up the druggie who killed Giliberti, the sooner this kind of stupid speculation will stop."

"It could heighten interest in the exhibition," a representative from the public information office offered. She was ignored.

Carole Aprile had the last word. "I'm relieved that this dreadful wanton act won't derail the exhibition. The administration remains fully committed to it. If problems arise with the Italian government over this, let me know." She whispered to Annabel, "A minute?"

They stood in a corner of the reception area, watched by the Secret Service agents. "I'm so sorry about what happened to you this morning, Annabel."

"Lucky, actually. Guess he could have killed me."

"Bad time to ask more of you, maybe, but I will. Court is very concerned about Luther's mental stability."

"Really? It sounds to me like he's simply distraught over his friend's death."

"I agree. But Court seems sincerely troubled by Luther's behavior. His reputation as a curator might be more secure than his psyche. I wondered if you'd make it a point to get, and stay, close to him until the exhibition opens. You know, keep in touch with him, read his moods, and let me know if in your judgment there's anything to worry about—including *his* judgment."

"I'll do my best. We're not close friends but—"

"Your best is more than sufficient, Annabel. You weren't hurt at all?"

"Bruised a little. Nothing a little liniment and a good night's sleep won't cure."

Carole kissed Annabel on the cheek. "You're a trouper. Keep in touch."

At five-thirty that afternoon, Annabel turned the last page of the mug-shot book placed before her by Steve Jordan. "Sorry," she said, "but I see nothing that even resembles the man who came into my gallery this morning. As I said, all I really remember were his hat and coat."

"A long shot, Annabel, but worth taking. We put out a bulletin on what the guy was wearing. Every cop in town will be looking for him. Not that that's much consolation. Maybe he was a nut case, smashing it as an act of protest."

"Against what?"

"Against art, or pre-Columbians, or beautiful gallery owners. Hungry?"

"Surprisingly, yes. Mac said he'd join us at six-thirty."

"I might have to bail out before he arrives. One of the kids is sick, and I promised Ruth I'd get home early to spell her. It's her class night. She's studying calligraphy. But we can at least have a drink and appetizer together."

"Time enough to proposition me?"

"I wouldn't put it that way." His grin was pleasingly boyish. "To make you a proposition you can't refuse. Besides, I never try to hit on women taller than me."

Bill Wooby's Collector Gallery and Restaurant, located on the ground floor of the Dupont Plaza Hotel, had become the gathering spot of choice for Washington's artists, a place where the gossip was as juicy as the steaks, backs were bitten, and useful information was occasionally exchanged. Washington's artist population was America's fourth largest, according to Washington artists.

Wooby, whose grandmother had been a bareback rider, knife thrower, and tattooed lady in Buffalo Bill's Wild West Show, was a prime influence on what went on artistically in the city, his restaurant a rallying point for social, charitable, and artistic causes dear to his heart. The art featured on The Collector's walls was rotated on a monthly basis. This month it featured the black-and-white works of photographer Kathleen Bober.

As Steve Jordan and Annabel entered, Wooby was winding down a cocktail party honoring students of the Corcoran Gallery's art school. He spotted them and led them to a table, saying to Jordan as they passed through the bar area, "I still intend to get your name on my ceiling one of these days."

They stopped and looked up. The ceiling was covered with signatures and salutations from artists, politicians, and other regulars.

"Not until I retire from the force," Jordan said. "It wouldn't do the career any good to end up next to an art forger or thief on your ceiling."

Wooby sat with them. "What's new on the murder?"

Jordan shrugged. "Nothing you haven't heard on television. Did you know Carlo Giliberti?"

"As a customer. I wouldn't call him a regular, but he did come in now and then. He had a thing going with a local artist and used to bring her here."

"We're still trying to figure out what he was doing in Rock Creek Park at that hour," said Jordan. "As far as we can piece together, he wasn't the kind of guy to be prowling a park after midnight. He's married, got a couple of young adult children. No sign of drug use. Hard to figure."

"So, Steve, what is this mysterious proposal you wish to make?" Annabel asked after Wooby had gone in search of a waiter.

He grimaced against what he was thinking, then said, "I may be way out of line in asking this favor of you, Annabel. But I'll end up kicking myself for not trying."

"I'm listening."

"You can tell me to back off any time."

"All right."

"Are you aware that there was a theft at Dumbarton Oaks six months ago?"

Dumbarton Oaks's original mansion and added wings occupied sixteen acres of lush gardens on the crest of a wooded valley in Georgetown. The Dumbarton Oaks Research Library and Collection, incorporated in the District of Columbia and administered by the Trustees for Harvard, contained outstanding collections of Byzantine and pre-Columbian art.

"No," Annabel said. "I'd heard something about a 'problem' with the pre-Columbian collection, but not about a theft. I can't believe something like that could happen and escape the gossips."

"I've been waiting for M. Scott Pims to report it ever since," said Jordan.

"What was stolen?"

"Three things. A were-jaguar, a black basalt serpent, and a gold monkey."

"And they've managed to keep it quiet for six months?"

"Yeah. Their call. They figure that if enough time passes, whoever took the pieces would get around to trying to sell them through the underground. Looks like enough time has passed. The word is they are for sale, right here in D.C."

"By the person who stole them?"

"Probably not. I'm convinced it was an inside job. The pieces had been taken off display during a renovation. They disappeared from a storeroom. I figure someone with access lifted them and sold them to a middleman. The middleman now wants to unload."

"Shouldn't be hard to do," said Annabel. "There are plenty of crooked collectors always looking for good pieces at bargain prices, no questions asked."

"And that's where you come in."

"Me?" She laughed. "I'm not a crooked collector."

"But you could become one."

"I could?"

"Sure.

"I think I know what you're getting at, Steve, and I'm not sure I like it."

"I won't say another word."

Their white wine and a shared order of smoked-duck ravioli were served.

"Steve," Annabel said after tasting her wine.

"Yes?"

"Tell me more."

His smile said much. "Not a lot more to tell, Annabel. Word is that the three pieces are for sale here in Washington. My concern is that if I don't act quickly, they'll end up in Europe. South America."

"What would I have to do if I—?"

"You don't *have* to do anything."

"I know that. But if I did agree? What then?"

He replied casually after a taste of ravioli, "I'd put the word out underground that a local pre-Columbian collector was in the market for gold monkeys and were-jaguars. No questions asked. I'd set you up with a studio, probably in the Atlas Building. We've used it before in these kinds of stings. Give you a phone, answering machine, a special number. The seller calls—if he does—and you convince him you're ready to buy. You arrange a meet. We're there. He's arrested. The pieces end up back at Dumbarton."

"Just like that."

"Just like that."

"Would I actually have to meet with the seller?"

"No. We'd be there in your place. What do you think?"

"I don't know."

"I thought of you because you've already got heavy credentials in pre-Columbian. I think it would work."

"I—"

"You'd be doing a real nice thing for Dumbarton, Annabel. Shame to have those important pieces end up in the collection of some slob who'll stash them away purely for their monetary value. They'd never be on display again for millions to enjoy."

Annabel laughed softly and tasted the ravioli.

"You're very persuasive, Steve. I'd have to ask Mac."

"You know lawyers. They always find a reason to say no."

"I was a lawyer."

"But now you're a gallery owner." He checked his watch. "I have to run. Think about it overnight. Give me a call tomorrow."

"All right."

"Before I go, tell me about your trip to Italy with Giliberti. I was reading the other day about the upcoming Caravaggio exhibition and that you represent the White House."

"That's right. Mac and I were with Carlo last night at the black-tie dinner. I liked him very much."

"He say anything, do anything, that might have indicated he was in some sort of trouble?"

"Absolutely not. He was happy and gregarious. He played the perfect host for me in Rome. No sign of trouble."

"Mess things up for the exhibition?"

"I don't think so."

"What's the skinny on *Grottesca?* Almost too good to be true."

"A remarkable find by Luther Mason."

"You think it's legit?"

"Of course. And if it isn't the gallery experts will find out quickly enough. That particular Caravaggio will be scrutinized like no other painting in history. Every scientist at the gallery and every Caravaggio expert will pore over it. Frankly, I don't think they'll find anything amiss. Luther Mason's connoisseurship and honor are too great for him to have the wool pulled over his eyes. He stakes his reputation on it. That's good enough for me."

"I hope you're right. There's Mac."

The men exchanged greetings and the detective left.

"Anything come out of staring at mug shots?" Mac asked after settling in with a single-barrel bourbon on the rocks.

"Afraid not."

She told him of the noon meeting at the National Gallery. "They're concerned about the impact of Carlo's murder on the exhibit. I don't see where it will have any, except in a macabre way. More intrigue about the artist and his works." She also told him about the tabloid reporter's piece, 'The Caravaggio Curse Threatening Washington.' They both laughed and agreed that there were worse threats in Congress.

After a dinner of Maryland crab cakes seasoned with Old Bay served with a lemon-chive sauce, and salads tossed with raspberry–and–toasted almond vinaigrette, he said, "Well, Annabel, it's been quite a day for you. Ready to go home?"

"Yes. I'm exhausted. Emotionally drained."

"That's obvious from the look on your lovely face. Your eyelids are at half-mast."

She smiled. "Maybe in memory of Carlo."

They stood. "Mac, let me give you a tip."

"You have me confused with the waiter."

"I love you."

"Oh, that," he said in a mock brush-off. "I love you, too—more. My week hasn't included a masterpiece, a murder, a smashed and beloved figure, and a madman swinging a hammer in the gallery. You wanted me to retire. Now, it's you who's keeping life interesting."

FIFTEEN

"STEVE? It's Annabel."

"Hi. Did you sleep on my proposition?"

"Fitfully. I'll do it."

"Terrific. What did Mac have to say about it?"

"I didn't tell him. He has enough on his plate these days with students, deans, a dog as big as a horse, a house, and being out of the criminal loop, without having this to worry about."

SIXTEEN

LATER THAT DAY

"MR. WHITNEY, Luther Mason on line two."

The director picked up the phone in his office. "Feeling better?" he asked.

"I wish I could say I did, Court. The fact is I think I'm about to unravel."

"I understand," Whitney said, continuing to read an article from the *New York Times* about the Caravaggio exhibition.

"I need to get away."

"Of course." Whitney wedged the phone between his ear and shoulder and kept reading.

"I thought I'd visit my mother in Indiana. Maybe go on to Italy."

"Odd itinerary. Any reason to go there?" Whitney asked, thinking budget.

"There are always loose ends to tie up. Maybe drop in on Alberto Betti, the minister of culture. He's a loose end himself, capable of undoing everything."

"Frankly, Luther, you'd be better served going to a spa. If you're in as bad shape as you say you are—and I don't doubt you for a moment—solid rest in one place would do you more good than globe-trotting."

"Maybe I'll do just that, Court. Can you spare me for a week?"

Whitney had spent much of the day being questioned by law-enforcement officials about Giliberti's murder. The list of press people to call back had grown taller. His wife, Sue, was angry that their plans for a weekend away had to be scrapped because of what had happened. And WJLA, a local television station, was putting together a three-part investigative series on the physical condition of the National Gallery's West Building, based upon a report compiled earlier in the year by a group of consultants Whitney had hired. The report, which had been leaked—no surprise in a town of leaks, wet and dry—concluded that many masterpieces on the gallery's walls were at risk of serious damage due to faulty skylights, malfunctioning humidifiers, and an antiquated climate-control system. Some problems did exist, Whitney knew, but he was on top of it. Congress had already authorized funds to modernize the skylights and to install a monitoring system for the building's climate-control protocols.

"I think we can spare you for a week, Luther," Whitney said. The edge in his voice had nothing to do with Mason. The writer of the *Times* piece had ended by questioning the authenticity of

Grottesca. Whitney scribbled a note to prod Don Fechter to complete his scientific evaluations ASAP.

"Court? Are you still there?" Mason asked.

"Yes. Go rest, Luther. Feel better. Call in once or twice." Not having to ride Mason's emotional roller coaster for a week would be a welcome respite.

"Of course. You know I always do."

Mason was poised to make another call from his apartment when the phone rang.

"Luther, it's Annabel Reed-Smith. I just wanted to say how sorry I am about your friend Carlo. I didn't know him well, of course, but I liked him very much."

"He was a dear friend, Annabel. He'll be missed."

"How are you holding up?"

"All right. Well, perhaps not. I just got off the phone with Court. I'm getting away for a few days."

"Sounds like a good idea. I heard there was talk of delaying or canceling the exhibition."

"I want to but Court won't hear of it. You do understand my feelings on it, don't you?"

"Of course. But I think—"

"I'll talk to him again when I get back. Maybe you could put in a word of reason. Yes. Of course. He might listen to you, speaking for the White House as you do."

"I—when are you leaving?"

"Soon."

"A pleasant destination I hope."

"Yes. Not quite sure where." He injected a single laugh. "Play it by ear."

"The best way. Well, Luther, again my condolences at losing your friend. We'll speak when you get back."

"Yes. Thank you, Annabel."

As Annabel left a message with Carole Aprile's office—she wanted to brief her about her conversation with Luther and the fact that he'd be away at some unknown destination for a week—Mason dialed a number in San Francisco.

"Who's calling?" a man asked.

"Luther Mason. From Washington, D.C."

It seemed to take an inordinate amount of time for del Brasco to come to the phone. "Yes," he said. "What's going on?"

Franco del Brasco's loud, gruff voice caused Mason to hold the phone away from his ear. "Mr. del Brasco, I'm sorry to disturb you."

"Is there a problem?"

"As a matter of fact, there is. It's important that we talk."

"Go ahead."

"Not on the phone. I'm flying to San Francisco tonight. Can we meet?"

Mason heard a series of grunts. The sound of thinking? "Tomorrow. Noon. At my house."

Del Brasco wasn't suggesting a time and place. It was a command.

"That will be fine," Luther said. "Noon. Your house."

The phone rang almost immediately after Mason had concluded his conversation. He hoped it wasn't the police again. They'd been at his apartment to interview him only a few minutes after he'd returned home from work. The plain-clothes officers were pleasant enough, and Mason was confident his case of nerves had not been too obvious.

He let the phone ring six times before picking it up.

"Luther. Scott here."

"I can't talk now, Scott."

"I called you at the Gallery. They said you'd gone home sick. The flu? I hear it's going around. A rare Asian strain. Like Imelda Marcos."

"Scott, please, I'm very busy. I'm leaving tonight for—"

"Another trip to Italy?"

"I'm going to California."

Scott laughed. "Disneyland?"

"I'll call you later."

"Need a ride to the airport?"

"No."

"What time shall I pick you up?"

Mason sighed, "Sometime after dinner. I'll call you."

"Why don't we have dinner together?"

"Scott—"

"No arguments. My treat. Talk to me later this afternoon."

Luther pulled a suitcase from the closet and opened it on his bed. He'd packed the plaid boxer shorts he was fond of wearing when the phone rang again. It was his son.

"What is it, Julian?" he asked.

"I'm in jail."

It wasn't the first time he'd heard that from his only child.

"Did you hear me?" Julian asked, his voice surly. "I'm in goddamn jail."

"Why?"

"Because I was arrested. I got into a fight at a bar."

"Good Lord," Luther muttered.

"I need bail money."

"Where are you?"

Julian told him. Bail was five hundred dollars. Luther said he would be there as soon as possible.

He realized he'd forgotten to check flight availability that night to San Francisco. He considered calling SATO, the travel group servicing many federal institutions, including the National Gallery of Art, but thought better of it. He dialed an airline directly and was told there was a flight to San Francisco, via Dallas, leaving National Airport at nine. He booked a first-class seat using his American Express card, then reserved a room at his favorite hotel, the Westin St. Francis on Union Square.

He didn't return home from bailing out Julian until almost five. Pims was waiting in the lobby of his apartment building. "You don't get rid of me that easily," Pims said, pushing his bulk up from the chair.

"I forgot to call," Luther said. "Julian was in trouble. I had to get him out of jail."

Pims's laugh was loose and gutteral. "More like Caravaggio every day."

"I'd rather not talk about it."

"Packed for your trip to la-la land?"

"Yes."

"Get your bag and let us proceed to dinner. I'm famished. You can hear my stomach growl. Sounds like the zoo."

They went upstairs, where a flickering light on Luther's answering machine indicated three messages. The first was from Lynn Marshall, a young assistant curator on his staff. "They told me you'd gone home because you were sick," she said through the speaker. "You must be feeling better because you're not there. I'm calling to say I'm sorry about what happened between us the other night. I shouldn't have said what I did, and I can understand why you became so upset. I think we should talk."

Mason looked over his shoulder at Pims; the expression on the rotund critic's round, pink face said he'd found the message interesting.

The second message played: "Luther, it's Annabel Reed-Smith. It occurred to me and Mrs. Aprile that something could come up while you're away that might necessitate speaking with you. If you get a moment, please give me a call and let me know how to reach you. Leave it on my machine if I'm not here. Not trying to intrude on your much-needed R-and-R. Just being compulsively pragmatic. Have a wonderful trip." She left her number.

The third call was from a man introducing himself as an attorney for Luther's second former wife, Cynthia. He asked in a bored voice for Luther to call him concerning certain works of art in Luther's possession and left his number.

"Sounds like the vultures are circling lower," Pims said.

Mason didn't respond. He watered a few plants, prompting Pims to question how long he would be gone.

"Just a week," Mason said, adjusting blinds in the living room and bedroom, turning on a radio so there would be sound in the apartment in his absence, and taking a final look around. He never traveled without consulting a printed list of things to do, and to take. Satisfied everything had been crossed off, he picked up his bag and asked, "Where are we eating?"

"Since you'll be dining on that dreadful California cuisine of sprouts and skinless chicken, I've made reservations at La Colline. I've been thinking about breasts all day—duck breasts with cassis, that is."

SEVENTEEN

THE VIRTUALLY empty first-class cabin of Luther's flight to Dallas provided welcome solitude. There was much to think about. He settled back and mentally rewound the video that was his life up until a year ago, when this dramatic new leaf in it had sprouted and begun to take shape.

The audacious adventure started as nothing more than a whimsical notion. A flight of fancy. Mason and his colleagues at the National Gallery often reflected over coffee in the Refectory, the employee dining room, how it was to lead a modest life economically, with all the priceless art surrounding them. And how one could profit from the proximity. Playful conversations, plotting murder mysteries set against the scrim of the esteemed National Gallery of Art.

What if this, what if that . . . ?

What if, Luther sometimes pondered, he were to learn of the availability of a rare painting that had been stolen—find a wealthy collector who would advance the money to purchase it—have a perfect copy made to pawn off on the collector—and wing off to a faraway land, the original master-piece clutched to his bosom like a shield?

It remained only that, of course, a what-if ex-ercise.

Until the day Carlo Giliberti told him that a newly uncovered painting was for sale in Italy. When Giliberti said it was the *Grottesca,* Mason couldn't believe his ears—and fantasy began to blend with harder thoughts.

What if?

What if he could come up with a wealthy, un-scrupulous collector—not a rare breed—to ad-vance the money to purchase *Grottesca* from Giliberti's source in Italy?

Luther had kept his daydream to himself until one night, when drunk, he shared it with his good friend, gadfly and television commentator M. Scott Pims. Pims found the whole exercise to be "high fun" and encouraged Mason to continue his conjuring.

When Luther brought up the question of how a perfect copy might be made, Pims said without hesitation, "Jacques Saison, of course."

Mason was dimly aware of the Frenchman's reputation as a master forger of fine art. "How much does Saison charge?" he asked Pims.

"Depends upon the work in question," Pims replied. "Of course, you might be better off with two copies."

"Two? Why?"

"Well, let's be logical. This wealthy collector, whoever he may be, will want solid verification of the authenticity of his 'purchase.' And who could blame him?"

"Still, why two copies?" Mason repeated.

"What better way to authenticate a lost masterpiece than to have your beloved National Gallery do it?"

"Give the original *Grottesca* to the Gallery? Ridiculous! If this were possible, if this fantasy were to become reality, I would want to end up with the original."

"Of course. And you would. I love this! What fun. Listen carefully to me, Luther. I'll make it simple for you. One, you arrange with someone, this mythical collector, to advance you the money to purchase *Grottesca.* Do you have anyone in mind?"

"I was thinking of someone in California. San Francisco."

"Franco del Brasco."

"Yes. You know him?"

"I know only two things about the man. One, he is wealthy and has been looking for an original Caravaggio for years. Two, his is not 'old' money in the traditional sense. His 'family' has a long Italian name. Broken kneecaps rather than textiles or steel. All right, Luther, let us say it is Mr. Franco del Brasco who advances you money to go through with your tantalizing little scheme. In return for your delivering *Grottesca* to him, he pays you a handsome 'finder's fee.' Say, a million dollars."

"I wouldn't want the money."

"Quiet, Luther. Don't interrupt my flow of thought. You purchase the original from Carlo's source in Italy, using del Brasco's front money. You take it to Jacques Saison—there are other forgers, but Saison is the best—and have him make *two* copies."

Luther started to say something, but Pims held up a fat hand. "You then announce to the world that you, Luther C. Mason, the world's leading Caravaggio expert, have 'found' *Grottesca* in Italy. With me so far?"

Luther nodded.

"You arrange for the original to come to Washington to anchor the Caravaggio exhibition. You'll be a hero with your employer and all of America. Maybe even parades, Luther. Twenty-one-gun salutes."

Mason couldn't help but laugh.

"The original will be authenticated for del Brasco's sake by none other than America's Museum. Unassailable. Beyond debate."

"Yes. I see."

"Then, my friend, one of the copies is returned to Italy, the other goes to del Brasco. Del Brasco pays you your fee. You, the money, and the original *Grottesca* wing off to find the meaning of life. Brilliant?"

"Inventive."

"The key is the National Gallery's connoisseurship. God, Luther, sometimes I even amaze myself."

They were sitting in Pims's living room. Pims leaned close to Mason and fixed him in a serious stare. "So, Luther, this coinage of your fertile brain *has* gone beyond wishful thinking."

Luther averted Pims's probing eyes. He looked at his shoetops, then up. "Yes," he said.

"Splendid. Go for it, Luther!" His booming voice reverberated about the large room.

Luther didn't make his decision to "go for it" until a few days later. Pims kept up his enthusiastic encouragement. Carlo Giliberti urged Luther to make up his mind. "My source in Italy will not wait much longer," he said.

And so straight-arrow, law-abiding, ethical, and honest Luther Mason *went for it.*

He contacted Franco del Brasco, who agreed to put up the money.

Luther met with Giliberti's Italian source, the old mafioso Luigi Sensi, and bought *Grottesca.*

Because he was reluctant to bring the painting himself to the alcoholic French forger, Jacques Saison, Carlo Giliberti did it, after Luther agreed to give him a greater share of del Brasco's fee.

Adding the old defrocked priest, Pasquale Giocondi, to the mix was Giliberti's idea. He felt that Mason's claim to have discovered *Grottesca* in Italy needed to be supported by a third party. And so he turned to Giocondi, who'd done him a few "favors" over the years.

All in all, Luther mused, as he accepted a drink from the flight attendant, things had gone remarkably well.

Until now.

Because he was not a greedy man, Mason did not understand greed on the part of others. Sensi's greed, and Giliberti's willingness to feed it, had probably gotten his dapper little Italian friend murdered. And the priest had now made noises about wanting more. At least Scott Pims wasn't asking for money. His payoff seemed to be meeting the challenge—and being in on it.

It occurred to Mason that this mission to Franco del Brasco might get him killed, too. Once you caved into demands for more money, where did it stop? Still, he felt he had to try. Carlo might be dead, but that wouldn't deter Sensi from going after Luther directly for the money, possibly using the same men who worked for the Italian Embassy, and for Sensi. All he needed was enough time for the original Caravaggio to be exhibited and for the copies to be distributed. Then . . .

He wiled away the hour layover in Dallas nursing a drink in the airport bar. The flight to San Francisco was full. Seated next to him was a stout woman, the flesh of her stubby fingers partially obscured beneath a dozen large, ornate rings. Her perfume was repugnant. Luther would have changed seats had there been another open. He pressed himself against the wall of the aircraft, placed a pillow between it and his head, and attempted to sleep away this leg of the trip.

But sleep escaped him. His mind was too active to shut down.

Where would he go once it was over? He'd have to make that decision soon. He blotted out the incessant whine of the jet's engines and allowed a familiar fantasy to consume him. In it, he'd taken *Grottesca* to a warm place where, in a simple and sparse apartment painted stark white, Caravaggio's masterpiece was displayed for his eyes alone. His life in this dream was as simple and spare as his apartment. He didn't need a lot of money, just enough to live out his life in serenity, and with the *Grottesca* to nourish his soul.

His imagined white apartment had a small balcony overlooking a body of water, preferably an ocean, but an inlet, a lake, even a stream would do. He'd find a cafe close by at which to take his meals. He'd use a new name. Jones? Smith? "Ah, Mr. Smith, your usual table?" They would consider him a nice man, a quiet, unassuming American who'd retired from his job as—Executive? Teacher? Librarian? Yes, a librarian. Like his mother.

He was not alone in this pleasant vision. There were women, too, but never one he'd met at an art gallery or museum. Too risky. One might recognize the Caravaggio as the real thing. The voluptuous young women in his dream shared his bed, but not his mind. They knew nothing about art. "That?" he'd say when they commented upon *Grottesca.* "Just a cheap print." If celibacy became necessary to preserve the peace, so be it.

In his fantasy he sent money to his mother and to Julian. A hundred thousand each. More if he could afford it. He would not become penurious in his new life.

Although Luther was exhausted when reaching San Francisco, the cab ride into the city rejuvenated him. San Francisco was, for Luther, still a magical place, filled with memories of when he and Juliana had lived there. As he stood in front of the St. Francis, a sense of urgency overcame him. It was as though a doctor had given him only a few days to live in which to re-create those carefree, pleasurable moments. A drive to the wine country, tasting along the way. He and Juliana had once taken a mud bath at a spa in Calistoga. (She'd loved it, but the heat had caused his sensitive skin to break out into an itchy rash that lasted for days.) Picnics beneath 250-foot-tall redwoods in Muir Woods, across the Golden Gate. Pasta and jazz in North Beach. Cheap wine parties with artist friends. Walks hand in hand, leg muscles aching after reaching the top of the city's fabled hills.

He crossed the black marble lobby with its gold-topped columns and peered into the Compass Rose Bar, where he and Juliana had toasted special occasions, surrounded by the room's exquisite dark woodwork and served by bartenders who resisted conversation with customers.

"Yes, Mr. Mason, we have your reservation," said the desk clerk.

"Would the Windsor Suite happen to be available?" Luther asked.

"The Windsor?" The young man at the desk raised his eyebrows. The Windsor Suite, home-away-from-home for Queen Elizabeth II, Emperor Hirohito, and numerous presidents of the United States, cost $1,500 a night. "You'll be staying for just one night?"

"Yes."

"I'm afraid there's a party in the Windsor."

"Another suite?" Luther said.

"The Bayview is available. Next to the Windsor."

"Fine. Then I'll stay in the Bayview tonight."

"Of course." The young man quickly added, "The Bayview is twelve hundred for the night."

Luther placed his American Express card on the counter.

The bellman pressed a button upon entering Suite 3178, causing electronically operated drapes to open, exposing an outstanding view of the bay and Bay Bridge, the Santa Cruz Mountains, and the lights of the city. Luther unpacked and neatly arranged his clothing in drawers and closet. He hadn't eaten on the Dallas–San Francisco flight and was hungry. He considered room service but opted instead to walk to the bustling Kuleto's a few blocks away, where he sat at the counter and ordered antipasti—oysters on the half shell with mignonette, grilled radicchio and pancetta with goat cheese–and–basil vinaigrette, and a selection of marinated vegetables. Two pleasant glasses of Franciscan Zinfandel went well with the food.

He walked after dinner, no destination in mind, just enjoying the feel and look of the city. He returned to the hotel at midnight and arranged for a wake-up call and for breakfast to be delivered at eight. It occurred to him as he fell asleep in the king-sized bed that staying in a twelve hundred dollar a night suite represented the most extravagant act of his life. Which was all right, he decided, as light from a full moon streamed through the windows, casting a moving pattern over him. Because he'd chosen to abandon his mundane, predictable life, a burst of extravagance seemed in order.

Franco del Brasco lived in a mansion in the Nob Hill section of the city, a few blocks from the Mark Hopkins Hotel, in a home that seemed almost as large. The lavish house was listed in sight-seeing guides as a prime example of the opulent turn-of-the-century architectural style that characterized the area.

Del Brasco's renovation had cost millions, and his exterior decoration included an eight-foot-high brick wall topped with coiled barbed wire, and an elaborate electronic security system. Floodlights illuminated the exterior. Every window in the twenty-one rooms was fitted with electronic shutters that rolled up and down at the touch of a button.

His three-person house staff lived in apartments above a six-car garage. There was a Mexican housekeeper and cook, a Chinese "manservant," and a middle-aged Brit who functioned as del Brasco's chauffeur, as well as overseeing the gardeners who arrived each day.

Del Brasco did not live in the house alone. A wing on the southeast corner housed two young men, whose function was to protect their boss and his possessions and to be on tap when he was in the mood for a game of chess, or darts, or billiards.

At eleven that morning, del Brasco sat in his private office staring at a computer screen. Financial symbols and numbers swam across it in a ceaseless stream. Gina, the housekeeper, had delivered breakfast—fresh fruit, a dry English muffin, and a silver pot containing green tea. He was dressed in pajamas and robe. The electronic shutters were closed on all windows except the one immediately next to the desk, affording him a view of an elaborately simple Japanese garden.

He rubbed his eyes. He'd stayed up until three that morning playing chess with one of his bodyguards. After dismissing him, del Brasco did what he usually did before retiring. He walked from room to room admiring his collection. Some of the rooms were arranged as they might be in an eclectic gallery. One featured California artists. Another contained some of the best examples of Chinese art. The two largest rooms, joined by a wide, soaring archway, were reserved for Old Masters, and younger ones—the Spaniards de Goya and Murillo; a magnificent nude by the German Cranach; and representative works by Clouet, Delacroix, Sargent, Picasso, and Velázquez, the Velázquez painted early in his career, while he was under the influence of Michelangelo Caravaggio.

On some nights, del Brasco ended his tour in the basement, where two climate-controlled rooms the size of ordinary tract houses warehoused dozens of other valuable works of art whose provenance was not as pristine as those in the collection upstairs.

He looked up at a large antique clock on the wall. Eleven-fifteen. That faggot Mason would be arriving shortly. He went upstairs to the 20 x 20 master bath, one of six. The marble was Italian, the fixtures solid gold. A steam room occupied one corner, a Jacuzzi another. He removed his robe and pajamas and examined himself in a floor-to-ceiling mirror. At sixty, he was in excellent shape, thanks to a fully equipped gymnasium in the basement, the daily arrival of a personal trainer, and a healthy diet. His six-foot body was lean and well defined. Living in California agreed with him.

He lifted his head and turned it left and right, chagrined at a slight accumulation of flesh beneath his chin. He leaned closer to the mirror and vigorously ran his fingertips through white hair the consistency of a wire brush. Dark circles under his eyes seemed more pronounced this morning. Time for another spa visit.

By the time he'd dressed in a white silk shirt, black trousers, and black loafers *sans* socks, and returned to his study, Luther Mason had been waiting a half hour. The muscular young man who'd met him at the front gate looked sinister to Mason, despite a helmet of soft, blond curls falling gently over his forehead and neck. He'd led Luther to a small anteroom and told him to wait.

A half hour later, Blond Curls escorted Mason to Franco del Brasco's study, where the owner posed by a fireplace, his elbow resting casually on the mantel. "Mr. Mason. Excuse me for keeping you waiting. I had other business to attend to."

"That's all right, Mr. del Brasco. Your house—I suppose I should call it a mansion—is magnificent." Mason's only other meeting with del Brasco had taken place in a restaurant in Sausalito.

"And expensive to keep up. Would you like a cup of tea?" He hadn't moved.

Mason declined. He didn't want a situation in which a shaky hand was noticeable.

Del Brasco crossed the room to a table on which a scale-model of a series of buildings was displayed, motioning Mason to his side. "This new wing on the hospital bears my name, Mr. Mason," he said. "A children's wing. I paid for it."

Luther said, "I think that's—well I think that's a wonderful thing to do, Mr. del Brasco."

"I believe in giving back," del Brasco said. He abruptly left Mason's side and sat behind his desk. "Sit. Tell me what's on your mind. I have other appointments."

"I'm here because of *Grottesca,* of course."

"There is a problem?"

Luther shook his head. "Oh, no, everything is going just as we planned. The painting is at the National Gallery, being subjected to many tests to determine its authenticity. Obviously, there will be no problem in establishing that it is, in fact, the lost Caravaggio."

"Such tests can only decide that it could not have come from Caravaggio's hand. They can never prove it did."

"Good point, Mr. del Brasco. But between the testing, other Caravaggio experts coming in to examine the painting, and my own expertise, there won't be any doubt of its authorship. A copy of the original is being made as we speak. When it is time to return *Grottesca* to Italy, it will be the copy that goes there. You'll have the original."

"I can be certain of that?"

"Why yes. Of course. You don't think that—?"

Del Brasco shrugged. "You have a reputation as an honest man, Mr. Mason. Yet you are stealing a valuable painting."

"Not stealing," Luther said. "It had already been stolen. All I did was—"

"Enough," said del Brasco. "I simply make the point that despite your reputation, you are obviously not above breaking the law. Which is fine with me. But I *will* have the original *Grottesca.* Correct?"

"You can be assured of it." Luther drew a deep breath before adding, "It will be necessary, however, for more money to be paid to the individual in Italy who arranged this."

Del Brasco said nothing.

"I hesitated coming here today to ask for more. You've been generous in advancing all the funds needed up to this point. But you know how these people are."

Del Brasco said, "Tell me how 'these people' are, Mr. Mason. Tell me why more money is needed. There was to be no further payment until the painting was delivered to me."

"I know that. But my contact in Italy insists that unless a further payment is made, he will—"

Del Brasco stood and slapped his palms on the top of his desk. "He will *what,* Mr. Mason?"

"I don't know."

Mason's shaky voice and trembling hands now mirrored what was going on inside. "These people can be ruthless," he said. "My friend was murdered because of them."

"Giliberti," del Brasco said flatly.

"Yes. You heard."

"You take me for a fool?"

"Of course not. I would not be here unless I felt the urgency of this. All I ask is that you advance some of the money you were to pay after delivery of *Grottesca.* To ensure that things continue to go smoothly. An additional advance."

A smile twisted del Brasco's lips. "To save your neck."

"If you wish to put it that way. I don't seek trouble. There should be no trouble. Not if people act honorably. I have acted honorably and will continue to. But this man in Italy, he—"

Del Brasco slowly lowered himself into the vast leather chair, propped his elbows on its arms, and formed a tent with his fingers beneath his chin. His voice was low and lethal; Mason had to lean forward to hear. "There will be no more money until I have *Grottesca.*"

Feeling like a child in the presence of a stern

headmaster, Mason stood. He detested this man across the desk from him, so filled with arrogance born of power bought with dirty money. "I will do my best, Mr. del Brasco, to make sure that nothing interferes with our business arrangement. Thank you for seeing me today."

Del Brasco pressed a button on the side of his desk and Blond Curls appeared. "Show Mr. Mason out," del Brasco said.

"I took a taxi here," Mason said. "Would you be good enough to call one for me?"

"Call him a taxi," del Brasco said.

Back at Union Square, Luther stepped into a travel agency a block from his hotel. "I need to get to Rome as soon as possible," he told the lady at the desk. "A family emergency."

She punched entries into her computer. "I can book you on a flight leaving tomorrow at noon," she said pleasantly.

"Nothing sooner?"

"I'm afraid not."

"Please book me a first-class seat on that flight," Luther said, placing his credit card in front of her.

He stepped into a phone booth and called the Westin St. Francis: "This is Mr. Mason in the Bayview Suite. I would like to stay a second night. Is that a problem?" It wasn't. "And would you please make a reservation for one this evening at Victor's. A window table. At eight."

"Of course, Mr. Mason."

Luther and Juliana had celebrated their first anniversary at the hotel's famous, expensive restaurant; the taste of braised celery hearts marinated in a vinaigrette dressing and served with bay shrimp, known as Celery Victor, was as distinct in his mouth as that night many years ago when he and Juliana had ordered it. And were so much in love.

He took a cab to the M. H. de Young Memorial Museum, in Golden Gate Park, and spent the next two hours walking through it. Being back where he'd launched his curatorial career was, at once, a source of pleasure and of sadness. Those had been happy days, although at the time he didn't realize it. He thought of Juliana, of Julian, of the sum of his life.

He'd left del Brasco's mansion a shaken, defeated man, ready to fold, to curl up in a fetal position and quietly disappear from the tumult he'd created for himself.

But as he moved from El Greco to Rubens, from Cézanne to Gainsborough to Seurat to Cassatt, it was as though each artist reached out to touch him, to transmit the glory and beauty of their creations in a physical way.

Before leaving the museum, he stood in front of the large and powerful *Saint John the Baptist Preaching,* by the Baroque artist Mattia Preti. It had been Luther's favorite work at the de Young while apprenticing there. Preti's use of dramatic lighting, monumental scale, and theatrical composition was much like that of his Baroque contemporary, Caravaggio. As Luther admired the painting, he remembered what one of his mentors had once told him: "Art derives a considerable part of its beneficial exercise from flying in the face of presumptions."

Too much had been presumed about Luther Mason, by too many people, for too many years.

He left the museum with a full internal tank of resolve.

Let everyone presume what they would about Luther Mason.

They would be wrong.

He would go through with his wild ride in pursuit of one of the world's greatest art treasures.

His time had come.

EIGHTEEN

ROME

MASON WENT directly to the Valadier Hotel; room service, a hot shower, and fresh clothes refreshed him. He had no intention of contacting Italy's minister of culture. The fat bureaucrat provided nothing but complications, and Mason's new agenda was to simplify. Besides, the thought of spending time with the pompous Alberto Betti was too painful.

He called a number in Rome he'd been given by Father Pasquale Giocondi. A man answered. Mason introduced himself and said it was important that he speak with Giocondi. He gave the man the number of the hotel, saying he would be there most of the day.

Giocondi returned the call two hours later. He did not sound happy.

"Has anyone approached you since you returned?" Mason asked.

"*Si.* Of course."

"And you told them only what I instructed you to say?"

The smarmy priest responded angrily in a barrage of Italian: "This is no good. No good. You lied to me. Too many people asking questions. I can no longer live in my home. The press, it looks every day to find me. I have moved in with my cousin. *Idiota meschino!* This is not what I want."

The cousin was petty minded and an idiot, thought Mason. He tried to say something when Giocondi paused for breath, but he started in again. He wanted more money, a lot more, or he would go to the authorities and tell them everything.

Mason made a decision. He would not be blackmailed into giving him more. Not one more lira. "Now you shut up and listen to me," he said, surprised at the force in his voice.

There was silence on the other end.

"We made a deal," Luther said. "And you will live up to that deal."

"Signore Mason, I only wish to—"

"You only wish to rip me off."

"Non capisco."

"It doesn't matter." Luther Mason raised his voice to the most menacing level he could muster. "Remember one thing," he said. "The painting has come from very dangerous people here in Italy. Murderers, killers, mafiosi. You would not be the first man of the cloth to be found hanging in front of a church. *Capisce?" That* you *do* understand. Giocondi said nothing. Luther added to his threat:

"If you do anything stupid, I will see that you face *them.*"

"I understand. *Si,* I understand, Signore Mason."

The old man sounded frightened. Good. "Perhaps one day when this is all over, I will be able to arrange for you to receive a bit more money," Mason said.

"Grazie."

"I think it is good that you stay with your family. Your cousin, you say?"

The mention of the cousin set Giocondi off on another monologue, none of it flattering. He ended with, *"Scemo innato!"*

Whether the cousin was also a feebleminded fool was irrelevant. *"Arrivederci,* Father Giocondi. I will be in touch."

Mason hung up with a smile on his face. In this deal, he'd never been one to confront, to lay down demands. But that was before. He'd decided during the long flight to Rome that unless he stiffened his backbone and met challenges head-on, everything he'd put into play could be, would be, lost.

The next call, to Paris, was answered in what sounded, based upon background noise, like a restaurant. The man spoke a language Mason identified as Greek.

"Do you speak English?" Luther asked.

He said he did, but his garbled attempt said otherwise. Luther told him he wanted to speak with

Jacques Saison. "The artist. Upstairs." He realized he was shouting, which would do nothing to break through the language barrier.

"Saison? *Artiste?* Uh huh. Saison. You hang over."

Hang over? Mason heard the phone drop on a hard surface. Not yet. Hang *on* now, a pleasant hangover in Paradise later.

Jacques Saison spoke in French. He slurred his words. Was he drunk?

"Are they ready?" Mason asked. "The two copies. The painting Signore Giliberti brought to you."

"Ah. *Oui. Oui.* They are ready."

"I will be there to pick them up tomorrow."

"*Oui.* What time?"

"In the afternoon. You will be there?"

"*Oui.* You will have the money?"

"Yes, I will have the money."

The money. The money. It was the sound of the Greek chorus, and the Italian, and the French. Mason booked a flight from Rome to Paris, then went to a bank, where he withdrew the balance of funds from a joint account he'd shared with Carlo Giliberti, converting the lire to francs. He returned to the Valadier, where he packed his suitcase, placing most of the money beneath his neatly folded clothing.

He enjoyed an early, expensive dinner of *risotto fiori di zucca* at an outdoor table at La Maiella on the Piazza Navona, and a bottle of mineral water.

He was wide awake after dinner, despite his recent lack of sleep, and decided to walk back to the hotel. Mason walked slowly, admiring shops and busy cafes and the smart-looking men and women going in and out of them. But when he reached the via del Corso, he was suddenly overcome with fatigue. He took a table at a small outdoor cafe and ordered a *sambuca alla mosca,* more interested in the coffee beans on which to munch than the alcohol. It felt good to rest his legs. The travel, the anxiety, the talk of money had caught up with him. He needed to go to bed.

As he searched for his busy waiter to get a check, he looked into an adjacent cafe. He'd seen the man earlier that evening, remembered the colors: black raincoat, red beret, scraggly beard and moustache, a cigarette dangling from his lips. The man had passed several times as Mason ate at La Maiella. And he'd seen him again while walking to the hotel. Seeing someone twice wouldn't strike him as unusual. But three times in one evening? The chances of coincidence vanished. His stomach knotted, his heart pounded. *Sensi.* The man must work for Luigi Sensi.

How would the old mafioso know he was in Rome? Who knew he'd come there? Scott Pims. Court Whitney. The travel agent in San Francisco. None of them would have a connection with Sensi, nor would they have reason to hurt him.

He dropped lire on the table and left the cafe, turned the corner, and walked at a brisk pace to the next corner, where he stopped and looked back. The red beret had left his cafe and was looking in Mason's direction. Abruptly, Mason ran, cutting through a small park and down a narrow alley linking two streets, then stopping to lean against a tree in front of yet another cafe. His lungs threatened to explode. He went inside and joined a throng of drinkers at the end of a long bar. "Mineral water," he ordered, looking for a rear exit, looking to the front window. No sign of the red beret. He waited a half hour before venturing out to the street again. He told the cab driver to take him to the Valadier. Once there, he lingered in the lobby to make sure he wasn't being followed. Confident he wasn't, he went to his room, bolted the door, and stepped out onto the small terrace overlooking the Borghese Gardens. It took a long time for his nervous system to return to near normal. He sat in a white wrought-iron chair and looked up into a pristine night, the sky black, the stars unusually bright. He lingered there a long time, trying to sort through what was occurring.

He knew from the moment he'd turned fantasy into reality that there would be great risks. If he were caught, he would be branded a fraud and a thief. Everything he had worked so hard to gain professionally would be stripped away in an instant. Worse, he might be charged with theft, or fraud, or both, and face a jail sentence. That thought, during his darkest hours, frightened him.

But those potential ramifications seemed almost silly now. The one thing he'd never considered was murder. The murder of his good friend, Carlo.

Certainly not his own murder.

Fear and fatigue fought for control. Fatigue won. He undressed, brushed his teeth, slid beneath the sheets, turned out the light, and for the first time in years, prayed. The old expression, no atheists in foxholes, crossed his mind as he fell asleep.

As Mason drifted into unconsciousness, the man in the black raincoat and red beret ordered a cappuccino downstairs in the Valadier's small coffee bar. *"Grazie,"* he said to the young waitress. He sipped. Good coffee. Sometimes you get lucky, he thought. This was a good assignment.

NINETEEN

PARIS

"COURT?"

"Luther?"

Courtney Whitney III glanced up at his kitchen clock. Six-fifteen. Another early call from his erratic senior curator. At least this time he hadn't been roused from a deep sleep. He'd been up for fifteen minutes.

"Where are you calling from?" Whitney asked, measuring coffee into his coffeemaker's gold filter.

"Paris."

"Paris? I didn't realize you were going there."

"A last-minute decision." Mason laughed. "You know how Paris picks up the spirit. I'm feeling considerably better."

"Glad to hear it." Whitney punched on the coffeemaker and sat at the kitchen table. "Why are you calling?"

"Just following the rules."

"What rules?"

"About giving the National Gallery first dibs on some art I want to buy. Two pieces by an obscure artist. Gaisser. Jan Steen–influenced, but not quite as moralistic. A little saccharine for most tastes, but I rather like them. In any event, I've put a hold on both at a gallery here. The owner wanted eight thousand dollars for the pair, but I negotiated him down to five. I need a quick okay from you so I can complete the purchase and bring them back with me."

One of many ethics rules for employees of the National Gallery of Art was that anyone contemplating the personal purchase of art had to give the gallery first refusal, even if the pieces had already been paid for. Mason was not being quite honest. He'd already bought the paintings, which stood side by side next to him as he spoke to Whitney from his room at the George V. He judged the pair to be worth as much as ten thousand dollars in the United States. But he wasn't buying them to make a profit. Good thing, he knew. Under the National Gallery's ethics rules, if it decided to exercise first refusal rights, it was obligated to pay only what was actually laid out for the paintings— in this case, five thousand. Any increase in value would benefit the gallery.

"Gaisser?" Whitney said sleepily, carrying the phone to the refrigerator, where he removed a package of English muffins. "Name doesn't ring a bell."

"Check with Paul Bishop. I heard him speak once of Gaisser's work. As I said, strictly minor league, but of some scholarly value at a fair price. I would appreciate a ruling before going through with it."

"I'll check with him when I get in this morning. When are you coming back?"

"In a few days. I want you to know, Court, how much I appreciate your understanding. If I didn't take this trip, I don't know what might have happened."

"You needed a rest."

"Anything new on Carlo's murder?"

"No. The police are still questioning anyone who knew him, but I haven't heard anything new."

"How is the testing of *Grottesca* going?"

Sue Whitney padded into the kitchen in robe and slippers, her quizzical expression asking who was on the phone. Whitney placed his hand over the mouthpiece and said, "Luther Mason. From Paris."

She made a disgusted face and headed for the coffeemaker.

"*Grottesca?*" Whitney said. "The testing is proceeding nicely. Donald's nose was out of joint over the way everything's been handled. But he's caught up in the excitement of it now. He told me yesterday that from everything he and his staff could ascertain, it might well be the original lost Caravaggio. But as you know, Luther, all the testing in the world can only rule *out* authorship. It can never prove it."

"Of course. Well, Court, sorry to bother you so early in the morning. If all goes as planned, I'll leave Paris for Washington tomorrow night. May I call you later today, or tomorrow, to get a ruling on the two Gaissers?"

"Sure. I don't see any problem, but I'll follow the rules, too. Enjoy your stay in Paris."

"Thank you, Court. I already have."

Mason hung up and looked at the paintings he'd purchased. He wasn't interested in the artist, or his work, though what he'd said about the artist was true enough. When he went into the gallery he had only one criterion with which to judge what paintings to buy. They had to be the same size as the two copies of *Grottesca.* There'd been some modern works of the right dimensions in the gallery on Porte Maillot, but Mason knew that for him to buy such modern art would cause raised eyebrows. His scorn for most of it rivaled that of *60 Minutes*'s " Morley Safer, but on a more elevated, informed level. The Gaissers were perfect. What had Pissarro said? *"The most corrupt art is the sentimental, the art of orange blossoms which makes pale women swoon."*

The sentimental Gaissers suited his purpose.

As he climbed the stairs that afternoon to Saison's studio above the Greek restaurant on rue de la Huchette, he was almost cooked in the conflicting odors of the narrow stairwell. I'll have to get this suit cleaned the minute I get home, he thought.

Saison opened the door and narrowed his eyes.

"Bonjour, Monsieur Saison. Luther Mason." Mason extended his hand.

Saison didn't move to take it. *"Entrez,"* he said. *"Merci."*

The sight of Jacques Saison's studio was as revolting to Luther as the odors emanating from it. He'd never seen such chaos. Canvases were piled up and tossed haphazardly. Filthy plates and glasses covered most exposed surfaces. The man himself was a monument to dishevelment, badly needing a shave and a haircut, if not first aid. It looked to Mason as though Saison hadn't washed his hair since starting work on the Caravaggio knockoffs. Giliberti had sworn Saison was the best art forger in the world. How could he be? How could anyone do high-quality work in such surroundings?

Saison stumbled to where a half-filled bottle of whiskey stood on a dirt-crusted sink, poured some into a smoky glass, and lit a cigarette. *"Voulez-vous un verre? Cigarette?"*

The thought of whiskey and a cigarette caused Mason to wince. He conspicuously checked his watch. He wanted out of the studio and away from its occupant. "You have the paintings?" he asked.

"Oui." Saison continued to lean against the

sink, drawing on his cigarette and sipping his whiskey.

"I would like to see them," said Mason. "I have a busy schedule."

"The money. You have the money?"

"Yes," Mason said, sighing. "I have the money." He retrieved a fat envelope from his inside jacket pocket and looked for a place to drop it. A pile of old canvases seemed as good a place as any.

Saison opened the envelope and did a fast count.

"I assure you it's all there, Mr. Saison. And it is yours, provided the work you have done is satisfactory."

Saison's back was to Luther. He spun around, his face creased in a fuzzy anger. "You doubt my ability?"

"Oh, no, not at all," Luther said. "I have—I had great faith in Carlo. You heard about him, I assume?"

"Heard about what? He has been arrested?"

"You haven't heard. He's dead. He was murdered in Washington."

Saison mumbled French obscenities.

"You know you are to leave Paris for at least six months?"

Saison ignored his reminder. He belched, rubbed his eyes, and pointed to a closet at the far end of the studio. "In there. They are in there."

This was Mason's moment of truth. He was afraid to open the closet door for fear that what he would find would not be good enough to withstand the scrutiny of people like Franco del Brasco, or the Italians to whom one of the copies would be returned.

"Go on, go on," Saison said. "I don't have all day."

Luther opened the closet door, allowing light from the studio to spill inside. Leaning against the back wall, facing him, was one of the two copies. He couldn't believe his eyes. It was magnificent. A *remarkable* duplicate of Caravaggio's original. The second copy was behind it.

Luther slowly turned. "They look quite good," he said.

Saison guffawed. "It is better than good. I have worked day and night on them since Carlo brought me the original. Day and night. From the photographs. No rest, no food. It is not enough."

"What is not enough?" Mason asked, spirits sinking, knowing . . .

"The money."

"Nonsense! Caravaggio is not that difficult to copy, and you know it. He had no trademarks, no subtle signature techniques to be considered. Everything is strong and direct."

The anger flared up in Saison again. He advanced halfway across the studio to where Mason stood. "You tell *me* it is not difficult to copy Caravaggio?" he shouted. A torrent of obscenities passed his lips.

Mason held up his hands against what he thought was about to become a physical attack. "Please, Mr. Saison, no offense. The work you have done is splendid. *Magnifique!* But there is no more money for you." Or for anyone else, he thought. "You have been fairly paid. More than fairly paid. Enough to go away for a year, to lie in the sun on the Riviera, to do what you wish."

"Carlo is dead, huh? Maybe I am next. I want more."

A familiar panic returned. Was this madman about to deny him possession of the copies? He didn't have any more money to give. That was the simple truth. Whatever happened to honor? Then he remembered his resolve with the larcenous priest.

"No!"

Mason did something he never thought he could. He picked up the envelope filled with money, went to the door, placed his hand on the sticky knob, turned, and said, "Keep the paintings."

Saison's expression said he was stunned, confused. He spread his hands and smiled. A yellow, crooked smile. "The paintings are no good to me. What good are they?"

"That's your problem," Mason said. "*Au revoir,* Monsieur Saison."

He stepped into the foul hallway and slammed the door behind him. He closed his eyes, took a deep breath, and said aloud, softly, "What are you doing?"

The door opened. "Come in," Saison said. "No need for anger. Take the copies. I never want to see them again."

The sense of relief Mason felt was palpable. He followed the Frenchman back into the studio, went to the closet, and brought both copies to the center of the large room. "Do you have something I can wrap these in?"

Saison looked at him through bloodshot eyes. "You want something to wrap them with? That will cost you extra."

Mason glared at him.

Saison said, "A joke. Just a joke." He rummaged through a pile in a corner until coming up with two large pieces of cloth. He threw them at Luther, who immediately went to work wrapping the paintings, using masking tape to secure the flaps on the back.

"*Merci,* Saison." Mason held a painting under each arm as he headed for the door. "Enjoy your holiday. You've earned it." With that he was out the door and fairly running down the stairs.

He stopped on his way back to the George V to purchase a number of items, including framing tools in an art-supply store, then went to work in his hotel room. First, he dismantled the two Gaisser paintings. He carefully removed the *Grottesca* copies from their stretching frames, positioned them behind the Gaisser works, and put everything back into frames. He picked each up and examined every inch, front and back. It would work. He would get through Customs, even if one of Carlo's friends in the Italian Customs Service wasn't available to slide him through, as planned.

His call caught Court Whitney at the Gallery as he was about to leave. "Did you talk to Paul?" Mason asked.

"Yes. Frankly, Luther, Paul says you've been taken. He says Gaisser was worse than a minor artist. Sure you want to go through with this purchase?"

"Yes. I don't intend to hang them in my apartment. They're gifts." Why he felt the need to defend his artistic integrity was lost on him. "They'll make nice gifts. One for my mother back in Indiana. I'll give the other to Julian."

"Expensive gifts," Whitney remarked.

"Nothing is too expensive for my mother. You must meet her one day, Court. She's a darling woman. The Gallery has no interest in them?"

"That's right, Luther. Go ahead and buy them."

"Thank you, Court. As I said earlier, I'm feeling like the proverbial new man. Maybe minor, mind you, as I'm sure Paul would agree, but new."

TWENTY

"YOU READ this?"

Steve Jordan slid that morning's newspaper across the desk to his assistant, Gloria Watson, who'd joined the Washington MPD art squad after graduating with a degree in art history from American University. Being a cop seemed more exciting than working in the musty back rooms of museums, provided she could even find such a job.

She read the article:

LONDON—A major art-insurance fraud has been uncovered, according to officials of London's Metropolitan Art Squad. Lord Adam Boulridge, a descendent of the Duchess of Monmouth and a noted collector of works by British artists, has been charged with arranging to have a portion of his collection 'stolen' in order to profit from insurance on the works. Working closely with investigators from the insurer, Lloyd's of London, police authorities last night arrested Lord Boulridge at his castle on the Northumberland Coast. His Lordship, according to police, has confessed to the scheme. In a brief statement made while being led away, he said, "In this perilous economy, it is not easy being a peer of the realm."

"Not easy being royalty," Jordan said. "Especially when you're in jail. The British tabloids should have a ball with this for the next two years, the Royals having quieted down."

"It doesn't say whether they recovered the art," Gloria said.

Jordan laughed. "Probably being sold in Hong Kong or Beirut as we speak."

"What tops the list this morning?"

"For me? A meeting. For you? Get everything in place over at the Atlas Building for the pre-Columbian sting."

"Mrs. Smith still going through with it?"

"She hasn't told me otherwise. What's the matter? You look like you just sucked on a lemon."

"The Atlas. I hate going there. It gives me the creeps."

The Atlas Building, located on a decayed portion of Ninth Street populated by pornography shops and grim bars, near the National Portrait Gallery—and only a few blocks from the National Gallery of Art—had been a stately turn-of-the-century home to Washington's most prestigious law firms. But as the once-genteel neighborhood declined, and the lawyers prospered, they moved out. In the 1960s, the building's new owner turned it into a low-rent artist's colony, home to more than two hundred area artists over the ensuing years. The owner's decision to "support the arts" was not altogether altruistic. Renting to struggling artists meant few complaints about the building's deteriorating interior and exterior and lack of services. There was no water, and only occasional electricity. Break-ins were frequent, although the few artists remaining in the building pointed out that thieves never stole their art, just answering machines and small radios. But you couldn't beat the rent. Artist Richard Dana, a former intelligence officer friendly with Mac and Annabel Smith, paid $167 a month for a huge studio. Another Washington monument, in this case to decay.

Steve Jordan and his art squad sometimes rented space in the Atlas when they needed to front a sting. The building was seedy enough to be believable. It was known as an artists' haven. And the occasional use of it wouldn't threaten Jordan's budget—at all.

"Well, Watson, you may not like going there, but you will. The phone line comes in this morning. Jacob signed the lease. It went to the landlord first thing this morning."

Jacob Will, a Maryland artist, had been arrested by Jordan a year ago for laundering hot art. A deal was struck to avoid prosecution. When Jordan needed a front, in this case renting a studio in the Atlas Building on a month-to-month basis, Jacob provided it.

"Check in with me after lunch," Jordan told Gloria.

Jordan's meeting was at MPD Headquarters, Second District, on Idaho Avenue, N.W. Present were representatives from the law-enforcement agencies investigating the murder of Carlo Gili-berti. Jordan knew everyone in the room except for two men sitting together at the head of a confer-ence table. They were introduced by Washington MPD chief of detectives Emil Vigilio as New York City detectives.

One explained their reason for being there. "We'd been investigating Carlo Giliberti for six months," he said. "Customs tipped us to the pos-sibility that Giliberti was smuggling in stolen art from Italy and selling it to a gallery down in Soho. We put the arm on the owner. Helped him to see the light, and he decided to cooperate. The last stuff Giliberti brought in was a couple of paint-ings by an artist named—he consulted a scrap of paper—Preti. Mattia Preti."

"Stolen from San Francesco di Assisi, in Cosenza," Steve Jordan said.

"Right."

"Jordan heads up our art squad," Vigilio said. "Go on. We're listening."

"We couldn't do much with Giliberti. Diplo-matic immunity and all. Diplomatic impunity is more like it. We were ready to pass the information on to authorities in Italy when he got it in the neck, down here."

"What was his source of stolen art?" Jordan asked.

The New York cop again checked his notes. "Hard to say. From what the Italians tell us, stealing art is getting to be big business for the local mafiosi."

Which wasn't news to Jordan. Unlike organized crime in the States, with drugs, extortion, prostitution, and other crimes providing the major sources of income, art theft was an important criminal industry in Italy. The fact that Italy had more priceless art to steal undoubtedly had something to do with it, supply equaling demand.

The New York detectives completed their report, and after some discussion and a promise of further cooperation, left.

"Giliberti wasn't as clean as we thought he was," said Vigilio. "I'd say Mr. Giliberti's untimely departure from this world wasn't a random killing. Looks like a mob hit to me."

"Over some paintings?" one of Vigilio's detectives said, laughing. "Drugs, maybe. But art?"

Jordan had heard it before. In a city whose murder rate increased every month, his focus on recovering stolen paintings was viewed by many colleagues as dilettante police work. Who cared whether some rich art collector got ripped off when the city's citizens were being gunned down over a pair of sneakers, or a Washington Redskins jacket?

"You have any information on Giliberti smuggling art into the country?" Vigilio asked Jordan.

"No, but it's happening all the time through embassies. Diplomatic pouches are getting bigger and heavier every day." He opened a small notebook. "Italy leads the list, although there's plenty of action from other countries, too. The old Soviet Union for one. Italy's loaded with art, a lot of it in churches and convents. They can't afford to pay for security. Easy pickings." He went on to cite statistics from a conference in Rome he'd attended a few months ago. Drawing law-enforcement officials from sixteen countries, it had been held in conjunction with an unusual art exhibition featuring stolen art taken back by the art-recovery division of Italy's *carabinieri,* its police department.

"Twenty-nine thousand pieces of art were stolen last year in Italy alone," said Jordan. "They recovered maybe five thousand of them. The Mafia, as the New York guys said, is heavy into art theft over there. No doubt about that. Ten billion dollars worth of art stolen every year around the world." He looked at the detective who'd made light of stolen art. "Yeah, the numbers are worth killing for. I had a meeting last week with the Bureau's Interstate Theft Unit. They estimate there's at least fifty thousand pieces of stolen art floating around this country alone. We recover ten percent."

"Unless you get lucky like we did," said Carl Kelley, head of the National Gallery of Art's three-hundred-person security force.

"Caravaggio?" Jordan said. *"Grottesca?"*

"Right. Didn't take the police to find it. A curator. Luther Mason."

"We have to keep these curators off our turf," Jordan said, laughing.

"Amazing," said Kelley. "Finding it after a couple of hundred years."

"The *carabinieri* just recovered a Raphael missing for two hundred years," Jordan offered. "Worth a cool twenty-four million."

"I never worry about anybody stealing our art," Kelley said. "The wife buys it all at tag sales."

"Back to Giliberti," Vigilio said. "If he was killed by the mob for whatever reason—art, drugs, sleeping with the wrong woman, forgetting to kiss the godfather's ring—we can stop looking for the murderer in the general population."

"I'll do some more checking," Jordan said. "Maybe I can narrow it down a little."

"Yeah, do that, Steve," Vigilio said. "If it pans out to be a mob hit, we'll pass what we know on to the Italians. Anything else?"

The meeting ended.

In Cincinnati, Ohio, Harry Whitlock had recently received a generous bonus from his employer, prompting his wife to buy new furniture and to sell the old at a tag sale. The orange-and-white zebra-pattern couch went quickly. Cindy had returned to the flea market to buy another print from the dealer who'd sold her Fragonard's *A Stand of Cypresses in an Italian Park,* which had gone nicely with the old couch. The new couch was green: She bought a landscape by someone who'd signed it "Carracci" to hang over it.

No one at the tag sale showed interest in the Fragonard print until a couple stopped by, perused what was left, and huddled at the far end of the driveway, talking quietly. "I'm telling you, that picture is worth a lot of money," the man told his wife.

"I don't like it," she said.

"It doesn't matter whether you like it or not. They're selling what could be a rare masterpiece."

"Why would they do that?"

"Because they don't know anything about art. Like I do. I'll do the negotiating. They're asking thirty bucks."

A few minutes later, the couple left the Whitlock house carrying the Fragonard print, as well as a table lamp with a frayed cord. Cindy wouldn't take less than thirty dollars for the print but threw in the lamp.

TWENTY-ONE

ANNABEL AWOKE with a start. It was as dark outside as in the bedroom. Mac felt her sudden movement and sat up. "What's the matter?" he asked.

"I don't know. I—"

"Just a bad dream."

"Yes. No." She snapped on the reading lamp. "Mac. I think I know who smashed my Tlatilco."

His light came on, too. "Who?"

"I can't be sure. But I know how to find out."

They got up, showered, dressed, and sipped coffee in the kitchen until sunrise.

"What time does it open?" he asked.

"Eight."

When Annabel Reed, now Annabel Reed-Smith, closed her legal practice in search of fulfillment as a gallery owner, she had put the contents of her office in a self-storage facility in Alexandria. She hadn't visited those dead files in over a year.

"You don't remember his name?" Mac asked as they crossed the Potomac River on the Theodore Roosevelt Memorial Bridge.

"Cedro. Cedras. Something like that. They were Costa Rican. It shouldn't be hard to find the file. I had a special drawer for spousal-abuse cases."

Annabel's storage unit was on the ground floor of a two-story prefab metal building painted a garish pink. Mac opened the door with the key she handed him and rolled up the corrugated metal door. Inside, beige metal file cabinets were stacked on top of one another from floor to ceiling. Her desk, chairs, and other furniture were carefully placed on top and against each other to make optimum use of the space. Fluorescent ceiling lights cast a greenish glow over everything.

Annabel looked at labels on the front of each file cabinet. "This one," she said, kneeling, opening a bottom drawer, and fingering through the folders it contained. "Here." She withdrew one and handed it up to him. The label read: MARIA AND JOSEPH CEDRAS.

They stepped outside to read the folder's contents.

"You think it was him?" Mac asked after they'd finished going through it.

"I can't be sure. But he was the same size, same general appearance as I remember him from the one time he came to the office. He was furious that his wife was leaving him. I've had angry people in my office before, but he was frightening. He was so—irrational. He threatened her. Threatened me."

"You should have reported him," Mac said.

"I considered it but decided to give him time to calm down, get used to the fact that Maria wanted a divorce. That was the last I heard from him. He'd beaten her on a number of occasions. I got her into a battered-women's shelter and put through the divorce papers. He didn't formally contest the action. The last I heard, he'd gone home to Costa Rica."

"The wife?"

"Stayed around here, I think. I really don't know. I lost touch."

"What did he do for a living?" Mac asked.

"Had his own business. Import-export."

"Did Mrs. Cedras ever report being beaten to the police?"

"Once, I think. The last time it happened. She was scared to death of him."

"The police arrest him?"

"Yes. That was the day before he came to my office. That's what set him off."

"Good," Mac said.

"Why good?"

"Chances are MPD fingerprinted him and took his picture. We'll call Steve Jordan and go through his mug-shot books."

Two hours later they sat in Jordan's pleasant little art gallery–cum–office. A photograph of Joseph Cedras was already on the desk.

"Look, Annabel," said Jordan, "you may be right. You probably *are* right about this guy. But even if we pick him up, you won't be able to ID him. You said you never saw his face."

"But I saw his hat and coat. And his hammer. My read on him was that he was unstable, capable of violence. People like that sometimes don't hesitate to take credit for their violent acts."

"But violence against an inanimate object. Why?"

Mac asked his wife, "Did you give him your patented two-heads-are-better-than-one speech? You know, using the Tlatilco?"

"Not as I recall. Wait a minute. He and Maria ended up in a shouting match. *She* mentioned it because I'd given my what you call 'speech' just before he barged in."

"We'll issue a warrant on him, Annabel. If we pick him up—and if we come up with his favorite hat and coat—we'll do a lineup best we can."

"Thanks, Steve. I appreciate it."

"Keeping busy, Mac?"

"Uh huh, only the lady here these days is making me look like I'm retired. You?"

"Yeah. Got a bulletin this morning from Norway. They convicted the four guys who stole the Munch painting, *The Scream,* from the National Gallery in Oslo a couple of years ago. The art-and-antiques unit of the Yard posed as potential buyers and nailed them. Only took them three months. Know what I love?"

"What's that?" Mac asked as he helped Annabel on with her coat.

"They snatched the painting in less than a minute, and left a note that said, 'Thank you for little security.'"

Mac and Annabel laughed.

"Twenty mil. The legitimate art market may be depressed, but the underground is flourishing. How's the Caravaggio exhibit shaping up, Annabel?"

"Fine. Although Carlo Giliberti's murder threw things into a tizzy for a while. Luther Mason wanted to cancel the exhibition because of it."

"He *did?*" Jordan said. "From what I know of Mason, it would take mass genocide for him to call off anything to do with Caravaggio."

"He's changed his mind. Took a week's vacation in Europe."

"He does get around," Mac said.

"Seems to have done wonders for him," said Annabel. "At least according to Court Whitney. Anything on Carlo's murder, Steve?"

Jordan decided not to share what he'd learned from the New York City detectives and shook his head. "Thanks for coming in, folks. I'll be in touch if we come up with Señor Cedras."

Annabel was relieved Jordan hadn't hinted at the arrangement she'd entered into with him to help recover the missing Dumbarton Oaks artifacts. She'd intended to tell Mac about it since making the decision to help out, but the time never seemed right. Besides, she assured herself, nothing would come of it anyway. It was a shot in the dark. Her only obligation was to check the answering machine in the Atlas Building studio once a day, and she could do that by telephone. Her involvement was nothing more than a gesture, one she was glad she'd made. How often were you called upon to help law enforcement, especially when you would be helping recover what had become precious to you, pre-Columbian art? *Ask not what your country can do for you . . .*

Just as long as she didn't end up like the fools who'd broken into Watergate because they'd been duped into thinking *their* cause was worthwhile.

CHAPTER TWENTY-TWO

WASHINGTON

THE MONTHS flew by quickly for everyone involved in the exhibition. The paintings loaned to the National Gallery began to arrive by Alitalia, each protected in a climate-controlled box designed and built by conservator Don Fechter's staff. Most conservation work on the paintings had been accomplished at their sites-of-origin, although permission had been granted by some lenders for Fetcher's experts to complete the work in Washington, paid for through a private fund.

The publicity mill was in full gear. The media were bombarded with press releases, and the gallery's Speaker's Bureau fielded an unprecedented number of requests. As might be expected, most were for Luther Mason. To the surprise of the National Gallery's staff—Courtney Whitney III no exception—Mason graciously, even enthusiastically agreed to speak to the most important of the groups. He'd been reticent in the past about making public appearances. There were certain public relations efforts expected of curators—

scholarly papers presented within the National
Gallery and at other leading art centers, curatorial
conferences, an occasional presentation to the
trustees. Mason had always fulfilled those obliga-
tions, but not without his penchant for making
dramatic protestations:

"Must I again stare into a room of vacant faces
while I try to *explain* Caravaggio to them? Do you
explain Mozart? Perhaps if I were speaking about
a new Nintendo game or gene-splitting technique
they would be interested. Why are Americans so
comfortable with science but uncomfortable with
art?"

Not this time.

"I think it's wonderful," deputy director Naomi
Warren told Court Whitney over coffee in his office one morning. "It's as though Luther not only
discovered *Grottesca,* he discovered himself in the
bargain."

Whitney could only agree. Mason's calendar
was chockablock with talks and interviews. The
only problem Mason's leap into the spotlight created was the envy it generated in his senior-curator
colleague, Paul Bishop. Bishop complained regularly to Whitney that the exhibition was turning
into a circus, hardly befitting the reputation of the
National Gallery of Art. The considerable professional and personal attributes that had qualified
Whitney to be director of "America's Museum"
included the art of assuagement, which he found

himself having to practice with Bishop nearly full time.

Since returning from Paris, Mason seemed to find an extra hour in each twenty-four-hour day, causing security guards to question whether the senior curator was sleeping at the gallery. He was there day and night and insisted upon making the final decision on virtually every aspect of the exhibition, large and small, important and trivial. He challenged the design created by George Kublinski, chief of the Gallery's Design and Exhibition Department, including the choice of color for the walls. Like all good curators—and the best exhibition specialists—Luther knew the importance of color as a backdrop for works of art. Kublinski's plans called for the walls to be painted a burgundy thinned with a special white paint.

Mason disagreed. He'd spent days researching color and its relationship to Caravaggio's work. The walls would be a pale apricot tint.

He took the same hands-on approach to the framing of *Grottesca.* The Matting and Framing Department, which fell under Donald Fechter's conservation group on the National Gallery's extensive organizational chart, had chosen an elaborate, bordering on the ornate, cherry frame with thin gold-leaf inlay.

"Too big, too rococo," Mason insisted. "It detracts from the work. I want it kept simple, and smaller." When he announced he would seek outside consultation with Max Mowinkle, a New York framer, the Gallery's framers complained to Fechter. He dismissed their complaints. "The man is consumed by this show," he told them. "Let him pick his own goddamn frame and get on with other things. You'd think *he* was in the frame."

A week later, Luther attended a meeting of the Framing and Matting Department accompanied by Mowinkle, a diminutive man in his fifties who had a nervous tic in his left eye and spoke with a matching stammer. Mason presented the frame Mowinkle had created. It was cherry but considerably less bold than the original. There was no gold leaf, no elaborate carvings. It was slender and simple, barely protruding from the painting itself.

Fechter and his people were unanimous in their belief that Mason had made a bad choice. But again, Fechter declined to argue the point.

The next morning, Mowinkle dropped off a package at Mason's apartment. Inside were two identical copies of the *Grottesca* frame. The doorman accepted them and handed the framer a fat envelope Luther had left with him before going to work that morning.

The press breakfast set for the day of the Caravaggio opening was a week away.

So was the dinner.

All the loaner works were in Washington and ready to be hung.

The show was sold out.

The two copies of *Grottesca* were in the rear of Luther's living room closet, along with the duplicate frames.

"Mother?"

"Hello, Luther."

"How are you feeling?"

"I feel all right."

"Mother, I want you to come to Washington as my guest at the opening of my—our—Caravaggio exhibition." He'd sent her some clippings.

"I read about it. Sounds very nice."

"But only if you're here. This is the greatest moment of my life, mother. I want to share it with you."

She said nothing.

"Julian will be here. It would be a good chance for the three of us to spend time together. Please say yes. I'll send a first-class airline ticket to you by Federal Express. I've already booked a suite at the Watergate Hotel. You know that hotel. It was where Richard Nixon—"

"I know it. Why is it still open?"

"Will you?"

"Luther, I—"

"I won't take no for an answer, Mother. I insist."

She agreed, providing him with a profound sense of relief. It would be the last time he would ever see her.

TWENTY-THREE

"THIS HAS been a long and challenging undertaking," Court Whitney said as he wound up a Friday-morning meeting. I commend each of you for your dedication to seeing this challenging undertaking come to fruition. My suggestion is that we all get an early start on the weekend, rest up, and be ready to hit it hard again on Monday. Unless there are further questions, we'll meet next at eight sharp Monday morning."

Earlier in the day, Mason had stopped by the security office to scan the weekend duty schedule. A veteran member of the gallery's police force, Tom Morris, was due to come on duty at six Sunday morning. Good, Mason thought. He and Morris had a cordial relationship.

He left the Gallery and headed for home. As he looked in the direction of the Gallery's Constitution Avenue entrance, his heart tripped. A huge red-and-green banner with white lettering was being raised above the doors: GENIUS COMES TO

AMERICA: THE WORKS OF MICHELANGELO MERISI CARAVAGGIO.

"My God," he said aloud. "It's almost over."

The upcoming week promised to be relatively relaxed. Most loose ends concerning the exhibition had been wrapped up, leaving Mason time to tie up the loose ends in his personal life. Or to clip them off.

Scott Pims called at five to invite him to dinner at his apartment and to an auction the following day. "I've been toiling all day over a *coquilles Saint-Jacques au jus de truffe.* Morton was to dine with me but he stubbed his toe. I hate to invite you as a substitute, Luther, but better that than eating alone. You will come, of course."

Mason sighed. The thought of one of Pims's meals was attractive; he had little energy to prepare himself a meal, and the contemplation of eating out was equally unappealing. On the other hand, his instincts told him it would be prudent to content himself with something from the freezer and a good night's sleep. "I'm afraid I'm too tired to go anywhere tonight, Scott. You know the merry-go-round I've been on. With only a few days until the opening."

"Trash talk, Luther. I know you're tired. But I assure you, a few hours at my table will not only pick up your spirits but infuse you with renewed energy. Besides, I'm dying to hear the latest."

"Maybe I could—"

"Splendid. Seven. I have an excellent bottle of Chablis—Grand-Cru—which I will open with only slightly less ceremony than your Dago painter's show. After dinner, we'll watch my program together."

Pims's television show aired each Friday night at ten, taped earlier in the day. "There's a brewing scandal in Le Beaubourg. Actually, it's the Centre Georges Pompidou. But as you know, the French hate naming anything after a dead statesman. I have wonderful contacts in Paris. Come to think of it, I have wonderful contacts all over the world." His sudden, sharp laugh was a 4.7 on the Richter scale. "You'll love the show. I've managed to top even last week's production."

"All right."

"Seven then. Don't bother dressing. We'll make it an informal, cozy night."

After hanging up, Luther rationalized having dinner with Pims. In a sense, it would serve as a rehearsal for doing things he preferred not to be doing. Lord knew, there were enough of those situations to be faced over the next seven days.

SATURDAY

His calendar read: *Dinner, Lynn.*

Mason's affair with Lynn Marshall had commenced six months ago, two months after she'd come to work for him.

She'd been among more than two hundred candidates submitting résumés for the opening on Mason's staff. From those, he'd narrowed the field to thirty. And of the thirty bright, ambitious young people he interviewed, Ms. Marshall gave the most favorable impression. Her educational credentials in art history, along with a productive two-year stint as an apprentice curator at Washington's first museum—the prestigious Corcoran Gallery of Art—provided the background Luther sought. Her knowledge of the Old Masters was broad based. Most important, she'd presented an interesting philosophical view of many of the works they discussed during the hour interview in his office. She viewed Roman art as inferior to that of the Greeks, with which Luther agreed. An emphasis on learning how to *draw,* Lynn felt, was to the artistic detriment of Roman artists. It stifled their purely creative output. Score another for her, Mason thought. She considered artists of northern Italy during the Renaissance to have possessed even greater talent than their counterparts in Rome and Florence, although she was careful to pay homage to the Romans and Florentines: "I'm especially fond of Correggio," she said. "His experiments with movement and emotion created a remarkable bond between artist and viewer." Mason nodded.

It was when she began to discuss the Baroque period that she captured Mason's heart, and the job. She knew a great deal about Caravaggio and waxed poetic about his power and technique. Luther assumed she'd done her homework before the interview, having learned that Caravaggio was his passion. But that was in her favor. If she was energetic and creative enough to delve into the background of the person interviewing her, she would likely bring to the job a similar dedication and ambition.

Then, too, Lynn Marshall was attractive. Her features were too coarse to be considered classic, lips large and full, her nose broad. But the overall effect was proud sensuality, and the fleshiness of her body enhanced it. Mason was aware that she was subtly flirting with him during the interview, which he found pleasant, even flattering. What he most enjoyed was Lynn Marshall's easy laughter.

Her first overt sexual overture happened while they were working late, the merest brush of bodies in close quarters. Mason offered little resistance. He'd been celibate since leaving Cynthia three months ago, with the exception of a weekend fling in New Orleans with a middle-aged Dallas curator who'd latched on to him at a cocktail party and enticed him to her hotel room. Easily and quickly forgotten.

But sex was not the prime motivating factor in his affair with Lynn. "Torrid" was not the word

Mason would apply to their occasional nights together, nor would others observing those episodes. It wasn't in his nature to let himself go to that extent. But he did revel in her doting on him when they were together, complimenting his sexual performance in a way that caused him to ignore the possibility—no, probability—that she was being disingenuous.

They got together twice a week at best. Sometimes, weeks went by without their seeing each other outside the office. This was a controlled affair, not a brushfire. And she worked hard at her job. He'd hired smart.

Mason knew it had not been prudent to enter into an affair with a professional colleague, especially one reporting directly to him. Books on how to advance careers and manage employees counseled against it; so did common sense. But Luther didn't read such books or allow for common sense. Everything seemed distinctly irrelevant once the affair was underway.

As far as Luther knew, he represented the only male extracurricular event in Lynn's life. When she wasn't with him, she seemed consumed with the art lessons she took at the A. Salon of the Jackson School, a nonprofit arts group funded by the District of Columbia's Commission on the Arts and the National Endowment for the Arts. Her problem as an aspiring artist was that while her mind was willing, her brush was weak. Woefully so,

Mason knew upon first seeing the work that she'd pinned up on every inch of wall space in her small Capitol Hill apartment. Julian had produced better art in the sixth grade. Her paintings were without form, articulation, even content. Naturally, he did not express his opinion. The relationship was too important to him for honesty.

Instead, he praised her work in as elaborate and noncommittal ways as possible: "It has a certain raw, unleashed power." "You have an—interesting, original—approach to color." "What a pleasant, unforeseen melding of geometric shapes." And, of course, he spoke at length about the Dionysian quality of her painting, using the psychiatrist from *Equus* as an example.

It wasn't long before his artfulness led him into the inevitable. She asked him to arrange a gallery showing of her work.

Luther tried to ignore this unreasonable request, but she pressed. As she did, her exquisite female softness and bubbling laugh that so delighted him began to harden. After some months, she hinted for the first time that she might enjoy having others at the National Gallery know of their affair. "Wouldn't that raise some eyebrows, Luther? Wouldn't Court get a charge out of it?"

One night, while Mason and Lynn were having dinner in a Georgetown bistro, Julian arrived unexpectedly. He was accompanied by another young man. Mason invited them to join their table. He found it engaging at first that Lynn openly flirted with his handsome, strapping son. But as the evening wore on, it began to nettle him, to the extent that he abruptly called for the check before coffee had been served and whisked her out of the restaurant.

"You were pretty taken with my son," he said angrily as they drove to her apartment.

Her laugh, which he used to enjoy, now had a slight edge of cruelty. "So what?" she said. "I've always had this fantasy of being mistress to father and son."

That irksome incident was soon smothered in a tangle of soft, sweet-smelling sheets. Strangely, the intensity of the sexual act that night was of a dimension Mason hadn't experienced in a long time, going back to his earliest days with Juliana. And it was apparently the same with Lynn. Sexual competition with his young son? The stuff of talk shows and tabloid newspapers. He worried about it for a few days, but because he considered himself above such shabby musings, he stopped worrying. The Caravaggio took over all his emotions and fantasies.

One hot, sticky August morning, Mason drove to Rockville, Maryland, where a friend operated an art gallery in a mini-mall. With him in the car were four of Lynn's "best" works.

"I dropped the paintings off at a gallery," he proudly announced to her on the phone that night. "He said he'd get back to me in a few days."

His friend called the next day. "Luther, for God's sake, I may not have the keenest eye for art, surely not like yours, but this stuff is embarrassing."

Mason didn't tell Lynn of the phone call, deflecting her inquiries until the following weekend, when he picked up the paintings and returned them to her apartment. "He's booked quite far into the future, Lynn," he said. "But he thought your works—produced interesting emotions."

She gave him a sardonic laugh. "Who the hell wants to be exhibited in . . . where did you say? . . . Rockville, Maryland, anyway? I want a show in the District, or New York."

Luther considered approaching Bill Wooby, owner of The Collector Restaurant and Art Gallery. He knew Wooby respected him because of his position at the National Gallery but would smoothly, gently turn him down. Truth was, Lynn Marshall's future as a curator was bright. As for a life as an artist, the expression "Don't give up your day job" summed up his feelings.

Downhill from there.

The latest thorn in the bouquet of their relationship—Luther now wished he'd read one of those books about the pitfalls of office romance—arose when the unexpected departure of an associate curator created an opening one level above the position held by Lynn. She wasted no time letting Mason know she wanted the promotion—did her tone say *expected* it?

In his opinion she wasn't ready for it. Besides, there were two others on his staff in line to be promoted and whose experience better prepared them for what the job entailed. That was one of the things he hoped to accomplish at dinner—to dissuade her from pursuing the job.

The other matter on his dinner agenda was to put an end to their affair. He no longer had time for it, no time for anything but paying attention to every last detail of his plan. Their relationship would be over soon enough anyway, when he fled the country with *Grottesca.* But he didn't want to leave without some sort of closure. He owed her that.

Lynn was always content to have dinner in small, inexpensive restaurants—her pretensions were limited to her art. But Mason invariably chose fancy places. Was that something old men felt compelled to do with young lovers? Demonstrate power, affluence, and taste? Probably. This night he chose the Willard Room in the refurbished, venerable Willard Hotel on Pennsylvania Avenue, the place where Ulysses S. Grant coined the useful term "lobbyist" to describe power brokers lounging in the imposing lobby in search of influential elbows to rub and palms to grease.

Beneath a high ceiling that was a work of art unto itself, Mason ordered his favorite sweet corn–and–oyster soup. Lynn made a face when he suggested she try it and said she wanted shrimp cocktail.

"You must be pleased with the story in the *Post* this morning," she said.

"Of course."

"It was a nice picture of you."

"I thought it made me appear dissipated."

"You look tired, that's all. That sexy world-weary look."

"If you say so. Frankly, I was more impressed with the final results of Don Fechter's testing of *Grottesca*. It came from Caravaggio's hand."

"The *Post* also quoted Lafroing," she said.

"Posturing, pompous Peter Lafroing. Always willing to withhold judgment. Well, let him withhold his goddamned judgment. He's like a lawyer. You can never be wrong by saying 'no.' Or withholding judgment. Peter is jealous, that's all."

Lafroing was a freelance curator from California, one of two Caravaggio experts brought in by the National Gallery to provide independent evaluations of *Grottesca*. Lafroing stated that it was a "good possibility" that the painting had been rendered by Caravaggio but that he would withhold a final opinion pending further research and consideration.

Mason shook his head. "I will give Peter this.

He's his own man. Not like others whose opinions depend upon who's buttering their bread. Naturally, I would have preferred Peter's unqualified endorsement. But it isn't needed. Everything points to *Grottesca* as Caravaggio's. Of course, I knew that the minute I saw *Grottesca* in that—" He almost said "barn" but caught himself. "In that rundown church outside of Ravello. I knew it was the lost masterpiece. We have to go through this pro forma exercise, which I understand. In fact, I'm glad we did. Now, there is no question of its authenticity."

"I heard Paul Bishop make a strange remark the other day. He still doesn't buy the way you found the painting."

"Ah, Mr. Bishop at work again. Another case of jealousy, Lynn. Don't listen to what Paul Bishop says. Ever. He's lost touch. Who was he saying this to?"

She screwed up her face. "I think it was Naomi Warren. Yes, it was. Court was there, too."

Luther knew Bishop had been sniping at him to anyone who would listen. Under normal circumstances he might have confronted his colleague. But it didn't matter any longer. And he didn't want to risk a showdown. Bishop's attempts to discredit him and his work were a useless exercise. Soon, he would be free of backbiting and professional envy. As that realization replaced his pique, he settle back in his chair, a smile on his lips.

"Well, Luther, what about the promotion?" Lynn bit into a shrimp.

Reverie interruptus, Luther thought, sitting up straight and placing his elbows on the table. "Lynn, I would give you this promotion in an instant. But it's wrong for you at the moment. You are a year away from being able, being entitled, to carry the responsibility it entails. I think you will agree that I did the right thing in hiring you. I have never lost sight of the need to nurture your considerable talents, to bring you along at the proper pace. This premature promotion would set you back, not advance your career."

Her expression said she didn't buy it.

It had occurred to Luther that aside from the question of qualifications, and those in line to be promoted, there was another issue with which to contend. To choose someone, and then to leave, meant that his successor would be forced to live with Mason's choice. That wasn't fair.

He'd always wanted to do the right thing. But recently he'd become consumed with that need, perhaps to compensate for the large wrong he was in the process of perpetrating. Despite the romance with one painting, he wanted to be remembered as a good and decent man, generous and kind as well as the consummate professional who always had the best interests of his staff and the Gallery at heart.

How *would* he be remembered?

"Good ol' Luther. He really pulled off a coup. Masterly."

"He was a good man. I miss him, and I hope he's having a good time with his *Grottesca.*"

"Mason? Nothing but a common thief!"

Were Luther able to join in those conversations, he would tell them that when viewed against evil governments slaughtering innocents for the metaphor of patriotism, when compared to child molestation and stock manipulation, rape and murder and teens shooting teens, having "taken" one lost painting represented the most minor of infractions.

After all, who'd been hurt?

The National Gallery of Art?

Not in Luther's eyes. It had benefited mightily from having *Grottesca* secured within its walls: "The greatest one-month flow of private donations in the gallery's history," Court Whitney had proudly proclaimed. Not bad for Whitney's career either.

Franco del Brasco, who'd put up the money for a painting, not knowing that it allowed Mason to pursue his dream?

Del Brasco had lived his life hurting and taking from others. Ending up a million dollars poorer, and with a bogus Caravaggio, was his just due.

The Italian government? The Italian people?

The government was corrupt through and through. The politicians would only use *Grottesca* to enhance their ability to steal even more.

As for the people of Italy, what was one painting among thousands? Besides, the copy they would receive was so perfectly executed by the Frenchman, Saison, they would still have an excellent representation of the master's technique and style. A further rationalization: How many works of art attributed to the Masters had, in fact, been done by their apprentices? A tenuous undertaking, this business of art.

When engaged in such introspection, Mason often thought back to Thanksgiving dinners at his home, attended by relatives and family friends. A deceased uncle, Luther, for whom he'd been named, had abandoned his wife and four children to run off with a seventeen-year-old exotic dancer who'd come through town with a carnival. Everyone talked at dinner about his irresponsibility, his callous indifference toward his family, his foolish infatuation with the nubile young woman. But it was all said with a certain fondness and generally accompanied by laughter. Other deceased family members were mentioned only in passing. The smitten uncle was still prime-time table talk.

Which led Mason to believe that when you were dead—or in seclusion someplace in the world—the appreciation of your misdeeds was heightened by the break from convention they represented.

He hoped that would be the case for him at next year's Thanksgiving celebration.

"Then who will you give the promotion to?" Lynn asked. Her voice was hard. So were her eyes.

"I don't know yet. Look, let's enjoy this evening. It may not last."

"What may not last?"

Mason forced a laugh. "Anything. Life. I've been—thinking of leaving Washington."

Her eyes opened wide. "You have. Where? What will you do?"

He held up a hand against the fusillade of questions. "Just idle thinking, Lynn. After all, I am getting older. My pension won't be large, but enough to live a comfortable life in a less expensive place. I don't know. Maybe Indiana where I grew up. Spain. Or Paris."

"Paris is expensive. I just hope you'll make sure I'm taken care of before you do decide to—retire."

"You know I will."

The rest of the meal was consumed in the sort of stony silence one often sees with couples in restaurants who have had something unpleasant to say to each other earlier in the evening. Or in life. He took Lynn home; the silence in the car was as pervasive as it had been in the restaurant.

"A nightcap?" Mason asked, hoping she would decline.

"No. I think we need to talk another time."

"Of course. This week won't be good. Not with

the show looming. Once the exhibition is on, we can find some real time together. Would you like that?"

"What I would like is an opportunity to talk to you, Luther, about substantive things."

"Of course. I'll call you tomorrow."

"Tomorrow? I'm afraid I'm busy."

"Then I'll see you at the office on Monday."

Mason had two messages on his answering machine. The first was from Julian, who said it was important that they talk. It had to be about money, Luther decided, and could wait a day. He returned the second call, from Scott. "Wonderful dinner last night," he said, injecting buoyancy into a tired voice.

"And extremely pleasant company, I must say," replied Pims. "What did you think of my show? You never actually said."

"I thought it was fascinating. You certainly do have impressive contacts in Paris."

"And elsewhere. I might also say, Luther, my friend, that you seem to have things well under control in your, as you would put it, bareback ride in the moonlight."

"Perhaps I said too much," Luther said. For some reason—and Luther decided it would take years of analysis to understand it—he was incapable of ignoring his fat friend's persistent questioning.

"Nonsense. Everyone needs a willing ear. It helps keep us on an even keel, keeps us from making irrational, imprudent decisions. You'll be happy to know you missed nothing at the auction today. A few dreadful pieces, the rest worse than dreadful."

"Good."

"Where were you this evening?"

"At dinner with a colleague."

There was a pause. "A pretty one?"

"As a matter of fact, yes. I have a great deal to do before getting to bed, and I'll be at the gallery for most of tomorrow. Again, Scott, thank you for a lovely meal. I'll be in touch." Luther gently lowered the receiver into its cradle, cutting off his friend's words.

What Pims was about to say was that he, too, would be busy that evening.

Hours earlier, he'd received a long fax from Rome that he was scanning into his computer.

The sender of the fax had gotten caught in a sudden rainstorm and had removed his soaked red beret and black raincoat after entering the small shop in Rome that offered facsimile and other services to small businesses. Once the fax had been transmitted and he'd paid the fee, he put on his outerwear and went home to bed. He had to be up early the next morning for a trip to Ravello in search of a frockless priest named Giocondi.

SUNDAY

"Good morning, Mr. Mason."

Tom Morris had spent more than twenty years protecting the paintings hanging on the walls of the National Gallery's East and West buildings. He sat behind a desk this early Sunday morning at the employees' entrance to the West Building. "Early start for you."

Mason signed in. "As much as I love the Caravaggio exhibition, I'll be glad when it's over, Tom."

"You'll be taking a much-deserved vacation then?" said the uniformed Morris.

"You can count on that, Tom. Oh, I have something to show you."

Mason had with him the two framed Gaisser paintings wrapped in brown paper. He unwrapped one and held it up for Morris to see. The beefy security guard put on his glasses and leaned closer. "Can't say I recognize the artist," he said.

"Nor should you," Luther said pleasantly. "Obscure, but rather good, I think, in their way. I bought them in Paris."

Morris removed his glasses, sat back, and laughed. "That's what art should be about, isn't it, Mr. Mason? Buy what you like, not what you think is going to make you a fortune."

"Exactly," said Mason, securing the paper around the painting. "I brought these in for Paul

Bishop to look at. He has some knowledge of the artist. I want his professional opinion."

Mason used the underground concourse to go to the East Building. The moving walkway wasn't running, so he walked its length, pausing to admire the water from the outside fountain cascading down terraced steps to the glass curtain wall.

He took the elevator to the fifth floor, locked his office door behind him, took a key from his pocket, and unlocked a closet in which he kept personal effects and pieces of art he was in the process of evaluating. He placed the two Gaisser paintings against the back wall and covered them with the others, locked the closet, and sat behind his desk. If he had allowed himself, he might have nodded off. The previous night with Lynn Marshall had not been a late one, but tension had taken its toll.

He returned to the West Building and went to the gallery in which the Caravaggio exhibition was being readied. A guard at its entrance signed him in. You went nowhere in the Gallery without signing a piece of paper, no matter who you were.

Half the Caravaggios loaned for the exhibition had already been hung. Mason paused in front of each to admire the setting in which they'd been placed. His choice of a wan apricot for the walls was perfect.

The west wall was reserved for *Grottesca,* which hadn't been brought up to the gallery as yet.

Mason wished it had. To be able to breathe in its beauty would provide the elixir he needed for a case of nerves that had started building during dinner with Lynn and that was still with him. Soon enough, he told himself. *Grottesca* would be hung on Wednesday.

He chatted amiably with Tom Morris before leaving the gallery and heading for his car. The morning sky was crystal clear; a gentle breeze from the west was refreshing on his face. He took a detour on the way home to buy magazines and to pick up his favorite glazed apple turnovers, called *chasussons,* and coffee at Bakery Potomac Metro.

He ignored the message light on his answering machine, browsed that morning's *Washington Post* and the magazines he'd purchased, undressed, slipped into pajamas, and returned to bed. He got up at four and spent the rest of the day and early evening going over material he'd been collecting on destinations to which he might "retire."

His initial consideration had been extradition laws. But he decided that if he chose a place to live based on that alone, he would be cheating himself of the pleasures of being where he wanted to be. Besides, at his age, and considering the fact that what he was about to do paled when compared to other crimes, it was worth taking a chance.

Ravello was out of the question. South America or a small Caribbean island were also early considerations, but he ruled those out, too. Pedestrian choices. Nazis fled to South America. Unscrupulous investment bankers used the Caribbean to set up phony accounts in plaque banks. Distasteful.

He made his final choice at seven that night. Greece. The island of Hydra, a relatively barren island with a picturesque, colorful harbor three hours from the port of Piraeus. Luther had fallen in love with the island ten years earlier. He'd taken a mule ride to a series of monasteries sitting high in the mountains that provided a spectacular view of the harbor below. Scattered about the island were stately homes surrounded by pretty smaller white houses, some of which had signs in front indicating they were for rent. Who would bother looking for me there? he thought. Who would look for *Grottesca* on the island of Hydra?

That was it. He would check on travel to Athens and Hydra first thing in the morning. He wasn't sure when he would make his ultimate escape. That would have to be after one of the forgeries of *Grottesca* had been returned to Italy. Plans called for Luther to accompany the painting back to its country of origin. He had tried to get out of that assignment but hadn't been successful. He would go through with it, return to Washington, deliver the second forgery to Franco del Brasco, and then arrange for the original to be sent to Greece.

Making the switch within the National Gallery was one of the more problematic aspects of his plan. But he'd thought long and hard about it and was confident that the plan he'd come up with would work.

He returned his son's calls—Julian had left three more messages that day. He needed money. Luther told him he was strapped, prompting increased arrogance. "All right, Julian, we'll meet for dinner on Tuesday. I'll see what I can do by then." There was no thank you, no expression of appreciation.

Mason loved his son deeply and dearly but ached at his inability to express it freely and without reservation. It wasn't that Luther lacked the talent to demonstrate love. Feeding Julian's insatiable demands for money seemed to be the only expression of "love" the boy was willing to accept from his father. Love on the barrelhead. No credit. Cash-and-carry love.

Remarkable, Mason sometimes thought—and suffered guilt when he did—how one can, at once, love and hate one's own son.

MONDAY

Mason called Court Whitney's office first thing Monday morning to say he'd be a few hours late. He then drove to Alexandria, Virginia, where he went to a travel agency he'd never used before. After he told the agent he was thinking of taking a vacation trip to Turkey, or Crete, or maybe

Greece and some of its 437 islands, she gave him brochures and a tentative itinerary she'd be "happy to book once he'd firmed up his plans."

His day at the National Gallery was abbreviated by other appointments. He was to address a luncheon of art history students from George Washington University at the Hay-Adams Hotel and to confer in the afternoon at the offices of a Washington publisher interested in having him write a new book on Caravaggio, incorporating the discovery of *Grottesca*. That evening there was a dinner at the White House hosted by President and Mrs. Jeppsen, although Mason had heard that the president and first lady might be called away to attend the funeral of Mrs. Jeppsen's sister, who was close to death in a Wisconsin hospital. In that case, Vice President and Carole Aprile would host the evening. The guest list included Italy's minister of culture, Alberto Betti; Court Whitney and his wife, Susan; the president of Alitalia; two members of the National Gallery's Board of Trustees; and assorted others having to do with "Genius Comes to America: The Works of Michelangelo Merisi Caravaggio."

He stopped by Lynn Marshall's office on his way to the luncheon. "How are you?" he asked.

"Very well, thank you."

"About Saturday. I—"

"I really don't wish to discuss it. Frankly, I think there's been too much talk and not enough action."

He stepped inside and closed the door. "What do you mean by that? Sounds like a threat."

"Take it the way you will. I've been strung along by you for six months. Lots of promises, nothing delivered. I have tremendous respect for you, Luther. You've been a wonderful mentor, and I owe my job to you. But we have a relationship that extends beyond this building."

"A relationship that provided both of us with what we needed, I thought." That sounded weak, and Mason wished he hadn't looked in on her.

"Whatever," she said. "Just keep me in mind for that promotion."

He was tempted to explain once again his principles about the vacant job but thought better of it. So he said nothing. He left her office and walked slowly to his car, a yoke of apprehension and sadness weighing him down.

His talk to the students went well—they told him it had. So did the meeting with the publisher, despite his instant dislike for the editor, who seemed too interested for Mason's taste in turning a book about Caravaggio into a commercial success. Of course, it was all academic. He had no intention of writing another book about Caravaggio, or about anyone else for that matter. But it was necessary to go through the motions, maintain a credible schedule, to keep people from thinking any radical change in his life was on the horizon.

The lawyer for his ex-wife Cynthia called while he was struggling with his bow tie in preparation for the White House party. Struggle or not, no clip-ons for Luther Mason.

"You didn't return my phone call, Mr. Mason," said the attorney in the same bored voice Luther had heard on his answering machine.

"You are correct."

"Trying to avoid discussing this won't help either party, Mr. Mason. My client, your former wife, your second ex-wife, intends to pursue part ownership of what she represents to be your impressive and valuable collection of art."

Mason laughed. It felt good. "Let me tell you something," he said. "The art I own is marginally valuable. It represents certain things that tickled my fancy along the way. But I'll tell you what. I am extremely busy with an exhibition to open at the National Gallery this Friday. The first month of that exhibition will be especially stressful for me. When that month is over, I will call you and we will arrange to sit down. Frankly, I am not predisposed to give half of my art collection to Cynthia. I might give her all of it. But until the month is up, do not bother me again."

Guests for the dinner entered the White House through the oval Diplomatic Reception Room. Mason was no stranger to special rooms in the White House. Prompted by Mamie Eisenhower's efforts to return the presidential residence to its original state of decoration and furnishing—until she came on the scene, each administration simply got rid of most paintings and furniture and installed its own—President Lyndon Johnson appointed a standing Committee for the Preservation of the White House. Its members included heads of the Smithsonian Institution, the National Gallery of Art, and the Fine Arts Commission. The Committee was the final arbiter of how the public rooms were decorated; the first family was free to exercise its personal taste in the private quarters.

Wilfred Penny, a curator at the Smithsonian's Museum of American History, had been recruited by the Committee to curate the White House's substantial art collection. Mason and Will Penny were good friends; Penny frequently invited Luther on private tours whenever new works of art had been acquired.

Cocktails were served in the Blue Room, one of Mason's favorites, oval-shaped and approximately the same size as the Oval Office. He stood with a glass of white wine in his hand and looked out soaring windows to the Washington Monument. He was deep in a private reservoir of thought when Mac and Annabel Smith approached. "Good evening, Luther," Annabel said.

Mason turned, smiled, and shook Annabel's outstretched hand, then Mac's. "I'd forgotten you were on the guest list this evening," Mason said. "How nice to see you both again."

"You must be heady with anticipation," said Mac. "How many more days is it?"

"Three," Mason replied. "Then Friday morning's press breakfast. The show opens at noon. Never been such advance ticket sales for any exhibition in the Gallery's history."

"You must be bursting with pride," Annabel said.

"That, and hors d'oeuvres, and exhaustion."

Alberto Betti waddled into the room, accompanied by the Italian ambassador to the United States and his deputy. The two trustees from the National Gallery arrived in tandem with their wives; Mason realized he was the only one without a spouse or guest. He was also aware that neither the president and his wife, or Vice President and Mrs. Aprile, were on hand to greet their guests. He was thinking about that when a door opened and the Apriles appeared.

The vice president, who always appeared taller on television than he was, moved from person to person, a large smile on his face, his handshake firm. "The president and first lady unfortunately can't join us tonight," he told people. "Mrs. Jeppsen's sister passed away, finally. But the president let us borrow his house for the occasion."

Carole, Annabel noticed, didn't seem as ebullient as her husband. She was gracious to each guest, of course, and made the requisite small talk. But when she reached Mac and Annabel—by this time, Mason had wandered away to another group—she said, "Annie, can I speak privately with you for a minute?"

Mac and Annabel looked at each other. Carole laughed. "Nothing world-shattering, Mac. Just a girl sort of thing to straighten out. I promise I won't keep her longer than a minute."

"You can have her for two, but no more than that."

"Promise," Carole said, lightly touching Annabel's elbow and guiding her from the room.

The two women went up a narrow flight of stairs until reaching the State Floor, passed two Secret Service agents, and opened the door to the Red Room, a small formal parlor with, no surprise, crimson walls. Annabel crossed the room to admire two still lifes from the 1850s by Severin Roesen, then stepped back to better take in an Albert Bierstadt landscape. "The White House is an art gallery of its own, isn't it?" she said.

"Yes," Carole replied. "Ever since Mrs. Eisenhower, and of course Mrs. Kennedy, there's been a concerted effort to find the paintings and furniture that used to be in this house, buy them back, and reinstall each piece. We're making pretty good headway. Come, sit." She indicated an upholstered chair at a small, round Lannuier table and sat opposite. "I have my own office near Joe's in the West Wing, but I sneak into this room after the tourists are gone. Somehow, I just seem to think better here."

Annabel looked around. "I can understand why. It's lovely."

"Yes, it is. But I didn't bring you up here to admire the Red Room. Look." Carole slid a single sheet of paper across to Annabel.

She read carefully. It was a confidential dispatch to Carole from the American Embassy's Press Office in Rome, routed through the arts council office.

SUBJECT: Press inquiry re: Future Caravaggio Art Exhibition at the National Gallery of Art, Washington, D.C.

Recent inquiries have been made of this office by a journalist from *Time* magazine. His area of inquiry is the exhibition of paintings by the Italian painter, Michelangelo Caravaggio, to open next Friday at the National Gallery. Said journalist claims that the Italian parish priest, Giocondi, was dismissed dishonorably from his priestly duties for theft, rather than having retired as previously stated. Said journalist, who is preparing a story to coincide with the opening of the exhibition, questions whether Father Giocondi's veracity can be trusted, considering his background. Further, he speculates whether the authenticity of the painting purportedly discovered by a National Gallery curator in the parish once served by Giocondi should also be called into question.

"What do you think?" Carole asked after Annabel had dropped the paper on the table. Annabel shrugged. "Maybe the good father was a disciple of John Dillinger, robbing the church because that's where the money was. Sorry, Carole. Don't mean to be flippant. It would be a shame for such a story to run in conjunction with the opening. But I don't see any real damage to come from it, except to feed the skepticism of the already skeptical. If Father Giocondi had been the one to come forward with *Grottesca,* I would say the situation might be more serious. But Luther Mason was the one who found the painting in the church. With his credentials and credibility, the fact that the priest might have stolen something in the past, and was defrocked, doesn't mean too much. At least that's how I would respond, if we're challenged by *Time,* or anyone."

"I agree," Carole said.

"Not only that, the experts who've examined it, with one or two minor exceptions—and even they haven't ruled it out, just adopted a wait-and-see attitude—say it came from Caravaggio's hand. No, I really don't see any great harm from this, aside from having to explain it to another group of journalists who'll want to follow up. Which means even bigger crowds, not to sound cynical."

Carole Aprile sighed deeply, spread her hands on the table, and smiled. "You've made my evening, Annabel. I needed reassurance."

"Of course, Carole, my first response could be conditioned by what I *want* to come of it. Mac always says a person's hopes or wishes don't make for perfect prophecy. Naturally, we'll have to follow up. Do you intend to tell Court Whitney and Mason? Want me to do it?"

"Court has to be told, of course. I'll give him a call in the morning. No sense injecting this sort of thing into a pleasant evening. Thanks for leaving that handsome hunk of a husband. Even for two minutes."

"The old man does look stunning in a tuxedo, doesn't he?" Annabel said, her voice cheerful. Both women wore evening dresses they'd purchased at Claire Dratch's boutique on Connecticut Avenue, Annabel's of *guipure* lace the color of sandstone, Carole's dress a pale-blue silk.

"Let's get downstairs before we're missed," said Carole.

If the Italian contingent to the party expected the White House to do what the National Gallery had done at its first black-tie dinner—create a menu to honor their ethnic tradition in food—they were to be disappointed. Few knew that Vice President Aprile's dislike of pasta rivaled George Bush's hatred of broccoli. It could have created an international incident if it got out, to say nothing of a serious drop in pasta sales, so popular was the V.P. They dined on watercress soup with sesame seeds, roast tenderloin of beef in a truffle sauce, tiny roasted potatoes, *haricots verts* and baby carrots, and a mixed green salad with herb dressing. Lime sorbet with a wine mousse, fresh raspberries, and cookies constituted dessert. Accompanying the meal were three wines: a 1990 Cuvaison chardonnay, a 1970 Baulieu Vineyards Georges de Latour cabernet sauvignon, and finally a 1987 Iron Horse brut, Summit Cuvée. Chianti never came into it.

"A thoroughly delightful evening, Mr. Vice President, Mrs. Aprile," Mason said as he was leaving. He'd been spared sitting close to Alberto Betti. Mac and Annabel Smith had had that pleasure.

"So happy you could be here this evening, Mr. Mason," said the vice president. "From everything my wife tells me, you have performed a remarkable service not only to the world of art, but especially to the National Gallery."

"I am honored to have been able to do so," Mason replied. He turned to Mac and Annabel, who were next in line. "Good to see you again, Smiths. You'll be at the press breakfast, Annabel?"

"Wouldn't miss it," she replied.

Mason turned to head for the door while Annabel continued to talk with Carole. He was intercepted by one of the National Gallery's trustees.

"Donations are pouring in faster than ever," the trustee said, smiling.

Mason heard him. Simultaneously, he heard from behind what Carole April was saying to Annabel: "I'll call you tomorrow, Annabel, on this question of Father Giocondi's background. I'd like to discuss it further with you *before* I call Court."

"What?" Mason stared blankly at the trustee.

"The donations," the trustee said. "Many and large. Are you all right?"

"What? Yes. Good to hear about the donations. Yes, that's good news. I've never felt better. Excuse me. Looking forward to seeing you Friday morning."

He trembled so on the way home that he feared he might lose control of his automobile. *What question about Giocondi?* What had gone wrong?

He called M. Scott Pims the moment he walked into his apartment.

"Ah, back from a pleasant evening rubbing elbows with the high and mighty. Better than the rich and famous."

"A pleasant evening. A good meal, in fact. Scott, have you heard anything from Rome about—well, about the priest, Giocondi?"

"No, I can't say that I have. Should I? Trouble?"

"No. No trouble. It's just that there was lots of conversation about him, and I wondered whether he perhaps had been interviewed by some Italian scandal sheet."

Pims's laugh was long and hearty. "Wouldn't

that send you racing to the nearest drug store for a year's supply of Tums."

"Just thought I'd ask, that's all. If anyone was likely to know, you would." Mason felt momentarily relieved.

"Free for dinner tomorrow night? I'll make it my business to know more by then. Come to think of it, it *is* my business. We can discuss it at length."

"I'm having dinner with Julian."

"If he shows up."

"I think he will. He needs money."

"Yes, money. The great motivator. Well, Luther, you sound tired. Get a good night's sleep. We'll be in touch tomorrow, dinner or not."

TUESDAY

The minute Court Whitney got off the phone with Carole Aprile, he summoned Mason to his office. "Did you know about Giocondi's checkered background?"

"Checkered?"

"Your friendly parish priest with the lost masterpiece in his closet has a record—a little larceny in his history—and managed to get defrocked in the process."

"This is news to me, Court. My understanding was that he was retired."

"The Vatican's diplomatic way of putting it. I

think you should talk to this *Time* reporter. He called me a few hours ago. I put him off." He handed Mason the reporter's number in Italy.

"Of course I'll call him. But it all seems silly, don't you think? I mean, what does it matter? Father Giocondi hasn't profited from having *Grottesca* sitting in his parish. His background, whatever it might be, has nothing to do with the painting."

"But a nuisance. And to think we showcased one light-fingered, slippery little priest at our first dinner. Call the reporter and put it to rest."

"I'll let you know how the conversation goes."

MEMO

TO: Courtney Whitney

FROM: Luther Mason

RE: *Time* magazine

Had a pleasant twenty-minute chat with the reporter. He agrees that Father Giocondi's past means little. Except, of course, it makes for a story, and I suppose journalists are always looking for stories, no matter how inconsequential. The reporter is dealing only from rumor. Seems he hasn't been able to locate Giocondi. Reporter assures me the story focuses on the exhibition, on Caravaggio's life, and that the Giocondi story is nothing more than a sidebar.

Mason was somewhat relieved after his soothing telephone call to the *Time* reporter and spent
most of the afternoon overseeing the hanging of
four more Caravaggios. He checked in with Whitney at five. "Go on home, Luther," the director
said, hearing traces of tension and fatigue. "I'm
sure you'll want to be bright and bushy-tailed in
the morning when *Grottesca* goes up."

"Yes, I am looking forward to that moment. By
the way, Court, my mother is arriving tomorrow
from Indiana."

"Oh? To see her son bask in his glory?"

"Something like that."

"Luther."

"Yes?"

"You've done a remarkable job with this exhibition. I can only say that the trustees—and I, of
course—are extremely grateful."

"It makes me feel good to hear you say that,
Court. Very good indeed. Good night."

When Julian had first come to Washington from
Indiana to pursue his college education, his father
had tried to introduce him to Washington's better
restaurants. The city didn't always have a selection of good ones from which to choose, its reputation for inferior food honestly earned. But that
was no longer the case. Restaurants of every
stripe, and encompassing every ethnic taste, pro-
liferated.

The problem was that Mason couldn't get Julian to dress appropriately for the fancier establishments of which he was especially fond. And so he eventually came to grips with the reality that when going out for dinner with his son, he had better get used to a burger-and-beer menu. Even then, he had standards, having come to the conclusion that the hickory-smoked hamburgers and feathery fried onion rings at Houston's in Georgetown were a cut above the others.

Julian was his usual brooding self—generational, Luther had decided. Everyone under thirty seemed to be brooding these days. All the models in men's clothing ads brooded—didn't smile or shave. The young men working in hair-styling salons looked as though they carried the future of Western Civilization in their fanny packs; giving a good perm was hardly that.

He examined this young man across the table who was his son, yet who seemed a stranger most of the time. Julian had inherited his mother's Mediterranean looks: dark eyes, olive skin, inky black hair pulled back into a pony tail. He wore a lightweight black turtleneck sweater and jeans in which he'd deliberately cut holes. This wanton destruction of good clothing bothered Luther, but he'd stopped commenting on it because the more he protested, the larger the holes.

"When do you have to appear in court?" Mason asked.

Julian shrugged. "I don't know. I lost the notice. I guess I threw it away."

"If you don't show up they'll put out a warrant for your arrest."

"Big deal."

Mason couldn't catch himself. "Yes, it *is* a big deal, Julian. Breaking the law *is* a big deal."

"Hey, chill out," Julian said. "Jesus."

Mason willed himself into a calmer state. They ordered mugs of tap beer.

"What is it you want to talk to me about?" Mason asked. "To thank me for bailing you out of trouble once again?"

"I want to go to Paris."

"Really? On a holiday?"

"No. I want to live there. With Mother."

The mention of Juliana caused her face to flash in front of Mason. He hadn't seen her in many years; was the face he now saw an accurate reflection of what she looked like today? He asked, "Have you been in touch with her?"

"Yes. She wants me to come. She thinks I could learn a lot by studying there."

"I don't doubt that, Julian. But there are some fine teachers here."

The little chuckle that came from the boy was his substitute for outright laughter. "In this city? There's no art here. It's nothing but one damn big bureaucracy. Washington sucks."

Another familiar argument about to erupt. But also a solution.

"I think you should go live with your mother," Mason said, holding his voice steady. "You're obviously unhappy here and have been for a long time. Yes. move to Paris. Study there. I think it would do you a world of good."

"I can't afford it," Julian said, downing the last of his beer and motioning for the waitress to bring him another before he drew a breath.

"No, thank you," Mason said. "I don't wish another beer, but thank you for asking."

Julian ignored the sarcasm. He rested his elbows heavily on the table; his brow creased as he formulated what to say next. "I need money to do it," he said. "It will cost a lot to move there. And I'll need money to live."

"You'll live with your mother," Luther said. "That won't cost you anything."

"I don't want to live with my mother. I want my own place."

"Do you, now? Then I suppose you'll have to get yourself a job in Paris."

"Fat chance. I don't speak French. If you could give me enough to live for a year I could probably get something going by then."

The nerve, Mason thought. The sheer gall. Did he think that because he wished to become an artist the world owed him its support? The cities were filled with young, aspiring creative people waiting tables and driving cabs while learning their craft and seeking success as artists, dancers, musicians, or actors. The majority of them, of course, had no business, to say nothing of talent, to be seeking careers as artists. Lynn Marshall came to mind. All fantasy, movie-star stuff, or worse, Julian Schnabel, or Christo wrapping buildings and landscapes in plastic, of all things. If that had been the case with Julian, Luther would have attempted to dissuade him. But the truth was, Julian had talent. A great deal of it. Luther had seen steady progress in the work his son turned out since coming to Washington. One day, with the right additional training—and the right attitude—he could become a genuine artist with a following.

"I'll think about," Mason said.

"That's what you always say."

"It's the best I can do for now. Maybe in a few months. Something might be coming up that would enable me to help."

"Like what?"

"A book. I met yesterday with a publisher who wants me to do a new one on Caravaggio. It could mean a sizable advance. If it does, I'll help you move to Paris."

"When will you know?"

"A few months, I said. Maybe less." Luther waited for an expression of gratitude, but none came. It never did. It was as if at birth, Julian had been cheated of the gene of graciousness. He'd also never heard his son say, "I'm sorry." But when he thought back to Juliana, he realized those words hadn't been in her vocabulary, either. At least while they were together.

They ate their burgers with little more to say to each other.

Before leaving Houston's, Mason asked Julian for his mother's address in Paris.

"Why?" Julian asked.

"It's been a long time since I've had any contact with her. I thought it might be nice to write a letter, tell her how well you're doing, and let her know I approve in principle of your move to Paris."

"I think I have it here." He pulled a crumpled letter from the pocket of his jeans that bore Juliana's address. Mason dutifully copied it on a napkin and put it in his jacket pocket.

"Drive you home, Julian?" Mason suddenly felt a flood of warmth for his son.

"No. I'll walk."

"As you wish."

Once on the street, Mason clumsily attempted to hug his son, but Julian stiffened. "Find that notice of your court date, Julian. You don't want any trouble."

"Yeah."

Luther watched his son walk away, so tall and full of swagger. *Yes,* he thought, *go to Paris to study and be with your mother. Settle there and start to establish yourself in that city with such a rich history of art. Where you can breathe it in. I will help with more money than even you expect from me.*

Without warning, he began to weep. He quickly walked, embarrassed, to his car.

"Annabel? Steve Jordan. Hope I didn't wake you."

"No, but close. Mac and I are just getting ready for bed."

It was almost midnight. They'd been up talking about many things, including the dispatch to Carole Aprile from the Rome Embassy.

Annabel wondered whether Jordan had called to discuss some aspect of the sting in which she'd agreed to participate. She didn't want to have that conversation with Mac in the room.

But that wasn't on the art-squad chief's mind. "We found your Mr. Cedras," he said.

Annabel sat up straight on the couch. "You did? How?"

"Not a very pretty story, Annabel. Looks like the guy is more deranged than we figured. He used his hammer again, but this time it wasn't on a clay head. It was the real thing."

Annabel gasped.

"He found his ex-wife living in Adams Morgan. Beat her to death with that hammer. Neighbors called the police. When they got there he was sitting next to her body crying, the hammer in his hands."

"Oh, my God," Annabel said.

"What's wrong?" Mac asked, leaving his chair.

"Hold on, Steve." She whispered to Mac what Jordan had just told her.

"What a horrible ending to the story," Annabel said into the phone.

"Yeah," said Jordan. "Unfortunately, they end up that way too many times. When I get to see him tomorrow I'll ask about the Tlatilco."

"The Tlatilco sounds irrelevant now," she said.

"I know what you mean. But maybe it will help us put together a more complete picture of where this guy is coming from. Anyway, just thought you'd want to know."

"I appreciate the call."

She gave Mac a more complete accounting of the conversation once she'd hung up.

"All I can say is I'm glad he took it out on your clay figure instead of you."

"What pushes somebody like that over the edge, Mac? That line we all walk between sanity and insanity."

Mac shrugged, stood. "I think it's more a matter of how long you stay on the other side once pushed."

And how many people you annoy once you're there, thought Annabel.

WEDNESDAY

Until setting off on this Caravaggio odyssey, Luther Mason had always been a sleeper. No matter what turmoil surrounded him, he was able to sleep peacefully through the night.

Not this night. Sleep came in fits and starts. He gave it up at five Wednesday morning, showered, dressed in a gray tweed jacket, checkered shirt, yellow knit tie, slacks, and his favorite Rockport walking shoes, had breakfast, and was in his office in the East Building before seven.

This was the day *Grottesca* would be hung.

He checked with Design and Exhibition for the time the painting would be positioned on the wall. Nine-thirty, he was told.

He tried to pass the time handling paperwork, but he was preoccupied with other thoughts. Living on Hydra. Franco del Brasco. *Time* magazine. The ex-Father Pasquale Giacondi. Lynn Marshall. Julian.

He rode the interior moving walkway to the West Building and stepped into the gallery in which Caravaggio would be exhibited. *Grottesca* leaned against the west wall; two staffers from Conservation flanked it. Its frame was the simple one created by the New York framer.

Mason was transfixed as he stared at the painting, wanting to scoop it up and run.

"A beauty, isn't it, Mr. Mason?" a workman said.

"Yes. Oh God, yes. It is beautiful. Beyond description. He was the most revolutionary artist of his time, you know. Completely broke from tradition. No idealizing man and religion for Caravaggio. Everything was so dark and urgent, so real. Rembrandt was profoundly influenced by him. He—" Realizing he was giving the workman one of his lectures on Caravaggio, Mason smiled and said, "Yes, it's beautiful. Beyond description."

"I still think a more elaborate frame would serve it better."

Mason turned to face Don Fechter, who'd been eavesdroping.

"Don't you agree, Luther?"

Luther returned his attention to the painting and squinted. He used his hand to create an imaginary box around it, and said without looking back at Fletcher, "More elaborate? No, I think not. That's the usual Italian gallery approach. This is the perfect frame for it, Donald. We see the painting's strength, not the frame's."

Fechter stepped away as Whitney, wearing a new double-breasted gray suit tailored for him in London, lightly patted Luther on the back. "I knew I'd find you here," he said. "Excited?"

"Of course. This is a great moment for me. And for you and the National Gallery."

Luther, Whitney, Fechter, and others stood back as *Grottesca* was positioned in its place of honor on the wall. Luther saw now that he would have preferred it an inch lower, but those details had been painstakingly worked out earlier, the wall marked a week ago.

"Lunch?" Whitney asked as he and Luther headed back to the East Building.

"Love to, Court, but I have other plans. Perhaps another day. How is the breakfast shaping up for Friday?"

"Splendid. The biggest press turnout we've ever had for an opening."

"That's gratifying," Luther said.

Whitney stopped them before passing through glass doors leading to the ground-floor administrative offices' reception area. "I must tell you, Luther, that I had grave reservations about the *Grottesca* from the beginning. The unusual circumstances of finding it. The old priest. Your need to maintain secrecy, to use your own unnamed conservator. All of it. But I see now that everything you did was carefully thought out. A method to your madness." He grinned broadly. "Not only are you a curator without peer, Luther, you're a born public relations man. A real P. T. Barnum. All I can say is, well done! Bravo!"

Mason was astonished at how touched he was hearing the director's kind words. He said, "Your confidence in me means a great deal, Court. Thank you."

"Well, let's get upstairs and see what last-minute problems might have reared their ugly heads."

Mason had no sooner settled in his office than Lynn Marshall poked her head in. "Is it hung?" she asked.

"Yes. It looks wonderful."

"I'm sure it does. Luther, I—"

"I know what you're about to say, Lynn, but it isn't necessary. I would like to sit down with you tomorrow and have a long talk. Are you free for lunch?"

"I suppose so. But if you're not ready to—"

Luther held up his hand. "Don't jump to conclusions. Lunch tomorrow. I have something important to tell you. In the meantime, I would like a complete status report on our plans for returning *Grottesca* to Italy next month. Please have it on my desk by ten tomorrow morning."

"Including what?"

"Including everything. Logistics, packing, transportation, clearances, diplomatic plans, the reception in Italy. Whatever you can pull together."

"All right."

At noon, Mason drove home. Ten minutes later the doorman buzzed. "A man from a moving company down here to see you, Mr. Mason."

"Good. Send him up."

"You aren't planning to—?"

"Move?" Luther laughed. "No, Harry. Just planning to ship some nice paintings to my mother in Indiana. I'm running out of wall space."

The estimator from the moving company was a short, stocky young man wearing a black suit that was too tight for his body, who managed to be both ingratiating and condescending at once. Mason decided he'd sold used cars before going to work for the movers.

"Well, Mr. Mason, planning to move to Paris, huh?"

"I'm interested in what it will cost to ship everything from this apartment to Paris, France. I'm especially concerned about my paintings. I would want assurances that they would be packed in such a way that the chances of harm to them would be minimal. No. Nonexistent."

The young man slapped Mason's arm. Actually slapped his arm. "You bet," he said. "N-o-o problem."

"Follow me," Mason said, leading him to the bedroom at the rear of the apartment. The estimator carried a clipboard holding a form with multiple lines to fill in, and boxes to check.

"Are these famous paintings?" the estimator asked, looking at the art hanging in the bedroom.

"They are worth some money. Please, I must get back to work. Could you hurry a bit?"

"Sure. Only I want to do the right kind of job for you. We're not like other moving companies. They give you a lowball and then hold you up for more at the end. We pride ourselves on—"

Mason left him in the bedroom and went to the kitchen, where he took deep breaths and told himself to ignore the aggravation. Just get through it as quickly as possible.

A half hour later, the young man smartly removed the top copy of what he'd been filling out and handed it to Luther, snapping it like men on sidewalks handing out leaflets. "An honest price, Mr. Mason. A fair price. You can get another twenty moving companies to give you estimates. Most of them will come in lower and then jack you up at the end. Blackmail you, really. Not deliver your things until you pay up. You see, we've been in business for over thirty years and—"

"I am sure your company is an excellent one," Mason said, gently placing his fingers on the man's back and guiding him to the door. "Your estimate sounds just right to me. I'll need a few days to make final plans. I'll call you then."

"Better book us now," the estimator said. "This is a busy time of year. I'd hate to disappoint you."

"Good day, sir."

That night, Mason brought in Chinese food, put on a CD of Haydn's Symphonies No. 60, "Il Distratto," and No. 91 by his favorite chamber orchestra, Orpheus, and wrote a series of letters.

Dear Juliana:

I'm sure you'll be surprised, perhaps even shocked, to receive a letter from me after so many years without contact between us. As we agreed when we parted, it is better that we leave each other alone. Staying in touch after the candle of romance has dimmed, or gone out, only prolongs the hurt, I have always felt, and I know you share that feeling.

Still, I felt compelled to write after talking with Julian last night. He informed me that he was thinking of moving to Paris and studying there. I want you to know, Juliana, that I wholeheartedly agree with his decision and urged him during dinner to follow through on it. As you know, I am not one to compliment those not deserving of it—perhaps to a fault—even my own flesh and blood. But my eye tells me Julian has promise. He's quite talented. Studying with the right teachers in Paris, and falling under your benevolent spell, might be just what he needs to break through.

I am nearing retirement age, Juliana. Did I believe that day would ever come? Of course not. But it is, faster than I'm prepared to deal with it. When I do retire, I plan to leave the Washington area for some place less complicated, and less expensive. Because I have a penchant for ending and starting things cleanly, I will leave Washington without my furniture and the art I've managed to collect over the years. Some of that art comes from our earliest days together. Remember? We would seek out struggling young artists in San Francisco who we felt had talent, and one day would be famous. I want you to have those pictures, as well as others in my humble collection. If you decide not to keep them, feel free to sell them and use the money for your own purposes, and to help Julian get settled. I am also shipping you my furniture. Presumptuous of me, isn't it? But I don't know what else to do with it. It is an eclectic group; it's called Empire, although Art Deco comes more readily to mind. I would like to send it to Paris for you to dispose of, or to use. I have no idea of your living situation—you always favored sparse surroundings. If that is still the case, dispose of my furniture as quickly and profitably as possible.

This is the last time you will hear from me, Juliana. I will leave instructions with my lawyer about whom to contact when I die. You and Julian certainly top that list. I want you to know, Juliana, how much I've always loved you. We were both so young and unknowing. But we meant well, didn't we? I must admit that when you suggested my mother raise Julian, I was appalled. But that was because I was *supposed* to be aghast at having one's child raised by another. The fact is that I was as selfish as you. I did not want a child standing in the way of my career. To continue with this rare burst of honesty, I don't feel any different now, would not have done it any other way, even factoring in the wisdom I'm supposed to have gained with age.

You will find Julian to be a somewhat angry, brooding young man, not uncommon with his generation. Friends—one friend, actually—have likened him to Caravaggio. I have mixed feelings about that. I would hate to think of Julian ending up as Caravaggio did. On the other hand, the wild abandon with which Caravaggio led his life becomes more appealing as I slip into my declining years. Too late for me to shed my inhibitions and to run with the bulls, to ride naked and bareback in the moonlight? Probably. Then again, I might have one last gasp of irresponsible freedom left in me. Only time will tell.

Mother is arriving in Washington tomorrow to join me at the Caravaggio opening, which takes place on Friday. I'm apprehensive about seeing her. We were never especially close, and I am not looking to establish a closer bond than we currently have. But I felt it appropriate that she share this moment of triumph, if you can call it that, with me. You and she got along quite well, and I will give her your fond regards. She did ask for you the last time I spoke with her.

And so I close, Juliana, wishing you only good things, hoping your life is fulfilling and happy and that your memories of me are not all unkind.

Love,
Luther

Dear Julian:

By the time you receive this letter, I will no longer be in Washington. Instead, I will be where I can live out my remaining years in peace.

I have written your mother in Paris informing her of my support for your plan to move there and to study in that glorious city. I will also have arranged for my worldly goods, as they are called, to be shipped to your mother, including such artworks as I possess. You might find some of the furniture included in that shipment useful, should you decide to set up housekeeping in Paris.

You will undoubtedly hear stories about the unusual circumstances under which I seek a new life. Many of them will be true, although embellishment will warp that truth as time passes. The interpretations of my decision should matter little to you, Julian. We do what we must. As one of your icons, now deceased, put it, "Life is what happens while we're making other plans." I wish it had been one of my icons who'd said it, because I rather like the sentiment behind the saying.

What does matter, it seems to me, is that I love you very much. Perhaps even more important, I believe in you and your gifts. You could, should you apply yourself properly, achieve success as an artist. You were born with talent. What you do with it is now squarely up to you. My most fervent wish is that you make the most of it. That means hard work and a dedication to excellence. Only time will tell whether you have it in you to succeed.

Because I am your father, I am unable to curb the temptation to give you advice. I know how much you hate receiving advice from me. You might have noticed in recent years that I have given less of it, certainly when sitting across a table from you and running the risk of your angry reactions. Why so much anger, Julian? What is there to be angry at?

That you were not born to perfect parents? That you perceive yourself as having been "abandoned" by your mother and father, left to be raised by your stern grandmother? When you think about it, my son, your grandmother raised you in a loving and nurturing environment, more so than either your mother or I were capable of providing. We did what we thought was best under the circumstances, best for all parties involved. But I won't offend your intelligence and sensibilities by saying we did it for your own good. We did it for the mutual good of all the human beings involved, as silly and misguided as they might have been.

If your anger stems from the circumstances of your youth, I suggest you look in the mirror and acknowledge the fact that you are no longer a young boy. You are a man. Your life is here and now, and you must discard what I consider to be any sophomoric tendencies to blame everything that happens to you today on what went before. If you fail to do that, you remain a perpetual child, and your distasteful temper tantrums will continue until the day you die.

There is much about which I should feel guilt. But I do not. I have done my best in this life in all things, and with all people, failing miserably at times, succeeding nicely at others. Your mother and I leave you with what I consider to be a legacy upon which you can build a rich professional and personal life, should you desire. But no matter which road you choose to take, know that I love you and want only for good things to happen to you.

We will not see each other again, unless there is some unusual circumstance beyond the unusual circumstances that will separate us again. I will think of you every moment, Julian. Perhaps one day I shall anonymously visit your one-man show in Paris, or Rome, or even the National Gallery of Art, and will bask anonymously in the light of your talent, just as I have always done with the great artists whose work has been placed in my hands.

Love,
Father

Dear Cynthia:

By the time you receive this letter, I will not be reachable by you or your sour attorney. The art you and your attorney wish to confiscate will no longer be available to you. It has been donated to a worthy charity.

I do not believe in holding grudges. Carrying anger toward another person is a hurtful exercise that burdens one with unnecessary baggage as we go through life, particularly the later stages of it. But I'm afraid I must make an exception in your case, Cynthia. There is little I regret having done in my life. You represent an outstanding exception. I don't believe you ever cared about my well-being, nor that of any others with whom you came into intimate contact. Despite that, my dear, I shall demonstrate a largeness of spirit in forgiving you and hope that what is left of your life provides you with the sort of spiritual nourishment that seems to have eluded you so far.

I have found that elusive, precious commodity called *freedom.*

Sincerely,
Luther

My Dearest Lynn:
They say that as you grow older, you are supposed to become more conservative because you have more to conserve. I find my life taking a path quite contrary to that belief. I grow more liberal with each passing day, perhaps not politically, but certainly in the way I choose to live my life. If what I am about to do represents a liberal act, then I join the ranks of the great left thinkers.

Of course, someone once said that there is nothing sadder than an old liberal. I believe they were referring to Hubert Humphrey. But I find it even sadder when I see old men attempting to rejuvenate themselves on the arms of young women. Did people look at me that way when you and I entered restaurants, or the theater? I wince at the thought. A man my age can only take from vivacious and beautiful young women like you. For you have much to give, and I have little. Money? I don't possess much of that, as you know. Wisdom? Fatherly advice? A distinct possibility, although once we shared a bed together, my fatherly role, if that is what it was, was immediately tangled in the sheets we dampened together.

I have not always done the right thing with people, although Lord knows I've tried. I certainly want to do the right thing where you are concerned. Perhaps by the time you receive this letter, my suggestion that you be considered for the promotion on my staff will have become reality. I certainly hope so. I can do no more than to strongly urge that you be given the slot. If you are turned down, don't become disheartened. You have a bright future ahead of you as a curator, and I take pride in having helped create the foundation upon which you build your career.

You have given me much pleasure. For that I am grateful. You renewed my spirits, to say nothing of my slumping libido. Thank you for that, too. But we both know that the relationship we forged outside the walls of the National Gallery was meant to last only a moment in time. That it came to its logical and preordained conclusion now is fortuitous. I shall be leaving Washington under a cloud of accusation, perhaps disgust, on the part of those who view my actions from their own perspectives. I care not what they think. But I do care what you think of me, of our time together, of my hand in helping develop your already sensitive eye toward things of beauty. I take comfort in the fact that *my* eye has not lost its keenness. You are a thing of beauty, Lynn. A lovely painting that I had the pleasure of enjoying for however brief a time.

Be well. Think of me fondly and know that I have, at last, found the sort of true happiness I have sought my entire life.

Love,
Luther

TO: Courtney Whitney III

FROM: Luther Mason, Senior Curator

SUBJECT: My Resignation

This is to inform you in writing that effective this date, I am leaving my post as senior curator for the National Gallery of Art.

I view my years at the National Gallery with a sense of pride and accomplishment. Since joining this wonderful institution, I have not only watched it grow both in size and esteem, I immodestly take my share of credit for having contributed to that growth. I will have submitted the appropriate paperwork to the Personnel Office (one day the National Gallery must join the twentieth century and rename its Personnel Department the Human Resources Department, or some other euphemism, as others have) to arrange for my pension, 401K, and other benefits to be distributed to those I name. I will be seeking solitude in my retirement and thus will leave no forwarding address.

I wish you and your excellent staff every success in the future.

Sincerely,
Luther Mason, Senior Curator

Mother Dearest:

I write this letter on the eve of your arrival in Washington. I look forward so much to seeing you and to having you share in the celebration of the opening of my greatest achievement as a curator, the exhibition of works by Michelangelo Caravaggio.

Spending this time with you is especially important to me because it will be the last time we will see each other. I have made long-range plans, necessitating leaving my post at the National Gallery and going far away to live out what years I have left. Please don't misunderstand. I am not sick, not facing a terminal illness. But I have come to the conclusion that a man (or, of course, a woman) must pause at some point to assess what life has been so far and to determine how to face mortality in a way that will bring the maximum contentment. I believe I have come to the proper decision. Although it is fraught with potential problems, I am confident it will proceed as planned.

I have always wanted you to be proud of me. I know I have done things in my life of which you disapproved. Leaving Julian with you and going off to pursue my career certainly must head that list. But as I have written Julian, it was in the best interests of everyone concerned—Julian, Juliana, me, and, I am convinced, you. You did a wonderful job of raising my son and for that I shall be eternally grateful.

Because I will be dropping out of sight under unusual circumstances, I'm afraid it will be impossible for me to maintain contact with you, or with anyone else for that matter. Please try to understand. My silence shall not be born of neglect, simply pragmatic necessity.

I am not sure when I will be leaving, but I wanted this letter, as well as others, written and ready to be delivered when that time comes.

Thank you, Mother, for bringing me into this world and for nurturing my love of art. A parent can do no more than to prepare a child for a productive and fulfilling adult life. You did that for me.

I could go on, but there seems little more to say except that I love you very much and pray that you will think of me often, and in a positive light.

Love,
Your Son, Luther

He stopped writing, with a mist of tears in his eyes. He carefully addressed each envelope, inserted the letters, sealed them, and placed them in a small locked box he kept in the back of the closet. Writing the letters had been exhausting. He quickly cleaned up the kitchen, took out the garbage, dressed for bed, poured himself an unusually large snifter of brandy, and looked through the first Caravaggio book his mother had bought him so many years ago. He'd done it thousands of times; the pages were dog-eared and stained. He soon dozed off.

Waking at three, he stumbled into the bedroom and fell on the bed.

His dreams that night were torturous.

THURSDAY

After an abbreviated lunch with Lynn Marshall at which Mason announced that he intended to recommend her for the promotion—amazing, he thought, how pleasant things become when you're giving someone what they want—he met his mother's plane and took her to the Watergate. "You settle in, Mother. I'll pick you up for dinner at six."

He returned to the National Gallery and looked in on the Caravaggio gallery, where final touches were being put on the exhibition for its opening at noon the following day. He then checked his office for messages before heading home for a quick shower and change of clothes. The phone rang as he was about to leave. He debated; he was running late and didn't want to keep his mother waiting. But his hand automatically went to it. "Hello."

"Signor Mason?"

"Yes. Who is this?"

"I am calling on behalf of Mr. Franco del Brasco." The heavy Italian accent caused Mason's heart to thud against his chest.

"Mr. del Brasco wants to know whether everything is in order."

"Why wouldn't it be? Everything is—who are you? What's your name?"

"Mr. del Brasco wishes you to know that he expects your business with him to be carried out as agreed upon."

"Of course. As agreed."

"I will tell Mr. del Brasco. He wishes you to telephone him at your earliest convenience."

Luther wanted to say that he was not about to discuss anything with someone who refused to give his name but wasn't sure that was prudent. "Tell Mr. del Brasco," he said, "that everything is going as planned. And I would appreciate it, sir, if neither you nor Mr. del Brasco telephoned me here. He has my home number."

"Of course. Congratulations on your exhibition. I look forward to seeing *Grottesca.*"

"You? You have a ticket?"

"I understand it is very beautiful."

"The breakfast? Will you be at the breakfast?"

"Have a pleasant evening, Signor Mason. *Arrivederci.*"

He tried to put the call out of his mind during dinner at J. D. Cook's, choosing to take his mother and Julian there because it represented the quintessential Washington power restaurant, at least for the moment; there would be a D.C. celebrity or two to point out.

The maitre d' raised an eyebrow (Julian wore his favorite black turtleneck sweater; at least he hadn't worn pants with expensive holes) but said nothing. Sadly, there were no familiar faces in the restaurant that night, just dark-suited lobbyists, back room power-brokers whose effectiveness depended in part upon a lack of public recognition.

Mason felt very much the spectator during dinner, as he often had when his mother and Juliana forged their close relationship. Now, he welcomed it. Julian demonstrated a surprising spark while talking with his grandmother, and her spirits seemed buoyed by being with her only grandchild, her eyes glistening a few times when Julian recounted stories from his teen years with her.

"Your father says you want to move to Paris," Catherine Mason said as dessert was served.

"Yes. To live with Mother. And to study."

"Your father says he likes the idea."

The son looked at his father and managed a smile.

"I think it's a good idea, too," she said.

"I'll be helping him get settled there," said Mason. "Paris is expensive."

"You should," his mother said.

"I'll be sending Julian money."

"Sending?" Julian said.

"Yes. I mean, not all at once. Not right away."

"I can help you, Julian," his grandmother said.

"Would you?"

"There's no need," Mason said. "I will have—I may write another book about Caravaggio. The advance will be enough."

"But I need some now," Julian said directly to

his grandmother. "I can't stand it here in Washington any more. I'd leave tomorrow."

Mason felt a flush spread over his cheeks. "We can talk about this at another time." He knew his mother had some savings, enough when combined with her pension and insurance proceeds to live comfortably in Indiana. That Julian would use this dinner to seek money from her was inappropriate, he thought. Sad, but not surprising.

"I'm sorry, Grandma, but I have to leave," Julian said after finishing dessert. "I'm meeting someone."

"So soon?"

"I'll see you tomorrow at the opening." Julian stood and kissed her forehead. Then, as an afterthought, he bent over and awkwardly embraced her. "Good night, Dad," he said.

"Such a handsome boy," Catherine said when he was gone. "He looks like Juliana."

"Yes, he does, doesn't he? About moving to Paris—there's no need for you to give him money. I'll be able to support him until he's settled and has a job."

His mother smiled sweetly. "That's good," she said. "He's your only son. You should help him any way you can."

"Well," Mason said, placing his hands on the table and sitting upright, as if injecting energy into his posture, "What would you like to do for the rest of the evening?"

"I'm very tired," she said. "The flight made me tired."

Luther was not unhappy to hear that because he was exhausted. "Then I think the best thing to do is take you back to your lovely suite in the Watergate and let you have a good night's sleep. It's a fine hotel. Glad the break-in and all the notoriety didn't spoil it."

"It spoiled Mr. Nixon," she said. "He wasn't a bad man."

Mason called for the check.

Once she was safely ensconced in her room, Mason said he would send a car for her at eight the following morning. "I'll be tied up with the press breakfast," he explained. "The exhibition formally opens at noon. I would come and pick you up myself except that I—"

"A car? You mean a limousine?"

"Something like that. Not quite as fancy. The driver will call your room when he arrives. When you get to the Gallery, just tell the guard to contact me."

"All right, Luther. Where are you going now?"

"Straight home." He kissed her cheek, smiled, and added, "I'm glad you're here."

While the three Masons dined, Annabel Reed-Smith was having dinner at I Ricchi with an old friend, Carolyn Stoltz, a psychologist in private practice in Washington. Her clients, many of them

Washington movers and shakers, went to her for her professional insight as well as for her reputation for discretion. Her approach to psychotherapy was short-term, as opposed to the Freudian analytic model, which she sometimes referred to as "wasteful archaeological digging."

Dr. Stoltz was also one of the city's leading forensic psychologists. When not seeing high-powered clients in her office, she could be found at the city jail, interviewing and evaluating accused criminals for either the defense or the prosecution. She'd spent that morning with Joseph Cedras, having been appointed by the court to evaluate his mental state. Because her involvement with Cedras had been court-ordered, the traditional doctor-patient relationship did not apply and she was free to discuss the case with Annabel.

". . . and he's clearly schizophrenic," Carolyn said. "His delusional, obsessive personality certainly doesn't come as any surprise."

"Funny," Annabel said, "but I can better understand a sick man murdering another *person* than I can smashing an inanimate object like my Tlatilco."

Stoltz, who wore a tailored black suit, a white silk blouse with a large bow at the throat, and oversized round glasses, said, "It has to do with a lot of factors, Annabel. I won't bore you with the Freudian theories of prephallic phases of psychosexual development, as opposed to the phallic-oedipal phase, but—"

"Thank you," Annabel said, laughing.

"It could get worse," Stoltz said, joining her. "I could launch into the whole fixation of libido at the anal-sadistic stage—but I won't do that either. In simpler terms, it has to do with what's called the Myth-Belief Constellation."

"Oh?"

"A fascinating thesis. We all have a series of myths laid on us while growing up. This is fine as long as we recognize that they are just that, myths, and don't turn them into our adult beliefs. Cedras believes two things. First, that the sole cause of all his problems—his business folding following his divorce—was his wife, Maria. That's a myth, of course, but it became his belief. But people like this can also fixate—become obsessional—on inanimate objects like your pre-Columbian statue. In a sense, you gave it 'life' by using it as a metaphor for cooperation. I believe he thought that by smashing the statue, he would be rid of the things that were causing so much torment in his life."

"If that had been the case," Annabel offered, "his wife would be alive today."

"Yes. But people with an obsessional neurosis are in great and constant pain, always looking for an external reason for it. If they can identify and get rid of it, they believe their pain will go away. Of course, it never does because it comes from within."

"I assume you're telling the court that he's insane, at least to the extent of not being responsible for his actions."

"Sure. That's the only professional conclusion I can reach. We all have our obsessions, our compulsions. The difference is that most of us don't cross that line into an irrational playing out of them, at least not in an antisocial sense."

"Mac said the other day that it isn't so much crossing the line but how long we stay on the wrong side—and how many people we annoy."

Stoltz laughed. "Well put. Does Mac have obsessions?"

"Oh, yes," Annabel replied. "Little ones that make our life better. He can't go to bed unless he's mixed a certain blend of coffees and gotten the coffeemaker ready the night before. Big ones like responding like a firehouse dog to any criminal case that comes along. And being obsessed with my personal safety, keeping me out of harm's way."

"Harmless enough," Stoltz said. "You can understand his concern for you. It's when people act upon their obsessions in a way that hurts someone else that we have problems. Like Cedras. Like men or women who become fixated upon another person and end up stalking them, sometimes with dire results. I treated a man not too long ago, an otherwise upstanding member of the community, good job with the government, wife, two-and-a-half kids, not a blemish on his record. He became obsessed with a friend's collection of autographs of famous people. So much so that he stole it."

"My goodness," said Annabel. "Was he arrested?"

The doctor shook her head. "He confided this to me during one of our sessions. It took a few weeks, but I convinced him to return the collection to his friend and to admit he'd taken it."

"Did he? Return it?"

"Yes. His friend was understandably upset, but my client's honest confession went a long way toward restoring their relationship. The point is, admiring that autograph collection, even wanting it badly, was okay until he acted. Maybe I shouldn't have painted him as quite as normal as I did. Down deep he suffered a lot of pain having to do with his childhood. Not a very happy one. As far as he was concerned, he had everything he could possibly want, but the pain wouldn't go away. He believed that if he could only have that collection, everything would be fine."

"Does Mr. Cedras admit having smashed my Tlatilco?"

"Yes. And he justifies it, exactly as having murdered his wife is justified in his twisted thinking."

As they parted on the sidewalk, Annabel said, "I must admit I do have one obsession, Carolyn.

There's a piece of pre-Columbian I sometimes I think I would give my right arm to have."

"Don't do it," Stoltz said. "But if you decide to, call me, day or night. Two arms are better than one."

The women went in opposite directions. As Annabel neared her car she remembered she hadn't checked the answering machine installed in the Atlas Building by Steve Jordan and his art squad. There was a phone booth on the corner. She removed a slip of paper from her purse, on which she'd written the number, and dialed it. As her outgoing message played, she punched in the two pre-programmed numbers that would play back what messages had been received. Until that moment, the only thing she'd ever heard was an electronic male voice saying, *"You have no messages."*

This night, that same grating voice said, *"You have one message."*

Annabel held her breath as she heard the tape rewind. Then, a man's voice, distinctly human, said: *"I have objects that I understand you might be interested in purchasing. I will call you tomorrow night at this same number at eleven. If you are interested, be at your phone to receive my call."*

Annabel quickly dialed another number. It was answered by Ruth Jordan, Steve Jordan's wife. "Mrs. Jordan, this is Annabel Reed-Smith. Sorry to bother you at home, but something important has come up I thought Steve would want to know about."

"Of course. I'll get him."

Jordan came on the line.

"Steve, it's Annabel. I just called the answering machine in the Atlas Building. There's a message on it." She told him what the caller had said.

"Okay," Jordan said. "Looks like this little adventure might pay off. Can we get together tomorrow at your gallery, say noon?"

"Afraid not. The Caravaggio exhibition opens tomorrow, and I'll be tied up from early morning until sometime in the afternoon. Could we make it later? Three?"

"Sure. Three o'clock, your place. See you then."

FRIDAY

The cameraman focused tightly on the painting, then pulled back to include Pims in the shot. Pims wore a red double-breasted blazer, a pink-and-white striped shirt, and a large floppy bow tie in a Picasso print. "I am M. Scott Pims, your benevolent host of this week's *Art Insider,* brought to you through the extreme generosity of viewers like you who support this public station. Behind me is a work of art called *Grottesca,* painted toward the end of the sixteenth century by a most talented and disturbed artist, Michelangelo Merisi Caravaggio. It appears at our esteemed National Gallery of Art for the next thirty days as the shining focal piece of a six-month Caravaggio exhibition. How it ended up here, after it had gone missing for hundreds of years, is a story as fascinating as the artist himself. Courtney Whitney III, director of the National Gallery, is with me to explain."

The cameraman stopped taping as Whitney stepped into the frame, shook Pims's hand, and faced the camera.

"Roll," Pims said.

"Speed," the soundman said.

"Well, Court, you've mounted quite a spectacle," Pims said.

"All I can say is that this remarkable work behind us not only represents the ability of an artist to create great art, it testifies to the dedication of the men and women of the National Gallery to bring it to the American people."

"Luther Mason topping the list, of course," Pims said.

"Luther, our senior curator, and every other employee of this gallery."

"Not bad, either, for the National Gallery's bottom line," Pims said, accompanied by his patented chuckle.

"But not in the way you mean it," Whitney said, his smile less spontaneous. "This institution is run with federal money appropriated by the House Appropriations Subcommittee of Congress. The increased donations we're enjoying mean a greater private fund from which to purchase even more great art. And," he added politically, "to reduce the need for money from government. Nice to see you again."

"One last question," Pims said. "What about recent reports that this building is in such disrepair, many of the masterpieces are in physical jeopardy?"

"As Mark Twain might have said, the reports of our deterioration are vastly exaggerated. Now you must excuse me. Enjoy the exhibition."

Luther Mason stood with his mother and Lynn Marshall while Pims looked at Whitney's retreating figure. He'd asked Lynn to escort his mother during the breakfast to free him up for media interviews he'd agreed to give.

"Luther," Pims said. "Come. Time for your fifteen minutes of fame."

Mason excused himself and joined Pims. "Ready?" Pims asked the cameraman. He got the nod, smiled into the camera, and said, "With me now is National Gallery senior curator, Luther Mason, one of the world's acknowledged Caravaggio experts and the person who found

Grottesca in that small, run-down church in Italy. Quite a coup you've pulled off, bringing it here first to Washington's National Gallery."

Mason managed a lank smile as he said, "It was just a matter of time before someone found the *Grottesca*. I happened to be in the right place, at the right time."

"A shining example of modesty in speech, but excelling in action. *Grottesca* will be with us for one month only. Then back to Italy. I understand you will accompany it on its journey home."

"Along with others." Mason's eyes danced over the hundred faces watching the interview. He saw Annabel Reed-Smith standing with Don Fechter and George Kublinski. Court Whitney's attention was on what a trustee was saying, something funny, because Whitney was laughing, or not funny but getting a laugh anyhow, the other man being not only a trustee but a major donor. The Italian ambassador to the United States was flanked by a half-dozen members of his staff, including the two men who'd so intently observed Luther and Carlo Giliberti talking the night of the first black-tie dinner. Had one of them been his caller the previous night? A macabre thought came and went: *They won't kill me on television.*

"Congratulations, Luther," said Pims. "The art world shall be forever in your debt."

Luther walked away as the Italian ambassador, accompanied by a public information aide, joined Pims on his makeshift set.

"Sorry I can't spend more time with you this morning, Mother," Luther said. "Have you had enough to eat?"

"Oh, yes."

"Luther." Lynn Marshall motioned him away from Catherine Mason. "She wants to leave. Wants to go back to Indiana this afternoon."

"Why?"

"I think she feels out of place."

"I'll try to—"

"She's fine, Luther. But maybe she should go back. She's an old lady."

Mason thought for a moment. "Yes, she is. Would you check on flights this afternoon? She's booked tomorrow. Maybe they can change it."

"Of course."

"Surely she'll stay for the opening."

"I'll see that she does. I know how important it is to you." She looked fondly into his eyes.

At one, an hour after the doors opened for the ticket-holding public to view the Caravaggios, Luther put his mother in a chauffeured car for her trip to National Airport. "Remember," he said, "I'll be taking care of all of Julian's needs in Paris. No need for you to give him any money."

"I'm very proud of you, Luther. You are quite the celebrity."

"For today," he said.

In a little over a month he would be a celebrity of a different stripe. Would she live out the rest of her life ashamed of her only son, unable to face neighbors and friends? Would the media want to interview her? "What was he like as a child? Any signs of criminal behavior? Did he torture small animals?"

"You take care, Mother. Thank you for coming. I love you."

"Thank you for having me, Luther. My, how impressed my friends will be."

He watched her leave, feeling at once pain and relief. He went back inside, where he was intercepted by Matt Miller, assistant director of personnel. "Got a minute, Luther?" Miller asked.

"Of course."

"It's about Ms. Marshall. The committee turned down your request for her to fill the opening on your staff. She's obviously bright and talented, but there are others with credentials and seniority that better match up with the opening. Sorry."

"Yes. I'm disappointed, of course. She will be, too."

"Her future's bright. Just a matter of time."

"I'll tell her."

Mason hoped he could postpone telling Lynn the bad news, but she was at his side the moment Matt Miller walked away. "What was that all about?" she asked.

Mason drew a deep breath. "Afraid—the personnel committee turned down my request for your promotion."

Her earlier adoring look turned to one of anger and suspicion. "They wouldn't override you," she said.

"Afraid they would, and did. Matt says your future is bright and—"

"Did you stand up for me?"

"Yes. Stand up? There's really not much I can do, Lynn. I tried my best for you. You'll just have to have patience."

" 'I tried my best for you,' " she mimicked. "Like you did with my gallery showing?"

"Lynn, stop being ungrateful. There is only so much I can do. Now I suggest—"

"Suggest nothing. I'm going home. I don't feel well."

Scott Pims and his crew left the gallery at two. "I have to put tonight's show together in a rush," he told Mason. "I have a number of elements to weave into it. You will, of course, watch it with me tonight."

"I hadn't planned on it."

"Well, change your plans. I think you'll find it immensely interesting. I-m-m-e-n-s-e-l-y!"

"Really?"

"An M. Scott Pims money-back guarantee. Be at my apartment at eight. I won't have time to prepare a meal with my own hands, but I've already ordered in from the European Market in Rockville. My production assistant is picking it up and delivering it to the apartment at seven. Wonderful conveniences, production assistants. They'll do almost anything to please. But then you already know that with Ms. Marshall. Their sardines are fiery good sprinkled with *piri piri* and grilled. And their *presunto* hams are better than prosciutto. Did you know, Luther, they let them hang for six months or more? And rub them with coarse salt and white wine and paprika and olive oil?" He slapped his large hand over his heart. "That, and more tonight for the curatorial toast of Washington, Luther Mason. Ta-ta. Mustn't disappoint my panting public."

The exhibition closed at four. Fifteen minutes before, Mason stood admiring the *Grottesca* anew, along with the last group of spectators to enter the gallery that day. As he felt himself drawn into the painting, a voice from behind snapped him out of his trance. He turned to look into the face of one of the two men from the Italian Embassy who Carlo Giliberti had said worked for Luigi Sensi. "A most unusual piece," the man said in the same voice Mason had heard on the phone the previous evening.

Mason went rigid. "Yes, it is. I'm Luther Mason. You are—?"

"I know who you are, Signore Mason. Carlo spoke often of you."

"Carlo. What a tragedy. You work for the embassy."

"*Si. Buon giorno,* Signore Mason. "You have done well."

"Have more ham, Luther."

Pims had grilled the sardines and set out the other dishes from the European Market. He served a red Portuguese table wine from a vineyard in Dao with dinner and a tawny port after.

At ten, a sleepy Luther Mason watched as Pims turned on the television set.

"I am M. Scott Pims, your benevolent host of this week's *Art Insider,* brought to you through the extreme generosity of viewers like you who support this public station. Behind me is a work of art called the *Grottesca.*"

The brief interview with Whitney played out. Pims now spoke from his familiar armchair on the set. For the studio portion he wore a white shirt, a broad tie with an image of the Mona Lisa on it, her breast adorned with a red ribbon indicating solidarity with the AIDS movement, and a vermilion silk smoking jacket with black lapels.

"I have attended far too many openings to comment upon, or even remember, in my long and illustrious career. But I have never seen anything like this."

Visual images captured that morning at the National Gallery played on a large screen behind Pims.

"Despite the National Gallery's decision to issue tickets in advance for the first month of the exhibition, literally thousands of people showed up in a misguided attempt to enter on this first day of Caravaggio's naked presence in Washington. Of course, the incredible events leading up to the discovery of one of the artist's long-lost masterpieces, *Grottesca,* did nothing to quell public fascination with this exhibition, which will run for six months, but with *Grottesca* on display here for only the first of those months."

A closeup of *Grottesca* now dominated the screen.

"This remarkable painting was discovered in a run-down former church outside the town of Ravello, Italy. The National Gallery's senior curator Luther Mason came across the missing painting in that church and arranged for it to be brought to Washington to join some thirty other Caravaggio works. Circumstances surrounding this discovery—

which might rank as one of the most important in the history of art—were unusual, at best. Living in the church was an old, retired priest by the name of Giocondi."

The mention of Father Pasquale Giocondi caused Luther to sit up straight and lean toward the large television set.

"But perhaps Father Giocondi was not all he represented himself to be."

Luther's eyes widened as the screen behind Pims filled with an exterior view of the small, decaying church in Ravello. "Scott, what are you about to—?"

The big man held up his hand for silence.

"According to official Vatican records, Father Giocondi was honorably retired from the priesthood. But rumor has it that this sweet, gentle little old man was actually drummed out of the spiritual corps for having taken money from his parishioners."

"Scott!"

"Hush, Luther."

Father Giocondi was now on the screen talking to an unseen person, his remarks translated into English.

"Vicious rumors," he said. "Jealousy. What is important is that this work of art by the genius Caravaggio has been restored to its rightful owners, the people of Italy. Signore Luther Mason is a wonderful man. *Grottesca* will be at his famous museum in Washington, D.C., for only one month. Then it will be returned to our country. I thank the Lord Jesus Christ for giving me the opportunity to serve him and mankind in bringing this important work to the attention of Signore Mason."

"Scott, what the hell do you think you're doing?" Luther fairly shouted, getting to his feet.

Pims smiled up at him. "Relax, Luther. Sit and wait until the end of the program."

Pims signed off twenty minutes later:

"A remarkable story, of course. Was the Italian cultural attaché to the United States, Carlo Giliberti, murdered over this long-lost Caravaggio? Possibly. Was Father Pasquale Giocondi dishonorably discharged by the Vatican? Perhaps. But that is not important. This humble little priest does not profit from the discovery of *Grottesca*. Nor does the esteemed curator who discovered it in Giocondi's church, Luther Mason. The only profit derived from the discovery of *Grottesca* falls to the millions of people who will be inspired as they stand and gaze at it in a gallery in the West Building of the National Gallery of Art, right here in Washington. And then, the citizens of Italy shall bask in its glory for all time—provided, of course, that someone doesn't decide to steal it again.

"I am M. Scott Pims, your eyes and ears on the world of art. See you next week. And remember, 'All passes. Art alone enduring stays to us. The bust outlasts the throne.' *Ciao!*"

He clicked off the set.

"Where did you find Giocondi?" Mason asked, unable to discipline his anger. "Why did you have to bring up the question about his background?"

"Dear Luther, please. Your glass is empty. More port is in order. Help yourself."

Mason did as he was told and resumed his chair. His hand shook; the liquid in his glass undulated in small amber waves.

"Luther, I have done you a great service with this report. I was obligated to bring up the rumor. *Time* is running the story this week, and I hate to be scooped by some reporter from a magazine who knows less than I do. The fact is, I have debunked the rumor in my own inimitable fashion. As for finding your priestly friend, you know I have contacts everywhere. I must admit it wasn't easy, but I reward my network of correspondents well for good information."

"I just wish you'd talked to me before you did this," Mason said, attempting a sip from his glass. Some port missed his mouth and went down his shirtfront. He pulled a handkerchief from his pocket and dabbed at it.

Pims laughed. "You really weren't made for a life of crime, Luther."

"Don't ever refer to it as that," Luther said. "I must go."

"Of course. Nothing like a good sleep after such a monumental triumph. My program aside, it was a splendid day for you, wasn't it? You even had your mother here to share the glory. You say she left this afternoon? Terribly short stay."

"She was uncomfortable being away from home. I don't think she's left Indiana in twenty years."

"Julian took her to the airport?"

"No. I hired a car and driver." He was doing it again, answering every question put to him by his friend. "Good night, Scott. I'm sorry if I had too negative a reaction. I see your point. It was a good report."

Pims struggled from his chair and accompanied Luther to the door. "You still plan to switch the paintings in Italy?" he asked.

Mason hesitated. "Yes," he said.

"I suggest you reconsider."

"Why?"

"Too unpredictable. It will be chaotic there. Far better to accomplish the deed in familiar surroundings. Like the National Gallery."

"I see your point. But I haven't given much thought to doing it there. I thought—"

"Ah, my dear Luther, in a world of clods and louts you provide a refreshing ray of sunshine. Sit a few more minutes and allow me to outline how it can be done. Unlike you, *I* have given it considerable thought."

A half hour later Pims wrapped his sizable arms about Mason and hugged him. "Safe home. No detours through Rock Creek Park. One murder over Caravaggio is quite enough."

His answering machine was filled with messages when he returned to his apartment. Most were congratulatory calls, warm and glowing expressions of praise. He hoped Lynn was among the callers. Surely she'd realize how untenable his position was and apologize. Her voice was not among the callers. Nor was Julian's. His son had stayed at the opening only briefly and had left without saying goodbye.

He reviewed the report Lynn had left on his desk that morning regarding the return of *Grottesca* to Italy. It would be crated and transported there in thirty-two days. Luther consulted the calendar on his desk and circled a date one week after that.

He went to the Virginia travel agent Saturday morning and booked his trip to Hydra, walking out with the ticket in his pocket. He then returned home and arranged for the moving company to pack up his apartment the day before he would leave the country.

One month to go.

One more month to survive in a lifetime of months.

TWENTY-FOUR

ONE MONTH LATER

LUTHER MASON and Courtney Whitney III sat alone in the director's office, Whitney in a club chair, Mason on a matching sectional. An easel across the room held an Anne Vallayer-Coster still life recently acquired by the gallery through the generosity of an anonymous donor. The window draperies were open. Night was arriving. Powerful floodlights bathed the Capitol in a soothing, peaceful glow that did not accurately reflect what went on inside during the day.

"How do you feel, Luther?" the director asked.

Mason shrugged, exhaled. "Drained. And exuberant."

"Drained I can understand. Exuberant? About having *Grottesca* leave us?"

A smile crossed Mason's lean lips. "You know me too well, Court. I left out sad. Yes, there is a profound sadness at having *Grottesca* leave the National Gallery."

"They've planned quite a homecoming celebration in Ravello. Feel up to it?"

"I think so, although I could certainly do without this trip."

Whitney laughed. "I never thought I'd hear you complain about a trip to Ravello. But I know what you mean. There wasn't any decision to be made. The Italian government, Minister Betti in particular, insisted you be present. Hands-across-the-sea sort of thing. Actually, you should be flattered. The Italians could have told us to simply send the painting back without fanfare."

"Maybe that would have been better."

Whitney went to the window. "Looks like a beautiful evening. What time is your flight tomorrow?"

"Noon. I'll accompany the painting to the airport."

Without looking back, Whitney said, "Luther, I hate to delve into anyone's personal life, but I feel compelled to do that with you." He turned to face him. "Are you all right?"

"Of course. Why do you ask?"

"Your behavior since *Grottesca* arrived. Paul has expressed concern, too."

"Paul Bishop? Why would he be concerned about me?"

"I know there's little love lost between you and Paul, and a hell of a lot of professional jealousy. But Paul is a decent man. He has a personal fondness for you."

Mason wanted to laugh but didn't. Instead, he said nothing.

"I've also noticed what Paul's referring to," Whitney said. "I passed by the Caravaggio gallery the other day and saw you standing in front of *Grottesca,* staring at it as though mesmerized. I kept going. When I returned fifteen minutes later, you were in the same spot. You hadn't moved."

Luther replied, "You might say I've taken every opportunity this past month to soak it up. It's like knowing someone will die in a month and wanting to embrace that person for every possible living moment. I knew the minute it arrived that I would have this limited time to examine it, to revel in its detail. If that seems—well, if it seems weird to you and Paul, I can only say that it isn't. The study of Caravaggio has consumed my professional life. The last opportunity I'll have to appreciate the work is when they hang it in the church in Ravello."

Whitney sat on the arm of the sectional and placed his hand on the curator's shoulder. "Luther, my only concern is your well-being. I expect many more years of outstanding service from this senior curator and would hate to think the emotional, and I suppose physical strain of this exhibition might have depleted you."

"I assure you that isn't the case. But I appreciate the sentiment behind your words, Court." He stood. "I'm fine. A good night's sleep is all I need, and a pleasant flight tomorrow, accompanied by my friend, Signore Grottesca." He laughed. "I talk as though I'm accompanying a child."

"The Italian ambassador and his staff will be with you," said Whitney. Richard and Maureen from Public Information. Annabel Reed-Smith representing the White House. The journalists who've signed on—I think there are four, including your friend, Mr. Pims."

"Yes. Scott decided at the last moment."

"I sometimes wonder, Luther, how you can remain friends with him."

"Why?"

"He's so—he's so—I'll be direct—he's so—"

"Obnoxious?"

"I'm glad you said it, Luther."

"Scott can be overbearing. But there are redeeming qualities."

"I suppose there are. Just hard to see. Well, it should be quite a party in Ravello."

"And I'd better get home to pack," Luther said. I can only thank you again, Courtney, for your kindness and professional support."

"All of it heartfelt," Whitney said, his arm draped over Luther's shoulder as he escorted him to the door. "You ought to take a few extra days in Italy. Relax. Soak up some sun. You'll be in your favorite town."

"Maybe when the exhibition is finally over."

"You did a wonderful job, Annabel."

Annabel and Washington MPD art-squad chief Steve Jordan entered Dumbarton Oaks through the 32nd Street entrance, a block east of Wisconsin, and stood in the Veracruz Room, part of the wing housing the pre-Columbian collection. They then moved to the Post-Classic Room, stopping in front of a display case.

"There it is," Jordan said.

Annabel shifted her perspective to avoid encountering glare on the protective glass. Peering back at her was a gleaming gold monkey. She smiled. "Nice to see it back where it belongs," she said.

They admired a were-jaguar and a black basalt serpent in other cases.

Annabel said, "I can't believe this actually happened. It actually worked."

"Sometimes it does. Most times it doesn't. We got lucky, no small thanks to you."

"I did nothing. All I did was call to tell you that someone had left that message on the machine in the Atlas Building and then made one phone call to the—'perp.' Right? End of involvement."

"Which makes it even better."

"What do you mean?"

"Your cover wasn't blown. We never used your name, just put out the word that an important dealer in pre-Columbian was in the market, no questions asked. We did indicate it was a woman. If we'd been pressed, we would have used your name or had you do it. Frankly, the guy wasn't very smart. He knew nothing about art, didn't even ask for your name when you called back to arrange the meet. When we arrested him, he asked who you were. I told him you were a South American collector temporarily living in Washington."

"You never told me who he was."

"A fence who took the items off the hands of the pair who stole them. They weren't employed by Dumbarton. Outside contractors with access."

Because the theft had not been made public, the return of the items to Dumbarton Oaks was also kept quiet. As far as anyone knew—aside from Jordan, Annabel, a few other law-enforcement people, and Dumbarton Oaks management—the items had never left.

"Drive you somewhere?" Jordan asked as they stepped outside into crisp sunshine.

"Thanks, Steve, but a walk will do me good. Such a lovely day. I have to ask you one thing, though."

"Shoot."

"When you said that my cover hadn't been blown, what did you mean by that? No, strike that. I know what you meant literally. But I have the sinking feeling you're pleased my identify wasn't revealed because you might ask me to do this again."

"Would I do that to a beautiful woman like you? Especially such a tall one?"

She narrowed her eyes and cocked her head.

"You know something, Steve. I think you would."

"Enjoy your walk, Annabel. Best to Mac. What does he think of his wife's fling with crime?"

"He—no problem."

There hadn't been a problem with Mac because Annabel hadn't told him.

Why? she pondered as she took her time returning to her gallery, stopping to admire the pretty homes nestled together on Georgetown's narrow streets, laughing at one garage on which signs in six languages warned against parking in front of it, seemingly on pain of death.

Why hadn't she told her husband?

It wasn't a matter of deciding not to tell him. She had every intention of doing that. From the beginning, one of many bedrocks upon which their wonderful marriage was based was the absence of secrets. They didn't tell each other everything, of course. *Their* Constitution allowed for a reasonable amount of individual liberty, as well as strict adherence to the First Amendment.

But her cooperation with Steve Jordan was something she should have shared with Mac before she became involved, and she knew it. She envisioned the range of responses he might have had. Foolish of her to lend her name and reputation to criminal activities. Foolhardy to place herself even potentially in harm's way. She was busy enough as it was, with the White House arts group, running her gallery, keeping up with friends, tracking down a madman who smashed pre-Columbian objects and ex-wives—busy enough being a wife.

All arguments *she'd* raised over the course of their marriage when he strayed from his latter-day quiet, genteel life of college law professor to lend his name and reputation to solving murders or helping friends prove they hadn't committed them.

Placing *himself* in harm's way. Adding an unnecessary entree to an already full plate.

Being a husband.

She stopped at the French Market to pick up the makings of a salad, and French bread. She was on her own for dinner that night because Mac was dining out with an old friend. He'd asked her to join them, but she'd begged off. She needed an easy night at home with a low-calorie dinner and the chance to pack carefully for her trip to Italy the following day. She had the whole evening ahead of her. Mac was off after dinner to a monthly low-stakes poker game with high-stakes friends at the National Press Club. Shades of Harry Truman's famous gatherings.

The rest of the afternoon went quickly and smoothly, aside from an infuriating conversation with a representative from the insurance company who wanted to give her even less than the Tlatilco had been insured for because, he claimed, "Your security was not up to standards."

She returned home at six, slipped into a favored knock-around-the-house purple sweatsuit, walked Rufus, and prepared her salad. Silly, she thought as she washed lettuce and placed it in a plastic salad spinner, that she hadn't told her husband about her part in Steve Jordan's sting. Especially now. It had been a success. The pieces were safely back at Dumbarton Oaks, and she was safe and sound. "How childish," she said aloud, cutting an Israeli tomato into wedges. Chances are Mac would get a kick out of her adventure. She'd tell him the minute he got home.

But by the time he returned from his poker game at midnight, Annabel had been asleep for an hour. And then, somehow, in the bustle of the following morning, the opportune time didn't present itself. Mac had an early meeting at the university and was out the door by seven-thirty. He embraced her in a bear hug before leaving, kissing her softly on the lips, then harder. "I'll miss you," he said.

"I'll miss you too," she said. "Damn. Here I am making these all-expenses-paid trips to Italy, but every time I do you have a conflict."

"Don't make me feel guilty," he said. "The hell with expenses being paid. Let's make plans to go to Italy together. We'll sit down when you get back, compare our calendars, and pick a time that works for both of us."

After a stop at the gallery to brief a young part-time employee who would mind the store in her absence, she was driven to Dulles Airport in a Lincoln Town Car sent by Carole Aprile.

"All set for the hero's welcome?" Annabel asked Luther.

"Absolutely," he said.

"And well deserving of a hero's reception," Scott Pims boomed. The cameraman and soundman traveling with him sat off to the side on large black equipment boxes.

"And you're capturing it for posterity," Annabel said to Pims.

"Of course. Does a falling tree in a forest make a sound if no one is there to hear it? Luther is a stout redwood in the art world. I intend that everyone hear the noise he makes."

When he falls? Annabel thought. And then wondered why she had thought that.

Mason appeared to Annabel to be uncomfortable with the conversation about him. "All I want," he said, "is to live a life of beauty and calm."

"An so you shall," Pims said. "Come. Time to board."

Everything had gone so easily.

When Mason had first formulated what at the time seemed an outrageous fantasy—making off with an original Caravaggio—he had no idea how to go about it. But as things began to fall into place—Carlo Giliberti's discovery that the Italian Mafia, led by Luigi Sensi, actually had *Grottesca;* a source of funding with which to buy it, or, rather, pay off the intermediaries, provided by the unscrupulous collector Franco del Brasco; and the availability of master forger Jacques Saison to create the necessary copies—the biggest obstacle was how to physically spirit the original from the National Gallery after it had been authenticated and exhibited.

When he'd told Pims that he intended to make the swap in Italy, he was being truthful. At that juncture, it had seemed the most sensible approach. If something went wrong, it would be easier to extricate himself from any resulting brouhaha while far from the National Gallery.

But Pims was right. He wouldn't be able to predict the situation in Italy when the painting was returned. And so he changed his plans. The switch would be accomplished at the National Gallery itself.

Mason's reputation for being obsessed with *Grottesca,* at times to a point of irrationality, proved valuable; he played that card throughout the month, standing in front of it for hours after the tourists were gone. Everyone in the gallery started talking about his infatuation with the work. Early on, Luther wondered whether it would be better to adopt an aloof stance where *Grottesca* was concerned, make it seem that he didn't care that much about it.

But again it was Pims who suggested that to be half-crazed about the painting would work to Mason's advantage. "Like not picking a fight with a crazed man in a bar," Pims had said. "We don't mess with crazy people."

"I'm not crazy," Luther had countered.

"A matter of opinion. *Controlled* craziness, Luther. *Slightly* crazy about *Grottesca.*"

That was the way Mason played it, although it didn't take much playacting. He *was* "crazy" about *Grottesca,* about almost all of Caravaggio's work.

Another ingredient of the plan was for Luther to make a point of always carrying other paintings with him wherever he went in the National Gallery. "Now that the exhibition is underway," he told colleagues, "I can finally get around to studying these other paintings." And so he moved from West to East buildings, in one gallery and out the other, arriving at meetings and leaving them with at least two works of art under his arm or in an oversized leather portfolio.

He also made it a point of spending an increasing amount of time in the crating and shipping rooms, which fell under Don Fechter's jurisdiction, becoming especially friendly with those who worked there. At the same time, he deliberately became a minor meddling nuisance about how

Grottesca would be handled once its month at the National Gallery was up.

"Stop worrying, Luther," he was told, never harshly. Mason had working for him his sterling reputation and gentle manner; his occasional histrionic outbursts were considered part of his eccentric charm. And he was the National Gallery's most dedicated and famous curator.

From the moment *Grottesca* was taken down from the wall, Luther never left its side, shepherding it through every detail of preparing for its packing and shipment back to Italy. He knew that there was one final element of the plan that would be crucial to its success. Timing. Timing was everything, it was said. That was certainly true here.

An hour before the original *Grottesca* was to be placed in its climate-controlled crate built by Don Fechter's staff, Mason signed in and entered the secured area. With him was one of the framed forgeries sandwiched between two other works. He went to where *Grottesca* leaned against the crate, lowered the three paintings he carried to the floor, and let out a long, audible sigh.

The other two people in the room were members of Fechter's staff. Mason had noted during his frequent trips there that the guard at the door sat facing out into the hallway, more concerned with who might enter than what went on in the room once they were inside.

"I can't bear it," Luther said aloud.

"Can't bear what, Luther?" asked one of the staffers.

"That it's leaving."

"You really love that painting, don't you?" the other staffer said.

"More than you can ever imagine."

"Well, Luther, take a final look. We have to get it wrapped up and ready to go."

"Of course. Just give me a few minutes to stand here and take it in. One last impression to carry with me for the rest of my life."

The staffers glanced at each other, gentle smiles on their lips. Luther Mason was a strange bird. A nice man—but strange. How could anyone be *that* enamored of a painting?

Mason didn't know if he could cry on cue. He'd practiced in front of his bathroom mirror, feeling foolish but pleasantly surprised to find that he could. He applied what he knew of "method acting"—recalling a particular time in his life and applying it to the moment. He thought of Julian. "I'm sorry," he said, wiping tears from his face with a handkerchief. "It's just that—"

"Sure, Luther," one of the staffers said, motioning with his head for his colleague to follow him into a small supply room.

They gave him a couple of minutes for a final swoon; he needed less than one to switch paintings. When the staffers returned, they looked at *Grottesca.* The Jacques Saison version.

"Sorry, Luther. Time to put it away."

"I understand. Thank you for that courtesy. At least I'll get to see it one more time when they hang it in the church over there. Yes, thank you so much for those few minutes. Sorry for losing myself like that. Silly." He stepped closer to the forgery, gently placed his fingertips on the twisted face of the androgynous boy snared in thorns and serpents, and said, "Go in peace."

He quickly signed out as the staffers giggled and began securing the painting in the crate.

Mason went to his office, where he hid the original behind other works in the locked closet.

Later that night, he returned to his office, removed the original *Grottesca*'s frame, and concealed the painting behind one of the Gaissers he'd bought in Paris. The following day, with Tom Morris on duty at the employee entrance, he signed out.

"How did you make out with those paintings you bought in Paris?" Morris asked.

"Oh, those. Bishop said they weren't worth very much, but I'm pleased with my purchase." He unwrapped the package and again showed Morris the Gaisser.

"I kind of like it, Luther," Morris said. "I think you made a good choice."

"I think so. Well, have a good day, Tom."

He replaced the paper around the painting and went to his car, his heart threatening to burst through his ribs, rivulets of perspiration running down his nose.

He called Franco del Brasco that night from home. "Mr. del Brasco, Luther Mason. I just wanted you to know that the most difficult part is over. The original is in my possession. I'm leaving for Italy tomorrow. When I return in a few days, I'll see that it's in your hands."

"Good." Del Brasco hung up.

"Bastard," Mason said into the dead phone. "You'll get only the art you deserve."

His dreams that night transported him from Washington to a small, pleasant house on Hydra, the turquoise sea far below his balcony. *Grottesca* hung on the stark white living room wall. Anyone observing Luther Mason sleeping that night might have wondered why a smile kept forming on his lips. A sexual dream? A fond recollection of a childhood incident, or a special meal? Simple pleasure at contemplating a long vacation in a lovely place?

In fact, all of the above.

TWENTY-FIVE

RAVELLO, ITALY

THE BUILDINGS that defined Ravello's central piazza—a church with large black doors dating back to the eleventh century; a white-and-pink government building flying the Italian and the Ravello flags; a small hotel the color of fresh limes, with white wrought-iron railings defining tiny balconies on the front rooms; a market with freshly killed pheasants, ducks, and rabbits hanging from a red, white, and green canvas canopy; two restaurants, their outdoor cafes packed tightly with onlookers; and some private residences—had all been additionally decorated for the event with garlands of flowers, flags, and crude signs. The requisite fountain in the center of the piazza sent water into the air through the mouths of wild animals. Pretty schoolgirls in colorful costumes performed traditional folk dances to the dissonant music of old men in red uniforms with silver buttons, the music from their drums, tuba, trombone, cornet, and saxophone sounding as though each musician played a different song. The swelling crowd included press, priests, politicians, and townspeople.

In front of the fountain, facing the open doors of the church, was a platform on which stood two loudspeakers, a microphone, and a dozen folding metal chairs. Annabel looked up from the church steps into a cerulean sky marked only by an occasional puffy white cloud moving fast on unfelt upper-atmosphere winds.

"This is really exciting," she said to Don Fechter.

"And tiring," he said.

They'd been picked up before dawn at their hotel in Rome by a sleek, modern bus on which an elaborate continental breakfast was set up; the coffee was the strongest Annabel had ever tasted. And good. She felt as if the caffeine had been injected intravenously.

The crate containing *Grottesca* took up most of the vehicle's rear bench. Two armed guards assigned by the Ministry of Culture sat to either side of it. "You are never to take your eyes off it," Alberto Betti had instructed them. One slept for most of the journey; the other read popular magazines. The crate was placed on the platform along with the chairs and amplification equipment, flanked by the two sleepy guards. Pims, who'd traveled from Rome with his camera crew in a hired limousine, directed the taping of the event from a vantage point directly in front of the platform.

Ravello's mayor raised his arms and said, "*Signore e signori.* Your attention, please."

"Time for you to get up there," Fletcher told Annabel.

She joined the others on the platform, looked out over the faces, and saw Luther Mason step from the dark recesses of the church into the bright sunshine. With him were two priests, followed by representatives from the National Gallery's public information office. Workmen in white coveralls brought up the rear. The only conspicuous absentee was Father Pasquale Giocondi. When Annabel asked, she was told he had a previous commitment in Rome. "Signor Mason," the mayor said into the microphone. "Please. It is time."

Mason and the priests descended the church steps, threaded through the crowd, and joined the others on the platform. Once seated, the mayor said in Italian, "My dear friends, my fellow countrymen, I welcome you to Ravello on this most joyous of days. We gather here to celebrate the return of a magnificent painting by one of Italy's most honored geniuses, Michelangelo Merisi Caravaggio." The crowd applauded. "It is fitting, I believe, that this work, lost to us for so many years, was discovered here in our beautiful village. Ravello and its people are things of beauty, just as Caravaggio created things of beauty. It is appropriate that our lovely village be home to this important work of art for the next century and beyond." More applause.

As the mayor continued to speak, Annabel thought how wonderful it was that this small church, in such an idyllic Italian town, would be the final showplace for a masterpiece. It also crossed her mind that great paintings were routinely stolen from Italian churches. She glanced at Luther Mason, seated at the end of her row. He looked to her like one of the statues dotting the piazza, ramrod straight, his face set in a stony grimace, in marked contrast with the ebullient mood of everyone else. Annabel couldn't help but smile. When she'd agreed to join the White House Commission on the Arts, she'd never dreamed it would lead her to a tiny square in Ravello, Italy. She wished Mac were there to share the experience. Photographers hired by the town recorded the event; she would order a set of pictures to bring home to him.

The mayor said, "We are honored to have with us today a representative from the White House of the United States, Signora Smith."

Annabel stepped to the microphone and read a short statement prepared by Vice President Aprile's Press Office. Her remarks were repeated by a translator: ". . . and the president of the United States, and all Americans, thank the Italian people for allowing *Grottesca* to have spent a month in the United States at the National Gallery. And we praise Italy in constant astonishment for having contributed so much to the world of art."

Mason was next. He rose tentatively; from Annabel's perspective he seemed unsure whether to go to the microphone. With that same frozen, pained expression on his face, he pulled a scrap of paper from his pocket and said in halting Italian, "This is where *Grottesca* belongs. With the people of Ravello. It is yours to treasure for all time."

Short and sweet, thought Annabel.

The ceremony was climaxed by the playing of the Italian national anthem. Then, workmen took the crate from the platform and carried it to the church. The mayor had wanted to unveil *Grottesca* in the piazza, but the parish priests prevailed in their view that it was more fitting for it to first be seen in its religious setting than in a secular display. The actual hanging would be witnessed only by invited VIPs and town officials.

As Pims's cameraman captured the action, *Grottesca*'s protective wooden shell was carefully dismantled under Donald Fechter's supervision, his instructions translated into Italian. Once freed, the painting was carried to the chancel rail, where the priests, dressed in black cassocks covered by white surplices, blessed it. The air was thick with incense; liturgical music came from an unseen organist.

The priests beckoned those in attendance to come forward to admire close-up the now consecrated painting before it was lifted to its place of honor high above the altar. Annabel was the first to approach. She knelt at the rail—it seemed the appropriate thing to do—and stared into the face of Caravaggio's young male model. She hadn't experienced a visceral reaction to *Grottesca* during its residence at the National Gallery. But now, so close to it, the young boy's anguish was palpable. She envisioned Caravaggio working on the piece, becoming one with the young male model. The impact on her was painful; she had to look away—directly into the cameraman's lens.

One by one the invited approached to pay their respects to Caravaggio and his work. It was a bit too ceremonial for Annabel's taste, and it seemed to her that Christ was playing second fiddle to a violent painter. But then again, she'd never been a person to stand on ceremony or to insist on ritual. As she watched, her attention was captured by a man she'd noticed outside during the ceremonies. He wore a shiny raincoat the color of rust, its collar raised against wind and rain that weren't there. His hat was a slouch-brimmed leather fedora from Hollywood gangster films of the thirties and forties. What most interested Annabel about him, aside from his getup, was that once on his knees, he withdrew a large, round magnifying glass and began to examine the painting through it. Strange, she thought, looking at Luther Mason, whose expression continued to be grim.

Annabel looked again at the altar. The man with the glass continued to examine the painting until a priest whispered in his ear. He stood and retreated from the rail as the priests lifted the painting with great solemnity and carried it to the altar where workmen, ascending parallel ladders, hung it. The applause was spontaneous. Two spotlights came to life, bathing the painting in brilliant white light.

"George Kublinski would have a heart attack if he saw those lights," Don Fechter whispered to Annabel. "Feel the humidity in here? *I* may have a heart attack."

"Is that it?" Annabel asked Fechter. "It just hangs there? Not bolted to the wall?"

"I give it three months," he said.

"Who was the man with the magnifying glass?" Annabel asked.

"Joseph Spagnola. A Vatican curator."

"Really? What was he doing, making sure it's the real thing?"

"Who knows?" Fechter replied. "Luther and Spagnola hate each other. I was at a conference a couple of years ago where they both presented papers on Caravaggio. Luther really tore into him, said his research was faulty—no, I think the word he used was 'shabby.' I thought they might come to blows."

"Did Luther know he was going to be here?" Annabel asked.

"Beats me. I'm just glad I work in conservation. These curator types can get a little too flaky for my taste."

Annabel laughed quietly.

"You should have seen Luther this past month," Fechter said. "Really acted strange. Bizarre."

"Well, Caravaggio, and especially *Grottesca,* mean an awful lot to him," Annabel said.

"I know," said Fechter. "But there's a difference between liking something and becoming maniacal about it. I guess I shouldn't say that. I really do like Luther. Beneath that neurotic exterior is a very nice man. And smart. I never doubted that what he said to Spagnola at that conference was on the money. Excuse me, Annabel. I want to get that crate put back together before it ends up firewood in somebody's house. Cost a bundle to make it. Hopefully we'll get to use it again."

On the bus trip back to Rome, Annabel asked, "Where's Luther?"

"He went with Scott Pims in the limo," a National Gallery staffer replied. "Said he had to get back to Rome right away. He sure seemed upset."

Originally, Annabel had planned to fly to Washington the next day. But once back in Rome, she decided to catch a flight that night. She missed Mac, missed Rufus, missed her home.

The following morning, a jet-lagged Annabel,

and Mac sat in their kitchen reading the *Washington Post*. A small story appeared in the "Style" section about the return of *Grottesca* to Ravello, illustrated with a photograph taken inside the church of Luther Mason shaking hands with Ravello's beaming mayor.

"Did you ever see Mason again in Rome?" Mac asked.

Annabel shook her head. "He just disappeared along with Scott Pims."

"You seem worried."

"That business with the Vatican curator, Spagnola, or something, really upset him."

"You say they don't like each other."

"According to Don Fechter. It sure looked that way to me. I must call Carole this morning, tell her how it went."

"Later," Mac said, coming around behind, wrapping his arms about her, and allowing his hands to wander into the folds of her robe.

"A little amorous for so early in the morning, aren't you?" Annabel asked, jet lag falling away.

"I missed you," he said. "By the way, I stopped in to see Susan Shevlin. She can get us some wonderful deals on a trip to Italy. I left a note on your desk with dates that are good for me. If any of them match up with your schedule, I'll book it."

"Wonderful," said Annabel, pushing back her chair, which pushed him back, too. She stood, turned, wrapped her arms about his neck, and kissed him hard on the mouth. "You once asked me to come up to see your tattoos. Is the offer still good?"

"You bet it is, lady. Sure you're not too tired from your flight?"

"There's always time for sleep."

TWENTY-SIX

IF TIMING is everything, Mac and Annabel had lost their touch, literally and figuratively. The ringing telephone saw to that. "Let it ring," Mac said.

"I can't," Annabel said.

"Sure you can."

"I'll be quick."

"Not quick enough."

"Hello, Carole. You beat me to it. I was about to call you."

"Hope I'm not interrupting anything."

"Oh, no. We're just—talking. I wanted to give you a rundown on how things went in Ravello."

"That's why I'm calling—to get your view of what happened."

Annabel frowned. To get her view of "what happened?" "What happened?" she asked.

"You haven't heard, of course. You just got back. Can you be here in an hour?"

"At your house?"

"Yes."

Annabel glanced at Mac. "I can be there," she said.

"Good. I'll explain when you get here."

"Something's wrong," Annabel said after hanging up.

Mac looked up from his magazine and grinned. "I noticed," he said, not referring to his wife's phone conversation.

"I'm sorry, darling," she said, slipping into a robe.

"I think you were right," he said.

"About what?"

"About there being a Caravaggio curse."

She laughed, dropped the robe to her feet—he gasped audibly—and got back in bed. Although Mr. and Mrs. Smith preferred their lovemaking to be leisurely, both were adept at responding to a sense of urgency.

An hour later Annabel arrived at the Naval Observatory, home of Vice President and Mrs. Joseph Aprile. To her surprise, Court Whitney was also there.

"Thanks for coming, Annabel," Carole said after they'd settled in her office.

"What's wrong?" Annabel asked.

Whitney handed Annabel a memorandum. The words SECRET—CONFIDENTIAL were written in big letters across the top. It was from Italy's minister of culture, Alberto Betti, and was addressed to Whitney at the National Gallery. Annabel read:

The accompanying letter was received by my office earlier today. The allegations contained in it represent a matter of monumental importance to me, my government, and to you, your museum, and the government of the United States.

I urge you to give this your immediate consideration, and to reply to me at once.

Annabel dropped it on the desk and looked to Whitney. "It refers to an accompanying letter," she said.

Whitney answered by handing her a longer document, addressed to Betti:

As senior curator of the Vatican, it is my responsibility to oversee all works of art belonging to the Holy See. In that capacity, I have taken upon myself to closely examine *Grottesca,* which was recently returned to Italy, its country of origin, by the National Gallery of Art in Washington, D.C. Naturally, the examination I conducted cannot be considered definitive. But it is my considered professional judgment that the painting returned to us did not come from the hand of Michelangelo Caravaggio. The brush strokes lack the authority of the master. It is possible, of course, that it was paint by an apprentice, whose talent was sufficient to cr a work approaching the standards of Caravaggio himself. But that is unlikely. It is well known that Caravaggio did not use assistants or apprentices. Therefore, if my judgment is correct, a fraud of extreme proportions has been perpetrated upon our nation, as well as upon the Vatican.

Because *Grottesca* was found in one of our churches, it rightfully belongs to the Vatican. That the Ravello church was chosen as its place of exhibition further solidifies that belief. Consequently, I request your cooperation in having the painting removed from Ravello and brought to the Vatican, where our experts can conduct a more thorough examination of the work. Simultaneously, I request permission to travel to the United States immediately to confront those at the National Gallery who might have had a hand in this, should my suspicions be validated.

Joseph Spagnola
Senior Curator, the Vatican

"My God," was all Annabel could muster.

"Court brought these with him after calling," said Carole. "I suggested we keep the use of fax machines to a minimum."

"That's prudent," Annabel said. To Whitney: "your read on this?"

"to assume a large mistake has been agnola is wrong in his assertion. some, an unneeded complication."

art," said Carole, "that the validation

process *Grottesca* was put through by his staff would certainly rule out Mr. Spagnola's contentions. Adding weight to that are Luther Mason's credentials and scholarship."

"What's the next step?" Annabel asked.

Whitney replied, "I'm inviting Spagnola to come to Washington to discuss it. I'm sure once he does, he'll realize he's making a mistake."

"I'd like you to attend such a meeting, Annabel," Carole said. "That is, if you can."

"I'll make a point of being available. Any idea when he'll arrive, Court?"

"No."

"Did you pick up any hints in Ravello, Annabel, that all isn't well there? Did you meet Mr. Spagnola?"

"No and no. Spagnola was pointed out to me by Don Fechter. He made a show of examining *Grottesca* in the church with a magnifying glass."

Whitney snickered. "Sherlock Holmes."

Annabel smiled. "There was an element of that. Hints that something might be wrong? Luther seemed upset. He left our group without a word and went back to Rome with Scott Pims and his crew."

"Why?" Whitney asked.

"I have no idea. But he and Mr. Spagnola a not friendly, according to Don Fechter."

"If they weren't friends before, they wor now," said Whitney.

"Have you spoken with Luther?" Annabel asked Whitney.

"Briefly. He's at home. I asked him to come in this afternoon."

"Want me to be there?" Annabel asked both Carole and Whitney. Carole nodded but Whitney said, "No. Better I go over this with Luther alone. I'll report back as soon as I have."

Annabel and Carole lingered in the office after Whitney left. "Level with me, Annabel," the VP's wife said. "Can you conceive of any way the original *Grottesca* might not have made it back to Italy?"

Annabel shook her head. "Not unless the world's greatest art forger went to work in the National Gallery while it hung there."

But on the way to her Georgetown gallery, Annabel had to mentally add to her answer: Or unless the forger made a copy *before* it ever got to the National Gallery.

Luther had fled Ravello with Pims rather than return to Rome on the bus because he felt he might ⎾isintegrate on the spot. Crumble into a pile of ⎾lering cinerous flakes. *"And your quaint honor ⎾lust. And into ashes all my lust."*

⎾*is fate?* he thought, as he tried to talk ⎾his agitated state. It was only nor- ⎾ous. What man wouldn't be? The ⎾gnificant enough to put anyone on edge, even if it had been the authentic *Grottesca* delivered to Ravello that morning.

But a forgery was being embraced and celebrated. Would it be discovered? Would he, Luther Mason, esteemed and respected senior curator of the National Gallery of Art—*America's Museum*—be led away in handcuffs by Italian police, tarnished and disgraced, a pathetic criminal doomed to a life in a dank prison, the subject of snide articles in the art magazines? That possibility, as remote as he intellectually knew it was, went through him that morning like a diuretic cocktail.

The imagery of how he might end up was bad enough: If all he had to fear was fear itself, fear was doing a good job.

The reality had set in when he arrived in Ravello.

As the bus pulled into the piazza, Luther saw the man in the red beret and black raincoat, a cigarette dangling from his mouth—the same man who'd followed him in Rome. Who was he?

Luther decided before exiting the bus that he would confront him. But by the time he got off, the man had disappeared. Luther searched for him in the crowd, in the church. Vanished. Just as well. What if it was Red Beret's mission to kill him? Better to stay as far away as possible. Stick with crowds. Control yourself, Luther. Think! Try reason, not emotion.

And then Spagnola showed up. Basta

hack. A scholar wannabe with his silly hat and a magnifying glass to demonstrate authority. What if he suddenly shouted, "It's a fake! A fraud has been committed and this is the criminal!" Fingers pointed at Luther. Police. The arrest. The pictures in the newspapers.

Once again, Luther force-fed his denial system. The Saison copy was too perfect for someone with Spagnola's limited talent to spot as a forgery. Unless, of course Spagnola knew something. Had been tipped. By whom? The old mafioso, Sensi? One of Sensi's thugs? Or someone in Franco del Brasco's employ?

Luther was proud of himself for the aplomb with which he'd handled his short speech and the unveiling inside the church, Spagnola's distasteful display be damned.

But to have to ride back to Rome on the bus and sustain a façade of normalcy was asking too much.

The presence of the crew members in the limo precluded any sustained conversation with Pims, so they passed the time with small talk. But when ⹁ limo pulled up in front of the Valadier Hotel, ⹁ccompanied Luther inside.

's wrong?" the jocular Pims asked. "You ⹁h you've seen a ghost."

⹁lowed."

⹁m?"

⹁ow. His name I don't know. He was

in Rome, then this morning in Ravello. Tall, black raincoat, red beret."

Pims looked at him like a father catching a son in a lie. "Come now, Luther, you are not yourself. A tall man in a red beret? The Cold War is over."

"Damn it, Scott, I'm not paranoid! And Spagnola being there. What if he—?"

"He won't. Saison's work will stand up. It will take a month of laboratory testing, and even that won't be definitive. By that time you'll be basking on a beach in—have you decided yet where to go?"

"Greece, I think. I need time to think."

"At times a dangerous luxury for you, Luther. How long will you stay here?"

"I don't know."

"I would stay with you, but I must be in New York tomorrow. Call me when you arrive. And calm down, for God's sake. The worst is over."

Mason checked in and sat alone on the balcony overlooking the Borghese. But after a few hours of aimless soul-searching, he checked out, to the surprise of the clerk who had just greeted him, and went to the airport in time to catch a flight to New York. The Amtrak train returned him to Washington.

The director was standing on his terrace looking out over the Capitol when Mason entered his office. "Court?" Mason said through the opening glass doors.

Whitney turned, his face as hard as his voice had been on the phone. He stepped through the open doors and went to a round table that served as his desk. On it were several sheets of paper. "Look at these," Whitney said, returning to the terrace.

Mason was almost afraid to pick them up, as though to actually read the words would seal his fate. He glanced at Whitney, then slowly picked up the first of the pages. It had come from Alberto Betti.

Mason dropped that page onto the table and picked up the next, the document to which Betti had referred in his transmission to Whitney.

As he read, Mason's heart became so heavy he feared it might drop to his stomach. Its beat was thunderous. His throat had gone dry; his teeth were clenched.

Whitney stepped back inside. "Well?" he asked.

Mason stiffened, turned, and forced a smile. "Much Italian ado about nothing," he said.

"That may be true, Luther. I suspect it is. But it raises a thorny issue that must be dealt with."

Mason shrugged. It was a calculated body His smile remained. "A shame you have to ond to such nonsense, Court. As far as d, answering them only dignifies their

ɔpagnola," Whitney said.

che misfortune of meeting him on a

few occasions. Conferences, mostly. He considers himself an expert. He isn't. He's a bureaucratic hack who has his job only because the Vatican keeps a bloated staff. He can't hold a candle to the experts you brought in to evaluate *Grottesca.* And, of course—"

"And, of course," Whitney finished the statement, "he can't hold a candle to you."

"I was too modest to say it myself," Mason said, turning his smile into a gentle laugh to reinforce the casual, unconcerned posture he'd assumed.

"Well, he might be holding a match. I'll have to meet with Spagnola. So will you."

"I have no problem with that."

"Mrs. Aprile and Annabel Smith know. I briefed them this morning."

"Was that necessary?" Luther asked, his throat parchment.

"Absolutely. Any expert suggestions on how to handle this?"

Mason was relieved at how firm his voice was as he said, "My suggestion is that you welcome Spagnola. No hostility. Kill him with kindness. We can easily allay his concerns. After all, we have the National Gallery of Art to back up the authenticity of *Grottesca.* There is no more credible institution in the world."

"I'll do just that. Where will you be the re the day?"

"In my office. Out and about the gallery."

"I'll find you. Thanks for stopping by."

The minute Mason was gone, the director called in Paul Bishop for his evaluation of the documents and their potential ramifications. Bishop was not nearly as reassuring. He went so far as to suggest that he'd had a sense for months that something wasn't right where *Grottesca* was concerned. "Think about it, Court," he said after accepting a cup of tea. "This masterpiece, lost for centuries, suddenly shows up in a church in Italy. Luther Mason is led to it by an old, retired priest, although it seems that 'retired' might not be the right word to apply to Giocondi, at least not according to the reports. Scott Pims brought it up on his show last week. It's all just too convenient, Court. And, of course, there's Luther's strange behavior over the past few months. If I were you, I'd take this very seriously and hope that it passes—but brace for the worst."

Later that afternoon, Whitney decided that his only course of action was the one suggested by Mason. Consider it a mistake, cordially invite ꞇgnola to come to the gallery to discuss the mat- ᴅ hope to dissuade the Vatican curator from ꞇtions. The way he now viewed it, he ꞇᴄh of a choice. If the painting that ꞇᴅ to Italy was not the original ꞇᴜn of good fortune he'd been experiencing as director of the National Gallery could come to an abrupt and painful halt.

M. Scott Pims had gone to New York that morning to investigate a brewing scandal involving a Soho art gallery. According to his inside information, the dealer had been the recipient of stolen Italian art for years, most recently three Mattia Preti paintings stolen from San Francisco di Assisi, in Cosenza. Pims's source told him that the paintings had been brought to the United States by the slain Italian cultural attaché to Washington, Carlo Giliberti.

Mason spent the remainder of the day secluded in his office, pretending to be busy but failing at the pretense. As he prepared to leave for home at six, his phone rang. It was Bill Woody, owner of The Collector Gallery and Restaurant, who asked if Mason could drop off two paintings by the impressionist Anthony Triano he'd taken a month ago to evaluate as a favor to Wooby. "Anthony's doing a show in Kansas City," said Wooby. "He'd like to take the works with him."

He delivered the paintings—"Excellent in my opinion"—and decided to have a drink and dinner before going home. He ate quickly and departed without saying goodbye. Wooby, observing Mason from the bar, turned to a friend, artist Ju Jashinsky, whose portrait of the restaurant ov greeted customers as they entered, and said, "Quite a coup he pulled off with *Grottesca*."

"Yes. An incredible story."

"I wish *I'd* find a long-lost masterpiece. If I did, I'm not sure I'd turn it over to anybody. Probably get on the next plane with it and live the opulent life in Brazil or on some remote island."

Jashinsky laughed. "You'd never last, Bill. Remote islands don't have causes."

"Did you get to see the *Grottesca* when it was here?" he asked.

"Of course. You?"

"I certainly did. There was something distinctly magical about seeing that work hanging on the walls of the National Gallery. I had this weird feeling that Caravaggio himself was there."

"Maybe he was," she said with a laugh.

Mason felt the effects of the drink and made himself a cup of strong coffee in his apartment. Feeling better, he called Indiana. "Just wanted you to know, Mother, that my trip to Italy went fine."

"I'm happy that it did," she said. "It was so od to see Julian again."

s. He's quite a young man, isn't he?"

him some money to help tide him over in

w much did you give him?"

d dollars. I told him I would send

"I wish you hadn't done that, Mother."

"Why? He's my only grandson."

"I know that. It was very generous of you, but I wanted to—"

"I think you should help him, too," she said.

"I intend to. I told you that. How are you feeling?"

"I have a cold. I hope it isn't the flu. The flu can be bad for someone my age."

"Did you get a flu shot?"

"No. I don't believe in them."

"Well, feel better. I'll be in touch."

He allowed his anger at the conversation to dissipate before making his next call. Franco del Brasco answered on the first ring. "Mr. del Brasco. Luther Mason here."

"I read about Italy," del Brasco said, the lack of affect in his voice now familiar.

"It went quite well, Mr. del Brasco. I have the painting for you."

"I will arrange to get it. What would be a convenient time?"

"I suppose any time would be fine. How do you want to do it?"

"I will have someone contact you. Someone who is intimately familiar with the artist's work."

Oh God—another expert, Luther thought. "Who?" he asked.

"He will identify himself when he calls. He need time to examine it."

"Of course. He can have all the time he wishes. And will he have with him the—money for me?"

"Yes. If he says I am getting what I paid for, he will turn the money over to you."

"The entire million?" Luther had trouble getting the words out.

"What we agreed upon."

"Yes. The million."

"You will be contacted in a few days. Good night, Mr. Mason."

After hanging up, Luther pondered what del Brasco had said. He hadn't counted on a third party coming between them, assuming all along that he would have to travel to California and turn over the copy of *Grottesca* directly to the buyer.

But as he thought about it, he realized that that was an unreasonable expectation. Del Brasco knew nothing about art. He'd probably stick *Grottesca,* or what he thought was *Grottesca,* in a vault and not look at it again for years. Mason, in fact, was counting on that. Surely even an evil boor like del Brasco would not show off a paint-ᵥ so recently in the news.

 question was whether the person acting on
ᵒ's behalf would have sufficient knowl-
ᵥaggio to raise a question about its
doubted it. Men who worked for
ᵤnco del Brasco weren't likely to be
ᵤuch beyond extortion and murder.

No, he decided, the copy was too good. It would fool anyone—except him.

But then he thought of Joseph Spagnola, who'd been astute enough to have picked up something wrong with Saison's forgery. The same could happen with the person examining it on del Brasco's behalf.

As of late, he was able to talk away such concerns. Time was on his side. It would take Spagnola months to prove that the painting hanging in the Ravello church was a phony. If del Brasco's so-called expert were to raise a question, Luther was confident he could finesse his way out of it. The trick, he decided, was to limit the amount of time del Brasco's man had with *Grottesca*. He wasn't sure how to accomplish that but was confident he'd come up with a way.

Although bone-tired, he couldn't resist taking the original painting from the closet—he'd marked its brown paper wrap with a tiny pencil dot to differentiate between the two versions—drawing strength and resolve from it, wrapping it once again, and carefully returning it to its safe haven.

The last thing he did before going to bed was to check the newspaper for the weather in Greece.

Sunny, highs in the 80s.

He fell asleep saying aloud a few simple Greek phrases he'd learned: *"Kalimera. Efcharisto. Ochi."* Good morning. Thank you. Yes. No.

Soon.

TWENTY-SEVEN

THE PHONE'S harsh ring jarred Mason into wakefulness. His eyes went to the red glow of his bedside digital alarm clock: 3:10. He searched for the phone in the dark and put the receiver to his ear. "Hello," he mumbled.

"Signor Mason?"

"Who is this?"

But he already knew who it was—the same man who'd called him at his office a few days ago and who'd approached him the day of the Caravaggio opening.

"Mr. del Brasco wishes to arrange a meeting with you tomorrow night."

Mason was still sleepy. Did he mean that night, the next night?

˙ caller anticipated the question. "Not this ˙ore Mason. Tomorrow night."

˙l Brasco coming to Washington?"

˙ing up and turning on a lamp.

˙co will send representatives to see

you. You will be called again tonight at seven. I suggest you be at this number."

Click.

To attempt to go back to sleep was folly. He made coffee and mentally went over the telephone conversation a dozen times. He was certain the caller had said representatives would contact him. Plural. More than one. He knew someone was to be designated by del Brasco to examine the painting before turning over the money. But who were the others? Del Brasco's henchmen? Blond Curls from San Francisco? Hired goons of the sort who'd murdered Carlo Giliberti?

It had never occurred to Luther in all his planning that he would have to take steps to protect himself physically from Franco del Brasco. Physical violence hadn't been factored into his thinking because violence wasn't part of his world. Would that be what ultimately brought him down, his naïveté?

Luther Mason had never been able to accept that child abuse took place because abusing a child was anathema to him. Just as bigotry was beyond his comprehension.

But that didn't mean, of course, that those things did not happen. It simply wasn't part of hi genetic and environmental mix.

He also detested hypocrisy yet knew he being a hypocrite. He was engaged in a cri act no matter how he tried to sugarcoat it. And he was certain as the monochromatic early morning light rendered everything in his kitchen gray, including him, that naive criminals must always be the ones who were caught and paid the price.

He told himself while showering that he must create a scenario for turning over the painting that would minimize physical risk. That meant two things: First, he had to be the one to determine where and when the exchange took place. Second, greed mustn't be allowed to cloud his judgment.

Luther's deal with del Brasco called for him to be paid a million dollars for *Grottesca*. A fraction of its worth.

But he didn't need a million dollars to live the remainder of his life in modest comfort. If the opportunity presented itself, he might be able to offer some of his million to buy a positive report from del Brasco's appraiser. Surely, anyone working for Franco del Brasco would not be a stranger to bribery.

He also decided (along with the realization that planning a crime was the most exhausting mental ~rcise he'd ever gone through) that it might be ¹e to limit the amount of time the appraiser ᵗhe painting. He could ask for a small ᵗ against the million dollars in re- the appraiser to take *Grottesca* nia to be studied more closely. If gladly waive the balance owed him.

How much did he need? Half a million? Two hundred fifty thousand? His life was worth more than that.

He was about to leave the apartment for the Gallery when the ringing phone stopped him. The man again? There was no sense trying to avoid him. He answered and heard the bombastic voice of M. Scott Pims. "Luther, my friend. Scott."

"I thought you were in New York."

"I am. About to leave. Thought I'd best check in with my favorite wayward curator."

Luther winced at the characterization.

"Looks like your deceased Italian friend, Mr. Giliberti, was quite the artful smuggler."

"Was he? I wouldn't know about that."

A guttural laugh from Pims. "How are things progressing? You're nearing the culmination of your grand adventure."

"I can't talk now, Scott. I was just leaving for work."

"Loyal up to the last moment. I like that. You sound—well, you sound slightly shaken. A new and unpleasant development?" He didn't wait for a reply. "Free for lunch?"

"No."

"Then we'll make it dinner."

"Call me at the Gallery when you're bac Maybe we *should* get together."

The main entrance to the National Gallery the scene of a commotion as Mason drove

He pulled to the curb and narrowed his eyes to better read the message on signs carried by picketers: AMERICAN GALLERIES FOR AMERICAN ARTISTS. It was the same group of dissident local artists who picketed the National Gallery whenever a major exhibition featured a foreign artist. At least Julian wasn't with them.

He then noticed another picketer standing far removed from the group. Mason knew who he was, too. The Style Section of the *Post* had recently run a piece about an Italian-American who'd been picketing the Italian Embassy on Albemarle Street, acting on his complaint that the Italian government had allowed *Grottesca* to be first exhibited in the United States.

Luther attended an eleven o'clock meeting of the Exhibition Committee, at which Paul Bishop's proposed exhibit of British landscape painters, anchored by William Blake and Joseph Turner, with some Constable and Samuel Palmer thrown in to add spice, was discussed. Mason said that such an exhibition would be "characterized by a numbing sameness that would choke the spectator in de-
l." His evaluation did not sit well with Bishop.

on's growling stomach told him he was
aybe Lynn would like to have lunch. It
uous thought. They'd avoided each
onfrontation about her promo-
drawn to her office by a need to
contact. At least not yet.

Her office was empty. He was told that she'd called in that morning to say she was taking a personal day.

Strange that she hadn't called him, Mason thought as he walked through the East Building on his way to the employee exit. One rule of his department was that anyone calling in sick or intending to take a personal day inform him personally.

After a fast, solitary lunch at nearby Jaleo, he returned to his office and called Scott, catching the rotund art critic just as he walked through the door.

"Ah, Luther. Feeling better?"

"I would like to catch up with you later today. I thought maybe a drink after work."

"I think I could arrange that. I have to dash from here to The Collector. Our gregarious innkeeper-friend, Mr. Wooby, is about to open his annual exhibition from Life Skills Center. Always a lovely event, heartwarming and inspiring." One month each year, works by mentally handicapped artists belonging to Washington's Life Skills Center were displayed at The Collector, the best becoming menu covers that sold for ten dollars as a fund-raiser.

"I have to be home a little before seven," Mas said. Could you meet me at five?"

"Yes. Why do you have to be home a little b seven?"

Mason's initial reaction was anger. What business was it of his? "I'm expecting an important call," he said.

"Concerning your little adventure? You're coming down to the wire, aren't you?"

"Meet me in the lobby of the Four Seasons at five."

"Yes, *sir,*" Pims said, laughing. "Why do I have the feeling, Luther, that you are about to spring something dark and mysterious on me?"

"Because—because maybe I am."

He decided to leave early and called Court Whitney to let him know.

"Mr. Whitney is in conference, Luther," said Whitney's secretary.

"No chance of speaking with him for thirty seconds?"

"I'm afraid not. They just arrived, and—"

"Who just arrived?"

"Mr. Spagnola from the Vatican and two other gentlemen."

"I see. Please tell him I have a doctor's appointment and won't be back this afternoon."

"Anything serious?"

Just a stiff neck. I must have slept funny.

say anything about me attending the

been here all day."

ne on automatic pilot, unaware of

red his apartment at three-thirty,

and poured a glass of red wine. He needed something to calm his nerves; the wine seemed a more benign prescription than the Valium in his medicine cabinet. As he sat in a chair staring out his living room window, a horrifying thought came to him. What if del Brasco's representative, perhaps accompanied by two strong-arm men, insisted upon coming to the apartment? That was the *last* place he wanted to see them. It would be too easy to kill him there and walk away with the painting.

He had an equally potent revelation. They wouldn't kill him if he didn't have the painting for them to take. His gut twisted; how could he have been so foolish as to keep the original *Grottesca* here? The worst possible place. If he didn't have it, it would leverage his chances. He needed another safe place until he'd worked out arrangements with del Brasco's men.

"Of course," he muttered, opening the closet door. But as he peered into its recesses, he sensed something was wrong. The paintings weren't as he had left them. Or were they? He frowned as he tried to remember exactly how he'd positioned them. He was certain he'd lined them up one directly behind the other. But an inch of the original, which was behind the copy, protruded to the side. I must be wrong, he thought, as he pulled them out and put them in his large black leather portfolio, zipped it closed, went to his car, and drove to the Four Seasons Hotel on the fringes of Georgetown. "Calm down," he silently told himself as he chose an oversized stuffed chair in a corner far removed from the nearest seating area and absently stirred a Bloody Mary with a skinny red plastic straw until Pims arrived.

The large man paused at the lobby entrance, saw Luther, and laboriously made his way in his direction. "Started ahead of me, I see," Pims said, slowly easing himself into the next chair.

"I was early."

Pims's eyes went to the black portfolio resting against Mason's chair. "And what have we here?" he asked. The waitress requested his order. "Brandy and port, in equal amounts, in a snifter, no ice," Pims said.

The waitress asked him to repeat it.

"Tell the barman to place in a large snifter equal amounts of brandy and port wine. Very good for the stomach, my dear. Very soothing. More effective than blackberry brandy."

She smiled and walked away, eyebrows up.

"Now, Luther, my friend and irrepressible imp, tell me what has happened since I've been away. I told you about Carlo. He was obviously the perfect cultural attaché. Stealing culture from his native land to see that it received a wider audience. But I won't bore you with that. You can watch it on my show next Friday. Drink your Bloody Mary. You look like you need something. You're ashen.

The gray face of a man in a dilemma—or about to have a coronary."

"I feel fine, Scott. I believe that tomorrow night will be the end of all this." He continued to stir. "I received a call early this morning. They're calling back again at seven to set up a time to exchange the painting for money." He stopped talking as the waitress delivered Pims's concoction, which Pims lifted in a toast: "To my dear friend and curator without peer, Luther Mason. May all the days of your life be sunny and warm, and may you drink from the well of beauty forever more."

Luther touched the rim of Pims's snifter with his glass, placed it on the table, and said, "I want you to hold the two paintings for me for twenty-four hours."

The sudden worried expression on Pims's face was exaggerated, Mason knew. The big man said, "I was right. You are indeed suggesting something dark and mysterious. What paintings might these be that I would be holding in escrow for you?"

"Oh, stop it, Scott, will you!"

Pims drank from the snifter. "Usually, this wonderful mixture of spirits, which I learned from a Scottish bartender in Wick years ago, after making an obscenely rough journey to the Scottish mainland from the Orkneys, works almost instantly. But today, Luther, my stomach seems to be getting worse."

"Forget I asked," Mason said.

Pims placed his hammy hand on Mason's arm. "Don't be so touchy, Luther. Of course I'll do this favor for you. I just didn't want you to think it was an insignificant one. I want you to know that it marks the depth of the commitment I have to you as a friend, to say nothing of being an admiring critic. You want me to walk out of here with that portfolio."

Mason nodded.

"And to keep it safe until summoned by you to return it."

"Yes."

"And then, when you meet with your esteemed client and turn over one of the paintings to him in return for a fat envelope filled with negotiable currency, you wish to have me present to lend weight to your claim that what you're giving is the real McCoy, and perhaps more important, to lend my not inconsiderable physical presence to keep these same people from wringing your neck."

It hadn't occurred to Luther to ask Pims to accompany him to the meeting. But why not? He'd been the one to suggest it. And he knew everything about the scheme anyway.

A smile from Pims, and another reassuring placement of hand on arm. "Enough said," he said, sitting back and finishing his drink. "I offer myself as your aide-de-camp. In fact, this is all delightfully camp. When do you think this meeting will take place?"

"Sometime tomorrow night. I'll let you know as soon as I hear."

The waitress asked if they wished another drink.

"No, but give my friend the check," Pims said. When she went to get it, he said, "I think it appropriate that you pay for our drinks, Luther. But only because it will make you feel better. Make you feel less guilty about the awkward, dangerous position in which you place me."

"Jesus, Scott, will you please stop it. Either do this for me graciously or forget I asked."

They stood outside together. "Time for a quick bite?" Pims asked.

"No. I must get home for that phone call. And please go directly home yourself and put that portfolio where no one will find it."

Pims laughed. "You have placed it in the most capable of hands, Luther. You know that, which is why you chose me. I'm flattered."

You might be flattered, Mason thought, *but I'm feeling painfully empty-handed at this moment. Don't lose it, Scott. Don't have me end up a pathetic member of the Dortmunder gang in a Donald Westlake novel.*

While Mason waited by the phone in his apartment, Pims dialed a number from his. He'd unwrapped both versions of *Grottesca* and propped them against chairs next to his desk. "Remarkable," he said aloud. "Absolutely remark— Hello.

M. Scott Pims in Washington calling David Decker."

Decker came on the line. "Scott. How are you?"

"Splendid. Even better than that."

"How is the book coming?"

"You would ask that, being my editor. I was just in New York but didn't have a moment to call you. Tracking down another remarkable story having to do with a deceased cultural attaché from Italy who was more smuggler than attaché."

"Oh, yes, you mentioned Giliberti the last time we talked. Is that what you're calling about?"

"No. You know how delighted I am at having been brought into this inventive Caravaggio imbroglio. I mean, David, *really* being brought into it. Informed every inch of the way."

Decker sat in his cluttered office at the New York publishing house that had published Pims's last book and that had signed him up six months ago to do another.

"But just a few minutes ago, David, my inclusion on the margin of things suddenly put me in the midst. Things took a dramatic and unexpected turn. Can you keep a confidence?"

The young editor said, "I think so."

"The work in question. No, make that the *works* in question, sit mere inches from me as we speak."

Decker took his feet down from the edge of his desk, placed his elbows on the desk, and lowered his voice. "Are you saying—?"

"Yes, David. That is exactly what I am saying. You may have seen the best-seller potential when I first proposed this book to you. But that revered, albeit dubiously achieved status is now assured."

"When will I see the manuscript?"

"As soon as this adventure has played itself out to its logical conclusion."

"I can't wait. By the way, while you're on the phone, I've been playing with titles. I really like *The Caravaggio Conspiracy.*"

Pims laughed. "Good title, but unfortunately already taken. Peter Watson did a book about Caravaggio with that same title a number of years ago. Excellent work. I highly recommend it. Well, just wanted to touch base with my New York editor to let him know that his instincts for a good story are almost as good as mine. Ta-ta, David. We'll be in touch."

Pims placed both the original *Grottesca* and its copy on the dining room table and carefully rewrapped them in the brown paper. Luther had told him that the small pencil dot on the paper designated that package as containing the original. As he folded and taped the paper with the dot over the Saison forgery, he paused and looked up at the ceiling.

"Can you really do this to so fine a friend?" he asked himself aloud.

Then, looking down at the table, he laughed and said, "Of course you can."

TWENTY-EIGHT

As HE waited for the call from del Brasco's emissary, minutes turned into hours. Mason sat at his desk, his hand resting next to the telephone. But he'd decided to let his answering machine field the call first so that he could identify the caller before picking up.

It rang. Mason tensed. He waited for the machine's outgoing message to finish. Then, Pims's voice rattled the tiny speaker.

"Hello," Mason said.

"Heard anything yet?" Pims asked.

"I thought it was him," Luther said, exhaling breath he'd held in. "No. Will you be home the rest of the evening?"

"Oh, absolutely. I'm planted here awaiting your call."

The next call validated Luther's decision to let the answering machine act as a buffer: "Luther, this is Court Whitney. If you're there, please pick up. Luther, when you get this message, call me at my office immediately. I'm here with Mr. Spagnola from the Vatican, Mrs. Smith, and others. We're meeting about this controversy over *Grottesca* and will be well into the night. Call the moment you return."

Mason grimaced at Whitney's icy tone. Nowhere was it written that he had to be on call day and night. Let Whitney think he was out to dinner. He could call later, if he wanted to.

He looked at the clock again: 6:50. Ten minutes until the call from del Brasco's representative. Because he expected the ringing of the phone, the brusque buzz from his intercom startled him. He pressed the button: "Your son is here to see you, Mr. Mason," the doorman announced.

"Julian?" Luther muttered. His timing couldn't have been worse. "All right. Send him up."

He returned to his desk. 6:54. A knock. He drew a deep breath and opened the door. "Hello, Julian," he said. "I wasn't expecting—"

What Luther really wasn't expecting was to see the woman one step behind his son. "Lynn?" he said, face and voice mirroring his incredulity. "Why are you here?"

"She's with me," Julian answered.

"I can see that," said Mason. "But why?"

Mason looked into their eyes and read the answer. They were lovers. That night at the restaurant weeks ago. It must have started then.

But they hadn't come to announce their affair. It was something more important, he knew. Julian pulled Lynn into the apartment by the hand. She went directly to the closet and opened the door.

"Don't," Mason said, forgetting for the moment that *Grottesca* and its copy were no longer there.

"Where are they?" Lynn asked.

"Where are what?" said Mason.

"The paintings," Julian answered for her. *"Grottesca,* and the forgery."

"Are you both insane?" Mason said. *"Grottesca?* What in the world are you talking about?"

"This." Julian pulled Luther's airline ticket to Greece from his black leather jacket and waved it in his father's face.

"Where did you get that?" Mason asked, opening the desk drawer in which he'd left it. "Give that to me!"

Julian tossed the ticket on the desk. "Where are the paintings?" he repeated.

"I don't know what you're talking about," Luther said, knowing he'd been right. The paintings had been moved within the closet. He glared at his son. "You were in my apartment."

"I was in your apartment," Lynn said. "This morning."

"How did you—?"

Another question not needing an answer. He'd given her a key at the height of their affair and never asked for it back.

"I came up here this morning," Lynn Marshall said, her voice strangely bland considering the circumstances, "because I wanted to find out for myself what was going on."

"How dare you?" Mason was unable to generate the level of indignation he intended.

"It's all over the Gallery, Luther," Lynn said. "They're meeting now. Whitney. The curator from the Vatican. Police. Mrs. Smith from the White House."

Mason lowered his head and took a breath.

"Paul Bishop told me he had a hunch that the *Grottesca* that went back to Italy was a phony," Lynn said.

"Paul Bishop," Luther snarled. "Of course. Anything to tear me down. It's ridiculous. Absurd. You know me. Do you really think I would have any part of such a—?"

"If she doesn't, I do," Julian said. "Where are they?"

The phone rang. Mason spun around and looked at the clock: 7:05. His outgoing message on the machine was heard, followed by Court Whitney's voice. "Damn it, Luther, where are you? It's imperative that I reach you. Call me at my office the moment you hear this." He hung up with force.

"See?" Lynn said.

The phone rang again.

Mason stumbled to the desk and turned off the

answering machine. The phone continued to ring. "Please excuse me," he said feebly. "I'll—I'll be right back."

He slammed the bedroom door behind him, sat on the edge of his bed, and picked up the receiver. "Hello."

"Luther?"

He'd used his first name.

"Luther Mason?" There was no Italian accent.

"Yes," Mason said in a hoarse whisper.

"Peter Lafroing."

"Peter?" Lafroing was one of two other Caravaggio experts brought in by Court Whitney to evaluate *Grottesca.*

Luther cleared his throat. "Hello, Peter. I was expecting someone else. Hearing from you is a surprise. A pleasant one."

"Not purely a social call, Luther. I've taken on a freelance assignment that involves you."

"Oh?"

"Yes. I've been asked to appraise a certain work that I understand is in your possession."

Luther slumped on the bed as though the skeleton supporting his body had collapsed. Peter Lafroing working for Franco del Brasco? Outlandish!

As outlandish as he, Luther Mason, becoming involved with such a man.

"Del Brasco wants *you* to appraise the painting?" Mason said.

"I would rather not identify my client," Lafroing said, his voice filled with annoying light-
ness. "That wouldn't be professional. But I have
been asked to take a look before my client goes
forward with the purchase. Maybe we shouldn't
discuss it on the phone. Can we arrange to get together? I'd enjoy seeing you again."

Mason's initial reaction was that his dream was
about to come crashing down on him. Given
ample opportunity to exam the *Grottesca*, Lafroing was professionally capable of discerning
differences that would brand the Saison version a
copy. Show him the original and then try a switch?
No. Pulling off one switch had been nerve-racking
enough.

But then he remembered one of the "rules"
he'd formulated: Limit Lafroing's access to the
painting.

"Of course, Peter. Tomorrow night? That was
what I was led to expect."

"That's been changed, Luther. My client is anxious for the painting. He insists that I do it tonight.
Is it a problem?"

"You have the money with you?"

"I know nothing about your money arrangement, Luther. I'm with two other gentlemen sent
by my client to bring the painting back to him. I'm
sure they can resolve any questions of money between you and my client."

Mason wondered how much Lafroing knew. If

he knew everything and was willing to become part of it, he might be open to a bribe (he mentally changed it to "honorarium") to give a false report to del Brasco. If del Brasco was acting honorably, the men he'd sent would have a million dollars to give Luther pending Lafroing's examination of *Grottesca.* He could take Lafroing into his confidence, offer him a bigger fee than del Brasco was paying him. How much would it take del Brasco to buy someone like Peter Lafroing? Ten thousand dollars? Fifty thousand? Luther would give him double that. No, more. He'd offer him a half-million dollars.

"I would prefer that you examine the painting alone," Mason said. "Without these other men."

"I'm sure that will be acceptable to them. Where can we meet tonight? Say, eleven o'clock?"

Mason tried to organize his thoughts. Invite Lafroing to his apartment? Out of the question. It would have to be a neutral place.

"Luther?" Lafroing asked. "Are you there?"

"Yes. Just thinking of a place to meet. Not here. At my apartment. Too many people around. Maybe a restaurant."

Lafroing laughed. "Hardly the place to appraise a painting. Excuse me a moment."

Mason strained to hear a muffled conversation in the background but couldn't make out the words. Lafroing came back on the line. "Why not the Atlas Building?"

"The Atlas Building?"

"Yes. A dreary place, agreed, but we can be assured of being alone. A friend has a studio there. I have a key to it and to the building. Eleven o'clock sharp? I'll be inside the front door on the ground floor. I don't dare leave it open for you in that neighborhood."

"I suppose—"

"I must admit, Luther, that when I learned it was you who had the painting, I was—well, I suppose shocked is the word. I'm anxious to hear how it all came about."

"I—"

"There will be no problem, of course. I've already spent considerable time with the work when it was at the National Gallery. No question of its authenticity. Still, I have an obligation."

"Of course."

"It will be good to see you again. Eleven. The front door of the Atlas Building."

"Yes. But come alone, Peter."

"That shouldn't be a problem. Hold on." More muffled background conversation. "I'll be by myself," he said.

"You'll have the money with you?" Mason asked. "I can't turn the painting over without the money."

"I told you I have nothing to do with your financial arrangements. But I'm sure the gentleman is fair and honorable."

"You haven't met your client?" Luther asked.

"Not personally. We can go over all of this tonight when I see you."

"Yes."

"Good. Rest assured, Luther, your mischievous little secret is safe with me. My lips are sealed."

"Peter, perhaps you'd prefer to take the painting with you for a more prolonged examination. That would be acceptable to me, provided a good-faith advance was paid." Lafroing said nothing. "In the neighborhood of, oh, a hundred thousand dollars. I trust your client. Once you've validated the work's authenticity, he can send me the balance."

"That certainly sounds fair, Luther. I'll ask about it."

"Fine. Good. Eleven tonight."

Mason slowly lowered the receiver into its cradle.

Julian did the same with the desk phone.

When Mason returned to the living room, Julian and Lynn were sitting close together on the couch.

"Who was that?" Julian asked.

"Just a friend. Now, let's get back to this nonsense you were talking about before we were interrupted."

Julian stood and approached his father. "It's not nonsense and you know it. That Caravaggio you sent back to Italy was a phony. You have the original. Lynn saw it."

Mason turned to her. "If you were so sure I had the original *Grottesca,* why didn't you just take it when you broke into my apartment?"

Lynn, too, stood. " 'Broke in?' I had a key. You gave me the key."

"Because we were close."

"You were lovers," Julian said.

"And now *you* are," Mason said, barely able to contain his anger. And hurt.

"I didn't take the paintings because I didn't think it was right," said Lynn. "I wanted to talk to you about it."

"You didn't think it was *right?* What is right for you, Lynn? Using me to get ahead at the National Gallery? Sleeping with my son?"

"Why don't we just stop the BS?" Julian said. "Where are the paintings?"

"That is none of your business." Mason said.

"We're making it our business."

Mason felt weak, thought he might faint, and sat in the desk chair. It was incomprehensible to him to be confronted by his son this way. Like some lowlife extorting money from him. Of course, Julian had been doing that for years. The difference was that now, all pretense of subtlety had been abandoned.

"What do you want?" Mason asked, his thin voice mirroring his defeat.

"Let us in on it with you," Julian said.

"What do you mean?"

"Cut us in. You must have a buyer for the painting or you wouldn't have bothered with all this. It's worth, what, forty million? Fifty? How much are you getting for it?"

"I'd rather not say."

Lynn said, "You obviously had two copies made, Luther. One went back to Italy. The other one was in the closet along with the original. What are you planning to do, pawn the forgery off on a buyer and keep *Grottesca* for yourself?"

"I—"

"Don't be stupid," Julian said. "We can sell the original in Japan. Or South America. Why mess around with giving a phony painting to somebody in return for a few bucks?"

"Or," Lynn said, "for more than a few bucks."

Mason stood. "I'll have to think about it." They would never understand, he knew, that everything he'd suffered, all the scheming, planning, the pain and the fear, had nothing to do with money. Yes, he wanted enough on which to live nicely. But he hadn't stolen *Grottesca* to become rich. It was the work itself he coveted. These two greedy, ambitious young pups would never understand that. No one would.

"I'm meeting with people tomorrow night," he said. After I do, we can talk about this."

Julian and Lynn looked at each other, knowing he was lying. His meeting was that night, four hours from now. "Where will we meet tomorrow night?" Julian asked.

"Right here."

"You're sure you'll be here?"

"Have I ever lied to you, Julian?"

"Maybe you're lying to me now."

Mason had had enough. "Get out!" he shouted. "Just get out of here. The sight of you disgusts me."

"We'll be back tomorrow night," Julian said. Then he gave one of his small laughs. "Jesus, I never figured you had it in you—Dad."

Mason bolted the door behind them and called Pims. "I have to see you right away, Scott."

"I'm here, dear friend. I'm in the process of whipping up a lovely batch of *cape sante in tecia conchiglie dei pellegrini in umido.* I bought some delectable bay scallops, coral and all. I shall set the table for two."

"I'm not coming for food, damn it!"

"Of course not. But man must eat. Besides, nourishment is good for the brain, and I have a feeling you're going to need every gray cell you possess. Come on over, Luther."

"The forgery was done by a drunken French genius named Jacques Saison."

The meeting in Whitney's office on the seventh floor of the East Building had been going on for hours. Present were Whitney; Senior Curator Paul Bishop; Chief of Conservation Donald Fechter; head of the National Gallery's Public Information Office Philip Simone; Annabel Reed-Smith; Vatican senior curator Joseph Spagnola; Anthony Benedetto from the Italian Embassy; Steve Jordan, chief of Washington MPD's Art Squad; his assistant, Gloria Watson; and the National Gallery's head of security, Carl Kelley. Jordan had the floor.

"According to the information I've received from a colleague at Italy's Delegation for the Recovery of Missing Works of Art—they have fewer people working for it than there are words in the title—Carlo Giliberti personally delivered the original *Grottesca* to Saison in Paris. Saison, it seems, copied it, and Luther picked up the original and copy, although that isn't written in stone at this juncture."

Benedetto, the new cultural attaché to Washington, swore softly in Italian.

Jordan continued: "My counterparts in Italy are still trying to determine through Customs how Mason, or someone acting on his behalf, got the original and copies back into the States."

Carl Kelley interrupted. "That would be interesting," he said. "But I'm more interested in how the paintings got switched here in the Gallery. There's no question that what hung on the wall for that month was the real thing—is there?"

"Of course not," Whitney said.

"So at some point between the time it was taken off the gallery wall and the crate went back to Italy, Mason managed to swap the original for a forgery," said Kelley.

"I hate to play devil's advocate," Annabel said, "or be the lawyer again, but aren't we assuming too much to be accusing Luther? I mean, from what's been presented here so far, Carlo Giliberti took the original *Grottesca* out of Italy and gave it to this forger in Paris. You seem sure of that. You're also certain that the *Grottesca* delivered to the church in Ravello is a forgery. But I haven't heard anything that definitively links Luther Mason to those acts."

Paul Bishop said, "It had to be Luther. Put all the pieces together and the puzzle forms his face. His obsession with Caravaggio, especially *Grottesca.* The frequent trips to Italy. His close friendship with Giliberti." To Fechter: "Your people who crated *Grottesca* for the return to Italy told you that they left Luther alone in the room because he started to cry. Jesus, that painting should never have been left alone for any reason, under any circumstance."

Fechter started to say something, but Whitney waved him off. "The security guard has Luther's signature entering that room at precisely the time *Grottesca* was being readied for shipment. He had those few minutes alone, more than enough time to make the exchange."

"We all noticed," said Paul Bishop, "how Luther spent the month *Grottesca* was on exhibition carrying paintings everywhere he went. Always a couple of paintings, sometimes wrapped, sometimes in that big portfolio he's so fond of using. That must have been part of his plan. No one thought twice about his carrying art into the shipping room."

"I know, I know," Annabel said. "But we're still dealing with supposition."

"Go over again for us what Luther said when you showed him the correspondence from Betti," Kelley said.

Whitney replayed the conversation as best he could from memory, concluding by saying, "He dismissed it as being a stupid mistake."

"So did I," Annabel said. "With all due respect, Mr. Spagnola, you've only performed a cursory inspection of the painting in Ravello. Surely, it will take longer than that to ascertain whether it's a forgery."

Steve Jordan said, "True, Annabel. But we have the added information that the original *Grottesca* was taken to Jacques Saison in Paris and that he made a copy. You don't make a copy of a masterpiece unless you intend to lay it off on unsuspecting buyers. Or in this case a government."

"Any idea who that buyer might be?" Whitney asked.

Jordan shrugged. "There are dozens of rich collectors around the world willing to spend millions to get their hands on an original Caravaggio, especially one with the aura of *Grottesca*. A few of them have a standing order with the underground: Deliver me a Caravaggio, name your price, no questions asked. One interests me in particular. A notorious collector out in San Francisco, Franco del Brasco. Notorious because he not only collects art, he's connected—mob connected. Rumored to be a major buyer of stolen art. But that's all we've ever had, rumors, not enough to get a warrant to go in and search."

"Luther started his career in San Francisco," Paul Bishop offered.

"And we know he went out there recently," Jordan said. "Stayed at the Westin St. Francis in a twelve hundred-dollar-a-night suite."

"On a curator's salary," Bishop muttered.

Anthony Benedetto cleared his throat. "Gentlemen," he said, "all this conversation is good. But what is important now is not how it was done, but that the person responsible for this fraud perpetrated upon my people be found immediately. The original *Grottesca* is undoubtedly with him. Find him and we find the painting."

Everyone agreed, and the meeting broke up. Whitney said he would continue the search for Luther, and Jordan said he would send officers to

Mason's apartment. If the senior curator hadn't been found by morning, an all-points bulletin would be issued.

"Why not put out such a bulletin now?" Paul Bishop asked.

"Because I don't think Luther Mason is the kind of man to simply disappear," Jordan replied. "Too many strings to keep him here. His son, right? He has his connection to this gallery and his reputation to uphold. He's probably out enjoying dinner somewhere and hasn't the slightest idea what's going on."

Jordan walked Annabel to her car. "What do you really think of this?" she asked.

"More than I let on in the meeting. I owe you one, Annabel. And I know you can keep a confidence."

"I try."

"I think Luther Mason did pull this off. Or almost. And I also think the buyer for the painting is del Brasco in San Francisco, based upon what my counterparts out there have managed to track down. Del Brasco sent two of his 'assistants' to Washington yesterday. Art appreciation isn't their thing. Breaking knees is. Spagnola, from the Vatican, is no angel, either. Before he came over to see Whitney at the Gallery, he met with people in the Italian Embassy. Some of the people working in the Embassy are not what you would call diplomats. They have another function. Some have ties with intelligence services, some with business, some with organized crime back in Italy. There's an aging mafioso there, Luigi Sensi. Looks like the age of specialization hasn't escaped the Mafia. Sensi, along with committing other crimes, is their point man for stolen art. It's big bucks for the mob over there."

"It's my understanding that some people in our embassies aren't exactly diplomats, either," Annabel said.

"Everybody practicing diplomacy of a different kind," Jordan said. "I played down looking for Luther Mason tonight. But the minute I leave you, I'm getting over to his apartment. *And* I'm putting out that all-points. If he has the original *Grottesca,* and everybody's out looking for it, his health could take a sudden turn for the worse."

Annabel bit her lip. "I hope you find him," she said. "I know that if Luther's behind this, he's guilty of a crime. But not one worth losing his life over. By the way, Steve, what about the old priest, Giocondi, the one Luther claims had the painting in his parish all those years? He never showed up in Ravello."

"Disappeared," Jordan said flatly. "He could provide some answers—if anybody could find him. Gone. The Italian police are looking."

Jordan opened the car door for her.

"I never dreamed the world of art could be so evil," Annabel said. "I hope you find Luther before anything happens to him. Despite what he might have done—well, he's a nice man."

Mason was oblivious to everything around him as he left his apartment, got in his car, and headed for Pims's place. He did not notice a car parked across the street. In it were the two men from the Italian Embassy. They allowed Luther to proceed a block before falling in behind. Their presence was not lost on Pims, however, who stood at his living room window overlooking the street in anticipation of Luther's arrival. He saw his friend pull up to a vacant meter and park, get out, and scurry across. He also saw the car that had followed, whose driver parked at a fire hydrant and turned off the lights.

"What have we here?" Pims wondered aloud as he closed the drapes and went to welcome his good friend.

TWENTY-NINE

PIMS'S FLOOR-LENGTH purple silk robe was worn over a white shirt, his favorite Mona Lisa tie, gray slacks, and purple carpet slippers with gold embroidery, whose toes curled up over his instep. Although he expressed keen disappointment that Luther wasn't hungry, it didn't interfere with his readying of that evening's meal. Luther sat at the kitchen table as Pims removed leaves of radicchio from where they'd been soaking in extra-virgin olive oil in preparation for braising. ". . . which would mean giving up the dream that has fueled your plan from the very beginning," he said, his words accompanied by the steady chop-chop-chop of a large knife cutting through garlic cloves.

Luther was in a state of almost total physical, emotional, psychological, and spiritual collapse. He'd decided while driving there that he couldn't go through with the final phase of his scheme. Instead, he would give the original to del Brasco, take the million dollars, and escape the country without his prized possession.

Pims was appalled at that resolution. "Luther," he said, "money has never been the object. Not really. If it had been, I would have dissuaded you from the very beginning. If it was money you were after, I would have suggested you rob a bank, or swindle some rich little old lady out of the proceeds of her late husband's insurance. No! Your passion for Caravaggio, especially for *Grottesca,* is what enticed me to help you, to counsel you, to stand by you as you've gone through this remarkable exercise." *Chop-chop-chop.* "All will have been for naught if you succumb to this moment of weakness—which I assure you is only temporary—and turn over one of the finest paintings the world has ever known to that lowlife in California."

"I know, I know," Luther said, his elbows on the table, face buried in his hands. "But I just don't know if I can go through with it. When I discovered that Peter Lafroing had been hired by del Brasco to evaluate the painting, I almost threw up. And then learning that my own son was sleeping with Lynn Marshall, and that they know almost everything that's going on, was too much to bear."

Pims laid the knife on the counter. "And look at yourself, Luther," he said, turning and facing the curator. "Sitting at my table sniveling like some pimply schoolboy caught cheating on an examination and fearing expulsion. Snap out of it, man! *Be a man!*"

Luther raised his head. "You're right," he said.

"It isn't the money. I can return the original to the National Gallery. All I want is peace."

"Peace? Do you really think giving *Grottesca* back to Court Whitney and his bureaucratic cronies will buy you peace? It's too late for that, Luther. As we speak, your boss, and Lord knows who else, are planning your public hanging. Your only option is to go forward. I've examined both paintings very carefully. Saison did a masterly job. Lafroing, despite his impressive credentials, will have a bugger of a time branding it a forgery." His voice became louder. "Think of it, Luther. Think of having *Grottesca* hanging on the wall of your pleasant little apartment in Greece. Sunshine, soft breezes, no more groveling to the demands of the National Gallery and its artistic pretenders. Evenings on your veranda with nubile young women, a leaded goblet brimming with Metaxa in your hand. And when you choose to be alone, there will always be the majesty of *Grottesca* in which to bask."

Luther slumped in his chair. For the first time since launching his plan, he was incapable of making a decision. His internal reasoning circuits had shut down. That was why he'd come to Pims's apartment in the first place. He needed another person to think through this final phase. There was no one else in the world to whom he could turn. Pims had been along for almost every mile of the wild ride.

"I just don't know what to do," Luther said again.

"Your ability to make rational judgments hasn't been totally impaired. You had the wisdom to seek my counsel." He pulled out a chair and sat opposite Mason. "Actually, Luther, things are not as grim as you think. Consider. While finding out that your own flesh and blood has been sleeping with your former paramour has battered your male ego, it doesn't matter in the larger scheme of things. You're better rid of both, which you are. They think you're meeting these dreadful people representing del Brasco tomorrow night. But you're doing it tonight. Which means they are out of the picture. By the time they discover what you've done, you'll be on a plane to the Hellas, land of Homer and Hesiod, Demosthenes, Plato, Aristotle, *Iliad,* and *Odyssey.* Think of it, man! Greece! You and *Grottesca."* He chuckled. "A fitting reward for having endured the parasites who've dominated your life."

Detecting that his friend's spirits might have picked up a bit, Pims continued his lecture.

"You've thought things out very nicely, Luther, despite your tenuous emotional state. The two choices you contemplate make sense.

"You meet Lafroing at the Atlas Building at the appointed hour. I shall drive you and remain in my car at a respectful distance. But never out of sight.

"You tell Peter you will hand over the painting

to him then and there and that he has it for the next twenty-four hours. In return for this act of trust on your part, he is to give you a down payment on the million dollars. I rather think he will jump at the opportunity to walk away with the painting, probably cackling to himself about what a fool you are to have given it up so easily and for such a meager amount. But you, Luther, shall have the last laugh. You will have the original *Grottesca,* as well as the down payment in your pocket.

"How much should you ask? As in all things, it depends on what the market will bear. I think asking for two or three hundred thousand dollars is more than reasonable. Don't you?"

"I don't know if Peter will have money with him. The others—"

"The others will be in close proximity, I assure you. All Peter has to do is step out of the building for a moment and get the money from them."

Pims's clear, forceful presentation served its purpose. Luther was calmer now. "Yes," Mason said. "I see what you mean."

Pims wasn't finished. "Your other idea, of bribing Lafroing to give his client a false report, also has merit."

"Peter Lafroing is a legitimate and respected expert," Mason said. "For me to admit to him that—"

Pims smashed his padded fist on the table.

"Luther! Think about what you're saying. Peter Lafroing is knowingly taking part in a criminal act on behalf of Mr. del Brasco. He is well aware that he comes to the Atlas Building to examine a stolen Caravaggio. What makes you think he would not jump at the chance of putting an additional half-million dollars in his pocket?"

"I don't know," said Luther.

"And remember this, my friend, there is every possibility—probability is more accurate—that Mr. Peter Lafroing will proclaim that the Saison version is authentic. Legitimate. From the grubby hand of Caravaggio himself."

Pims's uncomplimentary reference to Caravaggio stung Mason. He rose unsteadily and went to the living room, where the wrapped paintings stood side by side. Maybe it will work, he thought.

He wrapped his arms about himself and rocked from side to side. Pims was right. Nothing he had done—the painful decisions, the sleepless nights, the frantic trips to Rome and Ravello, the tension of dealing with the defrocked priest Giocondi and with the drunken Frenchman Jacques Saison, the surly del Brasco—none of it had been for money. If he didn't succeed in flying away with *Grottesca* under his arm, it would all have been a useless exercise, a futile attempt to break the bonds of respectability that bound him.

Pims entered the room and extended his hand. "Come, Luther," he said. "Everything will be fine."

Luther picked up the wrapped paintings.

"Leave the original here," Pims said.

"No. I want them both with me."

"Good God, Luther, be sensible. What do you intend to do, make a decision on the spot which version to give Lafroing? Madness. He gets the copy."

"I want them both with me."

"You're liable to make a mistake—intend to give him the copy but hand him the original."

"The original has the dot on it."

"Here." Pims placed his index finger on the pencil dot and punched a small hole in the paper. "At least you'll know which is which without having to use a magnifying glass. And what will you do, place both on a table for Lafroing to see?"

"I want them both with me. I'll put one away before he comes."

"He's letting you in the building. You won't have the opportunity."

"I—I'll decide what to do before we get there. I'll leave one in the car with you."

"That's better," said Pims. "You're coming to your senses. Come. We mustn't be late."

They rode the elevator to the basement, where Pims garaged his Cadillac. The paintings were placed on the rear floor. Pims slowly drove up the exit ramp and turned right.

"Why are you going this way?" Mason asked. "The Atlas Building is—"

"To avoid company."

"What company?"

"Unwanted company. I'm not feeling especially sociable. The two men who followed you to my apartment. They parked behind you on the street."

Mason twisted in the seat to see through the rear window. "Them?" he said.

"Yes. I thought we might evade them coming out of the garage, but they're evidently smarter than they look. Moved their car to give them a view of both front door and garage. No matter. We can handle them if necessary."

Luther reached behind his seat and fingered the two versions of *Grottesca*.

"Still there?" Pims asked, with a light laugh.

"Who do you think they are?" Mason asked.

"Brokers of fine art. They also break things, I imagine."

It began to rain as they drove past the Atlas Building at ten-thirty, a half hour ahead of schedule. That strip of Ninth Street was dingy and dark. The yellow window of one of the pornography shops spilled a garish puddle of light onto the sidewalk. Young men loitered on the corners. A man wearing a tan raincoat came out of the porn shop and glanced left and right before lowering his head and walking away. No one stood at the entrance to the Atlas Building. Its chains and padlocks sent an ominous message.

Pims circled the block, followed by the other car. He pulled to the curb on Ninth, a hundred feet from the building's entrance, and shut off the lights. "I feel like a detective reconnoitering a den of depravity," he said.

The other car passed them and parked a block ahead.

What had been a lovely, gentle day in Washington had deteriorated into the leading edge of a storm roaring up the East Coast. The wind had picked up; the rain was whipped by it. Low, dirty clouds obscured the sky, the moon covered with cheesecloth.

"Have you made your decision?" Pims asked.

"Yes. I'll give him the copy. As planned. But should things go awry, you'll be here?"

"Oh, yes, Luther. I will be here guarding your treasure."

"Do you have an umbrella?"

"Of course." Pims reached beneath his seat and came up with a short umbrella that opened with the push of a button.

They sat in silence until another car turned the corner and stopped in front of the Atlas Building. Luther couldn't see through the vehicle's darkened windows, but there appeared to be three men in it. The back door opened and Peter Lafroing stepped out.

"It's him," said Luther.

"It certainly is," Pims said.

The car drove away and turned the corner in the direction of Constitution Avenue.

Lafroing unlocked two padlocks on the door, disengaged the chains, and disappeared into the pitch-black lobby.

"I suppose I should go now," Mason said.

"I suppose you should. Do you want to go over it with me one more time?"

Mason shivered against a sudden chill. "There isn't much to go over," he said. "Don't worry about me, Scott. I'll be fine."

"Of course you will, dear friend. It is almost over. After tonight, you're a free man. A bird on the wing."

Luther reached behind to grab one of the paintings from the rear. Pims reached, too, inserting his finger into the hole he'd made in the brown paper. Luther brought the other over the seat and into his lap. "That's it, Luther," Pims said.

Luther opened the door on his side and stepped into the soggy night. He hunched down in his raincoat as though to make himself smaller, closed the door, considered opening the umbrella, but decided the wind was too stiff and walked resolutely in Lafroing's direction, the painting cradled in his arms. He paused halfway there and turned to look at Pims. Pims snapped on the Caddy's interior lights and used his fingers to indicate he should keep going.

"There is weeping in my heart like the rain falling

on the city." Verlaine's line from *Romances sans Paroles* came to Mason as he stepped up to the Atlas Building's entrance.

Lafroing opened the door. "Come in, Luther," he said. "Miserable night."

That evaluation of Washington's weather was shared by everyone in the vicinity of the Atlas Building that night.

The two men from the Italian Embassy who'd met earlier in the day with the Vatican's Joseph Spagnola sat glumly in their car a block ahead of where M. Scott Pims waited.

Franco del Brasco's golden-haired bodyguard and a colleague recruited from New York had parked around the corner after dropping off Peter Lafroing. Blond Curls had traveled to Washington with clothing suited to a stretch of record-breaking heat in San Francisco and shivered and swore as he and his compatriot waited for Lafroing to rejoin them.

"What's this all about?" the New York man asked.

Blond Curl's teeth chattered. "Some painting my boss wants. This guy Lafroing is meeting, Mason, has it, only my boss thinks maybe Mason will try to pawn a phony off on him."

"A painting? What is it? Worth a lot?"

"Yeah. I don't know how much. Christ, I'm cold."

Julian Mason and Lynn Marshall left the bar of the 701 Restaurant at Seventh and Pennsylvania, a few blocks from the National Gallery and not far from the Atlas Building. He'd had three beers, she'd nursed a strawberry daiquiri. Neither had heeded the weather forecast. Lynn held a newspaper over her head while Julian expressed concern at what the rain would do to his leather jacket. They walked at a fast clip in the direction of Ninth Street.

It had been at least three years since Luther had been in the Atlas Building, his last visit having been to the studio of a friend, art conservator Hilary Daley-Hyme. As he felt his way up the dilapidated stairway to the second floor, a rush of emotions came and went like wind gusts. He was, at once, dreading this moment, yet exhilarated at its contemplation. Judge *Grottesca* as you will, Peter, he thought. Judge *me* as you will. It matters not.

They passed the door to Daley-Hyme's studio and went to the next, where Lafroing inserted a key. The inside was nearly black, illuminated only by ambient light through dirt-crusted windows. Lafroing found a lamp attached to a drawing board and turned it on. Hardly sufficient light to examine the painting, thought Luther. How convenient.

"So, Luther, here we are. You will, I assume, tell me what's going on."

"I would think it's self-evident."

"Some of it. What did you do, have a copy made to send back to Italy?"

"Yes."

"Who made it?"

"It doesn't matter. Look, Peter, I'd really like to get this over with as fast as possible. This is no place for you to examine it. The light. What I suggest is—"

"This is fine, Luther," Lafroing said. "Why not unwrap it and put it on this table. I don't need a lot of time or a lot of light." He laughed softly. "I spent hours with it at the National Gallery. Why my client is so concerned is beyond me. But he's paying me to do this, so I might as well go through the motions."

Mason placed the Saison copy on the table. "You unwrap it, Peter. Go ahead," he said, walking to one of the windows overlooking the street. He couldn't bear to look at the painting with Lafroing. And standing there helped obscure the light.

"Oh, yes," Lafroing said. "How beautiful." He gently ran his fingertips over the canvas, up and down, across, touching the boy's face, the animals, the twisted thorny stems. "We're looking at this on the right night. He was a stormy genius, Luther."

"I'm well aware of that," Mason said, at the window.

"The use of light," Lafroing said. "The naturalism that upset so many others in his time. Aha! You know, of course, that he started this work with the boy's ear, as he usually did."

"Yes, I know." Starting with an ear was a Caravaggio trademark. Saison had obviously known it, too. Score one for a drunken Frenchman.

"I love the way his *fattura* in this work is looser than some of his others. And that he chose—we know it was deliberate, don't we, Luther?—that he chose not to have certain figures cast a shadow even though the placement of the light source dictates that they should."

Mason continued to listen from his position at the window. Lafroing was showing off his academic knowledge of Caravaggio for Mason's benefit, so blinded by the need to impress that he was incapable of making a reasoned judgment about the painting's authenticity.

After another five minutes of posturing, Lafroing came to Mason, smiled, and slapped him on the arms. "One day I assume I'll read about this," he said.

"I hope not."

"Or hear about it on that pompous ass's television program—Pims."

"You'll report to your client that it's the original?"

"Of course. You mentioned the possibility of my taking the painting for a longer look."

Luther's heart sank.

"My client's colleagues asked that I give you this—*if* I judged the work to be genuine." He handed Luther an envelope.

Luther opened it. Inside was fifty thousand dollars and a letter:

I have instructed my representative to give you this cash if everything is in order and to take the painting with him. An equal sum will be delivered to you tomorrow at a place you designate. In addition, nine hundred thousand dollars will be deposited in a Swiss bank account bearing your name. The name of the bank and the account number will be sent to you. All, of course, dependent upon the final validation of the painting.

"Care to share what it says?" Lafroing asked.

"What? No. I really can't, Peter. Sorry. It says you are to take the painting with you. That's fine. The arrangements are fine."

Lafroing laughed. "I must admit, Luther, I never would have dreamed that you were capable of—well, of pulling off such a monumental theft. Awesome."

"Not something of which I'm especially proud, Peter. It just happened."

"Just happened or not, I am impressed. I take it you are now a rich man."

"Of course. Why else would I have done this *except* for money?"

"I can't think of another reason," said Lafroing.

"If I had the opportunity, I'd do the same. Take the money and run, thumbing my nose at the world all the way. Congratulations, Luther. Drop me a postcard now and then."

Lafroing started to rewrap the painting.

"Careful with that," Mason said. "Don't let it get wet."

"I will, I will. There'll be no rain on Caravaggio this night."

"How did you get here?" Mason asked after they'd left the building and Lafroing had secured the door.

"My client's colleagues. They're waiting for me around the corner. Ride?"

"No. I need a walk."

"In this weather?"

"I like the rain. Good night, Peter. And please tell your client I'm pleased Caravaggio's greatest work is in good hands."

Luther watched Lafroing turn the corner before allowing his glee to consume him. He laughed, more of a giggle. High-pitched. He wanted to leap and punch the air with his fist, a football player scoring a touchdown. Dance in the rain like Gene Kelly. He wanted to walk to Pims's car but broke into a trot. Still laughing. He couldn't believe it.

The men from the Italian Embassy watched Lafroing from their automobile as he headed with the package for the car containing Blond Curls and his associate. "That must be it," one said.

"What about him?" They both looked to where Mason had reached Pims's Cadillac and opened the rear passenger door.

"I don't know," his colleague replied in Italian.

Mason laughed and cried. Streaming tears of relief and joy. It had worked. Better than he'd ever imagined it could, or would. "It worked!" he shouted at Pims.

"Get in, man," Pims said. "The rain."

Luther pulled the other wrapped painting from the car.

"What the hell are you doing?" Pims asked.

Luther said through tears and blowing rain, "Walking, Scott. Running. It worked!"

"You're out of your mind. Get in the car!"

But Luther ran.

Pims's girth precluded him from reaching the rear door over the seat. He shoved himself from the car, came around, and slammed the door shut. "Luther, come on!" he shouted, the wind seemingly slamming his words back against his face.

Pims didn't know what to do. Pursue him on foot? Drive after him? By the time he had made up his mind to use the car and had wedged himself behind the wheel, Luther Mason was out of sight, having turned left on D Street and cut through the Navy Memorial in Market Square.

Lafroing was back in the car with Blond Curls and the New York man when they saw Mason running through the rain, a brown paper package held tightly to his chest.

"What's he got?" Blond Curls asked.

"I don't know," was Lafroing's reply.

"Looks like he's got the same thing you got," Blond Curls said.

Julian Mason and Lynn Marshall had been observing the Atlas Building from the protective overhang of a nearby doorway. They saw Lafroing leave, then watched as Julian's father came down Ninth Street carrying a rectangle wrapped in brown paper.

"Where's he going?" Lynn asked.

"Looks like he's heading for the Gallery." They followed.

Mason reached Constitution Avenue, turned left, and ran across the broad avenue and past the National Gallery's West Building, before turning right on to Fourth Street, which cut through the courtyard separating the West and East buildings. He looked to the fountains, jets of water caught by the wind and tossed into a swirl creating a grotesque series of patterns against the glass wall leading down to the interior concourse.

He went to the fountain and stood alone, the collar of his raincoat pulled up tightly around his neck. His shoes were soaked. He dropped the unopened umbrella to the ground and lifted his head into the wind and rain. Tears continued to flow; the rain was now a deluge. His body was numb, his mind very much alive. Visions of his mother, of Juliana and Julian, of the familiar comfort of his apartment and office at the National Gallery, of Lynn Marshall's warm body, of his friend Scott Pims, of Caravaggio, swamped him.

He felt small and lost and giddy. Like a child again.

He never saw the person approach, becoming aware only when a hand reached around him from behind and grabbed the package he held. The motion caused him to turn; he now faced his attacker.

Mason hung on to the painting. "Oh, no," he said, stumbling backwards in the direction of the tiny concrete steps over which the fountain's water cascaded down to the interior-concourse window.

"No," Luther shouted as he lost his grip. "Please. What are you—?"

The wet brown paper package was yanked from him with great force, sending him spinning out of control toward the man-made waterfall. He lost his balance and tumbled headfirst down the steps, propelled by the water's force, his face striking one step, then another and another, breaking his cheekbone, his nose, down and down—thud-thud-thud—until reaching the window, into which his face smashed. Luther Mason felt nothing in the few seconds of life left to him except the sensation of being alone, cold and wet. Then, the damage to his brain prevailed. Blood flowed freely from his nostrils, turning the water a pretty Poussin pink.

THIRTY

MASON'S BODY was discovered that morning by a National Gallery security guard. At first, the guard didn't believe what he saw wedged against the floor-to-ceiling window, the grotesquely misshapen face, the eyes opened unnaturally wide, the water gurgling in and out of the gaping mouth. Was it post-Impressionism? Performance art?

Now, at seven that morning, the exterior courtyard was filled with Washington police, the National Gallery's own security people, and a burgeoning crowd of onlookers.

Two MPD detectives, one using a small video camcorder, photographed Luther's body from the top of the steps leading down to the window; the other gave a play-by-play of what they were seeing: "Deceased is lying at bottom of steps—face against glass—Joe, get a closeup of the steps—there are—let me see, I'll count—ninety-six steps—no, I lost count—"

Suddenly, the fountain's twenty-four jets, which had been tossing water into the air, went dry.

"Who turned off the goddamn water?" a detective yelled.

"We have to get the body up out of there," another said.

"Turn the goddamn water back on until we finish taping—come on, get real—we need to show the body like it was, with the water running over it."

Word was passed; the fountain sprang into action again.

Videotaping completed, the water was once again shut off, and two criminalists from MPD gingerly descended the succession of tiny steps to the body. Minutes later Luther Mason's corpse was on dry ground, on its back on a piece of white canvas.

A forensics supervisor knelt next to the body, took Mason's jaw between thumb and index finger, and slowly moved it back and forth, saying as he did, "Rigor has started in the face." He looked up: "Get everybody out of here who doesn't need to be here."

As uniformed officers pushed back the crowd, the forensics chief pulled open Mason's raincoat, unbuttoned two shirt buttons, and inserted his hand beneath his armpit. "A little warmth, not much," he said to an assistant jotting down his comments. "But with all that water running over him, he's cooled off faster than normal."

After some debate about whether to attempt to

take Luther's temperature by inserting a thermometer into a body cavity, it was decided to rush the corpse to the forensics lab, where it could be done under less public scrutiny.

Two hours later, after preliminary forensic tests had been conducted in the lab, it was determined that the time of death had been approximately midnight, the cause multiple fractures of the skull.

Mason's possessions had been carefully catalogued. His wallet was intact. More important, an envelope was found in his pocket containing fifty thousand dollars in cash. If the deceased had been pushed down the steps to his death—and that was only a possibility; he could have fallen on his own—robbery was an unlikely motive. An assailant would have had to go down the slippery steps to retrieve the envelope. Of course, Mason might have been carrying something else that was taken from him prior to his fall.

That afternoon, MPD chief of detectives Emil Vigilio convened a meeting of homicide detectives. "First," he said, "let's deal with the obvious. There's no evidence to indicate the deceased was pushed down those steps. Is there?" Muttered negatives. "On the other hand, it doesn't make a damn bit of sense to me why this top guy from the National Gallery would be out there at midnight in the pouring rain, fifty big ones in his pocket, and just happen to take the wrong step. Anybody here explain that to me?"

"Doesn't make any sense." "Doesn't add up."

"So," Vigilio continued, "let's say somebody else was there and gave him a shove. Why? And if this somebody did it to kill Mason, is there any connection between it and the Italian cultural attaché, Carlo Giliberti, getting it in Rock Creek?"

"Why would there be?"

"They were good friends."

"Yeah. And they were both involved in the Caravaggio show going on at the National Gallery. I just got off the phone with Steve Jordan. There's rumors goin' 'round that there's been some hanky-pank where that one painting is concerned. What's it called? Grotesque?" He consulted a yellow legal pad. "*Grottesca.* Jordan says that Mason was under suspicion of pulling some kind of switch at the National Gallery. That could upset a few people, huh? Maybe enough to kill him."

One of Vigilio's detectives grunted and shook his head. "The two are so different, Emil," he said. "Giliberti got it with the ice pick in the back of the head, gangland style. Mason falls down the stairs and fractures his skull. If there was somebody else involved, sounds to me like he got into an argument and got this individual mad enough to take a swing at him. Give him a shove. Maybe a girlfriend—he's divorced, right?—or maybe a street guy looking to mug him."

"And this top curator just happens to be standing there in the rain," Vigilio said.

"What about that swap of paintings? This Mason pulls off a scam, hangs on to an original? Worth a lot of money?"

"Right," said Vigilio. "According to Jordan, Mason probably had the original of this—" He glanced at the paper again. "This *Grottesca*. Jordan says it's worth fifty mil. Maybe more. If Mason was walking around with that thing last night, it's like havin' fifty million bucks in your pocket."

"And fifty grand green in his pocket, too," said an admiring detective.

"Uh huh. Only if he did have the painting with him, *that* wasn't in his pocket. Let's say he's carrying the original on his way to meet somebody, maybe somebody interested in buying the painting. And let's say somebody else knew where he was going and why. Knew what he had. The guy Mason was supposed to meet doesn't show, or he's late, but this somebody else is there, grabs the painting, and shoves Mason down the steps."

Another detective, a grizzled old-timer who'd been silent, muttered, "Or maybe Mason was a fruitcake who likes walking in the rain. He slips, falls, and cracks his head. In which case, what are we messing with it for? It's an accident. Case closed."

Vigilio ignored him. "Until we prove otherwise, I'm treating this as a possible homicide," he said. "Let's check it out. Bobby, take somebody with you to the National Museum and talk to everybody who worked with him, worked for him, especially anybody who knew what was going on with this *Grottesca* thing. George, find out the players in Mason's personal life. Lovers, family, friends. Nail down where everybody was last night between, let's say, ten and one. I'm meeting with Jordan as soon as we break up to get a better handle on the art slant."

Michelangelo Merisi Caravaggio was being discussed late that morning by people with loftier titles than chief detective.

The president of the United States, Walter Jeppsen, received a special briefing by his vice president on the most recent of dispatches the VP had received from the Italian government.

"Why are they making such a big deal of it?" the president asked.

"I suppose because it *is* a big deal, Mr. President," Aprile said. "They don't view it as the irrational act of one man. They consider it some kind of grand conspiracy on the part of the United States."

Jeppsen leaned back in his Oval Office chair, clasped his hands behind his head, and mumbled an uncharacteristic four-letter word. "The Koreans are threatening to scrap the nuclear treaty," he said. "Castro is threatening to take over Haiti, as though he could. The French want to dismantle

NATO. I can't get new social legislation through on the Hill. Health-care legislation looks doomed again. My polls are the lowest they've been in a year. And we have to worry about a painting by an Italian madman. Who has the original?"

"As far as we can ascertain, Mr. President, this curator, Luther Mason, who was murdered last night, had the original and sent a forgery back to Italy. But the painting wasn't with him when he was found this morning. Your guess is as good as mine."

"Shouldn't be hard to find, should it?" the president said.

"Probably harder than you or I can imagine, Mr. President. The police are doing everything they can. One of my staff spoke with the head of MPD's art squad, as it's called. They're looking for it."

"Well," said Jeppsen, "one thing I don't need is the Italian government accusing the government of the United States of stealing one of its paintings. I have a reception to get to. Bring me up to date later tonight. Better, bring me a solution."

The assistant secretary of state for Mediterranean Affairs met in the modern State Department building on C Street, NW, with the Italian ambassador to the United States. He spoke soothingly. "We're well aware, Mr. Ambassador, that your government is extremely upset by what has happened. I can assure you that every possible avenue is being explored to find the original and to see that it is returned to you as quickly as possible."

"I am sure that is the case," said the ambassador. "I am also certain you can understand that what has happened here raises a serious question about the loaning of any future works of Italian art to your National Gallery—or to any other American museum."

"I don't think you need go to that extreme, Mr. Ambassador. This was the work of a demented person. Surely, you can't hold the United States government responsible for the works of one warped individual."

"It does not matter who did this or why this happened, Mr. Secretary. What does matter is that one of the world's most precious masterpieces has been stolen from us. What will be taken next by some 'demented person,' another Caravaggio currently on exhibition at your National Gallery? It is my recommendation to my government that the Caravaggio exhibition be canceled immediately and that all works of art be returned to Italy as quickly as can be practically arranged."

"I believe that would cause more problems than it would solve," said the assistant secretary. "I've met with the leaders of the National Gallery. They assure me their security is sufficient to protect works currently on loan from you."

"We were told that when we allowed Grottesca to

travel here under the most unusual of circumstances. No, Mr. Secretary, unless the painting is found and returned to us within the next few days, I am afraid I have no choice but to urge my government to close down your exhibition. At least our part of it. Thank you for your time. Good day."

Whitney, impeccably groomed as always, but his face a mask of stress, sat in his office with senior curator Paul Bishop. They'd just come from a series of emergency meetings.

"I can't believe they would cancel the entire exhibition," Whitney said to Bishop, pouring each of them brandy. "Do you really think they will?" "A damn good possibility." Bishop sipped. "Good brandy, Court. To get back to your question. Yes, I think they're serious about it. It would be a justifiable way to embarrass us."

"The United States of America?"

"And this institution. The Italians have always considered their museums superior to ours. Now they can make that point worldwide."

"What a mess. Do you know what, Paul?"

"What?"

"If I were able to confront Luther after knowing the turmoil he's caused, I would be happy to personally wring his neck."

Bishop laughed. "Just don't say I didn't warn you, Court. I told you the man had gone off the deep end."

"I don't need to be reminded of that."

"Anything else I can do for you tonight?"

"Yes. Deliver the original *Grottesca* to me."

"I wish I could," Bishop said, standing and going to the door. "If the Italians do insist upon pulling all the Caravaggios, we can play tough, too. Galleria Doria-Pamphili is asking us to loan them our two Titians, *Ranuccio Farnese* and *Venus with a Mirror.*"

"Right. We can play their game if we have to. Will you be going to Mason's funeral?"

"I suppose I'll have to. We all do."

"Frankly, I'll have trouble demonstrating sadness at his passing."

"So will I. But there is protocol to consider. Goodnight, Court. Have a pleasant evening, if that's possible."

Prompting people in high office to meet on his behalf would be nothing new for Caravaggio, had he been alive.

He'd been arrested fourteen times in less than six years while living in Rome but never spent more than a night in jail, thanks to highly placed friends, including Cardinal del Monte, and the French ambassador to Italy, who intervened on his behalf. Even papal authority was called upon to bail him out after he'd savagely attacked a friend. In another incident, Caravaggio lost money in a tennis match and attacked the victor with his racket. They dueled later that day, and Caravaggio ran the young man through with his sword, then fled Rome to the protective fiefdom of Don Marzio Colonna.

His rap sheet was as long as his list of paintings.

Caravaggio had captured the attention of two other prominent Washingtonians, Mackensie Smith and his handsome wife, Annabel Reed-Smith.

Annabel walked through the door just as Mac finished reading a newspaper account of Luther Mason's untimely death.

"I can't believe this is happening," Annabel said, tossing her coat on a chair, kicking off her shoes, and heading for the kitchen.

Mac followed. "What came out of the meeting?" he asked.

"The Italian government is threatening to cancel the Caravaggio exhibition."

"Really? Could start World War III."

Annabel poured a glass of grapefruit juice, took a long sustained swig of it, leaned against the sink, and directed a stream of air at a lock of hair that had fallen over her forehead. "You know what's so unfortunate about this, Mac?"

"Tell me."

"That in all that's going on, Luther Mason

being murdered seems almost irrelevant. He's been dead less than twenty-four hours, and the only thing everyone is talking about is Caravaggio."

"He does seem to have a certain presence," Mac said. "You're convinced Luther's death wasn't an accident?"

"Yup. And I think it had to do with *Grottesca* and Caravaggio."

"I'm sure your instincts are right." Mac picked up a raw carrot and took a crunchy bite. "Men have killed for less," he said. "A lot less."

Scott Pims left a building on K Street, NW, carrying a small shopping bag. He went directly home, changed into a tentlike pair of shorts and a size 52 T-shirt, opened a small tin of Sevruga caviar *malossol,* which he spread on thin water biscuits and garnished with finely chopped onion, poured a glass of vodka from a bottle encased in ice in an old milk carton in his freezer, settled at his desk, and opened the shopping bag. He stared at the sales slip from the CounterSpy Shop. "Bloody fortune," he mumbled, tossing the slip to the floor and removing his purchase, an "Electronic Handkerchief" that looked like a small tape recorder with a phone attached.

He read the directions. Simple to use. Replace an existing phone with the device, dial in the degree of change you want for your voice, and call any number. He experimented until settling upon a change in timbre and tone that pleased him. The booklet said no matter how drastic the change in voice, his words would be free of distortion.

He consulted his phone directory, dialed a ten-digit number, and checked his watch.

"Hello?"

"Mr. del Brasco please."

"Who's calling?"

"A very important person. It is in reference to a certain art purchase he recently made."

"What's your name?"

"Tell Mr. del Brasco to come to the phone. He will consider what I have to say extremely important. E-x-t-r-e-m-e-l-y important!"

He hummed "Whistle While You Wait" until del Brasco's flat, gruff voice came on the line. "Who is this?" he asked.

"The name is not important, sir; the message is. You have purchased what you assume is an original Caravaggio, *Grottesca* to be precise. You have been duped, sir."

"Duped?"

"*Duped.* Fooled. Conned. You have purchased a cleverly executed copy."

"What the hell you talking about?"

"Good evening, sir."

He'd had better caviar, but any caviar was better than peanut butter. He refilled his glass with the throat-numbing vodka and turned on his computer. This was going well. His book was becoming more interesting every day. And more salable. There was some danger he would become rich.

If only his friend Luther didn't have to die.

But how could he have anticipated that? He couldn't anticipate everything.

He started writing: *The unforseen and totally shocking death of one of my dearest friends, Luther Mason, left me shaken. It was as though Caravaggio's own hand had injected itself into the picture, striking down this gentle, sweet man who'd finally dared to flaunt convention in the interest of finding his own personal freedom.*

He sat back and sighed. "I am truly sorry, Luther," he said aloud. "Truly sorry."

His fingers flew over the keyboard.

THIRTY-ONE

TWO DAYS LATER

"ANNABEL. It's Carole."

"Hi. Anything new on the exhibition?"

"The Italians are still threatening, but no action yet. I've been trying to fax you."

"Machine should be on. I'll check." She returned a moment later. "Must have turned it off by mistake. What are you sending me?"

"Call me after you've read it."

Annabel read Carole's fax as it moved slowly through the machine:

THE ASSOCIATED PRESS

San Francisco—The body of noted art historian and freelance curator, Peter C. Lafroing 57, was discovered this morning in bushes surrounding Colt Tower, on Telegraph Hill. A sightseeing Japanese couple came upon the body. Lafroing, considered an expert on Italian Baroque art, was fully clothed, and his personal effects were intact, according to a preliminary statement by the police. A detective, speaking on condition of anonymity, stated that the circumstances of Lafroing's death were "suspicious." A final determination of cause of death is pending an autopsy. Lafroing, divorced, leaves two children, Stephanie, 28, of Santa Fe, and Peter, Jr., 24, of San Francisco.

"Carole, this is unbelievable. First Carlo Giliberti, then Luther Mason. And now this."

"I know. At what point does the link with Caravaggio cease to be coincidence?"

"Does Steve Jordan know?"

"Would you call him?"

"Of course."

As Annabel dialed the art-squad chief's number, Jordan and his assistant, Gloria Watson, were in his office reading a Reuters dispatch from Rome they'd received a few minutes earlier:

REUTERS

Ravello, Italy—Father Pasquale Giocondi, a retired Roman Catholic priest, in whose former church the lost Caravaggio masterpiece, *Grottesca,* was discovered by a curator for Washington, D.C.'s National Gallery of Art, was found hung this morning in front that same church. Italian authorities announced the priest's death as suicide, although the manner of death indicated a possible link to Italy's Mafia, particularly the Naples faction known as *Camorra*. He is the third person associated with the discovery of *Grottesca* to have met a brutal death. Italy's cultural attaché to the United States, Carlo Giliberti, was murdered in a Washington, D.C., park shortly after the announcement that the painting had been discovered. And a few days ago, Luther Mason, senior curator at the National Gallery of Art, who brought *Grottesca* to the United States, died of severe head wounds in a courtyard between that institution's East and West buildings.

Considerable controversy surrounds *Grottesca*. According to Italian authorities, a skillfully forged copy had been returned to Italy following its exhibition in the United States. It is believed that Mason possessed the original and was killed by whoever currently has the work. None of the murders has been solved, although there is still debate whether Mr. Mason was killed by someone or suffered a tragic accident.

"Make it four people," Steve Jordan said to Watson, pointing to the AP dispatch about Peter Lafroing.

"Will there be five?" she asked.

"Sure, why not? I don't believe in witches and curses, Gloria, but if somebody told me Caravaggio has cast a spell over everybody connected with *Grottesca,* he wouldn't get a serious argument."

He answered his phone. "Hello, Annabel."

"Hello Steve. Carole Aprile just faxed me an AP story about Peter Lafroing. He was another Caravaggio expert who—"

"I know."

"Remarkable, isn't it?" Annabel said. "Three people connected with Caravaggio—"

"Try four."

"What?"

"The ex-priest, Father Giocondi. Found hung in front of his church in Ravello."

Annabel's gasp was loud.

"How about we get together today, talk this out? Maybe you know more than you remember. Hold on." He cupped his hand over the mouthpiece and asked Gloria Watson, who was heading for the door, "Where are you going?"

"To buy a clove of garlic to wear around my neck, and a wooden stake."

"Annabel?"

"I'm here, Steve."

"Buy a couple of extra cloves," he shouted at Gloria's back.

"What?" Annabel asked.

"Garlic."

"Garlic?"

"I'll explain when I see you."

THIRTY-TWO

THE MARKET INN, located beneath the Southwest Freeway, was a Washington institution unto itself, a popular spot for locals seeking straight-ahead American food and round-the-clock jazz. Steve Jordan met Annabel at the door and led her to a booth in a secluded corner. Drinks ordered, she asked for his reaction to the murders of Peter Lafroing and Father Giocondi.

"Giocondi is simple enough. An Italian Mafia hit. Why? No details, except it's reasonable to assume it's connected with *Grottesca.*"

"Peter Lafroing?"

"A guy I went to school with heads up San Fran's art squad. We're pretty close. He told me just before I came to meet you that the Lafroing case looks like a professional hit, too."

"The same people?"

"I don't think so. But there's that damn Caravaggio again, maybe linking them—and maybe not. Giliberti. Mason. Giocondi. Lafroing. What do you hear from Mrs. Aprile?"

"She's shaken, of course. Besides seeing four people murdered, she's pivotal in trying to dissuade the Italians from closing the Caravaggio exhibition. And maybe some of our air bases by now."

"And?"

"So far just saber rattling. It's good they're nonnuclear. Where do you think *Grottesca* is?"

"Until he took his fall, I'd say it was with Luther Mason. The question is whether he had it with him that night. If he did, and if somebody pushed him down those steps, that same person might have it. Unless he had already sold it, which is unlikely. Did Luther have any contact with Peter Lafroing after the exhibition opened?"

"Not that I know of," Annabel replied.

"Lafroing was in Washington the night Mason died. We have his flight records. He flew in the day before, then back to San Francisco first thing next morning."

"Any idea what he did while in Washington?"

"A few leads. Nothing the night of Mason's death. The flight crew that worked his flight back to California is San Francisco based. My friend interviewed flight attendants who worked it. One remembers Lafroing carrying a package onboard the size of a painting. Kept it close to him all the way."

"That's interesting."

"Yeah. But he didn't have any painting with him

when they found his body. Wallet missing, leading you to believe it was robbery. But the Caravaggio link is just too strong, robbery too simple—though as I've learned, sometimes the complex is really simple. I don't know how this all comes together, Annabel, but I'll bet it does."

Just as Annabel started to speak, Jordan's beeper went off. "Excuse me," he said, heading for a phone. He returned a minute later. "Have to run. Or maybe you'd like to come with me."

"Why?"

"Your friend, Carol Aprile, received a call at her office from some guy claiming to know where the original *Grottesca* is."

"Oh."

"Secret Service called my leader, the commish. They consider the call threatening."

Annabel followed him to the door. "Based upon what's already happened," she said, "Secret Service made a good move."

After a stringent check of credentials at the security gate, and phone calls to the inside, Annabel and Jordan were escorted to Carole Aprile's office in the West Wing. Darkness had begun to fall. Annabel had told Mac she was meeting Jordan but wanted to let him know where she was now. She used a phone in Carole's outer office and got his machine, told him she was at the White House and would check in later.

With Carole were two Secret Service agents, two

plainclothes detectives from MPD, an administrative aide, and a woman from State who'd been meeting with Carole when the call came in. The Veep's wife provided a capsule account of what transpired.

"What did he say specifically?" Jordan asked.

"This," she replied. "All calls to the office are recorded."

The aide punched buttons on an elaborate tape recorder, and voices came through separate enhanced speakers:

"*Mrs. Aprile's office,*" an aide's voice said.

"*I would like to speak with Mrs. Aprile.*" The voice was male, deep and resonant.

"*Who's calling?*"

"*I would prefer not to identify myself. But Mrs. Aprile will want to speak with me, I'm sure.*"

"*I'm sorry, sir, but it is our policy not to take calls where the caller—*"

"*Please tell Mrs. Aprile I know where the original Grottesca can be found.*"

Carole's aide paused, obviously processing what the caller had said. One of the detectives spoke, but Jordan waved him off, leaning closer to the speakers.

"*It's very important that Mrs. Aprile speak with me,*" the caller said.

"*Please hold on.*"

There was a lull until Carole Aprile picked up her extension. "*Who is this?*" she said.

"*A friend, Mrs. Aprile.* Grottesca *is very important to you. I know where it is.*"

"*Where?*"

He laughed. "*I can't make it that easy.*"

"*Why not? If your motivation is to see the painting returned to its rightful owner, I'd think you'd
want to—*"

"*I've said enough for today, Mrs. Aprile. I'll contact you again.*"

"*Wait. I—*"

The line went dead.

"A nut," a detective said.

"We're taking him seriously," a Secret Service
agent said. "How many murders have there been
over this painting?"

"Four," Steve Jordan said. "At least three. We're
not sure about Mason's cause of death."

"We want to set up a trace on this line," said a
detective. "Any problem with that, Mrs. Aprile?"

She looked to the Secret Service agents. "Not if
it's okay with Mrs. Aprile," one said.

"Do you recognize the voice, Carole?" Annabel
asked.

"No."

"He said he was a friend."

"I took it to mean he was *acting* as a friend,"
she said. "Not a friend in the true sense. What's
next?"

A Secret Service agent answered. "We're going
to increase security for you, Mrs. Aprile."

She laughed. "I can't imagine more security than I already have."

"You won't even notice," he said.

Everyone left the room except for Annabel and Steve Jordan, at Carole's request. "What do you think?" she asked.

"I think you should take the call seriously in two ways, Mrs. Aprile," Jordan said. "Obviously, the safety of everyone involved with the Caravaggio exhibition is of concern. Second, the caller could be legit. He might really know the whereabouts of *Grottesca.*"

"That would be wonderful," said Annabel. "If the painting is recovered, it would take the pressure off the exhibition."

"Off all of us," Carole said.

"What do we do?" Annabel asked Jordan.

"Sit tight, I suppose. He'll call again. Or reach you another way. Maybe too canny to use the phone again. Maybe the trace will work. And you've got your recorder going, Mrs. Aprile. All we can do is wait."

"My least favorite thing," she said.

"First thing you learn as a cop, Mrs. Aprile. Patience. Especially in this type of situation."

"Annabel," Carole said as they prepared to leave her office.

"Yes?"

"Thanks for being here, for being along all the way."

"Just taking the bitter with the sweet, as my father used to say. It's been nothing but sweet fun, mostly. Now we're into the bitter."

"Has there been any progress in investigating the murders?" Annabel asked as Jordan drove her back to the Market Inn, where she'd left her car.

"Only what I told you earlier. We've been talking to anybody who was close to Mason. They all have an alibi for when he took his tumble. His son was at a bar with his girlfriend. The bartender isn't certain what time they left, but he thinks it was past midnight."

"Julian."

"Yeah. Right after he was interviewed he went to Paris."

"He was allowed to leave the country?"

"Homicide's ruled him out."

"I suppose that's reasonable considering Luther's *death* still hasn't been ruled a homicide. Has it?"

"No, it hasn't."

"What about his girlfriend?" Annabel asked.

"She worked for the kid's father at the National Gallery. Lynn Marshall."

"Yes, I know her. I mean, I've met her on a few occasions."

"The son, as I understand it, went to stay with his mother in Paris. He told us he had been planning to do that. Mason's first wife, the kid's mother. His second wife was visiting relatives in

Florida when he died. I know what I didn't tell you. The umbrella found at the scene belongs to that pretentious pantload, Mr. Scott Pims."

"It does? Was he with Luther that night?"

"Uh huh. He says he and Mason had an early dinner together at his apartment. Mason left around nine, according to Pims. Claims he doesn't know where he went after that. Pims stayed home to work on a book he says he's writing.

"Believe him?" Annabel asked.

"Yeah. He showed one of our people files logged on his computer with time-date stamps that have him there when Mason died."

"Those things can be doctored," Annabel offered.

"What are you saying, that you think Pims might have pushed his friend down the steps?"

"Just free-associating."

"Everybody who knew Mason at the National Gallery has an alibi, some that check out, some that don't."

"What about the ones that don't?"

"Lacking motive. But no one's been ruled out completely. Look, I'm assigning people to keep an eye on you."

"That isn't necessary."

"My call, Annabel. You won't even know they're around. Thanks for the help."

"Mac will. Know they're around. Oh, by the

way, you said after the Dumbarton incident you might want to use me again to recover stolen art."

His laugh was easy. "As I remember, you accused me of considering that. I denied it."

"And without conviction. I'll help in any way I can, Steve. Please remember that. I'm beginning to hate anyone stealing or destroying art."

"Yeah, except you don't make a very believable hater, Mrs. Smith."

THIRTY-THREE

WHEN ANNABEL walked through the door of their Foggy Bottom home, Mac was on the phone with a former law student who'd been offered two excellent jobs and was seeking his professor's advice on which to take. After the conversation, Mac joined her in the kitchen. "You were at the White House?" he said.

"You got my message. I was with Carole. She had a call from a man claiming to know *Grottesca*'s whereabouts."

"Oh? Who was he?"

"He didn't leave his name, said he'd call again. The conversation was taped."

"An interesting development."

"Mac, I have something to tell you."

"Yes?"

Annabel's phone rang.

"Tell me," Mac said.

She headed for the corner of the kitchen where a phone and her answering machine sat but didn't pick up. Her outgoing message played. Then, a male voice said, *"Good evening Mrs. Smith. I trust you are well."*

Annabel and Mac looked at each other. The voice was similar to the one Annabel had heard in Carole Aprile's office. The difference was this version had an Italian accent.

"I am calling because of your interest in Caravaggio and Grottesca.*"*

"Should I pick up?"

"Let it record," Mac said quickly.

"Grottesca *is for sale. If you are interested, I can arrange it. I will call again."*

Mac came to her side and picked up the receiver. Dead air. "First Carole, now you," he said gruffly. "Any idea who it might be?"

"No. Listen, Mac, we have to talk."

"Okay."

"Let me call Steve Jordan and tell him about this call. Will you dub the message onto another tape so we don't lose it?"

"All right."

While Mac went to his study to make a copy of the answering machine's tiny cassette, Annabel called Steve Jordan's office. "Good," she said, "you're still there. I just received a call similar to the one Carole got. What? Sure. Hold on." She placed her hand over the mouthpiece and yelled, "Mac, can we play the tape for Steve over the phone?"

He stepped into the kitchen carrying the original tape and a recorder. "I haven't dubbed it yet," he said.

They held the mouthpiece close to the recorder and played the tape. "What do you think?" Annabel asked Jordan when it was over.

"Could have been the same person. The Italian accent threw me."

"Did it sound authentic to you?"

"Hard to say. Hang on to that tape.

"Mac's making a copy."

"Good. I want to hear it again on good equipment, compare it to Mrs. Aprile's call. When can we get together? Can you come down to headquarters now?"

"No. I mean, I will if—"

"Not necessary. There should be an officer parked outside your house by now. Staying home?"

"Yes." She looked at Mac. "We may go out for dinner." Raised eyebrows asked for her husband's agreement. "Sure," he said, returning to the study.

"Annabel," Jordan said. "Take this seriously. Something's boiling here."

"Don't worry, I share your concern. I'll call tomorrow."

"Let's go to Citronelle," she said to Mac after he'd finished his dubbing chore. "We haven't been there yet."

"What was it you wanted to tell me?"

"Over dinner."

By the time they'd arrived at the trendy restaurant and settled in, Mac seemed to have forgotten that Annabel had an announcement to make. He dominated the conversation with his reaction to a Supreme Court decision announced that day with which he fervently disagreed. When he finished, he sipped his wine and said, "You haven't said much."

"You've been on a roll," she said.

He looked at her quizzically. "Is that a complaint?"

"Hardly. And I totally agree with you. It was a dumb decision. Speaking of dumb decisions, I have a confession to make."

"What am I about to hear?" he asked, his expression serious.

"Nothing worthy of Oprah," she said. "I haven't sold the gallery, nor have I called in someone to paint the shutters on the house."

"Thank God," he said, wiping imaginary sweat from his forehead with the back of his fingers. "I intend to get to the shutters this weekend."

"Mac, I did an undercover job for Steve Jordan and his art squad."

Mac sat back and lowered his chin almost to his breastbone. "You *what?* Worked undercover for—? I'm—"

"I didn't exactly go undercover . . . ." Annabel recounted her involvement in retrieving the three pre-Columbian artifacts for Dumbarton Oaks.

Mac maintained his posture throughout her story. Then he sat up. "I'm glad it turned out the way it did," he said. "But the much larger question, lady, is why you never told me about it."

"I know, I know," she said, touching his hands. "I should have, and fully intended to. I don't know why I didn't. Like not returning a phone call and finding it harder every day that passes. Maybe I was afraid you would tell me not to do it. I wanted to do it."

"Would it have mattered if I didn't want you to do it?"

"Of course it would have."

"But would you have gone ahead with it anyway?"

"I really don't have an answer for that. I like to think I would. After all, we've always operated on the premise that two fulfilled individuals make a better couple."

"Yep. And I still agree with that approach," he said. Espresso was served. He smiled, raised his tiny cup, and said, "To your successful foray into crime." They touched rims. "But let's have an understanding from this moment forward. We don't do things like this without telling each other." She started to respond, but he held up his index finger. "You have to admit, Annabel, that every time I've made the mistake of getting involved in somebody's murder, I filled you in from the git-go."

She nodded.

He raised his cup again. "To the peaceful life we've managed to achieve."

Her cup stayed on the table. "Mac," she said.

"Yes?"

"That call about the Caravaggio. Carole's call. If Steve feels I can be of help in recovering the painting, I want to do it."

Mac was silent until they were home again. "I don't think you should get involved."

"But if I could be of help—"

"The Dumbarton Oaks caper—I suppose we can call it that—involved little risk. But four people have already been murdered over *Grottesca*."

"We don't know how Luther Mason died."

"But it undoubtedly had something to do with *Grottesca*. He had fifty thousand dollars in his pocket. He was accused of having a copy made so he could steal the original. And what about Father Giocondi? And Peter Lafroing?"

"All the more reason, it seems to me, to be willing to lend a hand. If the painting is successfully recovered, maybe the murders will stop."

He said grimly, "Maybe stop with *you,* Annabel. No. Pardon me if I don't allow the person I love more than anything in this world to put her life in jeopardy."

"That's sweet, Mac." She didn't smile. "It also sounds slightly dictatorial, a tone I'm not used to hearing from you."

"I don't mean to sound that way, but I think you

know what I'm getting at. A couple of pre-
Columbian pieces is one thing. A Caravaggio
worth maybe fifty million bucks is another."

She sighed and tucked her bare feet beneath her
on the couch. "I suppose you're right."

"I'm not being critical of you *wanting* to do it. I
understand the motivation. And helping to recover a stolen masterpiece, maybe identify a murderer or murderers as a bonus. If suppose if I were
asked, I might—"

She placed her feet on the floor and leaned forward. "Yes?"

He couldn't help but smile. "I might rise to the
challenge."

"Why is it different with me?" She didn't allow
him to answer. "Because I'm a woman?"

"Hmmm," he muttered, biting his lip. "Because
you're my wife. My love." He paused. "Maybe that
is what's behind my objection. Surprised at how
chauvinistic I can be?"

She laughed. "Frankly, yes. Tell you what. If
Steve, or Carole, or whoever asks me to help, I'll
tell you immediately and inform you of every
move I make. No exceptions, no secrets. That way,
we'll be doing it together. As a team. We always
talk about what a great team we are. Is it a deal?"

"I don't know."

"Yes, you do," she said, leaving the couch and
kneeling next to where he sat. She touched her fingertips to his cheek and turned his face to her. "I

really want to do this if asked," she said softly, offering her lips. He kissed her and caved in. "Okay?"

"Okay," he said. "But if there's the slightest hint of anything that puts you in physical danger, we call it off. Right?"

"Right." She offered her hand the way a partner would. He shook it, smiling. "By the way," she said, "Steve has assigned some officers to keep an eye on me. Us. There should be one parked outside right now."

"Terrific."

"Just a precaution," she said. "Just until this is resolved."

"I have one more request," he said.

"Which is?"

"That we agree to stop shaking hands. There are better ways—for us—to make up."

THIRTY-FOUR

"I AM M. Scott Pims, your benevolent host of this week's *Art Insider,* brought to you through the extreme generosity of viewers like you who support this public station."

Mac and Annabel settled back in their study to watch Pims's weekly television show. The tall, obese critic wore a red-satin smoking jacket over a black T-shirt on which, in white, was a line drawing of himself. He smiled at the camera as it zoomed in for a tight shot of his face.

"As you know," he said, "recent events at the National Gallery not only have threatened to close down the splendid exhibition of Caravaggio works now on display, but appear to have rather stunning political implications as well. Naturally, you have kept up with this sordid tale through your conventional channels of disinformation—what a lovely word that is. But unless you join *me* each week, the true story will never be yours to know and understand.

"Here is what is at the *root* of it."

Footage previously taken of *Grottesca* and the crowds ran as Pims talked over it:

"This is the original masterpiece called *Grottesca,* painted hundreds of years ago by an Italian madman named Michelangelo Merisi Caravaggio. Mad, yes. Talented? Without peer. You know, of course, that this lost gem hung in our National Gallery for a month after having been discovered in Italy by a man who was not only senior curator at the gallery and an acknowledged Caravaggio expert, but who was my friend. Luther Mason. His untimely death shocked us all. I was especially devastated by it.

"Before his unfortunate demise, Mason was accused of having stolen the original of *Grottesca* and of having had a copy made—obviously an excellent one—which he returned to the Italian government in place of the original. Because of my close friendship with him, I find it incomprehensible that he would stoop to such chicanery. But if he did—and let us for the moment assume that he did—the monumental question remains: *Where is the original?*"

Mac scratched the groove between Rufus's eyes and muttered, "I really can't stomach him."

"It's only a half hour," Annabel replied. "Part of his charm, the reason people watch. He's smart and funny along with bizarre and outrageous." Rufus yawned and sprawled at Mac's feet.

"He's like an extra-large Truman Capote. Your last two adjectives could get him elected to Congress."

"Sad to report," said Pims, "that evidence recently uncovered lends a certain credence to the allegations against my dear deceased friend."

"Pims is a friend nobody needs," said Mac. "Sssssh."

"Luther had in his apartment an airline ticket to Athens, Greece, and additional travel documents from that city to the idyllic isle of Hydra, off the Greek coast."

"I didn't know that," Annabel said. "Steve never mentioned it."

"Probably because he didn't want it public," said Mac. "But Pims obviously knows. "It's public now. *If* it's true."

"I have also learned exclusively that Luther Mason had arranged for a moving company to empty out his apartment, all of it to go to his first wife, Juliana, in Paris."

Another tight shot of Pims, whose eyebrows went up unnaturally high.

"Hardly the sort of thing a man does unless—"

He shook his head sadly.

"Unless he was planning a swift and unannounced flight, perhaps with a work of art worth many millions of dollars on the open, albeit criminal, art market."

"He's playing judge and jury," Mac said.
"But what else does he know?" asked Annabel.
Pims answered her question:

"It has come to my attention through my impeccable sources that the original *Grottesca* has already left the country, Italy its final destination. Furthermore, although our well-meaning local police— particularly what is known as its Art Squad, headed by a charming gentleman named Detective Jordan— refuse to verify it, Luther Mason's death is being held open as a homicide. Which means, of course, that his assailant is the individual who has taken the original with him to Italy. Find that person and you find *Grottesca*—which is exactly what I intend to do, in your service."

Pims turned to other matters to round out his half hour, including an update on Jean-Baptiste Oudry's *The White Duck,* stolen in 1990 from Houghton Hall, the Norfolk house of the seventh marquess of Cholmondeley, England, and valued at more than $6 million. According to Pims, his "unimpeachable sources" were zeroing in on that painting's whereabouts, too.

"I am M. Scott Pims, your eyes and ears on the world of art. See you next week. And remember, 'All passes. Art alone enduring stays to us. The bust outlasts the throne.' *Ciao!*"

As Mac clicked off the TV, Annabel answered the phone. "Did you watch Pims tonight?" Steve Jordan asked.

"Yes."

"And?"

"Is it true about Greece and the movers?"

"Yes. It's looking more every day like Mason really did try to pull this off."

"I'm sorry to hear that. What about our tape?" She'd given him the tape from their answering machine the day after it had been left.

"Our tech people say it sounds like someone disguising his voice."

Annabel laughed. "Like putting a handkerchief over the phone?"

"Something a little more sophisticated. A favor?"

"What?"

"Mrs. Aprile has been very cooperative. But she's a busy lady, has more on her mind than Caravaggio and stolen paintings. I guess that goes with being the Veep's wife."

"Certainly *this* Veep's wife."

"The problem is, I need her clout with other art cops. Especially the Italians. With her on the case, they tend to be a little more attentive."

"What can I do, Steve?"

"Step up your involvement with her and the arts commission. Be my daily conduit into her. Not that you don't have a full plate, too. It's just that—"

"No explanation needed. I'll be as involved as Carole allows me to be."

"Good."

"Do you think Pims is right about the painting already being in Italy?"

"It's a good possibility. Those diplomatic pouches get fatter every day. Like Pims. I intend to talk to him again today. How's Mac?"

"He was fine until we watched Scott. Not his favorite television personality."

Jordan laughed. "The pompous bastard—pardon me—is out to show us up, solve the case by himself."

"I'm sure you'll take all the help you can get."

"That's right. But if you think Pims is insufferable now, imagine what he'll be like if he finds *Grottesca* on his own. I'll be in touch, Annabel."

Scott Pims watched in his apartment. He was

pleased with the show, although he made notes during it about certain production values he wanted changed. Too many crowds, too little art. Too tight on him in the closeups. Lousy lighting.

His phone rang a half-dozen times after the show, calls from friends congratulating him. "You're very kind," he said to them. "But one day, when I'm with a real network with money to back me up, you'll really see the art of investigative art reporting. Ta-ta."

At midnight, he placed a call of his own. It was nine o'clock in San Francisco. The call was answered by a man. "Del Brasco," Pims said through the voice-altering telephone, enhancing the change by adopting what he considered to be a mobster's voice, hoarse and guttural, word endings clipped.

"Who's calling?"

"Somebody who can make things right with your boss. Come on. I don't got all night."

"Sorry. He's not here."

"Not there, or don't want to talk to me?"

"Hey, look, I told you—"

Pims hung up.

He tried again at two o'clock his time. Del Brasco answered.

"How would you like the original *Grottesca* to replace the phony you ended up with?" Pims asked.

"Who the hell is this?" del Brasco snarled.

"A friend. Sorry about Lafroing. You must a' been really pissed off."

"How do I get *Grottesca?*"

"By doing exactly what I say. Interested, del Brasco?"

"Yeah."

"You'll hear from me again. *Ciao,* baby."

"Wait. I want to know what—"

Pims lowered the receiver into its cradle. Everything was proceeding very smoothly, like butt-ah. His smile turned to laughter as he pictured del Brasco looking at the original *Grottesca* and thinking it was a forgery, fuming at having laid out fifty thousand for it, enraged enough to have had Peter Lafroing killed, a turn of events Pims hadn't considered a possibility when he placed the call informing del Brasco he'd been taken. All these people dying over one painting, he thought; that rascal Caravaggio must be grinning from his chair in that section of the Forever After reserved for mad geniuses— but not his, M. Scott Pims's, fault, and certainly not what he'd intended.

He awoke Saturday morning to find a fax from Rome on his machine. It read: *Contact made. Awaiting next instruction.*

"Next instruction?" Pims mused over a hearty breakfast at a table set for one in his dining room. "Ah, yes," he said aloud, opening a file folder marked DUMBARTON. In it was a report he'd typed after a friend on Dumbarton's staff told him the story of the missing pre-Columbian pieces and of Annabel Reed-Smith's role in helping Steve Jordan's art squad recover them.

"Of course," he said, padding barefoot to the kitchen, carrying his dirty dishes. "Of course."

THIRTY-FIVE

THE DETECTIVE sitting in his unmarked car across the street from the Smiths' home in Foggy Bottom seemed embarrassed when Annabel waved to him Saturday morning as she stepped through the front door. The air was crisp and clear at seven-thirty. A "fat day," as Mac would say.

She retrieved their blue Caprice from their rented garage a few doors down the block and drove quickly through Washington's empty streets to the Naval Observatory on upper Massachusetts Avenue, where two Secret Service agents waved her through the entrance gate. She pulled up in front of the home of the vice president. The detective, who'd followed at a respectful distance, parked across the street. Another agent escorted Annabel inside, where Carole Aprile was waiting. After a hug and some preliminary chitchat, they settled in the Second Lady's small office at the rear of the house.

"Another call?" Annabel said, accepting a cup of coffee.

"Yes. Steve Jordan picked up the tape a few minutes ago."

"Who can it be, Carole? Is it some sick individual playing a hoax?"

"I don't know. Whoever it is knows a lot about what's going on. He mentioned you."

"Mentioned me?"

"Yes. Here. I transcribed his message." She handed Annabel a neatly typed note:

Now listen to me, Mrs. Aprile. If you and the government want this Grottesca *mess resolved, you do exactly what I say. You're a busy lady. But your friend, Mrs. Smith, isn't so busy. Tell her to have her bags packed and be ready to go. More later.*

"Did he leave this on your machine at the White House?"

"No. He called here on my private number. I picked up. The minute I realized who it was, I pressed a button on my machine that records both sides of the call."

"How did he get your private number?"

"I don't know."

"Was it the same voice?"

"No. This time it was high-pitched, a whiny voice. Kind of a 'dem and dose' speech."

"No Italian accent?"

She shook her head.

"Steve thinks it's someone disguising his voice, maybe using some sort of gadget."

"That makes sense considering it's different

each time he calls. Unless there's more than one person making the calls. What's Mac think of all this?"

"He's concerned."

"As well he should be. Annabel, when Steve heard the reference to you, he said he wanted to get us together, have a meeting, decide what to do if the caller gives instructions for you to follow."

Annabel frowned and chewed on the inside of her cheek.

"Not that you'd have to do anything if you didn't want to. But Steve made some comment about you being willing—no, he said you *knew* about this sort of thing."

"I suppose I do. Keep a secret?"

"Sure."

Annabel told Carole about how she'd helped Jordan recover the missing artifacts from Dumbarton Oaks. Carole listened with wide eyes and a bemused smile on her lips. When Annabel was through, Carole said, "I'm impressed."

"Don't be. I didn't do anything except act like a silly schoolgirl by not telling Mac about it until after the fact. I promised to let him know if I contemplated doing something like that again."

"Bring him to the meeting."

"I'll talk to him."

"I told Steve I had an hour today at four. Joe and I are flying tonight to Colorado. A party fundraiser. Back tomorrow."

"Four? I can make it. The new assistant I hired is a godsend. She treats the gallery like it was her own. You'll call me?"

"Yes. And bring Mac."

"Pims here."

"Scott, it's Will Penny." The White House curator, formerly with the Smithsonian Museum of American History, was calling from his apartment off Dupont Circle.

"Ah, Wilfred, my friend. I was meaning to call you. We haven't broken bread in ages. Free tonight?"

"As a matter of fact I am."

"Splendid. As I recall, you're especially fond of smoked trout."

"My favorite. But I wasn't calling to arrange dinner."

"But you will come."

"Of course. Strange things going on at the big White House, Scott."

A jovial, knowing laugh from Pims. "When aren't strange things going on there? I always think of Stuart's portrait of George Washington in the East Room as symbolizing the nonsense that goes on there." He referred to Gilbert Stuart's copy of his original portrait of President Washington, the only object still in the opulent East Room dating from its completion in 1800. Stuart painted copies in order to make a living. In the original, one of two books leaning against a table near Washington is *Constitution and Laws of the United States.* In his haste to paint this particular copy, Stuart misspelled a word in the book's title: *Constitution and Laws of the United Sates.*

Penny laughed, too. "I've always thought Stuart might have done it deliberately. His private little joke. Mr. Jordan from the MPD art squad has been spending plenty of time here. Mrs. Aprile has another meeting with him this afternoon at four."

"How did you learn that?"

"Her archivist. We're close. Mrs. Aprile is meeting with Mrs. Smith, Jordan, maybe others. Just thought you'd want to know."

"Oh, I do, Will, I do. You'll have more to share with me at dinner?"

"It must have to do with *Grottesca.*"

"Perhaps."

"By the way, I loved your show last night."

"Thank you."

"Poor Luther. I miss him terribly."

"So do I. One of life's truly decent people. And so knowledgable. And I say, so what if he wanted to abscond with the love of his life? More power to him. But to die over it?" He sighed long and loud. "One day we must go to Indiana to lay a proper wreath on his grave. Sweet, his mother asking that he be buried there. I only hope Luther has found the peace he sought. Perhaps it is better to die at once, Will, than to lose one's life a bit at a time, boredom nibbling pieces from you every day, frustration eroding your spirit, dreams dancing just out of reach. While we shall all miss our dear friend, we must celebrate his reach for his shining star."

Penny said nothing.

"Amen," said Pims. "Eight at my apartment. And bring good stories. You know how I love good stories. Must run. I have a difficult but necessary appointment this afternoon."

THIRTY-SIX

LYNN MARSHALL sat in her office at the National Gallery of Art. She hadn't wanted to work on Saturday, but Senior Curator Paul Bishop, who'd arranged for her transfer to his staff after Luther's death, needed a long report typed and edited by Monday morning. Dumb secretarial work, she grumbled, as she labored to decipher Bishop's scrawl. He'd promised her a more senior job in the near future; well, not exactly promised, but the hint was strong. Funny, she thought, how much she missed working for Luther. Bishop's brusque, often demeaning style was in marked contrast to Mason's gentler, albeit erratic, sometimes bristly approach.

What she'd quickly come to resent were Bishop's constant derogatory comments about Luther. He was obsessed with his colleague and competitor, even though the man was dead.

"Didn't you have even an inkling of what he was doing?" Bishop often asked. "You worked closely with him."

"I was as shocked as everyone else," Lynn replied.

"But you were personally close."

"Luther was like a father to me. A mentor."

"That's not what I've heard."

"People are wrong if they think anything else."

Once: "Would you have dinner with me, Lynn? My wife is visiting her sister in Maine and—"

"I'd love to, Paul, but I'm busy."

He hadn't asked again since his wife returned.

She worked faster to finish the report so she could leave to meet Scott Pims.

Pims had called that morning as Lynn was leaving her apartment. She barely knew the man except for his public persona and from the few times Pims and Luther had been together in her presence.

"And how are you this fine day?" he'd asked.

"Fine, Mr. Pims."

"Call me Scott. Luther told me on more than one occasion that Ms. Lynn Marshall has considerable artistic talent."

"I—"

"And I have always been vitally interested in nurturing young artistic talent. I'm sure you're aware of that."

"Oh, yes."

"I would like to meet with you to discuss what help I might be in furthering your career."

"That sounds—"

"No gratitude necessary. The least I can do is pick up on my dear departed friend's keen eye for talent and do what's right. Are you free this afternoon?"

"I'm on my way to work."

"As dedicated as Luther said you were. Surely you can break away for an hour. A relaxing drink at Adirondacks, in Union Station? Say six? They open then."

"I think so."

" 'Til then. You'll certainly recognize me. Hear from Julian lately?"

"No. He's—"

"He's busy setting himself up in Paris. Lucky lad. Well, Lynn—May I call you that?"

"Yes, I—"

"Six. I'd offer dinner but I'm having guests this evening. Ta-ta."

Pims's call was on her mind all day, slowing the hieroglyphic process of typing Paul Bishop's notes. Was Pims serious about helping her? It probably wasn't a pass. He didn't look the type. Probably liked cuddling up with his teddy bear. Well, nothing to lose by meeting with him. He was, after all, the most influential art critic in Washington, and she'd recently read that a national cable network was negotiating to carry his program.

She left the gallery at four, drove home, show-

ered, and changed into a pretty flowered dress.
Should she bring some of her paintings with her?
She decided not to. Too pushy.

As Lynn Marshall prepared, Mac and Annabel
Smith met in Carole Aprile's White House office
with Carole, Steve Jordan, and Courtney Whitney
III.

"I understand what you're saying," Mac said to
Jordan, "but that's assuming he'll follow through.
He could be—in all probability is—nothing more
than a crackpot making mischief."

"You may be right, Mac," Jordan said. "But let's
say he's not that. Let's say he was involved with
Mason in the scam, knew everything that was
going down, maybe even lent a hand. Maybe he's
the one who sent Luther down those steps at the
National Gallery. Maybe he has *Grottesca.*"

"Doesn't add up," Annabel said. "If he has
Grottesca, he wouldn't be calling *us* about it.
There's a ravenous underground market out there
for valuable art. The Italian government would
probably pay for its recovery. Why bring *us* along
for the ride?"

Carole Aprile, who'd been packing a small briefcase for Colorado, said, "Maybe because he
knows how much *we* want to be instrumental in recovering *Grottesca.* The Italians have given us
until next Friday to come up with it or they shut
down the Caravaggio exhibition."

"And they mean it," Whitney said. "De Montebello at the Met calls me every day. Twice a day. As though I have the ability to pluck *Grottesca* out of thin air and salvage the show. The Brits are talking lawsuit—against *us* for losing the damn thing and jeopardizing *their* Caravaggio show. De Montebello had the gall to say we aren't doing enough to find it. Lord knows I don't wish to be unkind, but when I think of the havoc Luther Mason has caused everyone, I want to—"

"Every art squad in the world has *Grottesca* as its top priority," said Jordan. "Anybody buying it—"

The ringing phone stopped all conversation. One of Carole's assistants picked it up in the outer office, opened the door, and said, "Him."

"Hello?" Carole said into her extension as Jordan activated an electronic device triggering a trace through C-and-P Telephone's central switching center and slipped on a pair of earphones attached to a reel-to-reel tape recorder that started to spin. The others in the room could hear only Carole's side of the conversation:

"Yes, I understand"—"But how do I know you have the original?"—"Trust you? Why should I?"—"It's not being traced."—"Wednesday? That's very short notice."—"Two million. Unmarked bills."—"Me? I can't—"—"How is she to—?"—"No, wait. I—"

Jordan rewound the tape and played it:

"*Good afternoon, Mrs. Aprile. I will speak quickly. Do not interrupt. Understand?*"

"*Yes, I understand.*"

"*I am giving you the opportunity to recover Grottesca—but only if you follow my instructions.*"

"*But how do I know you have the original?*"

"*You'll have to trust me.*"

"*Trust you? Why should I?*"

"*I asked you not to interrupt. I know this call is being traced.*"

"*It's not being traced.*"

"*Now listen. Grottesca will be available in Italy on Wednesday.*"

"*Wednesday? That's very short notice.*"

"*Come to Italy with two million dollars in unmarked bills.*"

"*Two million. Unmarked bills.*"

"*Bring the money personally.*"

"*Me? I can't—*"

"*Then send an emissary. The person I represent will deal only with someone representing the highest echelon of government. Mrs. Smith will do.*"

"*How is she to—?*"

"*Further instructions will be forthcoming. Goodbye.*"

"*No, wait. I—*"

There was the *click* of his hangup followed by tape hiss.

Jordan's cellular phone rang. "Okay," he said to the caller. "Good."

"What's up?" Mac Smith asked.

"They got a trace on it. The Atlas Building."

"The Atlas Building?" Annabel and Court Whitney said in unison.

"They're on their way." He looked around the room. "So?" he said.

Mac screwed up his face, walked to a window, and said, "He's making it sound as though this seller of the painting is the Good Samaritan, willing to turn it over only to the government."

"For two million dollars," Jordan said.

"A bargain," offered Whitney. "It's worth thirty times that." He took in each face. "I hope you aren't debating whether to meet his demands."

Carole Aprile's laugh was short and to the point. "Of course there's debate about it. The government of the United States—the White House—isn't in the habit of buying stolen art from criminals."

"I only meant," said Whitney, "that considering the tenuous state of relations with the Italian government, two million dollars to patch things up doesn't seem unreasonable."

"And to save your exhibition," Mac muttered.

"Is there anything wrong with wanting to do that?" Whitney asked.

Mac didn't answer. Instead, he sat next to

Annabel on a yellow-and-white striped loveseat and said to her, "We haven't heard from you."

"It's not my call," said Annabel. She looked to Carole Aprile. "You're right, Carole. I can't imagine the U.S. government authorizing payment to a crook to recover a painting that doesn't even belong to us."

Carole nodded as she sat stoically behind her desk, deep in thought.

"The government has done worse things," Court Whitney said. "CIA funds for drug runners. Paying the mob to do its dirty deeds."

Carole's stern look silenced the Gallery director. "Let me run this past the appropriate people," she said. To Annabel: "Obviously, I can't follow through personally with this person. It would have to be someone without official capacity. You seem to be acceptable to him. He's mentioned you on two of the calls."

Annabel looked at Mac. "Only if I'm with you," he said.

"I'm willing," Annabel said.

"It wouldn't have to be federal funds," Steve Jordan said. "We have sources of money for such things."

"Two million?" Mac asked, incredulous.

"Yeah. I'll check out availability. When will you know if it's a go, Mrs. Aprile? And you, Annabel?"

"Maybe by tomorrow morning, after I get back from Colorado."

"You don't have to, you know," Mac said, placing his hand on Annabel's.

"I know. Let's go home and talk about it."

Carole Aprile said, "I don't want to follow through, Annabel, unless I know you'll do it."

Annabel stood. "I'll do it," she said.

Jordan's cell phone rang again. After a few nods and grunts from the art-squad chief, he said, "The call came from an artist's studio in the Atlas Building. Nobody there. They're trying to contact the artist who rents it. Why don't we break this up and get back in touch with each other? Sorry," he said. "Don't mean to end your meeting, Mrs. Aprile."

"Feel free," she said. "I'm running late. Talk to you in the morning."

THIRTY-SEVEN

M. SCOTT PIMS held his breath against the building's odors as he hurried down the stairs, his voice changer cradled in a canvas shoulder bag. He sweated profusely as he waddled at full speed in the direction of his car at Pennsylvania and C Street, dropping down a grate the key he'd used to an acquaintance's studio. He drove home with the air conditioning running full tilt, plugged the machine into his phone jack, and dialed San Francisco. Blond Curls answered. "I don't have time for you," Pims said, out of breath. "Put your master on."

Del Brasco came on immediately. "Yeah?"

"Now listen to me, del Brasco," Pims said. "The original *Grottesca* is waiting for you in Italy. Wednesday. Bring the forgery with you. The seller wants it. And two million cash, unmarked bills, about a hundred thousand in lire."

"Wait a minute. Who the hell do you think you're talking to?"

"Be there if you want the original. I don't have time to argue. Check into the Raphael Hotel in

Rome, on the Piazza Navona. Be there by Tuesday night—with the forgery and the money. Check in under your own name. You'll be contacted." He hung up.

Pims sat in a favorite recliner and willed the pounding in his chest to stop. Sufficiently calmed, he sent an E-mail message to Rome: *Wednesday party on as scheduled. Will confirm reluctant guest.* He checked his watch. Time to go to Union Station. He made one more call, this to the young producer of his television show: "Is all the travel arranged for the crew?" he asked. She confirmed that it was. "Good. Keep your beeper on in case there's a change. I'll call later."

Driving to Union Station, Lynn Marshall had serious second thoughts about agreeing to meet with M. Scott Pims. She'd been too impetuous, allowed his fame—more important, his offer to help her career—get in the way of making a reasoned decision. She was certain of one thing: Julian would be furious.

Contact between Lynn and Julian had been sporadic, at best, since he left for Paris. Lynn missed him, although she didn't have any misconceptions about the true tenor of their relationship. She knew his interest in her had been primarily sexual and that it wouldn't last. That was okay. What had started to bother her was not knowing to what extent her relationship with his father had prompted

Julian to pursue her, sometimes speculating that he'd commenced the affair to hurt Luther by taking from him something important in his life. But that was too Freudian for her to digest in large bites. If that was the case, so be it. The sex had been good, and she'd taken a certain pleasure, as well as felt a modicum of guilt, from having participated in Luther's betrayal. He certainly had it coming the way he'd let her down.

She'd also wondered early in their furtive relationship whether Julian was using her to find out about his father's activities. He constantly asked questions, especially about the Caravaggio exhibition and *Grottesca.* Then, one day the questions stopped. Truth was, she'd had little to offer, knowing nothing about the switch of paintings until Julian told her.

"How did you find out?" she'd asked.

"Better you don't know," was his pat reply. "Just keep your eyes and ears open at the Gallery and tell me what's going on."

Knowing that her boss and former lover was about to pull off perhaps the greatest art scam in history was unsettling. At first, she dismissed it because she could not conceive of the usually meek and mild Luther Mason even contemplating such a thing. And then carry it off? Ridiculous.

But it didn't take Julian long to convince her that not only was he right, she could participate in his own plan to head it off. "I don't want to see my father go to jail," he told her one night after making love. "Do you?"

"Of course not."

"He'll botch it, Lynn," he said. "He'll sell it for a song and get caught in the bargain."

"We can talk to him," she said.

"Forget it. He'll never listen."

That was the night she agreed to go to Luther's apartment, use her key to get in, and see whether the original *Grottesca* was there. She wasn't capable of determining authenticity, but the fact that there were two versions of it gave credence to Julian's claim. When she reported back to him, he said, "Just go along with me. Don't ask any questions and do what I say."

"I don't want to get into trouble," she said.

"You won't. You're not doing anything. *He* did it. We can get him to share with us. I'll go to Paris and sell it for a hundred times what he'll get. Just don't worry, and keep your mouth shut."

Lynn drove Julian to the airport the night he left for Paris. He was unusually cheerful, thinking of the original *Grottesca* packed in with other worthless canvases he'd sent by Airborne Express.

"When will I hear from you?" she asked.

"After I find a buyer. I've already got a line on one in Italy. Big bucks, Lynn. As soon as I make the deal, we can hook up again. In Paris."

She looked into his cold, black eyes and knew he was lying about "hooking up again." That didn't matter. It was the money she'd begun to fantasize about. She'd never had money. With it she could study full time with the best teachers. That was all she lacked, she was sure, solid training to enable her to better execute her artistic visions.

He'd promised to be in constant touch, but he seldom called. She'd called twice, the first call answered by Julian's mother, Juliana, who promised to tell her son. When he didn't respond, Lynn tried again to reach him. He sounded angry, said he was about to leave for Rome and couldn't talk—not on the phone.

"I only wanted to hear your voice," she'd said, disgusted with her weakness.

"Now you heard it," he said.

She stiffened. "Maybe you're forgetting that you and I are in this together," she'd said. "Maybe you're forgetting what you owe me."

Her reminder softened him. "Look," he'd said, "I'm under a lot of pressure. I've got this contact in Italy that might pan out. It's not easy, you know? I'll call you in a few days."

"Promise?"

"Yeah. Promise."

Pims was at the far end of the bar when Lynn walked into Adirondacks. He stood, greeted her with a great flourish, and pulled out the adjacent barstool. After ordering her a rum and Coke, and concealing his distaste, Pims leaned close.

"Luther told me your work was worthy of a gallery showing."

"He did? He tried to arrange one for me but it fell through. Some gallery in the boondocks. Maryland." She sipped her drink through the tiny stirrer, which annoyed Pims. It was for stirring, not slurping.

Pims laughed. "Showing in a rinky-dink gallery in Maryland will hardly advance the promising career of any talented artist."

"I know," she said, sipping again.

"I can do wonderful things for you, Ms. Marshall."

Was he about to make some silly pitch? Not an unusual occurrence in her experience, but distasteful coming from him. Pims might be a powerful force in art, but he was personally offensive: grossly overweight, foppishly dressed, perspiring in the cool atmosphere of Adirondacks, lips too fleshy, nails manicured and polished, smile crooked, a true George Grosz character sketch.

"I know that," she said, adding, "and I would be very appreciative of any help you could give me. I was going to bring some of my work with me but—"

"Where is Julian?" Pims said abruptly.

"Julian?" She sipped. "In Paris."

"*Was* in Paris. Not any longer."

She turned to face him. "How do you know that?"

A half-smile. "I have sources everywhere, Lynn. Good sources. I know that he went to Rome for— a meeting."

"Really?"

"Don't come up coy with me, Ms. Marshall." His silky tone had segued to hard edge. She tried to avoid his eyes, but he directed her attention with a firm grip on her wrist. "We have something extremely important to discuss," he said.

"Let go of me."

His gentle voice returned as he removed his hand. "Of course. The gravity of the moment overwhelmed me." He then said, as though voicing an inner thought, "I can keep you and your boyfriend out of jail, Lynn Marshall."

It wasn't a laugh that managed to squeeze its way through her suddenly dry throat, more a feeble expression of incredulity. She finished her drink and looked about the room, which had begun to fill.

"And I can do wonders for your career. I think you'll agree that the combination is potent."

She summoned the courage to look him in the eye. "I don't know what you're talking about."

"Then allow me to enlighten you. Julian, son of my deceased and dear friend, went to Rome from Paris to arrange a transaction of sorts. I know because it was I who put him in touch with a potential business partner."

"You did? I don't understand."

"One day, my dear, I shall take the time to explain it to you at length. In the meantime, suffice it to say that your boyfriend's irrational stubbornness threatens my well-being."

"Why? How?" She'd mustered a certain steely calm now. "I'd like another drink."

"Of course. Sir, another for the lady."

"What do you mean you arranged for Julian to meet someone in Italy?"

He held up a hammy hand to silence her. "I shall talk, and you shall listen. I, after all, arranged for this pleasant festivity and am the one paying for it. Enjoy your rum and Coca Cola, Carmen Miranda." He winced. "And please stop using the stirrer as a straw. It offends me. Now, where was I? Ah, yes. You are to contact Sir Julian the moment you leave here. You are to inform him that he is expected to honor the arrangements I have made for him in Italy. Understand?"

"What arrangements?" Lynn asked, realizing that Pims was talking about someone to whom Julian could sell *Grottesca*. Why hadn't Julian told her?

Pims laughed. "I see many little wheels spinning inside that lovely head of yours, Lynn. Good. You're concerned that your lover boy might make his score, as they say, and leave you behind. M. Scott Pims to the rescue. Do what I say and I will see to it that your interests are protected."

"You want me to call Julian and tell him to do what you said?"

"Bravo! Very astute. And don't be reticent in relaying that message. Be firm, because you have a reason to be. Not only do I know the little secret shared by the two of you, the evidence I possess is sufficient to give both of you many years of solitude at taxpayer expense to develop your artistic talents. Or your abilities as a laundress. Do I make myself clear?"

"I—"

"No matter. The only thing you must do at this point is to apply your female charms to Julian in the interest of what we might call a greater good for all of us."

"I don't know how to reach him in Rome."

Pims handed her a slip of paper. "The number of his hotel. Instruct him to move to the Raphael, on the Piazza Navona, and to wait there for further instructions. *Capisce?*"

"What?"

"Do you comprehend what I have said?"

"Oh. Yes."

"Once you have talked sense into your mule-headed friend, I want you to forget any of this happened. I want you to go about your usual daily routine, work hard for Paul Bishop, continue to turn out your art which, I assure you, will be of great interest to me after this adventure is concluded, and wait to hear from me."

"All right. But I want you to know I had nothing to do with any of this. I didn't know what Luther was doing. And I wasn't the one who—"

He touched his index finger to her lips. "Please. Now, might I suggest you taste my drink, equal amounts of port wine and brandy? My stomach has been upset today; I imagine yours might be, too." He handed his snifter to her and she tasted. "A much more civilized libation than the national drink of the Banana Republic. Barman, our check, please." He laid cash on top of it. "Ta-ta, Lynn. This has been an extremely pleasant hour."

Lynn reached Julian at his hotel and told him what Pims had said.

"His contact offered two million. It's worth ten times that."

"Please, Julian, Pims knows everything. It isn't worth going to jail over greed. Two million dollars! A million for each of us." He said nothing. "Did you hear me?"

"Yeah. Maybe you're right."

"He wants you to move to a hotel called the Raphael. On some piazza."

"Piazza Navona. This other guy told me to go there, too."

"Well, go there for God's sake and get it over with. Who is this other man?"

"It doesn't matter. Name's Testa. Like testy, you

know? Filippo Testa. He's a middleman for the buyer."

"I'm coming to Italy." She said it despite Pims's admonition not to change anything about her life.

"Don't be stupid."

"I want to be there when you sell it."

"Don't you trust me?" He laughed.

"Of course I do. It's just that—"

"Just sit tight, Lynn. You're right. I'll do exactly what Pims told me to do. I'll call you as soon as the deal is made. You can come then."

Small tears ran down her cheeks. "All right," she said. "When will you call?"

"The deal goes down Wednesday."

"Call me before that. Call me every day."

"Yeah, okay. Love you. Have to go."

Pims's final act before beginning to prepare dinner for his friend Wilfred Penny was to use his voice-altering equipment to leave a message on Mac and Annabel's answering machine: *"Written instructions for your jaunt to Italy are to be found with the bartender at The Collector Gallery and Restaurant, on Dupont Circle."*

Unless, he thought, the homeless person to whom he'd paid ten dollars to deliver it to the restaurant fell down on the job. Maybe I should have paid him more, Pims mused as he prepared smoked trout delivered that afternoon from Cannon Seafood. No, he decided, ten dollars was more than sufficient. Besides, as a businessman he had to watch the bottom line.

The trout's robust smell spoke of wonders ahead—on the plate and, soon, bird in hand.

THIRTY-EIGHT

THE MOMENT Carole Aprile returned from Colorado and announced "agreement in principle" with the attempted recovery of *Grottesca,* Steve Jordan met in his office with the Smiths, Jordan's assistant, Gloria Watson, and a detective from the Italian *polizia* art squad, Paul Colarulli, who'd flown to Washington the night before at Jordan's request, and expense.

"It has to be that way," Annabel said in response to a cynical comment Jordan made about the conditions laid down by Carole Aprile, whose absence was conspicuous. "The government wants to take credit for recovering *Grottesca* in order to satisfy the Italians. But if something goes wrong, including an outright failure to obtain the painting, it's not to be linked to the effort."

"Convenient," Jordan said.

Mac said, "Look, let me level with you. As much as I appreciate Detective Colarulli's assurances that the Italian police will be working closely with you every step of the way, I want more of a guarantee of Annabel's safety." Colarulli had outlined commitments made by his people of manpower, surveillance equipment, and vehicles.

"Hopefully, there won't be a need for police involvement aside from arresting whoever's selling it and whoever's buying. If we get to that stage, Annabel's function will be over."

"Words like 'hopefully' and 'if' don't hold up in my court," Mac said.

"I'm sure everything will work out just fine," Annabel offered. "Steve and Detective Colarulli seem to have put together a sensible battle plan."

"Look, Mac," Jordan said, "if you have serious reservations about this, nothing says Annabel has to go through with it."

Mac thought for a moment before asking his wife, "You're comfortable with it?"

"Yes."

"Then I have to be. What's next?"

What was next was to make travel arrangements, with everyone involved taking as many separate flights as possible to avoid being seen together. Mac and two detectives loaned to Jordan's art squad by another Washington MPD division would be on the same plane. Gloria Watson was on Annabel's flight, seated two rows behind her in first class. Colarulli took the earliest flight to fine-tune things in Rome.

On Sunday night, Mac and Annabel packed in silence. Finally, she said, "Mac, I have to admit

I'm upset, not about what we're about to do but about your response to it. You seem—well, you seem angry at me for doing it. If I'd known that would be your reaction, I would have said no."

He stopped trying to fold a light sweater to perfection, sat on the edge of the bed, and said, "Did it ever occur to you that I might be worried about the woman I love?"

"Of course. But—" She joined him.

"And did it also occur to you that we are winging off to Rome based upon disguised voices and a note from what is undoubtedly a demented individual, someone who has set off a chain reaction involving police departments on two continents, the government of the United States, and Lord knows who else?"

"It has crossed my mind."

"And?"

"And it has also crossed my mind that not only will we be instrumental in recovering a masterpiece, and maybe identifying a murderer or two, we'll settle the mystery of Luther's death. And . . . " She smiled. "And, we'll have a delicious story to dine out on for the rest of our lives."

"It's the murderer part that bothers me. I don't want anyone dining on you. Four people have lost their lives over *Grottesca.*"

"And maybe it will stop once *Grottesca* is back in its rightful owner's hands. You know what, Mac?" She kissed his cheek.

"What?"

"We're finally going to Rome together. And at taxpayer expense."

"Well, yes—it is cost-effective." He couldn't help but grin.

"And romantic. You know how sexually charged you become when danger lurks."

"I *what?*"

They fell back across their open suitcases and kissed for a long time. "Let's get the packing out of the way," she said. "The handle on my suitcase is breaking my ribs."

Mac's flight got him and the two MPD detectives into Rome Monday night. They went straight to the Raphael Hotel, where Mac was booked into a room next to the one Annabel would be assigned when she arrived the next day. He didn't like having separate rooms but bowed to Jordan's wisdom. He'd been instructed to lay low, order room service, and, in general, act as though he wasn't there. He had trouble sleeping that night.

Annabel and Gloria Watson left the plane separately on Tuesday and took individual cabs into the city, Annabel going directly to the hotel, Gloria, whose large sunglasses, massive drop earrings, and red satin jumpsuit gave her the look of a jet-setting rock star, taking an hour's tour of the city before checking in.

The Raphael's gloomy, dimly lit lobby was off-putting at first for Annabel. But although her room was small, it was sunny and nicely furnished, providing a splendid view of the piazza. She unpacked, undressed, and wrapped herself in a terrycloth robe provided by the hotel. Like Mac, she'd been instructed to remain in her room until contacted, either by one of her team or by the unnamed person who would give her further instructions.

An hour later, Gloria Watson checked into a room at the other end of the hall. Jordan and his two borrowed detectives also had rooms on that floor, one by the elevator, one near the exit.

Annabel received a call from Jordan. "Welcome to Rome," he said pleasantly. "That husband of yours is driving me crazy wanting to see you. If I didn't know better, I'd think you were on a honeymoon."

"We intend to make it a second honeymoon," Annabel replied. "When *can* I see him?"

"After dinner. You'll each order separate room service. When you're done, I told Romeo he can sneak in to see Juliet."

"I love it," she said. "And thanks."

After dinner, and after carefully checking the hallway, Mac slipped into Annabel's room carrying a bottle of wine, a miniature cribbage board, and a deck of cards. They embraced like lovers separated by war. Mac opened the wine and set two glasses on a small table by the window. "Better draw the shade," Annabel said, doing so.

"What's the drill again?" Mac asked after they'd toasted, "To us."

She shrugged and said, "Wait until I receive a call."

"Tonight?"

"I hope so. Now that we're here, I want it to happen fast. The thought of sitting in a hotel room with Rome outside is depressing. Can you stay?"

"With you in this room tonight? I don't see why not. No one knows I'm here."

"Maybe you should clear it with Steve."

"I've cleared it with you. I'll go back to my room first thing in the morning. I feel like a college kid in a coed dorm."

"It's kind of exciting," Annabel said. "The sex therapists always suggest making love in new and unusual surroundings."

"In your own pool or kitchen, maybe. This is different. Besides, I'm beat. You should be, too."

"Too filled with anticipation to be tired. Go to bed."

He stripped down to his shorts and T-shirt and slipped beneath the covers while she sat up for hours watching him sleep, thinking how much she loved him and their life together; wondering what the morning would bring; and falling victim to occasional thoughts of waking him, packing their bags, and running away—from Caravaggio and his seemingly cursed *Grottesca,* from art thieves and murderers and twisted lives. She dozed off in her chair thinking those things, moonlight casting shifting light and shadow over her face, until three, when she jerked awake and joined him in bed.

They were awakened at seven by Steve Jordan's call and the sounds of another day starting outside on Piazza Navona. "Nothing yet?"

"I would have called you if there had been," Annabel said sleepily.

"I know. Christ, I hope this doesn't end up the proverbial wild goose chase. An expensive one."

"Not to worry," Annabel said. "It's backed by the full faith and credit of the United States Government."

"Only if we succeed. If we don't, they never heard of us. See Mac last night?"

"Yes. He's right—I did."

"Separate breakfasts in the room," Jordan said.

"Don't remind me. I'll call the minute I hear anything."

They whiled away the time playing cribbage. Annabel was about to win when the phone rang. She picked it up. "Signora Smith?" a man said.

"Yes. *Si.* Who's calling?"

"My name is Filippo Testa, Signora Smith. I believe you expected my call."

"I did."

"I have instructions concerning your business meeting."

"Good. What are they?"

"I prefer to tell you in person. There is a church a few blocks from your hotel, the Church of Sant'Agostino, on Piazza Sant'Agostino. Only a few minutes' walk. Meet me in the Cavalletti Chapel. Shall we say an hour from now? The last pew on the right."

"All right. How will I know you?"

"I will be the only person in that pew. Until then, signora."

Annabel called Jordan and told him of the arrangements for the meeting. "Okay," he said. "You stay in your room until we're ready to move. I'll call Mac."

"He's here."

"He's not supposed to be. Let me talk to him."

As Annabel dressed for her meeting, the team assembled in Jordan's room.

"So Testa's involved," Jordan said.

"You know him?" Mac asked.

Jordan and the Italian cops laughed. "Oh, yes," said Colarulli. " 'Count' Testa is well known to us. He bills himself as an art collector and dealer. Claims royal blood." He laughed again. "He deals in stolen art, nothing major, fencing pieces stolen here in Italy to buyers in other countries. Considers himself a dandy, but always broke."

"You think he has *Grottesca*?" Mac asked.

"No," Colarulli said. "Functioning as a middle-man."

"For who?" Mac asked.

Colarulli replied, "Lately, he's been associating with organized crime figures, one in particular, Luigi Sensi. Head of the *Camorra,* the Naples faction of the Mafia. Sensi is a major figure in art theft here, although he's as insulated from that as from every other aspect of his criminal activities."

"You seem to know a lot about him," Mac said.

"Knowing about people and being able to prove what we know is the most difficult thing, *si?*" he said to Jordan.

"That's for sure. Okay, folks, here's how we cover Annabel when she meets with Testa. Gloria, you and Jimmy play sightseeing American couple. Get going now. Stroll past that church, take pictures, wander inside, but stay far away from the back right pew where Annabel and Testa are meeting. Hang around the altar. Then get out, but stay in the area so you can see the door."

As Gloria and one of the Washington detectives left the room, Jordan said to the other American cop, "Bob, go with Detective Tedeschi in his car. Follow Annabel all the way. Park where you won't be seen but can see the door."

Paul Colarulli asked the remaining Italian detective, "Ready to join the priesthood again, Peter?"

Peter laughed and said in a heavy accent, "It is against the law to impersonate a priest, *si?*"

Colarulli said to Mac, whose expression was quizzical, "Peter makes a fine priest on demand. Come on, put on your clerical collar. You have official duties to perform in Sant'Agostino this morning."

They left the room, leaving Mac and Jordan alone. "What about me?" Mac asked.

"You stay here."

"Not on your life."

"Mac, this is a police matter."

"Annabel's not a cop."

"I know, I know. But don't make it difficult for me. Stay by your phone. I may need to get hold of you."

Mac sighed and said, "Okay. I'm trusting you, Steve."

"Good. I'll say one thing for whoever's behind this."

"What's that?"

"He knows his Caravaggio. The Church of Sant' Agostino has one. *Madonna di Loreto.* Caravaggio's model was a local woman who'd turned down a wealthy lawyer's marriage proposal. This lawyer confronted Caravaggio and accused him of being a heathen, or worse, so Caravaggio got mad, which he did pretty often, and ran the lawyer through with his sword. Had to skip to Genoa until things cooled down."

"Another murder," Mac muttered to himself. To Jordan: "You know your Caravaggio, don't you?"

"Been doing lots of reading. By the way, the party's getting bigger."

"What do you mean?"

"Got a couple of calls last night from home. M. Scott Pims, Washington's gift to television, is in Rome. They say he's here to do a documentary on the Museo Barracco."

"You sound skeptical."

"That's right. Museums like the Barracco have never interested Pims. Egyptian artifacts and classical sculpture. Not his cup of tea. Besides, along with the crew he brought from the States, he's hired two additional Italian video crews. Doesn't take three to shoot the Barracco."

"I see," Mac said.

"And Franco del Brasco evidently enjoys Rome this time of year."

"Franco del Brasco. Annabel mentioned him. The collector from an Francisco?"

"A very rich hood who also collects art—from any source. I've felt all along he might be the buyer Luther Mason had in mind when he grabbed the original and shipped the forgery back to Italy. Del Brasco flew here in a private jet with a couple of his goons."

"Do you know where he is in Rome?"

"No. My info came from San Francisco. No word from this end yet."

Mac's worried expression wasn't lost on Jordan. The detective slapped him on the back and said, "Don't worry, Mac. Nothing will happen to Annabel. That's a promise you can take to the bank. Come on. Let's brief her on what to expect before she heads out. I don't want any surprises."

Annabel walked with purposeful strides in the direction of Piazza Sant'Agostino. Not too fast, not too slow. She was aware of the car following her, containing the detectives, and fought the urge to look back. She paused a few times to look at goods in shop windows, but the items didn't register on her. She was too focused on the meeting with this wannabe count, Filippo Testa, whom Colarulli had described for her—tall and slender, slightly bent, balding but with wet dyed black hair swept back along his temples, charming, speaks excellent English (which she knew from their telephone conversation), mild in manner. She wasn't nervous. Excited was a more apt description of what she felt. It was actually happening. Within minutes she would be told how to recover *Grottesca*.

She passed an outdoor cafe on the piazza and was aware of male attention from some of the tables. She looked straight ahead, crossed the street, and stood in front of the Church of Sant'Agostino. The moment she climbed the short set of steps and entered, one of the men in the cafe got up and followed. He stepped inside the cool, dank church, removed his red beret, and looked to where Annabel sat in the rear pew on the right. She didn't see him. Her attention was on the unusually high nave, barely as wide as the aisles, dominated by a dome. A priest standing in front of a rack of flickering offertory candles appeared to be rearranging them. Annabel suppressed a smile; it was the Italian detective Jordan had told her would be there.

She sensed rather than saw the man sliding into the pew beside her. "Signor Testa?" she asked in a whisper, not turning.

"*Si.* A lovely church, you would agree?"

"Yes. Beautiful."

"Home of the Madonna del Parto, the Madonna of childbirth. Many women come here to pray to her for the safe delivery of their children. Couples without children pray to her to correct their situation."

"I didn't know."

"Caravaggio is here, too."

Annabel swallowed and faced him. Was it to happen so fast? Did he have *Grottesca* with him?

"Up there," he said, pointing to a pillar near the altar. "The *Madonna di Loreto.* A tragic tale behind it. And Raphael is represented, too. *The Prophet Isaiah.* So much art in Italy, *si?* So much beauty."

Annabel noticed as he pointed that the cuff of

his blue double-breasted blazer was frayed. He needed a haircut. He smiled at her; his teeth were yellow and had suffered neglect.

"What is it you wish to tell me?" Annabel asked, looking again at the altar.

"You have the money with you? Two million American?"

"Yes. Not with me, of course. Back at the hotel."

"And you have traveled to Rome alone?"

"Yes."

"Then the exchange will be made this evening, at six, at the Palazzo Madama."

"Where is that?"

"Only a few steps from your hotel. Across the Corso Rinascimento. The northwest corner at six."

"All right. I'll be there. Will you?"

"Unfortunately, no. It would be my pleasure to see such a lovely lady again, but my duties will have me elsewhere."

"Who will meet me?"

"In due time, Signora Smith. But he will know you. Such a striking beauty. I must leave. *Grazie.* It has been my pleasure. Enjoy my city. It has much to offer."

Annabel watched him leave the church before going to the nave, where the priestly detective continued to pretend to be busy. He smiled and walked away. She went to the pillar on which hung the Caravaggio and thought of Court Whitney's comment about the havoc caused by Luther Mason. "You're an accomplice, Mr. Michelangelo Merisi Caravaggio," she said to the painting. "And I hope you're satisfied.

"The Palazzo Madama," Steve Jordan said after they'd all gathered in his room.

"A problem with that?" Annabel asked.

Jordan laughed and shook his head. "Just another quaint Caravaggio connection. A cardinal named Del Monte lived at Palazzo Madama back in the mid–fifteen hundreds. He latched on to Caravaggio and gave him a studio and living quarters in his home. He painted a lot of his important works there."

"So now we sit and wait until six," Mac said.

"That's about it," Jordan said. "At least we have time to get everybody in place."

"I want to be there this time," Mac said.

"I figured you would," said Jordan. "There's an outdoor cafe on the opposite corner. You can watch from there."

Annabel smiled at Mac, who, after a moment, smiled back.

"Strange," said Detective Paul Colarulli.

"What's strange?" Jordan asked.

"Choosing such a public, well-guarded place as Palazzo Madama to exchange the painting for money."

"Well-guarded?" Mac said.

"Yes. The Palazzo del Senato is there, an important government building. A great deal of security."

"Glad to hear that," said Mac.

"But why?" Colarulli asked, as if to himself.

"Stop trying to be logical, Paul," Jordan said.

"I suppose you're right, Steve." The detective smiled. *Still, why?*

THIRTY-NINE

"SIGNOR MASON?"

"Yeah. Who's this?"

"Filippo Testa."

"What's going on, Mr. Testa? I've been sitting here all day waiting."

Testa laughed. "Ah, youth. So impatient. You have the product with you?"

"Product? Oh. Yeah. I have it."

"Good. Across the street from your hotel is the Church of Sant'Agnese. Be in front of it at five forty-five with the product. Be on time. A car will take you from there to your buyer."

"Hey, hold on a second. If you think I'm going to—"

"Mr. Mason, the last time we met turned out to be quite unpleasant. I am glad to see you've come to your senses."

"Where's Pims? I want to talk to Pims."

"Mr. Mason, please don't strain *my* patience. I understand you have agreed to the terms I previously laid out for you."

"You're stealing it."

"One, I am not the purchaser. Two, two million dollars is a great deal of money for such a—how shall we say it?—for such a controversial product. Five forty-five in front of the church—if you know what is good for you. *Ciao.*"

"Signor del Brasco?"

"Yes."

"Are you ready to own one of the finest works of art ever created by man?"

"Get to the point. Who am I talking to?"

"A friend about to fulfill your greatest wish. A car will pick you up in front of the Raphael at five-thirty. Have your money and the other version of the painting with you."

"Where are we going?"

"You will see. Don't be late. The driver has been instructed not to wait."

Filippo Testa hung up after making his second call to guests of the Raphael Hotel, on Piazza Navona, having stuck to the notes provided him by his client-master. He poured himself a large negroni—bitter Campari, sweet vermouth, gin, and Angostura bitters—from a pitcher he kept in his refrigerator, and downed it.

After checking his appearance in a mirror, he donned his red beret, went downstairs to where he'd parked his battered Fiat, and headed east on the A24 toward the Abruzzi region. He had to hurry. He didn't want to be late. As amusing as M. Scott Pims could be, Testa had seen his ugly side.

FORTY

ANNABEL REED-SMITH stepped through the front door of the Raphael onto the Piazza Navona. She was the last to leave the hotel; everyone else had departed at staggered intervals to take up their assigned positions. Mac would be seated in the outdoor cafe from which he could see the northwest corner of Palazzo Madama. Gloria Watson and one of the American detectives were again playing the touring couple. The other American and his Italian counterpart were in a car parked just off the square, on via Chiaca. Steve Jordan and Paul Colarulli idled in an unmarked police vehicle at Palazzo Madama's southeast corner.

Annabel's adrenaline drove her pulse. Her biggest fear at the moment was having two million dollars in marked currency in her oversized purse. What grand irony should she be mugged on her way to the rendezvous.

She crossed Corso Rinascimento and observed the street action by Palazzo Madama. It was relatively quiet. Two uniformed soldiers provided sleepy sentry in front of the Palazzo del Senato. Traffic was light, although there were many parked cars.

She calculated direction and looked northwest. No one conspicuously stood holding what might be a painting. Then her eye went to a large, black, four-door Mercedes with opaque windows. Maybe he's waiting inside it, she thought, crossing the street and approaching the vehicle.

She stood next to the car and squinted in an attempt to see inside, but the black glass effectively prohibited it. A door opened; Annabel leaned forward to better see the person sitting in the rear compartment. Her first attempt at saying his name came out as air. She did better the second time: "Julian Mason?"

Annabel instinctively stepped closer and saw the painting he held. *Grottesca!* It was as though the canvas emitted a magnetic pull, a positive force drawing Annabel's negative field to it. As she stepped still closer, the front passenger door opened and a man hopped out.

Mac jumped up in the cafe, nearly knocking over his small table, speaking, below a shout, "No, Annabel. Watch out!" Others in the cafe smiled at his actions.

The man who'd come from the front of the Mercedes shoved Annabel onto the rear seat, slammed the door behind her, and scrambled into the passenger seat. The car roared away.

Mac was running. "Stop them, stop them," he yelled into the air.

Jordan and Colarulli had been taken by surprise. When it registered, Colarulli spun rubber and headed for Mac, who'd almost reached the scene of Annabel's abduction. Jordan was on the radio, calling for the backup car.

"Get in," Colarulli shouted.

Mac seemed stunned, immobile.

"Get in," Jordan repeated, reaching behind and opening the rear door. Mac fell in and they sped after the Mercedes.

"Catch them," Mac said, leaning over the seatback. "*Damn* it, pull them over."

Colarulli held up his right hand, his left on the wheel. "Let's see where they're heading."

"I don't care where they're heading. Call for help. Set up roadblocks."

Colarulli ignored him, speaking to Jordan. "They don't seem to be trying to lose us."

"Maybe they don't even know who we are," Mac said angrily.

The car containing the American and Italian detectives made radio contact with Colarulli in Italian. "What did they say?" Mac asked.

"They're with us," Colarulli said. To Jordan: "They're heading for the A24."

"Where's that lead?" Jordan asked.

"East. The Abruzzi region," Colarulli said, swerving to avoid a gaping pothole and tossing Mac against the door in the process.

Ahead, Annabel sat wide-eyed next to Julian Mason. Her question of the men in front, "Who are you?" was answered by a revolver leveled at her over the seat back. Once she'd regained enough composure to speak again, she turned to Julian. "You?" she said, looking at the painting he held close to his chest.

"I didn't know it was you coming to buy it," he said, his quivering voice mirroring his fright. "They didn't tell me."

"That's *it?*" she said. "The original *Grottesca?*"

He nodded, tightening his grip on the painting.

"Julian, what about your father? Did you—?"

"It was an accident. He fell."

"Fell? You were there?"

His silence answered affirmatively.

She was about to ask more when the driver entered the A24 and pushed down hard on the accelerator, pressing Annabel and Julian Mason back against their seats.

"We'll lose them," Mac said as he saw the Mercedes suddenly increase the distance between them. He twisted and looked through the rear window. The second car of detectives was right behind

them. "Can't you stop them?" he yelled at Colarulli.

Again, the detective's right hand came up.
"Trust me," he said.

"Trust you? That's my wife, damn it!"

"Easy, Mac," Jordan said. "Everything's going
to be okay." It didn't sound to Mac as though he
believed it.

As the Mercedes with Annabel and Julian Mason,
and the police cars with Mac, Steve Jordan, Paul
Colarulli and other detectives continued traveling
east from Rome, a surrealistic calm settled in.

Annabel and Julian rode in silence, trapped in
their thoughts.

Mac thought of the now infamous O. J. Simp-
son Bronco "chase" and wondered if this would
look the same were it televised. The only difference
was speed. The Bronco had been going thirty-five
miles per hour. They were doing seventy or better.

The Mercedes exited A24 and continued on A25.

"Cocullo," Colarulli said to no one in particular, indicating a town they'd just passed. "They
worship snakes there."

"What?" Mac said.

"Snakes. Snake worship. Looks like he's heading for Pescara."

"Pescara?" Mac repeated.

"On the coast. The Adriatic. Too polluted to
swim."

The last thing on Mac's mind.

A25 cut north, up through breathtaking snow-capped mountains, the towns of San Pelino and Caporciano a blur through the window. "You're losing them," Mac said as the Mercedes disappeared over a crest, only to reappear again on the other side. It was almost twilight; shards of shadow sliced across lush valleys and onto mountaintop villages with barns constructed of reeds, as they had been for centuries, and over old men and women shrouded in black. The road had turned chiaroscuro, sun to shade, shade to sun, the air cooler through a window Mac had cracked open.

The Mercedes slowed as it entered Pescara and navigated narrow streets, then broke free again on a ribbon of road leading to the seacoast's rugged beaches.

"Where the hell is he going?" Jordan said.

"Up there." Colarulli pointed to the crest of rocky hill growing up out of the beach to a plateau studded with scraggly pines. Although it was still light, an eerie glow came from the plateau, light of a different genesis than the horizon's pumpkin-colored scrim.

The Mercedes started up a one-lane road. Colarulli stopped at the foot of it. The second Italian police car pulled up alongside.

"*Pazzo,*" the Italian detective said to Colarulli through an open window.

"What's crazy?"

"Going up there. There's no other way down. This is the only road."

"How do you know?"

"My family's from here. I came every summer to swim."

They got out and stood by their cars.

"Lupi mannari," said the detective whose family was from Pescara.

"What's that mean?" Mac asked Colarulli.

He screwed up his face, said to the other detective, "Werewolves?"

"Si."

"Werewolves?" Mac said. "What the hell are you talking about?"

"This is a superstitious area. They used to practice sorcery, witchcraft, other such things."

"The caves are up there," the other detective said.

"What caves?" Colarulli asked.

"Where the hermits performed their ceremonies. The Middle Ages."

"What are we going to do now?" Mac asked.

"Looks like they can't go anyplace," Jordan said. "You have backup coming?" he asked Colarulli.

"I requested it. They said they would. Maybe."

"Maybe?" Mac said, his voice filled with frustration. "Maybe?" he repeated, louder this time.

The sound of approaching vehicles caused them to turn. Three marked *polizia* cars from Abruzzi's capital, Aquila, came to a dusty stop, and a half-dozen uniformed officers joined them. Colarulli engaged in a spirited conversation with the squad's chief before saying to Mac and Jordan in English, "They're trapped up there. No way out." He said to his two detectives, "Come with me." The chief of the uniformed contingent told his men to join them.

"Where are you going?" Mac asked.

"Up," said Colarulli."

"Not without me you're not," Mac said.

"Please, it is better that—"

"He's coming with us," said Jordan, knowing there was no way to prevent it.

"As you wish," Colarulli said. "But stay back. Behind us."

They started up, the police fanning out across the road, guns drawn, Mac in lockstep with Steve Jordan.

Jordan waved the party to a halt. "Whose car is that?" he asked, referring to a silver-gray Mercedes parked beneath some trees.

No one had an answer.

They continued to climb, slower now, more alert, senses tuned to their surroundings. They reached a relatively level dirt area where the black Mercedes that had led them to this lonely, lovely, forbidding spot was parked, along with four other vehicles—a muddy brown Mercedes and three Volvo panel trucks. Jordan and Mac checked the cars. Empty.

"What the hell is going on?" Jordan asked.

He was answered by a sudden burst of light emanating from behind a row of trees separating them from the hill's plateau. They tensed; the officers crouched, held their weapons in both hands, and pointed them toward the trees.

"Slow," Colarulli said, leading a further advance.

They reached the trees and peered beyond. The lights originated from floods mounted on stands and taped to trees, powered by large generators that had been trucked in. Mac spotted Annabel at one end of the clearing with two other people, one of whom held a gun. He strained to make out the other face. "Julian Mason?" he said.

At the opposite side of the tract stood three men, none of whom were familiar to Mac. One had a helmet of Harpo Marx–style blonde curls that appeared to have been pasted on his head.

An amplified voice cut through the evening. "Come up and join us."

"He's got a bullhorn," Jordan said.

"Those are cameras over there," Paul Colarulli said, pointing to a raised area formed naturally by a rock shelf worm smooth over centuries by wind and rain.

"Jesus," Mac muttered. "That's Scott Pims." Next to him stood Count Filippo Testa.

"Come, come," Pims said through the battery-powered bullhorn. "The party's just beginning."

Mac stepped away from the police and into the glare of the lights. "Come here, Annabel," he shouted, beckoning her with his hand. "Let her go."

"All in due time, Mackensie," said Pims. "First, there is business to be conducted."

All eyes were on Pims, who was dressed in black trousers and a billowing black shirt with puff sleeves. Draped behind him was a huge blowup of an ink-on-paper drawing of a bearded young man. As everyone watched, Pims said into the camera:

"I am M. Scott Pims, your benevolent host of this week's *Art Insider,* brought to you through the extreme generosity of viewers like you who support this public station. And I welcome those of you now able to join me on this visionary cable network."

He indicated the drawing.

"Behind me is the face of one of the world's great artistic geniuses, Michelangelo Merisi Caravaggio. It is in his honor that we gather here this evening on a windswept plateau in Italy overlooking the magnificent Adriatic. It is here that we invoke the spirit of Caravaggio—and solve the mystery of *Grottesca.*"

"The son of a bitch is turning this into a TV show," Mac said to Jordan.

"Looks like it."

"We have many distinguished guests on this week's program,"

Pims said.

"The government of the United States, which was terribly embarrassed when it lost *Grottesca,* is represented by one Annabel Reed-Smith, who appears here as an emissary of the White House's Commission on the Arts. Welcome, Mrs. Smith."

A camera captured Annabel, Julian, and the two men standing with them, then zoomed in on the *Grottesca* Julian held. Mac looked across the small clearing at his wife; she appeared to be as dumbfounded as he was.

A gust of wind sent Pims's sleeves fluttering as he raised his arms and continued:

"Also joining us this evening is the noted San Francisco art collector, Mr. Franco del Brasco, who has flown here at great expense in pursuit of the remarkable work from Caravaggio's hand known as *Grottesca.*"

Del Brasco and his henchmen took in the scene, impatient to act, nervous in the light. The blond man looked as though he might bolt at any second. Del Brasco's *Grottesca*—the original—became the subject of another camera closeup.

Steve Jordan, who'd been standing with Mac

Smith, stepped into the center of the area and shouted, "Don't forget to introduce us, Pims. The police, and plenty of us, American and Italian."

Pims clapped his hands and laughed. "Would I forget you, Detective Jordan? I would be keenly disappointed if you hadn't decided to partake in the festivities." He said to the camera,

"We are also joined by law enforcement from both the United States of America and Italy. These dedicated men and women have been searching 'round the world without success for *Grottesca*. Fortunately for the art world, I have been conducting my own exhaustive search, which has proved far more fruitful than their efforts.

"My other guest, no less significant than the others, is senior curator of the Vatican, Mr. Joseph Spagnola."

Spagnola had been in the shadows behind the sketch of Caravaggio. Carrying the third *Grottesca,* he stepped into the light and stood at Pims's side. A stronger gust sent Pims's hair flying, and he placed his hand atop his large head.

"The details leading to this remarkable evening will be revealed to you from a studio, in less turbulent conditions. But now, it is time to right wrongs."

"Aren't you going to move on him?" Mac asked Jordan.

"Let's hear what he has to say. Nobody's going anywhere." The uniformed Italian police and the detectives were poised for action once the word was given. But they, too, seemed transfixed by the scene.

Pims pointed to where Annabel and Julian stood. "Come forward," he said. To the camera:

"This young man is Julian Mason, son of the deceased Caravaggio expert, Luther Mason. He has with him *Grottesca,* which he intends to sell for two million dollars to Mrs. Smith, representing the White House. Have you consummated your sale, Julian?"

"Hold on," del Brasco barked. "That's mine." He started walking toward Annabel and Julian, flanked by the young blond man and his colleague, both of whom had pulled handguns from their jackets.

"Aha," Pims said.

"Mr. del Brasco is heard from. He, too, has in his possession a version of *Grottesca* which he believes to be a forgery."

Del Brasco brashly tossed the *Grottesca* he carried to the ground as he continued in Annabel's direction.

"Stop him," Mac said to Jordan, taking a step toward the advancing del Brasco. The blond saw Mac, stopped, and pointed his revolver at him.

"Come now," Pims said through the bullhorn. "There is no reason we can't resolve this like ladies and gentlemen."

"Let's go," Jordan said to Colarulli, who motioned the others to follow. The police went to the center of the area. "Drop the weapons," Jordan shouted. Colarulli repeated the order in Italian.

The del Brasco men were unsure.

"Drop them," Jordan said. "On the ground."

The men who'd driven Annabel and Julian to Pescara tossed their weapons in front of them.

"You, too," Colarulli ordered del Brasco. "Tell your men to give up their weapons."

"Get the painting," del Brasco growled. The blond and his partner hesitated, then lunged at Julian and Annabel. Mac also made his move, but too late. Annabel, who'd been standing with her hands shoved into the pockets of the light windbreaker she wore, pulled them out in an involuntary gesture of self-defense. The blond turned his revolver on her. Julian also acted without thought. Still cradling *Grottesca* in his arms, he stepped in front of Annabel as the discharge of the blond man's weapon snapped through the air like a whip. The bullet passed through the chest of the sensuous young model in *Grottesca* and entered Julian's chest to the left of center. He slumped silently to the ground, first on his knees, then toppling forward on top of the Jacques Saison forgery.

The uniformed police from Aquila opened fire. The blond thug was hit in the shoulder and thigh, his revolver sent spinning into the air. His companion, who'd fallen to the ground unhurt, pushed his weapon away from him, covered his head with his hands, and pleaded to not be hurt.

Mac reached Annabel's side and held her close. "You okay?" he asked.

"Yes. God, poor Julian." They dropped to their knees, and Mac gently rolled Julian on to his back. "Julian?" Annabel said.

"Sorry. I didn't mean to—"

"Don't talk," Annabel said. "You'll be all right."

One of the uniformed officers, clearly trained as a paramedic, started to work on Julian Mason while another ran to the cars to call for an ambulance.

Detective Colarulli ordered two policemen to place del Brasco under arrest.

"For what?" del Brasco asked, his attention on the *Grottesca* Julian had been holding that now lay in the dirt, a gaping hole through its center. "I did nothing."

"Not true," Pims blared through the bullhorn. The sound of his voice made everyone aware again that what had played out had been captured on videotape by the three cameras that continued to roll throughout. "You bought *Grottesca* from Luther Mason knowing it had been stolen. That makes you guilty of receiving stolen merchandise. You bankrolled Luther from the beginning."

"Prove it," del Brasco said.

"What about them?" Jordan asked, turning his attention to the two men who'd brought Annabel and Julian to Pescara.

Colarulli, who'd been questioning them, said, "Private detectives from Rome. Hired by Mr. Pims."

"That right, Pims?" Jordan shouted at the fat man.

"That is correct."

"You kidnapped my wife," Mac said to them.

They responded with a fusillade of Italian.

"Let's get out of here," Mac said, his arm around Annabel. As he started to lead her in the direction of the road, Pims said, "You can't leave now. Dinner hasn't been served yet."

Mac and Annabel stopped. "Dinner?" they said.

"Yes. Over there. To celebrate the recovery of *Grottesca.*"

"A badly damaged *Grottesca*," Steve Jordan said, picking up the one with the bullet hole in it.

"A badly damaged forgery," Pims said through the bullhorn. The original is there." He pointed to the painting del Brasco had thrown to the ground.

"What the hell are you saying?" del Brasco snarled. "That's a phony."

"To the contrary," said Pims, lumbering down from his slate stage, picking up the painting, and returning to his position in front of a camera. He faced it and held up *Grottesca.*

"*This* is the original *Grottesca,* ladies and gentlemen, now recovered and saved for eternity by none other than me, your benevolent host. The government of the United States has been spared further embarrassment, saving in the process two million dollars of taxpayer money. I hereby return this masterpiece to its rightful owners, the government of Italy."

He realized the Vatican's Joseph Spagnola was standing behind him holding the forgery Luther Mason had sent to Italy following *Grottesca*'s exhibition at the National Gallery.

"Ah, yes," said Pims, "yet another beautiful rendering of the original."

He took it from Spagnola and held it up to the camera.

"I had it," del Brasco said to the officers who'd handcuffed his hands behind his back. "It was mine all the time. That bastard who called lied. Damn him."

"*Non capisco,*" one of the officers said, shrugging to the other.

"That concludes this live portion of the program. I will interview the participants at dinner and wrap this up from the studio."

Filippo Testa came to Mac and Annabel. "Ah, Mrs. Smith, I am so happy you are safe. Had I known what—"

Pims now came down off the rock, patted his hair with his hand, approached, and extended his hand. Neither Mac nor Annabel moved to take it. "Exciting, yes?" Pims said.

They maintained their silence.

"You *will* stay for dinner? I've arranged for a typical Abruzzian celebratory feast back in Aquila. *Le virtù,* created of seven pastas and seven different vegetables; *diavoletto,* the hottest red peppers in Italy; a divine soup called *mbusse;* and *torrone* for dessert. Humble—but honey and almond have never reached such heights before."

Mac and Annabel continued to stare at him.

"You must join us. Besides, I want to interview you, Annabel. My report will not be complete without it."

It happened so quickly Annabel didn't realize what occurred until it was over. Mac's right hand came from low and behind, catching Pims squarely on the jaw and sending the corpulent TV host tumbling to the ground.

"Oh, Mac," Annabel said.

"I shall sue," Pims said, struggling to get up.

"You'll sue from jail," Mac said. "Come on, Mrs. Smith. Your job is over."

FORTY-ONE

TWO MONTHS LATER—
THE NATIONAL GALLERY OF ART,
WASHINGTON, D.C.

THE DINNER was held in the room in which the Caravaggio exhibition continued to be displayed to the public. The artist's magnificent works looked down upon the two dozen people seated at four closely grouped tables, there at the invitation of Courtney Whitney III and the gallery's trustees.

Because Vice President and Mrs. Aprile were honored guests, security that night was impenetrable. Secret Service agents had spent the afternoon going over every inch of the gallery in preparation for their arrival. Agents, some with dogs, patrolled access corridors to the room and entrances to the gallery itself.

Conversation was spirited.

"I just commissioned a Virginia Daley landscape for the house," Carole Aprile told Annabel. Mac and Annabel already owned a landscape by Daley, one of Washington's preeminent artists.

"Anything new on Pims?" Mac asked MPD art squad chief Steve Jordan.

Jordan gave out with a low, dirty laugh. "M.

Scott Pims?" he said, mimicking Pims's speech. "The DA thinks the grand jury might indict on withholding evidence. Conspiracy? Probably not. He's got his new cable TV deal, and his book, but we're working with New York on their son-of-Sam law. Hopefully, he won't be able to profit from this. Unless, of course, he's acquitted on the evidence charge."

Mac speared a cherry tomato from his salad plate. "He's a madman. Manipulating everyone, creating that scene in Pescara, setting up del Brasco and Julian, dragging Annabel into it through Mrs. Aprile. He's certifiably insane."

"You must admit, Mr. Smith, that his sense of the dramatic is without peer," a trustee at the table said, chuckling.

Mac ate another tomato, an excuse not to respond.

"Lynn Marshall's due here tomorrow from Seattle to give a statement," Jordan said to Mac. "I could feel sorry for her if she hadn't been so ruthlessly ambitious."

"The young lady who once worked here?" the trustee asked, adding, without receiving an answer, "Terribly poor judgment on Luther Mason's part, hiring her, wouldn't you say? Then again, Luther's judgment left much to be desired in many quarters."

Annabel ignored the comment and talked with Carole.

A trustee at Court Whitney's table compli-
mented the gallery director on his appearance on
Pims's TV show the previous week. "Took courage
to go on," he said. "You handled yourself beauti-
fully."

"Not difficult," Whitney said. "As much as I
personally abhor the way he did it, we all have to
admit that the *Grottesca* mess was resolved because of Pims."

Mac overheard the comment, turned, and said,
"And partly engineered by him." He whispered in
Annabel's ear, "I'm not sure how much longer I
can take this."

"What?" someone at the table asked.

"I was just telling my wife how proud I am of
her role in recovering *Grottesca.*"

"Oh?" the man's wife said. "Were you there,
Mrs. Smith?"

"I—Yes."

"Did Pims really hire an Italian witch doctor to
attempt to contact Caravaggio's spirit?"

"Ah, here's the soup," Mac said.

"All in all, an amusing little adventure," said a
matronly woman at another table. "Certainly
spiced up life at the National Gallery."

A succession of the dead people crossed
Annabel's mind: Carlo Giliberti, Luther Mason,
Peter Lafroing, Father Pasquale Giocondi. What
does she do for entertainment, Annabel wondered?

"It didn't take much to get Lynn Marshall to admit she was with Julian the night his father died and saw it happen," Jordan said to Mac.

"Do you believe her?" Mac asked, "that it *was* an accident, that all Julian did was to pull the painting away from him?"

"Yeah, I do. This is a son I'd just as soon not have to claim as my own, but I believe him. Arrogant as hell. Recovering nicely at his mother's house in Paris, I hear. I'm told he's a pretty good artist, in fact . . . the next Caravaggio?"

"He has the temperament. And the start of a record. What about del Brasco?"

"This I love," Steve Jordan said, breaking off a breadstick. "Based upon the *Grottesca* case, San Francisco police obtained a warrant. Interesting basement, climate-controlled, state-of-the-art, and filled with stolen art. *And,* I learned this morning, the Feds have turned one of his people in the Lafroing murder. Mr. del Brasco's attorneys are about to make a lot of money."

Mac and Annabel knew through Jordan that little had taken place in Italy regarding the *Grottesca* caper. Business as usual there. *Grottesca* was safely at the Vatican. "Count" Filippo Testa seemed to have vanished, his last sighting Morocco, where he was trying to sell two silver plates that probably were, according to Jordan, as authentic as his title. Father Pasquale Giocondi's hanging remained just another Mafia murder: Ask for more than you deserve, and you get more than you bargained for.

Court Whitney stood and asked for everyone's attention. He welcomed the guests, then asked Vice President Aprile to say a few words.

Aprile said without standing, "All I can say is that relations with Italy are pretty good these days." He smiled and said to Annabel, "You might consider a job with our State Department."

"No, thank you, Mr. Vice President. I'm perfectly content owning an art gallery and playing wife to this gentleman." She kissed Mac on the cheek.

"Court is quite right," said a trustee at Whitney's table. "Without M. Scott Pims, we'd still be in the mess Luther left us."

Mac couldn't contain himself, despite Annabel's restraining hand on his arm. "M. Scott Pims," he said to anyone listening, "could have prevented this from happening in the first place if he hadn't been so damned full of himself. Not only did he make sure Luther Mason went through with it, he saw his so-called good friend die. As far as I'm concerned, Mr. Pims deserves a place alongside Caravaggio himself—wherever he might be."

Everyone turned to their soup.

"You really popped him one," Jordan said to Mac quietly. "Good thing you did it on Italian soil. They're not big on personal liability suits over there."

"Actually, I was ashamed of myself. On the

other hand, it felt good," Mac said. "What about the Frenchman, Jacques Saison?"

"He'll die of cirrhosis before the French government does anything. Everybody copies other people's pictures, Mac. He just does it better than most."

While dessert was being served, Jordan pulled a wrapped package from beneath the table, tapped his glass with a spoon, and said, "May I have your attention, please." He looked directly at Annabel. "It has been decided by everyone present that a gift for you is in order."

"Gift? For me?"

"Absolutely." He said to Carole Aprile, "Would you do the honors, Mrs. Aprile?"

She shook her head. "No, I think I'll give that pleasure to Court."

Whitney stood, buttoned his jacket, looked at Annabel, and said, "We are all grateful for what you did, Mrs. Smith. We've had many discussions about what would constitute an appropriate expression of our gratitude, and we all agree that what we are about to present you represents exactly that. Actually, it was Mrs. Aprile's idea."

Jordan unwrapped the flowered gift paper and turned the painting so Annabel could see it.

"I don't believe this," she said.

"Don't get too excited," said Court Whitney. "It's not the original. But in all my years in the art world, I've never seen a better forgery—despite the unsightly bullet hole in the boy's chest. There is, however, one caveat."

"What is that?"

"That you make it available whenever the Italian government wishes to mount an exhibition of stolen and forged artworks. Other than that, it's yours to hang in your home as a reminder of your little adventure."

Annabel stood and accepted the painting from Jordan. "I'm touched by the sentiment behind this. Thank you, Carole, for putting such faith in me." She took in faces at the tables. "I would like to propose a toast," she said, lifting her wine glass. Others did the same. Mac looked up at her quizzically.

"To Luther Mason, a good and decent man who made one mistake in an otherwise good and decent life."

She looked directly at Court Whitney, who didn't seem quite sure what to do. He reluctantly joined in the toast.

Later that night, Mac and Annabel sat on the couch in their study. They'd taken down a favorite acrylic by Washington artist Sherry Zvares Sanabria and replaced it with the bullet-riddled Jacques Saison copy of *Grottesca.*

"Interesting, isn't it?" Annabel said as they looked at the painting.

Mac grunted.

"Amazing, the trouble one man can cause."

"Luther?"

"Caravaggio. Oh, I almost forgot." She handed him that day's *Washington Post,* which he hadn't gotten to, and pointed to a headline: ATLAS BUILDING BURNS—ARSON SUSPECTED. Mac read the short article. The fire had started in the pornography shop downstairs. The few artists left in the building reported extensive damage to their works. Police were investigating. A capsule history of the building ended the piece.

"Do you know what I'm thinking?" he asked after tossing the paper to the floor.

Annabel looked into his eyes. "That Rufus has to go out?"

"That—and—"

"Do it."

He removed *Grottesca* from the wall and replaced it with the painting it had displaced. Rufus got to his feet from where he'd been sleeping in a corner, went to *Grottesca,* and sniffed it.

"Quick, get him out," Annabel said. "And take Caravaggio with you. Pick an honored space in the garage. This house just isn't big enough for the three of us."

FORTY-TWO

As MAC and Annabel slept peacefully in their home, Gino Bonovolanta broke the lock on the rear door of Rome's Church of Sant'Agostino, on Piazza Sant'Agostino, went to a pillar in the Cavalletti Chapel, and, using a short crowbar, pried loose Caravaggio's *Madonna di Loreto*. He considered taking another painting, Raphael's *The Prophet Isaiah,* but that hadn't been on Sensi's list. Why anyone would pay money for such junk was beyond him, he thought as he left the church, the Caravaggio tucked under his arm.

In Hong Kong, a steamer trunk unloaded from a Dutch merchant ship contained four small still lifes by the Dutch master Willem Van Aelst, pieces stolen six months ago from the home of a wealthy Amsterdam collector. Their new owner anxiously awaited their arrival.

Jacques Saison started work that day on a copy of a Sisley landscape ordered by a well-to-do French banker, whose home was decorated with copies of masterpieces he claimed were authentic to those guests who didn't know better—which comprised most of them.

And in Cincinnati, Cindy and Harry Whitlock purchased a print of Gauguin's *Parau na te Varua ino (Words of the Devil)* at a flea market. Cindy wasn't sure whether to buy it. "Is it too risqué?" she asked her husband.

"Nah. That's the way artists are. They're all sex fiends. Besides, it'll go nice with the new chair."

All in all, just another week in the art world.

ABOUT THE AUTHOR

MARGARET TRUMAN, a former actress, singer, and "First Daughter," is the author of the highly successful Capitol Crimes series of mystery novels, as well as two best selling biographies, of her mother and father respectively. Her most recent book, *First Ladies,* goes into the White House to examine the lives of these extraordinary women.

Margaret Truman lives in New York City with her husband, former *New York Times* editor and book editor E. Clifton Daniel, Jr.

Look for these and other Random House Large Print books at your local bookstore